SECOND STRIKE

Also by Peter Kirsanow
Target Omega

SECOND STRIKE

A MIKE GARIN THRILLER

PETER KIRSANOW

DUTTON

DUTTON

An imprint of Penguin Random House LLC
375 Hudson Street
New York, New York 10014

Copyright © 2018 by Peter Kirsanow
Penguin supports copyright. Copyright fuels creativity, encourages diverse voices, promotes free speech, and creates a vibrant culture. Thank you for buying an authorized edition of this book and for complying with copyright laws by not reproducing, scanning, or distributing any part of it in any form without permission. You are supporting writers and allowing Penguin to continue to publish books for every reader.

DUTTON and the D colophon are registered trademarks of
Penguin Random House LLC.

LIBRARY OF CONGRESS CATALOGING-IN-PUBLICATION DATA
Names: Kirsanow, Peter N., author.
Title: Second strike / Peter Kirsanow.
Description: First edition. | New York, New York : Dutton, [2018] |
Series: A Mike Garin thriller ; 2
Identifiers: LCCN 2017034560 (print) | LCCN 2017039416 (ebook) | ISBN
9781101985335 (ebook) | ISBN 9781101985328 (hardcover) | ISBN
9781101985342 (softcover)
Subjects: LCSH: United States. Central Intelligence Agency—Fiction. |
Intelligence officers—United States—Fiction. |
Terrorism—Prevention—Fiction. | GSAFD: Suspense fiction.
Classification: LCC PS3611.I769845 (ebook) | LCC PS3611.I769845 S43 2018
(print) | DDC 813/.6—dc23
LC record available at https://lccn.loc.gov/2017034560

Printed in the United States of America
1   3   5   7   9   10   8   6   4   2

Set in Warnock Pro Light
Designed by Cassandra Garruzzo

For Solveig

We shall fight on the seas and oceans, we shall fight with growing confidence and growing strength in the air, we shall defend our island, whatever the cost may be, we shall fight on the beaches, we shall fight on the landing grounds, we shall fight in the fields and in the streets, we shall fight in the hills; we shall never surrender.

—WINSTON S. CHURCHILL

SECOND STRIKE

PROLOGUE

Pain is functionally irrelevant to the doomed.

Pain is an alarm, an early warning signal to the living: Damage has been done to the body, damage that, if not abated, could lead to disability or death. It is the basest of survival mechanisms.

But for the doomed—more precisely, the very soon to be dead—pain is superfluous. It serves no useful purpose.

To Michael Garin, whose timeline was almost at zero, the deep gash on his right shoulder that trailed nearly to his elbow was, therefore, a temporary irritant. The guard, now deceased, who had serendipitously inflicted it had caused little more than a distraction. Garin's objective remained uncompromised.

A mistake had to be rectified, a mistake that was potentially catastrophic. Garin, moving silently up the stairs toward the lower level of the fuel fabrication facility, M56 submachine gun pressed against the lacerated shoulder, was charged with correcting that mistake. Successive administrations had let the problem fester, hoping that it would resolve itself or that China would assume some measure of control over its lunatic client. But the lunacy grew unabated until it became clear that a crisis was emerging, one that would escalate from peninsular conflict to regional battle to war.

Garin's Omega team—comprised of eight tier-one special operators trained to interdict and destroy rogue WMD programs—should have been deployed sooner, but political advisors in the White House and careerists in the State Department had insisted on a graduated diplomatic approach to induce Pyongyang to curb, if not abandon, its nuclear weapons program. The approach failed. Nuance and sophistication had rarely been effective approaches toward the hermit kingdom.

President Clarke, with just over a month left in his administration, opted to launch a series of cyberattacks against North Korean nuclear weapons facilities and its missile launches to sabotage its nuclear program.

The cyberattacks succeeded, causing their missile payloads to crash into the Sea of Japan. But then someone got too clever and decided to disguise the attacks as South African. Until then, the North Koreans believed the misfires had stemmed from ineptitude, but once they discovered the true cause, they employed remedial measures to thwart the attacks. But not before their mercurial leader ordered the missile program to be ramped up significantly, creating a dangerous instability in the region.

The incoming Marshall administration determined direct action was necessary. As a feint, reports were leaked that SEAL Team Six had been deployed for a decapitation strike against North Korean leadership. The rumor was that the team was aboard the aircraft carrier USS *Vinson* in the Sea of Japan. This, planners expected, would cause North Korea to harden its defenses on its east coast. Omega, however, would enter the country from Korea Bay, on the opposite coast, and make their way inland to the nuclear weapons complex at Yongbyon, approximately seventy miles north of Pyongyang.

It had taken the Omega team more than eight hours to stealthily maneuver around the dense coastal patrols and move just one mile inland. From there they rendezvoused with a civilian contractor for the South Korean National Intelligence Service, who conveyed them forty miles by panel van to the outskirts of Yongbyon. They breached the heavily guarded perimeter of the Yongbyon Nuclear Scientific compound, crawling through a claustrophobic tunnel constructed by another group of civilian contractors, and emerged in a storage room in the subbasement of the nuclear fuel rod fabrication plant.

Garin led the team cautiously down a long, dimly lit concrete corridor under the main floor of the facility. Intelligence indicated that the facility would be largely empty of personnel at this time of night, with only a handful of security guards on the main floor. But, then, intelligence had failed to anticipate the guard in the stairwell with a bayonet affixed to his rifle. Garin, having dispatched the guard with a thrust of a tactical knife to the throat, moved slowly nonetheless, his team following in intervals of five to six feet. Each wore a balaclava and was outfitted exclusively with weapons and gear used by the Korean People's Army Special Operations Forces to limit evidence of any US involvement in the operation. Of course, if any of them were killed it would be clear the team was of Western origin; thus, their unstated protocol was that none of them would be captured.

Following immediately behind Garin was John Gates, who moments before had deposited twenty kilograms of Semtex beneath the center of the main floor. Behind him was Gene Tanski, a former Delta operator, who deposited another twenty kilograms of Semtex. Two other quantities of Semtex had been placed at opposite ends of the facility—one between powder vaporization and powder production and the other at powder processing. The engineers assured Omega that simultaneous detonations would collapse the facility. They'd already planted two other packages of Semtex at strategic locations in the adjacent reprocessing building, where weapons-grade plutonium was separated from spent fuel rods.

Garin began moving his team more quickly, with only minutes before the packages were to be detonated. Four facility guards appeared around the corner ahead. Garin struck the lead guard in the left eye socket with an SOG tactical knife, then spun to his right and whipped his arm toward the second guard, the knife penetrating the guard's right temple. Before the trailing guards could react, John Gates sprang forward and jammed his own blade in the third guard's solar plexus, withdrew it, and, with an overhead arc, thrust the blade into the throat of the last guard. Elapsed time: a shade under five seconds.

Garin signaled to his team to move forward, the group continuing to quicken their advance. As they neared the entrance to the tunnel, obscured behind and between two massive compressors, Manny Camacho, bringing up the rear, stage-whispered to Garin, "Boss, you need to see this."

Garin glanced back at Camacho, who was pointing at the entrance to a room to the right. The look on his face was one of astonishment.

Garin turned back and entered a room that appeared to be for storage—but the only items within it were four high-backed metal chairs with what appeared to be a human being strapped to each. Their faces were mutilated and their scalps had been pulled from the tops of their respective skulls down to their shoulders, the skin hanging limply across their chests like bibs. Pools of blood were congealed on the plastic-covered floor beneath them. A scene that transcended hell.

Garin knew they needed to keep moving, but as he motioned his team onward he had a sickening sense that he would soon encounter the author of that scene.

CHAPTER 1

**LOGAN AIRPORT,
AUGUST 14, 6:35 A.M. EDT**

It was all so much nonsense, she thought. Deliriously theoretical nonsense. Almost science fiction. Nonetheless, Meagan Cahill—no-nonsense big-firm litigator Meagan Cahill—sat at the counter of an eatery in Terminal B of Boston's Logan Airport, sipping iced coffee and listening as Ryan Moore Hammacher once again expounded ominously on something called the Arlanda Event.

She listened because Ryan happened to be her current romantic interest. She listened because he was endearingly earnest and because there was, frankly, little else to do as they waited for their flight to Reagan National to begin boarding.

Most of all—she admitted to herself with a twinge of guilt—she listened because railing about an impending apocalypse had proven to be remarkably lucrative, and Ryan had spent a not inconsiderable portion of his earnings on Meagan.

They'd met a little more than two years ago when the MIT professor of electrical engineering and computer science retained her firm, one of Boston's most prominent, to sue a Route 128 corridor tech company for appropriating software he'd developed for the Defense Advanced Research Projects Agency (DARPA). She obtained a sizable settlement for Ryan and shortly thereafter he called her for drinks. They'd been seeing each other ever since.

Her trial lawyer instincts telegraphed that Ryan would propose marriage sometime after they arrived in D.C., perhaps after his testimony later that morning before the House Committee on Transportation and

Infrastructure, but more likely after his afternoon testimony before the House Committee on Science, Space, and Technology.

She would accept, sincerely but pragmatically, knowing that she wouldn't find a better partner. And he was not unattractive, although his large head, spindly arms, and awkward gait made him resemble a giant marionette. A mischievous and vaguely lustful recess of her mind flashed to an image of his head atop the body of Corey Raines, the brawny Red Sox catcher she'd briefly dated, but she banished the thought with another twinge of guilt.

This would be the fourth time she'd accompanied him to Washington for testimony before some obscure committee of Congress. Each time previously the hearing had been anodyne. Only a few congressmen, a smattering of staffers, and a few other witnesses had been present. No C-SPAN; no print reporters.

Yet after each hearing, Ryan's speaking fees, as well as the number of requests, rose. After the first hearing, he was tendered a consulting agreement from a defense contractor nearly equal to his annual salary at MIT. After the last hearing, he'd entered into another for more than twice the cumulative earnings from his entire academic career. And DARPA had recently retained his services to develop certain software in collaboration with cybersecurity experts. All because Ryan Moore Hammacher was the Herald of Doom.

As the coffee parted the early-morning fog in her brain, she listened to him finish his latest jeremiad, just as the gate attendant announced that boarding would begin in a few minutes. ". . . And there's no way of preventing it, at least not on an individualized basis. They'd become weaponized. Scores of catastrophes combined to create an event without parallel in history."

Meagan heard herself say "horrible" for perhaps the third time that morning.

"What's more, they know it. But they haven't created the systems or countermeasures to prevent it. Unforgivable." Ryan fished in his pocket and placed a tip on the counter. "Watch my bag? Quick dash to the men's room before we board."

Meagan finished her coffee as she watched him cross to the lavatory on the other side of the concourse, politely dodging and yielding to travelers headed toward their gates. She smiled. A kind, sweet man playing Chicken Little on a grand scale. Thankfully, he'd already made his small fortune, because news reports showed that the president, Congress, and the military now were more concerned about the threat of electromagnetic pulse, or EMP, attacks, understandable given the recent Russian-Iranian efforts in that regard. It was the EMP experts' turn to become wealthy preventing Armageddon, while Ryan retreated to the ordinary life of an academic.

A minute later, priority boarding for the flight to D.C. was under way. Meagan gathered her belongings and Ryan's bag and proceeded to the line at the gate.

As regular boarding began, she glanced back toward the men's room. Ryan's dash had stopped being quick several minutes ago. A dozen passengers more and the door to the Jetway would soon close. No time for subtlety. Meagan walked briskly to the entrance of the men's room and called Ryan's name.

No response.

She called again. Nothing.

She took a few tentative steps toward the entrance. "Ryan, boarding's about done. We gotta go." A beat. "Ryan?"

She cocked her head and listened. "Ryan? Hello?"

She peeked around the corner into the brightly lit, white-tiled lavatory lined with a series of sinks on the left wall and a half dozen urinals on the right. Between them, lying spread-eagled on the floor and staring at her with lifeless eyes wide open, was Ryan, his chin resting in a pool of foamy saliva.

Meagan's screams echoed off the restroom walls and into the concourse just as a voice announced the final boarding call for United Flight 7181, scheduled for a seven A.M. departure to the nation's capital.

CHAPTER 2

Sean McDermott hated being afraid. He hated having to concede he was afraid as much as the sensation of fear itself.

He knew that to others he didn't look like the kind of man who was afraid of much. He was big—a former heavyweight wrestler in college— with a head shaped like an anvil and a face resembling a bulldog's. In fact, nothing much did scare him. But flying did, even though he had more hours in the air than some commercial pilots. As human resources director for a multinational steel company with facilities across the globe, he flew several days a week.

And each time petrified him. He knew the fear was irrational. He'd read the literature on the odds of a plane crash, that he'd have to fly for centuries before there might be a catastrophic event. None of that mattered when he was in the air.

Turbulence, of course, was his greatest concern. The slightest bump, shallowest dip, weakest shudder, set his nerves aflame. He couldn't help it, no matter how hard he tried.

During a flight McDermott was alert to every change in speed and altitude, every call button signal, every movement of the flight attendants. He knew when to expect the sound of the landing gear retracting after takeoff and lowering upon landing, the sound of the wing flaps, the bellow and whine of the engines.

Several of his most frequent flight paths had been committed to memory. Looking out the cabin window, he would identify mountains, rivers, lakes, and monuments marking the points at which the plane should be at cruising altitude, banking toward a final destination, beginning initial descent, or making final approach. Any deviation caused him to perk and wait for some sign of assurance that all was well.

McDermott took pains never to betray his fear. Whenever one of his flights did experience rougher than normal turbulence, his face would remain placid, almost serene, the only evidence of tension being the bulging veins on the backs of his hands as they gripped the armrests.

McDermott was on board a 737, the second leg of the flight from Detroit to Seattle, with a connection in Salt Lake City. He'd flown this particular route eight times in the last six months to attend union negotiations at one of his company's pickling and slitting facilities outside of Tacoma. By the third trip he'd memorized all of the landmarks along the flight path denoting the various stages of the flight.

He could see the Columbia River to the north. By his estimate they were about seventy-five miles south of Pasco, Washington, and little more than a hundred miles southeast of Hanford, which at one time was home to nine nuclear reactors, and now, after their decommissioning, contained much, if not most, of the high-level radioactive waste in the country.

McDermott calculated that in a minute or so he would be able to see the plumes of steam coming from the cooling towers on the commercial nuclear power plant that remained in operation at the Columbia Generating Station. They would then proceed northwest for another twenty minutes before beginning their initial descent into Sea-Tac.

Except they didn't. McDermott first sensed a slight drift northward in the direction of the Hanford site, then a faint bank to the east, the starboard wing dipping modestly. He swiveled his head to look about the cabin to see if it had captured anyone else's attention. Nothing. Some passengers dozing, others scanning devices in airplane mode, others playing sudoku.

McDermott gazed out the window. Despite the northerly drift, he could see the billowing clouds of steam from the Columbia Generating Station's cooling towers to the west. Likely just a minor course adjustment, probably to accommodate some traffic in the vicinity.

A few seconds later, however, the plane banked to the west, a more pronounced dip of its portside wing, the northerly drift becoming northwesterly. McDermott once again glanced about the cabin. A few more passengers were looking up, curious if not concerned.

The cooling towers grew larger in his window as the plane continued to bank in a northwesterly direction. The flight attendant from the main cabin passed him on her way to first class, where she spoke briefly to another attendant, who then picked up the wall phone opposite the flight deck. After a brief conversation, she turned to the other attendant with an urgent expression and said something to which the attendant replied with a curt nod before returning to the main cabin.

Seconds later, the plane began to descend noticeably, far too soon and steep for initial descent. They were probably a good two hundred miles from Sea-Tac and still around a cruising altitude of thirty-one thousand feet.

The seat belt sign illuminated. A couple of seconds later the voice of the flight attendant came on the speaker. "Ladies and gentlemen, the captain has turned on the seat belt sign. Please return to your seats and make sure your seat backs and tray tables are upright and in their locked position and your seat belts are securely fastened for the remainder of the flight. We're experiencing a few minor bumps before landing. We'll be passing through the cabin to collect any remaining service items."

McDermott, affecting an attitude of nonchalance, began tightening his seat belt just as the plane shuddered violently and pitched in a steep dive to the west. Panic spiked from McDermott's stomach through his throat, which struggled to suppress a cry of terror. He watched the attendant in first class get knocked off-balance and fall against the seatback of 4A—opening a deep gash on her right temple. Baggage flew from the overhead compartments and oxygen masks dipped to screaming passengers, many of whom were too preoccupied with bracing themselves to even notice.

Amid the shouts, cries, and prayers McDermott, strangely, found himself becoming composed. It was as if the overwhelming sensation of fear had tripped some gauge in some gland that flooded his brain and body with serotonin and endorphins, producing an incongruous sense of calm and ease. He quickly considered and dismissed possible causes for the impending disaster, as if he'd be able to correct the problem upon identifying it.

The roar of the engines grew louder and swiftly changed to a high-pitched whine. McDermott closed his eyes and the screams of the passengers and the whine of the engines receded into white noise. He shook his head once at the irony that all of his worst fears of flying would be confirmed by his own death.

But in the very next second the whine of the engines dropped several octaves, the volume of noise dropped almost to normal, and the plane began to level and stabilize.

McDermott's eyes snapped open and he looked out the window. The plane appeared to be at between fifteen and twenty thousand feet, far higher than he'd expected; it felt as if they'd been diving for much longer.

He heard whispers, gasps, and sounds of relief from other passengers. The flight attendants, including the one who'd hit her temple, were moving about, checking and comforting the passengers.

McDermott did a quick personal inventory to confirm he hadn't been hurt and waited for the captain's voice to come on the speaker with assurances and an explanation of what had gone wrong. But after several minutes of waiting, it became clear that no explanation would be coming.

They don't know why it happened, he thought.

For Sean McDermott, the lack of an explanation didn't matter. In fact, for his purposes, there was no possible explanation that would've mattered. Because at that moment, Sean McDermott resolved never to fly again.

CHAPTER 3

Todd Wells was in agony.

The hot, dry air seared his lungs as he gasped for oxygen. His legs were engorged with lactic acid, making both his quadriceps and his hamstrings feel as if they were about to tear with each step he took. His heart rate was in the red zone.

Yet disbelief nearly dwarfed his agony. The rookie—the no-name—was winning. Beating the toughest, fittest man on the planet. That's what Wells was, after all. He'd proven it by winning the Crucible two years running.

And the rookie was not just beating him; he was *smoking* him. In fact, the last event wasn't even close. The rookie had finished the forty-by-forty-yard shuttle run a good *nine seconds* ahead of Wells. Impossible.

But he'd prevail still. One event remained in the Crucible, a five-day competition created by a former German decathlete who'd graduated to a career as an operator in GSG-9, the vaunted German counterterrorism unit. Convinced that other extreme physical competitions tested only a limited range of physical prowess, he developed the Crucible to measure every aspect of physical fitness.

The Crucible included multiple sprints, 5K, 10K, and marathon runs, a variety of obstacle courses, surface and underwater swims, graduated power cleans, dead lifts, squats, and reaction drills, all with barely a pause between events. The competition was capped by a series of one-on-one fights, consisting of three one-minute, no-holds-barred contests, scored on a point system: the Cauldron.

It was this last event that Wells was depending upon. It had provided his margin of victory the last two years. The rookie, Tom Lofton, presently held a seven-point lead in the overall competition. In six years of competing in the Crucible, Wells had never lost a Cauldron match. As he stood hunched over, he looked at Lofton. Though he appeared exhausted, his expression was placid and his body relaxed. But his eyes had an intensity Wells found somewhat unsettling. No matter. Lofton would be toast in the Cauldron.

Mike Garin, the man known to the other competitors as Tom Lofton, was doing the math. He held a seven-point lead on the reigning champion with only the Cauldron remaining. The winner of the fighting competition would get ten points, the runner-up seven, third place five, fourth three, and fifth one. Therefore, all Garin had to do to win at least a share of the championship was to come in fourth place or higher in the final event. But if he did that, with all of the attendant notoriety of being champion, someone might discover that Tom Lofton was actually Mike Garin, former Omega special operator.

So, quite simply, he'd make sure to come in no higher than fifth. In other words, he had to lose. Not something he relished doing.

Garin rose upright, placed his hands on his hips, and scanned the sidelines, ringed with TV cameras, judges, and support team personnel. The other competitors had three or four team members each. Garin's support consisted only of Luci Saldana, and that was sufficient. She was already jogging toward him with an ice pack and a bottle of diluted Gatorade, looking cool and comfortable in white shorts and T-shirt.

Luci draped the ice pack over the back of Garin's neck and handed him the Gatorade.

"You didn't pace yourself, Tom," she admonished. "You need to have something in reserve for the Cauldron."

"How much time do we have?"

"First round starts in twenty minutes. You need to get out of the sun. Go into the tunnel to the locker room. That's the coolest place in the stadium. They've got examination tables you can lie down on. I'll rub you down to keep you loose."

Several of the competitors were beginning to make their way to the tunnel. "Thanks, but I'll stay here—too crowded in there."

"That's crazy, Tom. The sun will take it out of you. They've already taken four people to the urgent care."

"I've been in worse."

All of five foot three, 105 pounds, Luci Saldana looked up at Mike Garin with a stern expression. "No self-respecting support member would let their competitor do that. You could get heatstroke. Go into the tunnel. Right now."

"I'll be okay out here, Luci. Besides, it's going to smell like a zoo in there."

"I don't care. Go in there."

"No."

Luci was furious. "Then just remember, if you don't win the competition, it's because of this boneheaded decision."

And that's precisely what Garin was hoping Luci, and everyone else, would think.

CHAPTER 4

A lone figure with a patrician bearing stood on the second-floor balcony of the large beach house, smoking a Winston and watching the gulls skim across the surface of the ocean searching for prey. It was a hot day, but the northerly breeze skirting along the coast made it bearable. Comfortable, almost.

His cell phone rang as expected, the ringtone reserved for a specific caller. He transferred the cigarette to his left hand, reached into his pocket with his right, and spoke without any salutations or pleasantries. "Status?"

"Double-blind staging is almost complete," the assassin replied.

"Implementation?"

"Forty-eight hours."

The patrician paused for a moment, drew the cigarette to his lips, and then expelled the smoke slowly. "Begin to execute."

"The impediment, however, remains."

"The impediment is not operational."

"The impediment remains formidable," the assassin insisted.

The patrician was unused to the assassin expressing concern about obstacles to mission success. He brought the cigarette to his lips again, inhaled deeply, and scanned the horizon for several seconds before speaking. "Where is the impediment?"

"Secured."

"How much time is needed to address the impediment?"

Silence for two beats. It also was unusual for the assassin to hesitate. "Unknown."

The patrician was neither surprised nor perturbed by the response. Their previous experience with the impediment demonstrated it was the most truthful answer.

"We have ninety-six hours to execute. Use whatever assets are necessary to eliminate the impediment."

Ending the call, the patrician turned around and walked casually to the picture window facing westward to gaze upon a mainland that soon would be changed forever.

CHAPTER 5

Of the forty remaining competitors, those who ranked among the top eight were chosen to compete in the Cauldron. As the competitor with the most points thus far, Garin was the number one seed. His opponent was the eighth seed, Magnus Olsen, with the winner advancing to the semifinal match.

At six foot four, 250 pounds, Olsen had accumulated much of his point total in the strength events, but he was surprisingly agile and had impressive endurance for a man his size. According to the media guide, he'd been an All–Big Ten tight end at Minnesota before spending several years in the Marines. He now was a construction contractor. Solid, but under ordinary circumstances he wouldn't last more than fifteen seconds against Garin's speed, skill, and ferocity. More lethal fighters had lasted even less.

But this was Magnus Olsen's lucky day.

Garin's was the last of the four matches in the preliminary round. Wells had already prevailed in his.

The match took place in a conventional boxing ring in the center of the football field. No holds or punches were barred, save for strikes to the eyes, throat, and testicles. Points were awarded for punches landed, takedowns, and knockdowns.

A buzzer signaled the start. Magnus Olsen strode purposely from his corner toward Garin, fists up, weaving from side to side. Garin stood his ground and assessed: ponderous; poor weight distribution. If this were a true fight out in the field Garin would've incapacitated him with a single blow.

But he endeavored to make it look like a fight, a real struggle. As Olsen got within arm's length to deliver a blatantly telegraphed left hook, Garin dropped to the canvas, wheeled his right leg toward Olsen's calves, and swept his legs, sending him crashing onto his back.

Rather than seize the advantage, Garin rose sluggishly and withdrew, allowing Olsen to roll away and get back to his feet.

Garin advanced toward Olsen with his hands down and an air of cockiness. Olsen spun to his right, slamming his right elbow into Garin's left cheekbone. Garin crashed to the canvas as if falling through a trapdoor. Although the blow was quite painful, Garin remained in complete command of his faculties. He made a show of rolling about for a second on the floor, then staggered to his feet in time to receive a knee to his abdomen before he could stand fully erect. He suppressed the instinct to jam the heel of his hand into Olsen's foolishly exposed face and instead permitted his opponent to throw an uppercut into Garin's purposely exposed jaw, snapping his head back. Again, he dropped to the canvas.

That really hurt, thought Garin. He'd resolved to lose, not get injured. He rolled about on the floor for a few seconds. Olsen didn't press, knowing the match would be over in seconds and that he led on points. The buzzer sounded. Garin succeeded in dropping out of medal contention and remaining in relative anonymity. A fairly credible performance, thought Garin. No one would think that he tanked it.

Murmurs of disappointment came from the crowd, which, like most sports crowds, had been rooting for the unknown rookie who looked on the verge of upsetting the champ. No one, however, looked more disappointed than Luci. More accurately, no one looked more bewildered. She knew Garin's capabilities, watched him train at the Dale City Recreation Center, where she worked part-time. His workouts were brutal. She'd never seen anyone with an even remotely comparable pain threshold. Olsen's blows wouldn't even have slowed the Tom Lofton she knew, which made her angry.

Lofton stepped out of the ring and proceeded to the locker rooms as the next match was set to begin. Luci ran up beside him.

"That was a hell of a performance," she hissed. "Why'd you take a dive?"

Garin was startled. "What are you talking about?"

"You heard me. You were going to win the championship. Prize money. Endorsements, fame. Why on earth would you tank it?"

"He beat me."

"Bullshit, Tom."

"Okay. You're right. I should've listened to you. I was drained. Had nothing left."

"Again, bullshit. You always have something left."

More than feeling guilty for deceiving Luci, he regretted disappointing her. This wasn't just his competition. She devoted time and effort to be his support team, too. Being the trainer of the best-conditioned person on the planet could have done wonders for her career. He stopped and looked at her. "There's always next year, Luci. And I can always do Badwater or CrossFit."

"They're already over."

"Then next year." Garin put his hand on her shoulder. "Stick with me, okay?"

Luci knew she would. When he'd first come to the rec center a few months ago, she'd been instantly attracted to him, as had most of the other female members. He rarely spoke to anyone other than her, and even then, only a polite greeting with a voice so deep it was unnerving. He'd disappear, sometimes for a week or two, but when he returned, he'd resume his workouts—the intensity of which suggested he lacked the governor in his brain telling him when to stop—as if he'd never left. Yet despite his apparent surfeit of testosterone, he was a gentleman, very old-school, as if he'd stepped out of a time machine directly from the Battle of Agincourt, removed his armor, and put on jeans. She had no intention of leaving him.

"Skip the shower. Let's get you back to the Omni. I'll get some bags of ice so you can soak in the bathtub, and then I'll rub you down. You're going to be in a lot of pain tomorrow."

Garin gently squeezed her shoulder, sending a charge up her spine. "You got it, boss."

CHAPTER 6

Olivia Perry was growing impatient sitting at the witness table. Several members of the Senate Select Committee on Intelligence were huddled around Chairman Harlan McCoy, discussing something out of her earshot. They seemed unconcerned that they were nearly thirty minutes behind schedule. Perry and her boss, National Security Advisor James Brandt, both sticklers for punctuality, had arrived fifteen minutes ahead of schedule. Brandt was seated behind her, Arlo, his German shepherd guide dog, lying by his side.

This was her second appearance before the committee since the commencement of the bombing campaign against Iran three weeks ago. Brandt also had testified previously. The hearings were related to the congressional investigation surrounding the thwarted Russian-Iranian attempt to strike the United States with an EMP four weeks ago. The catastrophe had been narrowly averted, prompting massive retaliation against Iran by the United States. Chairman McCoy continued reading something in front of him before nodding confirmation to his colleagues flanking him that the hearing was about to begin.

"Thank you, Ms. Perry, for returning to the committee. We very much appreciate your continued cooperation."

"My pleasure, Mr. Chairman."

"Excellent. Committee staff have prepared a summary of essential facts adduced thus far, and . . ." McCoy fumbled with a sheaf of papers for several seconds before resuming. "Here we are. I'll give you the condensed version so we're all on the same page, okay?"

"Yes, Mr. Chairman."

McCoy brought several papers closer to the glasses perched midway down his nose and began speaking.

"On or about July 11, seven of eight special operators known as Omega—" McCoy stopped suddenly and looked up, indignant. "I have to tell you, Ms. Perry, despite the fact that I'm chair of Senate Intelligence of the United States of America, I'd never even heard of this Omega before. Not a thing. Neither had any of the forty-plus witnesses who have appeared so far before this committee, with the exception of DDCI Kessler." McCoy repeatedly stabbed the dais with his index finger. "Did you know about them?"

"Neither Mr. Brandt nor I was aware of Omega's existence until the crisis began unfolding," Perry answered truthfully.

A staffer rose from behind and whispered into McCoy's ear. Olivia Perry suspected that the senator's "extemporaneous" remarks were a rehearsal for when the investigation became public, an attempt to deflect attention from the fact that it was McCoy's closest confidant, Senate Intelligence counsel Julian Day, who had been funneling intelligence to the Russians—and by extension the Iranians—to facilitate the EMP strike. All right under McCoy's nose.

"As I was saying, this Omega team went into Pakistan—without that government's knowledge or permission—to prevent an attempt by terrorists to acquire a nuclear weapon." McCoy looked up again with theatrical magnanimity. "Now, I should say in all fairness, they were successful, though that doesn't excuse this administration's duplicity in keeping this team secret."

Once again he returned to the script. "In the process of preventing the acquisition of nuclear weapons by the terrorists, team leader Michael Garin apparently came into possession of information about the Russians and Iranians. He believed it would lead to the discovery of Iran's program—with Russian technical assistance—to construct and launch intercontinental ballistic missiles carrying nuclear payloads." McCoy gazed up. "How am I doing, Ms. Perry?"

"So far everything you've said about the Omega operation is consistent with our understanding."

"Within forty-eight hours of returning to the US from the successful operation in Pakistan, every single member of Omega, save for Mr. Garin, was assassinated. Seven members killed in a manner suggesting the sole surviving member of the team, Mr. Garin, was the assassin. Accordingly, given the extraordinarily sensitive nature of the matter, the FBI conducted a hunt for Mr. Garin, the scale of which, as I understand, was unprecedented. Nonetheless, Mr. Garin successfully eluded capture for several days.

"We now know Mr. Garin was innocent, but throughout the search the FBI and various intelligence agencies were fed information from a source within the government suggesting Garin was the assassin."

A different aide whispered into McCoy's ear. After a brief exchange, McCoy said, "Ms. Perry, it is our understanding that while Garin was a fugitive, you and Mr. Brandt were in contact with him. Is that correct?"

"I was. Mr. Brandt was not."

"But you conveyed information from Garin to Mr. Brandt; isn't that true?"

"He was never aware of Mr. Garin's whereabouts, Senator McCoy."

". . . to conveniently maintain plausible deniability regarding the whereabouts of a fugitive . . ."

Angered, Olivia began to respond, but Senator Brad Cross, ranking member of the committee, interjected.

"Mr. Chairman, the evidence makes clear that the reason Mr. Garin was a fugitive in the first place is because disinformation about his culpability was spread through law enforcement and intelligence services. At least some of this information came from counsel to this very committee. I respectfully suggest we return to the focus of the inquiry."

McCoy's face was flushed. The counsel to whom Cross referred, Day, was killed—some reports suggested he actually committed suicide—after his involvement with the Russians became known. To this point no one had made "public" reference to Day's involvement in the EMP plot. A shot across McCoy's bow.

The room remained uncomfortably silent for several seconds, aides looking at the floor and senators inspecting their paperwork. When

McCoy resumed speaking, his voice was neutral and measured. "It is our understanding Mr. Garin determined that his team was assassinated by a Russian operator with ties to President Mikhailov. The operator had somehow infiltrated and become an Omega team member. Is that your understanding as well, Ms. Perry?"

"That's correct, Senator. We determined the Russian operator had become a member of Omega more than two years ago under the name John Gates. We don't know how. His true name is Taras Bor. He was able to make it appear as if he had been assassinated along with the rest of the team."

"Unbelievable."

"Bor was directing the activities of Iranian Quds Force operators here in the US to effectuate the EMP attack."

McCoy shuffled papers, skipping several pages. "On or about July 17, and while still a fugitive, Garin received information from an Israeli agent, Ari Singer, that a clandestine Iranian effort to construct a nuclear weapon and place it on an ICBM had reached completion and the missile would be launched within hours. Accurate?"

"It is, Senator. Mr. Garin determined that three ICBMs armed with nuclear warheads were to be launched imminently. The ICBMs were constructed in and for Iran—largely by Russian personnel—with assistance from North Korea. Two of the ICBMs were targeted at Israel. The third, with a one-megaton yield, was targeted at the United States, to be detonated at an altitude of one hundred miles between Chicago and Kansas City, thereby creating an electromagnetic pulse that would cover most of the continental United States. The EMP would knock out anything and everything that uses electricity, sending us back to the Dark Ages."

"We've heard from witnesses who estimate that the death toll from disease, starvation, and unrest would be in the millions in the first year alone," McCoy informed the room.

"Conservative estimates put the death toll at twenty percent of the population," Olivia confirmed.

"How did the Iranians think they could do that without massive nuclear retaliation on our part?"

"The Iranians believed all three ICBMs were targeted at Israel. They didn't know one was targeted at the US. The Russians had controlled the entire project, permitting Iranians to assist only with the warhead, so that the nuclear signature would be Iranian. Thus, the entire world's tracking systems would've seen the ICBM launched from Iranian soil. The Russians would've been in the clear."

McCoy's brow furrowed. "Ms. Perry, in anticipation of your appearance, staff has examined all of the FBI, NSA, CIA, and DIA reports on the matter and found absolutely no intel gathered by such agencies showing Russian, Iranian, and North Korean involvement in constructing an Iranian ICBM ostensibly designed to detonate a nuclear device and set off an EMP. Yet this administration launched a massive bombing campaign, still under way, premised on Iran's having deliverable nuclear capability poised for imminent use against the US in the form of an EMP. When and where did the administration get that info?"

"From the Israeli operative, Ari Singer, who prior to his death had relayed it to Mr. Garin."

McCoy raised a skeptical brow. "All of this came from Singer?"

"Yes, Senator, most of it."

"Most of it," McCoy repeated. He glanced back at an aide, who nodded in return. "And where did the rest of it come from?"

"I'm afraid I don't follow, Senator."

"I'm certain that you do, Ms. Perry. Where did the rest of the details concerning the imminent EMP attack come from?"

Perry hesitated a moment. McCoy filled the void. "They came from the very same Julian Day whom my colleague Senator Cross referred to a few moments ago, didn't they? Except they weren't supplied by Mr. Day voluntarily, were they, Ms. Perry?"

Olivia shifted in her seat. "I was in the room when Mr. Day provided the details of the EMP strike. He provided the locations of launch sites, payload capacities, and timing of the launches. The warhead that was going to detonate over central United States was to have been launched from an underground facility at the base of Mount Azud Kuh in the North Alborz Protected Area of Iran."

"But again, he did not supply that information voluntarily, did he?" McCoy asked.

"I don't quite follow, Senator. He may not have *wanted* to supply the details because doing so confirmed his complicity in treasonous activities, but upon being caught, he provided them."

"My point, Ms. Perry," Mr. McCoy said harshly, "is that Mr. Day supplied that information only after being tortured by Garin, isn't that true?"

Olivia appeared shaken. "I observed no evidence of torture, Senator. I was in the room when Mr. Garin interrogated Julian Day. At no time did Mr. Garin make any physical contact whatsoever with Mr. Day."

"Isn't it true, Ms. Perry, that you were in the room with Garin and Day for only part of the time? Isn't it true that Garin was alone with Day for several minutes before you entered?"

The hearing room was absolutely silent but for the voices of the senator and the witness. The purpose of McCoy's line of questions was plain to everyone in the room. This was his preemptive attempt to shift attention from his aide's traitorous conduct to alleged torture by Garin. The media was almost certain to seize upon the torture angle, which, in their judgment, would eclipse Day's treason.

"Senator, I was in the very next room when Mr. Garin and Mr. Day were alone together for, perhaps, a few minutes. I heard no evidence of torture when I was in the next room and I observed no signs of torture when I entered the room."

McCoy held up a sheet of paper. "According to this affidavit from a member of FBI HRT who was present after Mr. Day emerged from the room you and Garin were in, Day looked, quote, stunned, terrified, and exhausted, end quote. What do you think accounts for Mr. Day's condition at that time, if not torture?" McCoy asked sarcastically.

"Perhaps, Senator, he was *stunned* at having been caught, *terrified* of the consequences, and *exhausted* from the effort in avoiding detection of his involvement in a plan that would have resulted in the deaths of millions." Olivia's voice became more strident with each word, a small vein pulsing at her left temple. "Mike Garin was singularly responsible for preventing an extraordinary catastrophe, and he did so at great risk to himself and his family—all while members of this body were sticking their heads in the sand and behaving as if the world is populated by unicorns threatened only by American imperialism; and all the while your assistant was conspiring with the Russians." From behind, Brandt kicked the back of Olivia's chair. She was swerving precariously close to contempt of Congress. "Michael Garin should be given an awards ceremony by this committee. Respectfully, Senator."

A scowl grew on McCoy's face as it turned crimson. His aides seated behind him winced and looked down at the floor. McCoy would have to find another diversion.

Senator Cross spoke up. "Mr. Chair?"

"The Chair recognizes Ranking Member Cross."

"Thank you, Mr. Chairman. Ms. Perry, it's our understanding that the Russian agent involved in this entire matter evaded capture and disappeared. It's only logical that he put as much distance between himself and the United States as possible. I'm sure his whereabouts are at least as big a concern to you as they are to everyone on this committee, but the FBI and every other law enforcement agency we've asked has no idea what happened to him. Do you or anyone on the staff of the NSC have any information as to his whereabouts?"

Olivia Perry felt a familiar twinge of anxiety for the first time in weeks.

"We do not, Senator."

O livia cast a shy smile at the security guard whose eyes were riveted to her.

As she stepped out onto the sidewalk and into the brilliant sunshine outside the Hart Senate Office Building, she was still on edge from the hearing and walking at a brisk pace, not the best speed for a hot, humid August day in Washington, D.C. Pedestrian and vehicular traffic were slow. Bureaucratic Washington was on cruise control during the August recess, the committee hearing one of the few signs of political life in the nation's capital.

The swarm of cabs that usually patrolled the streets of Capitol Hill had winnowed considerably, so Olivia headed in the direction of Union Station, where they remained omnipresent. She needed to get back to her office at the Old Executive Office Building, known to Washingtonians as the Eisenhower Building or OEOB, and draft a memo recounting the hearing while it remained fresh in her mind. She had a meeting with Brandt and Iris Cho to discuss the hearing and what, if anything, Brandt should tell the president about it.

Her mobile device vibrated gently in her hand. She pressed the icon, raised the device to her ear, and heard a familiar voice.

"Now that you're famous, I expected someone else to be answering your phone for you." It was Laura Casini, Olivia's former Stanford classmate, now an analyst with the National Geospatial-Intelligence Agency.

"With fame comes neither fortune nor privilege."

"Very Churchillian. But try being a worker bee like me."

"Not only have I tried it, it stuck," Olivia replied. "What's going on?"

"I thought you might be interested in something I happened to notice in the last day or two. Thought maybe you'd like to drop by."

Olivia's focus sharpened. The last and only time she had "dropped by" Casini's office was to view highly classified satellite imagery revealing peculiar production patterns at Russian industrial sites, patterns that only later became alarmingly decipherable.

"I take it you can't give me a preview over the phone," Olivia said.

"That Stanford education really didn't go to waste, did it? When should I expect you?"

"About twenty minutes after I find a cab, which at this rate should be early September."

"I'll be here."

O livia stood behind Laura Casini as she tapped commands onto a keyboard and a blurred image appeared on the seventy-two-inch screen in front of them. Casini manipulated a mouse, causing the resolution to become sharper.

"That looks familiar," Olivia said.

"It should. It's one of the same places you had me call up last time." Casini pointed to the screen depicting a mammoth industrial facility. "Do you remember which one that is?"

"Arkhangelsk."

"Right. Notice anything interesting?"

Olivia scrutinized the screen. "Not really. Looks about the same as I remembered it."

"That in itself should be interesting, don't you think? Mountains and mountains of electrical equipment lying about? Going nowhere?"

Olivia shook her head. "The EMP never went off; nothing got fried. So there was no market for replacement equipment."

"Fair enough," Casini said, producing an even sharper image with a single keystroke.

Olivia was astounded by the clarity of the image. "That's scary."

"Brought to you by your friendly neighborhood KeyHole 13 satellite dealer," Casini said. "We can spot dandruff on top of Yuri Mikhailov's head with this. Notice anything interesting now?"

"Forklifts. Some of the equipment's loaded on the forklifts."

"Got your attention now?"

"When was this shot?" Olivia asked.

"Today, 6:15 A.M. our time."

"Can you go back a few days?"

Casini hit a few more keys. Another image appeared. "From three days ago."

"There's actually more product there. Hard to tell, admittedly. But there seem to be at least five more rows of generators. And hardly any forklifts in sight. What about the other sites we looked at before?"

A few more keystrokes later, another image appeared on the screen. "Murmansk, earlier today," Casini said.

Olivia scrutinized the screen. "Go back a few days."

"There you go."

"Again, more product," Olivia said. "Just like Arkhangelsk. Now go back a little more."

Casini did so. Olivia scanned the image slowly. "The difference isn't as apparent as in Arkhangelsk, but it still looks like there's less product in the later image. What do you think?" Olivia asked.

"I concur."

"Can you do a split screen?" Olivia asked. "Arkhangelsk, Murmansk. Shots from today on one side and shots of the same locations from a few days ago on the other side?"

Casini tapped the keyboard, producing the requested grid of images. The two stared at the screen for a long time in silence. Olivia spoke first.

"Each site appears to have less product in the later image. Hard to tell how much less, but product's definitely being moved. What do you make of it, Laura?"

"You're the big brain. When you saw something similar a few weeks ago you concluded the Russians were up to something sinister. When the bombing campaign against Iran began, the Russians stopped moving equipment. Now they've resumed. So you tell me."

"Could be nothing."

"Come on, Olivia. You work for James Brandt. According to him, everything the Russians do is sinister."

Olivia remained silent, pondering the range of implications from what was on the screen. The one she thought least plausible was also the one that posed the greatest threat. That threat was at a level she could discuss with only a handful of people, and her friend Laura wasn't one of them.

Without another word Olivia Perry turned from the screen and left the room to hail a cab to take her to the White House.

CHAPTER 7

Garin stepped out of the ice bath Luci had prepared for him, toweled himself off, and examined his face in the mirror. Other than a small welt on his cheek where Olsen had struck him, he was in pretty good shape. The cheek ached a bit, but the ice bath had done wonders for the rest of his body.

He put on a pair of linen trousers and opened the bathroom door. Luci had arrayed tubes and bottles of ointments and analgesics on the nightstands flanking the queen-size bed. She shook her head, pointing accusatorially at his pants.

"That will not do, mister. No. No way. Off with them."

When Garin hesitated, she continued, "I can't do much for your legs and glutes with those on. Don't worry, I've seen the male form once or twice before."

Garin disappeared into the bathroom and dutifully returned seconds later, a towel draped modestly around his waist. Luci rolled her eyes. "I never would've pegged you for the shy type." *Not with a body like that,* she thought.

She waved him to the bed. "On your stomach first."

Garin lay diagonally across the bed and Luci straddled his hips, applying lubricant to his shoulders and back, using her fingertips to define the individual muscles, expertly kneading them to drive out the lactic acid. If the man had a single fat cell on him, she couldn't find it. It felt like she was kneading iron.

Luci felt featherlight astride Garin's back and was quite adept at what she was doing. He'd eschewed rubdowns as a waste of time in the past, all the way back to his college football days. He submitted now partly to mollify Luci as well as to assuage his guilt for having deceived her. But this felt very good.

She massaged in silence for nearly ten minutes, then: "I saw you at Saint Francis of Assisi a couple of weeks ago," Luci said, referring to a small church near the Marine base at Quantico, Virginia. "It was during the week, midafternoon. You were by yourself in one of the first pews. No Mass. No priest."

She paused and continued kneading iron; then, with a genuine curiosity in her voice, she asked, "What were you doing there?"

"What were *you* doing there?"

"Come on, Tom. You make people pee their pants just by saying 'hi.' I mean, you have a *look*. Seeing you at a human sacrifice? Plausible. Church? Not so much."

Garin shrugged and said nothing.

Luci slid down to straddle his thighs so she could work on his hips and buttocks. Still iron, molded and contoured.

"The ladies at the rec center have a pool going. Just pennies. They're betting on what you do for a living. The winner tries to talk to you."

No reaction.

"Want to help me win?"

"You're already talking to me, Luci."

She slid down to his ankles to work on his thighs and calves for a while. She had treated some of the Baltimore Ravens a few years back during an undergrad internship. Superb physiques and conditioning, yet nothing like this. This body looked and felt like it had done something serious.

"What do you do, Tom? I mean, seriously."

"Not much of anything right now."

"Then how did you pay for our travel and rooms?"

"General frugality."

She slapped his side. "On your back."

Garin rolled onto his back and Luci straddled his hips again, kneading his chest, shoulders, and arms. All bulges and veins and striations.

She took her time with each trapezius, each deltoid, each biceps, each brachialis. Then the pectorals, where she scrutinized a four-inch scar over his heart. Something had been able to penetrate the iron.

She hunched over to take a closer look, her hair falling over her face and onto his chest. She traced the scar with her index finger.

"What's this?"

"Nothing much."

Luci snorted. Tom Lofton, inscrutable to a fault. Placing her palms flat on his chest, she leaned forward a bit more, examining his eyes with a hint of frustration. And a bit of something else.

Garin liked Luci's eyes. They were big and intelligent, set deep in a bronze face. He liked her body, too. Fit and firm. He liked Luci.

"Ms. Saldana, you were at church on a weekday afternoon?"

"Just like you." She smiled.

"I bet you went to Catholic school as a kid."

"K through eight."

"Then you know the imperative to avoid the near occasion of sin," Garin said.

Luci stopped kneading, blinked several times, and grinned. Where did he keep that damn time machine?

Luci scooted off Garin onto the floor, still grinning.

Bemused, she stared at him for a second, then rubbed her hands together. "How about some dinner?"

"Sounds good. I could use a wheelbarrow of carbs right about now."

"Take a shower. Get dressed. You want carbs? How about pasta? There's a place down East Las Colinas."

"I could use some turmeric and ginger."

"I picked up both this morning. They're in my room."

"Marry me."

Lofton disappeared into the bathroom to change, leaving a grinning Luci to ponder her situation. She was alone in a plush hotel room with the most dangerous-looking male in the Western Hemisphere, who nonetheless behaved with altar boy rectitude. She expected to feel disappointment, frustration. Instead she felt a sensation akin to elation, anticipation at the very least. This wasn't a rejection. It was something closer to . . . respect, chivalry.

Luci's eyes flitted about the room as she waited. The sliding mirrored door to the closet was open and she glanced inside. No clothes on the hangers. Only a pair of running shoes on the floor and a black gym bag on the overhead shelf. Spartan, like everything else she'd observed about Garin. Yet he'd flown them first class from Reagan National and booked two rooms for five nights in a luxury hotel.

Garin emerged a few minutes later. The linen pants were accompanied by a white linen shirt. He held his arms at his sides and raised his eyebrows.

Luci nodded in approval. "Nice. I should go back to my room to shower and change too."

"You're fine as you are, Luci."

"Will only take a minute. It was hot out there and I've got analgesic all over me."

"All right," Garin said, nodding.

"You can wait for me in the room." She cast a mischievous look. "I'll keep the bathroom door locked to avoid 'near occasions.'"

Garin smiled, an event that occurred with the frequency of a lunar eclipse. He followed her to the door and she opened it.

For Garin, the milliseconds slowed to seconds and the seconds to minutes. Standing in the hallway outside the door were two men dressed in sport coats with PB-6P9 handguns raised at eye level, suppressors attached.

With his left hand, Garin jerked Luci back into the room behind him as he crouched and thrust his right hand toward the pistol of the man to Garin's right. He grasped the barrel just as the weapon discharged, striking the man to Garin's left in the neck. Garin ripped the pistol from the grasp of the shooter on the right, then reversed its grip and fired two suppressed rounds into the assailant's chest, followed by another just above the bridge of his nose. Without pausing, Garin pivoted to the man on the left, now lying on the hallway floor, and fired an insurance round into his forehead as well.

Elapsed time from door opening to dead shooters: a tick under four seconds. Speed, Garin always maintained, kills.

He quickly examined the hallway. Empty. He noticed something amiss with the bottom hemisphere of the surveillance camera affixed to the ceiling down the hall. The shooters had, thankfully, disabled it.

Garin secured both weapons in the process, then quickly dragged the bodies of the shooters to the emergency exit stairwell two rooms down, depositing both on the landing. When he returned to the room, Luci had staggered to her feet, her eyes wide with panic and bewilderment. Garin wrapped her in a brief bear hug and then held her at arm's length, looking dead into her eyes.

"Grab every single thing that belongs to you here and in your room as fast as you can. Time to check out."

CHAPTER 8

Piotr Egorshin should not have been nervous.

Piotr Egorshin was a star, and stars shouldn't get nervous, or, on the rare occasion when they might, it should not be noticeable.

Yet it was painfully apparent to Egorshin's driver that his boss was nervous, if not downright fearful. Though he appeared to be reclining comfortably in the expansive back seat of his Kortezh limo, his driver, looking in the rearview mirror, could see his body was tense, his fingers drumming rapidly on the armrest.

Not only was Egorshin a star, but his stardom was on the ascendancy, with no apogee in sight. At age thirty-eight he had rocketed through Russian military intelligence, the head of a special cyberwarfare unit within the Glavnoye Razvedyvatel'noye Upravleniye, or GRU. The unit sat at the pinnacle of Russia's vast cyberwarfare apparatus, an apparatus that transcended government agencies, coordinating cyberespionage, counterintelligence, degradation of foreign information services, distributed denial of service attacks, and other informational war capabilities among an array of military, intelligence, business, and cybercriminal networks.

The unit had no name, purposely so. The West had not even heard rumors of its existence, though its effects were spectacular.

Because there was scant daylight between military cyberwarfare efforts and those of the highly sophisticated Russian cybercriminal syndicates, it was staggeringly difficult, if not impossible, for the cyberforensics of Western intelligence services to attribute, if not trace, cyberattacks—whether inconsequential or devastating—to the Russian government. This permitted the GRU to engage in all manner of mischief with near impunity.

Egorshin's operation was assisted by a familial connection in the SVR, Russian foreign intelligence, who had, over the course of several decades, succeeded in planting agents within the US National Security Agency—the most powerful signals intelligence agency in the world. Egorshin's uncle, Sergei, had run a string of NSA mules for the KGB beginning in the early 1980s. US intelligence believed they had rolled up all such moles during Operation Global Story in 2010, but most of the SVR agents arrested in the operation were mere decoys. The SVR agents who remained within the NSA relayed information on the Five Eye encryption to Sergei, who relayed such information to his favorite nephew. Consequently, Russian military intelligence was able to monitor much of the West's most highly sensitive communications in real time.

Egorshin's family had been among the Soviet and Russian elite for decades. His grandfather had been a confidant of Kosygin and his father an associate of both Brezhnev and Andropov. After the collapse of the Soviet Union, the Egorshin family had prospered in business through its connections with powerful former KGB officials. Piotr, considered the most talented of the four Egorshin siblings, studied at both Harvard, where he acquired an air of privilege, and Oxford, where he cultivated a patina of unflappability.

So Colonel Piotr Egorshin had every reason to be calm, even arrogant. But as his car navigated through the surprisingly warm Moscow night, the closer it drew to the Kremlin, the faster his fingers drummed.

And that was because of one man: Aleksandr Stetchkin, head of the Twelfth Chief Directorate of the Ministry of Defense. Stetchkin was perhaps Russian president Yuri Mikhailov's closest associate. Stetchkin, like Mikhailov, was former KGB. And Stetchkin was second only to Mikhailov as the most feared man in all of Russia.

The basis for the fear was not hypothetical. Beyond the rumors that inevitably surrounded high-level Russian officials, there were sufficient documented cases of Stetchkin's ruthlessness that it would be unreasonable not to have a degree of trepidation meeting with him.

It didn't help matters that the meeting was called for four A.M. Nothing mundane happens at such an absurd hour, thought Egorshin.

Two other facts conspired against Egorshin's remaining calm: This was his first meeting with Stetchkin since the latter had become Egorshin's direct supervisor, if not officially, then functionally.

Ivan Uganov, Egorshin's former boss, had been removed from his position for indeterminate reasons, although reports circulated that Uganov's offense was to have questioned Stetchkin's intelligence. The hyperactive rumor mill of the Russian intelligence community suggested that he now resided somewhere deep in the bowels of Penal Colony Number Six of the Federal Penitentiary Service—the infamous Black Dolphin Prison. Consequently, the second-most feared man in Russia now would be scrutinizing Egorshin's every move.

But a far more important reason was that Russian history—world history—was scheduled to change in less than ninety hours. And Colonel Piotr Egorshin, whose vehicle had just arrived at one of the most imposing edifices in the world, was at the fulcrum of that change.

CHAPTER 9

Georgia state trooper Jim Benton sat in his cruiser along I-85 as early evening began to fade to night.

For Benton, dusk was approaching literally and figuratively. The twenty-eight-year veteran of Georgia State Patrol was approaching retirement, and although he hadn't set a fixed date, he suspected he probably wouldn't finish out the year. He'd had a fine career. Commendations and awards aplenty. But the cumulative breaks, strains, and bruises were catching up to him. In fact, his current detail was his third light-duty assignment in as many years, the latest a consequence of injuries received in a tussle with a trucker he'd pulled over for a moving violation who happened to have a load of methamphetamines in his trailer.

Benton was one of the sharper knives in the drawer of Georgia law enforcement. Not only was he experienced, but he had the innate intelligence and eye for detail of a physician, the occupation chosen by his two older brothers and sister. Benton had also seemed destined for a career in medicine, but physiology intervened; not the class, but his own. He was six foot four, 260 pounds of muscle softened only a bit by age—dimensions that had steered him toward a stellar college football career as a defensive end for the Georgia Bulldogs, as well as a preference for a physical, action-oriented profession. So, after college and a brief stint as a Cobb County deputy, he became a Georgia state trooper, resisting numerous attempts by superiors to steer him into supervisory roles that could desperately use his talents, preferring to remain where the action was.

Thus, the most overqualified traffic cop in the state of Georgia was sitting in an idling cruiser on the right berm of the highway shielded from the view of drivers by the pillars of an overpass, scanning traffic for speeders, DUI, and other suspicious activity.

To this point it had been an unremarkable evening. But as the first stars began to appear in the darkening eastern sky, a southbound gray 2015 Ford Transit van caught Benton's eye. Not because it was speeding, driving erratically, or had an expired tag, but because it was a Ford Transit. Benton could recall seeing few, if any, of that make and model along the highway. So as the vehicle approached from the rear at a steady sixty miles an hour, his gaze rested a second longer than usual on the front-seat occupants.

And that was all it took. It was only a glimpse, partially obscured by the head of the person in the passenger seat. But enough for the shrewd, experienced eye of the veteran trooper to send a signal to his brain. Not of alarm or concern, but of curiosity. That signal pulled up an image from a page with a series of photographs—head shots of certain suspects drawn from the sprawling terrorist screening database on the basis of sightings or reports suggesting such subjects might be in the northern Georgia area.

Benton hesitated a moment before shifting his vehicle into gear, restrained if only for a second by the hours upon hours of training and admonitions against profiling and cautions about implicit bias. Many officers, some of them good friends, had gotten into trouble for acting on hunches that politicians, lawyers, and activists maintained were fueled by racial stereotyping—enough that almost every law enforcement person he knew paused before acting on the instincts developed by years of experience as a good cop.

But while some community activist might have counseled Benton to take that moment's pause to reconsider his implicit bias, chastise himself, and stand down, Benton used it to call for backup, giving a reason, location, license number, and description of the Ford Transit before placing his car in gear and accelerating into the right lane approximately a quarter mile behind the van.

Abu al-Basri. That was the name Benton had given dispatch. And although he remembered the name, he couldn't remember the man's alleged infractions—just that he was on the terrorist watch list and had been engaged in some type of violence. Benton knew under such circumstances his call for backup, even unsupported by outstanding warrants, would trigger a quick response. If he was wrong, his retirement might be moved up involuntarily.

Within a few seconds, Benton had overtaken the van, pulling even with the driver's-side window in the left lane. Glancing over at the driver, Benton felt a pang of uneasiness. The driver resembled al-Basri, but there were no definite telltale markings. A plaintiff's lawyer would claim that the only reason the driver had been pulled over and humiliated was because Benton had engaged in racial profiling.

But Benton's unease lessened a bit when, looking behind the driver, he detected what appeared to be several men who appeared to be of Middle Eastern origin. The instincts that had served him well for three decades told him something was amiss. Benton radioed his findings, and dispatch reported that the van had been rented from Avis by a Seamus McCourt of Augusta. Ignoring the many hours of sensitivity training he'd received over the last decade, Benton noted that the driver looked nothing like a Seamus McCourt.

Benton saw that the driver continued looking straight ahead, not casting even a glance at the state trooper. In his rearview mirror, Benton caught two cruisers, light bars flashing, vectoring onto the highway from an on-ramp. Benton lit his light bar also, capturing the attention of the driver, whom he motioned to pull over.

The driver complied, coasting to a stop on the berm, the police vehicle behind him.

Benton resolved to be alert but courteous in the event, as was reasonably probable, the driver was simply an ordinary citizen motoring down the freeway. Three troopers, including Benton, got out of their vehicles, Benton approaching the driver's-side door with his hand on his weapon while the rest remained in tactical positions to the rear. Stopping several feet behind the door, he called for the driver to get out of the vehicle. Almost immediately, the door opened and the driver stepped onto the berm. A second later Benton heard the sound of the passenger door opening also, the occupant appearing around the front of the van as he approached the driver's side.

Cops hate sudden movement and surprises. All three began shouting for the passenger not to move. The passenger raised his palms outward and upward in a display of confusion and innocence but continued moving toward the driver, his movements phantomlike in the twilight. The cacophony of shouting grew louder and sharper, the troopers converging, pistols drawn, upon the Phantom.

Benton's last conscious memory was of the Phantom's eyes. Wolf's eyes. Predatory. Then a telescoping baton materialized in the Phantom's right hand and with astonishing speed struck a vicious backhanded blow across the bridge of Benton's nose, sending the big man crashing unconscious to the pavement. Before the converging officers could react, the Phantom pivoted toward them and with grim precision swung the baton first at the trachea of the approaching officer to his left and then backhanded toward the trachea of the officer to his right. Each collapsed helplessly to the pavement, gasping desperately for air through crushed and useless windpipes, eyes wide in pain and terror.

For several seconds, the only sound in the approaching twilight was the idling of the vehicles and the futile gurgling of the officers writhing on the asphalt. Then there was a metallic clicking sound as the Phantom collapsed the baton, which disappeared as if by magic into an unseen pocket in the Phantom's loose-fitting cargo pants.

The driver stood frozen next to the van. The other nine occupants sat rigid in the gloom of the rear of the van, stunned by the cold efficiency they'd just witnessed.

They saw the Phantom disarm one of the officers.

Nine methodically placed shots rang into the hot Georgia night, two in the torso and one in the head of each of the troopers.

The assassin could hear the crackling of the patrol car radios. He knew he must now abandon the van. He looked down the highway. He needed to and would procure another vehicle for the group.

They were still on schedule for the event. Later generations would say that the world had never seen anything like it before.

CHAPTER 10

NORTHERN GEORGIA,
AUGUST 14, 9:12 P.M. EDT

It would have to do. Approaching from the south less than a mile away was a white Econoline van. Not as large as the Transit, but they didn't have the luxury of selectivity. They had to get out of there right now. It had been several minutes since he'd killed the troopers. He'd made productive use of the time since then, placing the bodies in one of the cruisers and driving all three of the police vehicles into the woods adjacent to the highway. Sparse traffic favored him. The disposal was accomplished without notice, only one motorist passing before he'd completed the task—and all that motorist would've seen was a van and one patrol car—nothing particularly alarming.

But with each second the lack of communication from the officers was certain to arouse concern with dispatch. Another set of patrol cars was sure to appear in short order. He needed to abandon the Transit and get its driver and passengers to a secure location off the highway, preferably as far away as possible. Sometime tonight an APB would be issued, and he had no idea if any of the slain officers had radioed dispatch that the Transit held nearly a dozen occupants. If they had, any vehicle within a hundred-mile radius capable of transporting that many passengers would be targeted by law enforcement.

So the assassin stood in the middle of the highway waving his arms at the approaching van, certain it would stop. Not because of the disabled vehicle on the berm, but because no one stands in the middle of a highway at dusk waving their arms at a speeding vehicle unless it is a matter of urgency.

The Econoline slowed and halted twenty feet from the assassin, who could see that the driver was alone. The face looking through the windshield with a quizzical expression belonged to a young man, perhaps a college student. The face appeared earnest and willing to help a fellow motorist in distress. A face that sat framed on his parents' fireplace mantel.

The assassin approached the open driver's-side window, pulled the Glock 43 he'd taken from one of the officers from his waistband, and put three 9mm rounds through the center of that face.

The assassin gestured for two of the former occupants of the Transit to come over to the Econoline.

"Get him out and put him in the woods with the others."

Both seemed to recoil slightly, something the assassin found peculiar given their participation in the event. But after a brief pause, they complied with his command.

Another vehicle approached in the distance as the young man's body was being secreted in the woods. The assassin held his breath for a second as he tried to determine if it was a patrol vehicle. The headlights were on but he didn't discern a light bar on the roof. Could be unmarked, but the odds were it was another civilian vehicle. He glanced at the Econoline and then back at the car. It had enough room to maneuver around the van, but not if he stood in the other lane, which he did, waving his arms again.

The vehicle, a Buick LaCrosse, slowed to a stop almost even with the van. The assassin approached and the driver lowered the window.

"Looks like you could use some help." It was the voice of an elderly man. The voice of someone who knew how to fix things. The voice of a little girl's grandfather. The assassin withdrew the Glock 43 from his waistband and with two rounds to the head silenced that voice forever.

The assassin summoned the body removers, who placed it with the others in the woods. They now had two conveyances. Less crowded. More options.

But those were ancillary considerations. The primary reason the assassin stopped the second vehicle was for emphasis. He'd observed the reaction of his ten charges when he'd shot the troopers. They were frightened. Fear was a wonderful behavioral tool, one he employed often. The killing of the Econoline's driver was both a necessity and a statement. The killing of the LaCrosse driver was an exclamation point: The assassin is in charge. Listen to every word he says. Don't deviate one scintilla. Obey him to the letter or die.

Body dispersal complete, the ten gathered around him expectantly, awaiting further instructions.

"Who else has a license?"

A hand went up.

"Drive the car. Three of you go with him. Follow the rest of us in the van. Not too close."

They obeyed. A minute later they were headed north, hovering around the speed limit. They drove for little more than a hundred miles, crossing into South Carolina.

The assassin, seated in the front passenger seat of the van, directed the driver toward a small farmhouse that sat nearly a half mile off the road behind acres of corn. The car followed closely behind. The two vehicles pulled up the drive to a semicircle in front of the house and stopped. Everyone but the assassin was apprehensive. Everyone but the assassin expected the inhabitants of the house to be executed.

The assassin examined his watch. They were still on time.

CHAPTER 11

CENTRAL TEXAS,
AUGUST 14, 7:18 P.M. CDT

Luci Saldana's emotions swirled. She couldn't separate them, figure out which should be given primacy, which should govern her actions, which would enhance her safety or survival.

Tom Lofton had killed two men. She'd been less than ten feet away when it happened. They'd held guns on him, surprised him. Yet they were outmatched. He'd overwhelmed them as if they were infants.

And now they were driving down the highway in the Challenger he'd rented for the week of the Crucible. Despite the unwavering intensity in his eyes, he appeared calm. Save for a few brief commands at the outset, he had not spoken since the shootings.

"You killed two policemen, Tom. You killed two cops."

"They weren't cops."

"They had guns. They were dressed like cops, like detectives."

"They weren't cops."

"How do you know? How can you be sure?"

"Cops don't use suppressors."

"What?"

"Suppressors." Garin paused. "What some call silencers."

They drove for another twenty seconds.

"Are you sure, Tom?"

"I'm sure."

"Then it was self-defense?"

"I prefer to call it preemption."

Another ten seconds of silence.

"Then we need to go to the real cops. If those guys were going to kill us, we need to let the cops know now, Tom. Otherwise, when they find the bodies, they'll think you—we—killed them for no reason. It'll make things worse."

"Can't do it."

"Why?" Luci's voice went up an octave. "Why not?"

Garin didn't reply. Five more seconds of silence.

"Who are you, Tom?"

"Someone who knows we can't go to the cops," Garin replied. "And even if we could, it would be useless."

"What in the world does that mean?"

"It means if we go to the cops, we're dead. Both of us. No maybes. Dead." Garin's voice was low but emphatic. "But I can keep us alive. At least for a while."

"Who are you, Tom?"

"No one important."

"A man who two guys with silencers tried to kill, who can keep us alive even though the cops can't, is important to something. Or someone."

A no-nonsense reply. Yet another reason for Garin to like Luci.

"Not anymore."

"I deserve some answers, Tom. You know that. A few hours ago I was your trainer. Now, for all I know, I'm your accomplice. Whether you're a good guy or a bad guy, I'm in serious trouble. You admitted as much; if we go to the cops we're dead. You can't stonewall me, Tom. I didn't buy into this."

Garin remained silent.

"If you won't tell me who you are, then tell me who they are. Who did you just kill?"

Garin remained silent.

Luci's voice became more strident. "Tom—"

"My name is Michael Garin."

The shock was naked on Luci's face. "What?"

"Mike Garin. I use Tom Lofton on occasion."

"Are you hiding? A fugitive?"

A reasonable assumption, thought Garin. "No."

"Who do you work for?"

"Currently unemployed."

Luci gazed out the windshield down the endless stretch of highway, absorbing the events of the past few hours and Garin's revelation. Computing, reasoning.

"Who *did* you work for?"

"I can't tell you."

"You a cop?"

"No."

"Are you a good guy or bad guy?" There was a bit of trepidation in her voice.

"Depends on who you ask."

Frustrated, Luci pivoted. "Tom . . . Mike. Should I call you Mike or Michael?"

"Your choice."

"If you can't tell me who you are, Mike, do you at least know who they are?"

"I'm not completely sure," Garin acknowledged.

"Then how do you know we're dead if we go to the cops?"

"Because something similar happened about a month ago."

"This happens to you *monthly*?"

The tone of Luci's voice caused him to rewind the last minute of conversation and play it back in his mind. He conceded to himself that from her perspective, the conversation, if it weren't so frightening, would be absurd. He'd placed her life in jeopardy because he'd forgotten how dangerous his own was. Yet as much as she deserved answers, he couldn't provide them—at least not yet.

"Luci, I can tell you this much: This is very serious. It's highly probable more people will be coming to kill me and that whoever sent them has extensive resources and won't stop until I'm dead or they're dead. It's highly probable they know who you are and will eliminate you if it serves their purposes. And it's highly probable they will succeed if you don't follow my directions."

Neither spoke for several minutes. To Luci, the man sitting next to her had been an enigma since she'd first met him as Tom Lofton, yet even now, she felt safe with him.

"What are your directions?" Luci finally asked.

"First we need to put some distance between us and Dallas. Then we need to ditch the Challenger and get another car. And then I'll take you to people who can protect you while I set things right."

"How are you going to do that?" Luci asked.

"I'm working that out."

For her part, Luci was beginning to suspect it was highly probable he would find the people behind the assassination attempt. And it was highly probable he'd kill them.

CHAPTER 12

MOUNT VERNON, VIRGINIA,
AUGUST 14, 9:45 P.M. EDT

The story of the massacre was on all the cable news shows.

According to CNN, two Georgia State Patrol vehicles were dispatched to assist another trooper who had requested backup regarding a suspicious driver. After dispatch was unable to contact the troopers, several other vehicles were dispatched but found no vehicles at the last reported location. Fox News reported that after several additional cars were dispatched on a thirty-mile stretch of I-85, aerial surveillance was deployed using infrared scopes.

MSNBC reported that a team with search dogs located the bodies of three troopers and two civilians next to three patrol cars and a Ford Transit in the woods near the last reported location. Each of the victims had been shot multiple times, including what the reports described as a coup de grace—a single shot just above the bridge of the nose.

Dan Dwyer, a former Navy SEAL and owner and CEO of DGT, a mammoth military and security contractor, watched all three broadcasts intermittently on a bank of monitors located in a multimillion-dollar secure communications room in the subbasement of his sprawling home in Mount Vernon, Virginia. The grisly story had been playing on all the news outlets, interspersed with vapid political commentary and news of the tropical depression that appeared to be evolving into a hurricane off the eastern coast of Cuba. Until the reference to the single shot to the bridge of each victim's nose, it had all served as background noise while Dwyer studied financial and operational reports. Asleep at his feet were Max, his giant geriatric Newfoundland, and two German shepherd pups, Bear and Diesel.

The detail about the shot to the bridge of the nose, however, gave him pause. It reminded Dwyer of the favorite maxim of special operations legend Clint Laws that "there are no coincidences in this business."

A shot to the bridge of the nose was, indeed, an effective act to ensure the victim never posed a problem again. It was not unique in the business of death, but that particular signature had played a minor role in a series of events that had culminated in the current US bombing campaign against Iranian nuclear facilities.

After the story was replayed for perhaps the third time, Dwyer switched the monitors to an all-sports network. Preseason college football practices had begun and analysts were speculating about the race for the national title. A former assistant coach at Annapolis, Dwyer also had a rooting interest in the Wisconsin Badgers, his home state team. He snorted derisively when the consensus had the Badgers at twenty-fifth, well below Big Ten rivals Ohio State, Michigan, and Michigan State.

Just as one of the commentators was concluding what Dwyer considered to be a sophomoric analysis of the state of the Southeastern Conference, a buzzer sounded, signaling an incoming call. Bear and Diesel perked. Max remained asleep. Dwyer moved to the deep-cushioned captain's chair in the center of the room and pushed a button on the console embedded in the armrest, activating a speakerphone.

"Need help."

Now Max perked, recognizing Garin's voice.

"Whoa, whoa," Dwyer said. "No salutations? No witty byplay? No prefatory explanations? I have to conclude that your miserable butt is, once again, in an impressively deep pile of excrement."

Dwyer was, perhaps, the only person in the world who would dare address Mike Garin in that fashion. The two, after all, shared a long and varied history. Dwyer, several years Garin's senior, had unsuccessfully recruited the latter to play football at Annapolis, Garin choosing to attend Cornell instead, where he became an honorable mention all-American at free safety. A few years later Dwyer was one of Garin's instructors at BUD/S, the SEAL training program. Despite excelling at

BUD/S, Garin one day disappeared from the program, only to inexplicably reemerge in time to save Dwyer's life during a mountaintop operation in Afghanistan.

By then, Garin's reputation in the special operations community had assumed near-mythic status. The two went on to found DGT along with Bob Thompson, a fellow operator. A few years later Garin cashed out handsomely and once again disappeared. It wasn't until earlier in the summer that Dwyer had learned that Garin led the Omega team, a clandestine unit of tier-one special operators tasked with destroying or compromising rogue WMD programs on foreign soil. Garin had turned to Dwyer when every member of Omega had been assassinated and Garin was being sought as the chief suspect. Their collaboration discovered and thwarted an EMP attack against the United States. Since then, Dwyer had been trying to convince Garin to return to DGT.

"You conclude correctly," Garin responded. "A couple of hours ago two shooters tried to take me out."

Dwyer felt a twinge of anxiety. No coincidences in this business. He hit another button on the armrest console and the monitors switched back to the cable news shows. CNN and Fox were running the Georgia massacre loop.

"Where are you?" Dwyer asked.

"On I-45 southbound from Dallas."

"It's not over. He's back," Dwyer said.

"What do you mean?"

"The news shows are reporting a mass shooting in Georgia. Three state troopers and a couple of civilians. Each had been shot—"

"In the forehead just above the bridge of the nose."

"Bor." Dwyer nodded. "When the news first hit it stuck in the back of my mind. But I thought we killed all those bastards."

"All but Bor," Garin corrected.

"And we're bombing Iran back into the Mesozoic era. But now that you tell me someone tried to hit you . . ."

"No coincidences."

"Never," Dwyer affirmed. "What could they be up to now?"

"If it's Bor, it's something very bad."

Dwyer registered the unease in his friend's voice. Bor was the only person Dwyer had seen produce apprehension in Garin. In many ways, Bor and Garin were alike—physically, temperamentally, and operationally. There was, however, one quality peculiar to Bor. During his career in special warfare, Dwyer had encountered some of the most dangerous human beings mankind had produced. Bor, however, was unequivocally the closest thing to unadulterated evil Dwyer could imagine.

"If our recent experience is any guide, whatever big and bad thing Bor's up to is going to happen fast. The man's efficient. Practically supernatural." Dwyer paused. "Now is the time for all good men to come to the aid of their country, Mikey. Retirement's over. It's not you anyway."

"It wasn't retirement; it was a hiatus," Garin corrected.

"What do you need from me?"

"I need protection for a civilian. She's with me right now."

"A babe, I hope?"

Garin ignored the comment. Dwyer was both a savvy and successful businessman and a proficient operator, yet regardless of almost any circumstance, his approach was that of a college sophomore at Mardi Gras.

"Luci Saldana. They'll no doubt come for her."

"Your trainer for the Crucible? FYI—a hiatus implies relaxation, buddy, not radical physical torture. But I expect you cruised," Dwyer said. "Keep going south on I-45 toward Houston. Then take, I think, 59 southwest or maybe 90A to Sugar Land Regional Airport. You'll find it. I'll put Congo Knox on one of the Gulfstreams. He should be there in"—Dwyer examined a digital clock on the wall—"three to four hours. Go to the southernmost end of the runway off 90A near the old Central Unit 2 Prison. We have a small facility nearby that provides logistics support for our oil well, platform, and refinery security operations. I'll make sure the manager is there to meet you. Austin Danzig. Good man. Former Air Force PJ. He'll babysit Ms. Saldana until Congo arrives."

"Thanks."

"You're racking up quite the chit, man. This, plus the support for the last time bad guys were trying to kill you—"

"We'll settle up later," Garin interrupted. "Right now I need you to contact Olivia."

"I heard she's been seeing some senator since our last encounter," Dwyer said. "You know, though, she still only has eyes for you."

"Thanks for the tabloid newsflash, Dan, but you need to let her know we suspect Bor's back in operation."

"Olivia? Why not Kessler?" Dwyer asked, referring to the deputy director of the CIA.

"We can't trust anyone other than Olivia and James Brandt. The EMP operation was assisted, maybe even guided, by someone very high up in this government. We still don't know who that person is. Until then, we have to operate as if everyone's a potential mole. Same protocols as the EMP operation."

"Okay. I assume you're on a throwaway?"

"SIM's coming out and it's going out the window as soon as I get off this call, which, as far as I'm concerned, has already been too long."

"My lines are completely, one hundred percent secure," Dwyer said indignantly. He spent a small fortune on state-of-the-art surveillance countermeasures and was proud of it.

"My systems will screw up any . . ." Dwyer stopped. Static was coming over the speakerphone.

CHAPTER 13

The barn had a low plywood platform used for stacking produce, large enough to easily accommodate all ten of them.

They had arrayed their sleeping bags in a neat row next to one another with a foot or two separating each. To a man, they were relieved the assassin hadn't executed the elderly couple who lived in the farmhouse out front, but to a man they were expecting the assassin to do so before sunrise.

Taras Bor would not. Not unless they gave him a very good reason for doing so.

The couple were George and Allie Nichols of Abbeville County, South Carolina, both in their late seventies. They had been born Oleg Nikolin of Leningrad—now Saint Petersburg—and Aleksandra Ivanova of Moscow. They were not married, although county clerk records claimed they were. The neighbors thought it was a shame they'd never had kids. They would be the perfect parents and grandparents.

Although every official document stated, and everyone who knew them believed, that they had been born in the United States, they hadn't arrived until the late seventies, as sleeper agents under the supervision of the First Chief Directorate. Since then, they'd lived a typical American lifestyle in every respect. They worked their modest farm. They attended Saint Matthew's across the county line. For a period during the late eighties, Allie was even a member of the county planning commission, impressing several residents enough to urge her to run for the state legislature. She didn't, citing family farm obligations.

George supplemented their modest income as a talented handyman.

They also received irregular cash stipends from the KGB and SVR. Not much, so as to discourage anything but modest purchases that wouldn't attract attention. They paid all of their taxes on time but every few years remembered to make inconsequential errors on their forms so the filings wouldn't be suspiciously immaculate.

The last forty years for George and Allie had been unremarkable. With the collapse of the Soviet Union they'd made a seamless transition from working for the KGB to working for the SVR. In practice and substance, nearly everything remained the same. They were rarely pressed into service, and then only to provide a temporary accommodation for the occasional KGB or SVR agent. The years had seen them evolve from revolutionary communists to ardent nationalists to senior citizens. In all that time, Bor's team was by far the largest and most consequential they'd ever accommodated.

The Nicholses knew nothing of Bor, only that he and his companions would be stopping by during the night. Upon learning the size of the entourage, the couple were concerned about what would happen if someone was to drop by. They were assured that everything would be all right; the group would be arriving at night, and even if a curious neighbor or law enforcement officer should visit, their guest was quite adept at managing fluid situations.

Although they were unfamiliar with Bor or his reputation, George, having raised a variety of farm animals over several decades, knew something of predators, and he was certain Bor was just such a creature. He was quite pleasant, his mannerisms almost charming. But his eyes were uncompromising and his body was designed for destruction.

He was sitting casually in George's modest den, watching the story about the Georgia massacre. The Nicholses were unaware, of course, that Bor had anything to do with the massacre or had sanction to kill them both—a sanction directly from Yuri Mikhailov himself. For although Bor occasionally reported, as circumstances might warrant, to either Aleksandr Stetchkin or the chief of the general staff, he was answerable to the president of Russia alone. In a very powerful circle in Russia it was said even Stetchkin afforded Bor something of a broad berth.

Bor's only concern regarding the news reports related to the reference to each of the victims having been shot at the bridge of the nose. He was certain that if Michael Garin heard the report he would conclude that Bor was in operation, and Garin was the primary impediment to the success of the operation.

Bor was scheduled to receive a call any moment confirming Garin's death. And while Bor patiently awaited the call, he thought the odds he would receive a favorable report were bleak. Garin had frustrated their plans in the past, and absent Bor's direct involvement in his demise, it was best to assume Garin would do so again.

That was okay. Bor desperately preferred Garin's elimination, but Russians played chess while Americans continued to struggle at checkers. The shots to the bridge of the nose were not a mistake. Whether Garin survived, or even if he didn't—the placement served a purpose. It facilitated the double blind.

George came into the den and placed a cup of tea on the table next to Bor. "Let me show you something, friend," George said, waving him to a corner of the room. "You'll get a kick out of it."

Bor shrugged and rose from the chair. "Sure."

Before he could move toward George, Bor's cell vibrated. He pressed the phone icon on the screen and put the device to his ear.

"Yes?"

"Trident is down," the voice on the other end said. It was the voice of an agent of the Russian foreign intelligence service.

"Both of them?"

"Yes, I'm afraid."

"What is the location of the subject?" Bor asked.

"Unknown."

"You had two surveillance teams."

"The subject eluded them somehow."

Of course, thought Bor, *just as I suspected.*

"My teams will be there shortly. We will discuss this further," Bor said curtly and ended the call. The asset on the other end felt a spike of terror.

Bor, his expression relaxed, returned his attention to George. "Now, what do you want to show me?"

George grinned again and bent down to lift a three-by-four-foot section of flooring in the corner of the room behind the television. A trapdoor. He laid the section next to the opening and began to descend some stairs.

Bor followed the old man to a cellar the size of a small bedroom. The walls were completely lined with magnesium incendiaries that, when ignited, burned at more than two thousand degrees Celsius, turning everything within the cellar into an unrecognizable and indecipherable cinder.

Most of the cellar was stacked from floor to shoulder height with boxes and crates containing several generations of computer equipment, communications devices, and weapons—most of which had never been used.

A small museum of the Cold War, a war that many American politicians failed to recognize had never ended.

Bor took particular interest in the weapons: two Makarovs, a PSS-2, a KS-23 shotgun, and, of course, the ubiquitous AK-47, all lying atop a container with stenciled markings. Bor was intimately familiar with them all. He was sure the Nicholses were familiar with none. Numerous boxes of the appropriate ammunition lay unopened next to each.

"We have our own little armory down here," George said, like a boy showing off toys in the attic. "I have no illusions about the guns. But I imagine one day we'll get to use some of the equipment."

Doubtful, thought Bor.

George pointed to a switch on the wall next to the stairs. "That's on a thirty-second timer. There's an identical one upstairs next to the front door. If I flip it on, this place gets incinerated. Given the temperature of the flames, probably the house above goes too."

No doubt, thought Bor.

"What do you think, *tovarishch*?" George asked.

For a fraction of a second, Bor's hand moved toward the pistol in the waistband under his shirt. George had made a grievous mistake, perhaps the only one of his long and uneventful career. Speaking Russian, even in the cellar of a safe house on an isolated farm, could get someone caught or killed. This wasn't the seventies, eighties, or even nineties. There were satellites, drones, directional microphones, and listening devices everywhere. Even in rural South Carolina.

But Bor caught himself. George's one mistake in forty years, and only a few years left. Was it truly worth a bullet to the head? Besides, the important thing was they were still on time.

George caught the glint of anger in Bor's eyes and shook his head. "That's never happened before," he offered contritely, disappointed in himself. "It will never happen again, friend."

Bor nodded dismissively and ascended the stairs, followed by George.

As the old man replaced the heavy flooring over the cellar opening, it slipped from his grasp, slamming sharply to the floor of the den with a loud crack that echoed out the open window into the warm night.

Every single body lying in a sleeping bag in the relative coolness of the barn flinched.

CHAPTER 14

Luci Saldana stood next to Austin Danzig outside a small cinder-block building off the southeastern end of the runway at Sugar Land Regional Airport watching the Gulfstream taxi to within about a hundred feet.

Mike Garin had instructed her to follow Danzig's directions to the letter and do the same with Congo Knox when he arrived. Then, after assuring her she was in the best of hands, the enigma formerly known to her as Tom Lofton disappeared into the night.

Danzig was tall and wiry, with short, prematurely gray hair brushed back from his forehead. He looked to Luci like someone who kept his pens and notepads in neat rows on his desk and could recite the precise number of paper clips stored in the top drawer.

The whine of the Gulfstream's engines slowed, grew mournful, and stopped. A minute later the front hatch opened to the steps. A six-foot-four, 220-pound bolt of muscle, bone, and sinew dressed in black cargo pants and a dark gray T-shirt appeared at the door. His ebony head was shaved and he wore a goatee that descended into a sharp point beneath his chin. Although it was nighttime, a pair of Oakley sunglasses sat atop his head.

Luci watched as Danzig went to greet Robert "Congo" Knox with the sort of deference she'd seen privates accord superior officers on TV. Danzig had much more seniority than Knox, who'd joined DGT barely a month ago, but Knox's reputation preceded him. A former sniper for the First Special Forces Operational Detachment-Delta, Knox had more than eighty confirmed kills, including one at nineteen hundred yards using a fifty-caliber McMillan TAC-50 while adjusting for an eight-to-ten-mile-per-hour crosswind. He was known to his superiors as a problem solver: Whenever removal of a bad guy proved particularly nettlesome, they'd deploy Knox. One shot, problem solved. He retired as one of the deadliest snipers in American military history.

Danzig shook his hand and escorted him toward Luci.

"Mr. Knox, this is Ms. Saldana. Mr. Garin left her with me a short time ago and asked me to put her in your custody."

Luci extended her hand. "Nice to meet you, Mr. Knox."

He shook her hand. "Please call me Congo," he said, his voice a low rumble that resonated deep in his chest like the prelude to a volcanic eruption.

Luci's face betrayed unease, a reaction Knox had seen before.

"Political correctness offends me, Ms. Saldana; my name doesn't. Call me Congo."

"Okay," Luci said sheepishly, suspecting more than a few administrators on her campus would faint before doing so.

"You're welcome to sit in my office and have some coffee while you wait for the pilots to do whatever they need to do," Danzig said, gesturing toward the cinder-block cube. "I expect it should be a short turnaround."

The inside of the building was neat, almost severely so. One wall was covered with multicolor maps, another with time zone clocks, underneath which was a cot where, Luci surmised, Danzig slept when working long nights such as this. Atop Danzig's desk was a computer and short-wave radio. On a metal table next to the desk was a coffee machine with a full pot of steaming coffee, a stack of paper cups, and a pile of MREs. Two gray metal folding chairs were on either side of the table.

"The coffee tastes like paint thinner but it's got a kick like crystal meth—so I'm told."

Danzig poured two cups and handed one each to Luci and Knox. "Help yourself to the cream and sugar," he said, pointing next to the pot. "I run our petroleum-related operations for the Western Hemisphere out of this little place. We share a warehouse space out back with an aircraft fractional company. They use their portion as a hangar. We use ours mainly to store supplies. From here I can move everything from clothing to RBIs onto the drilling platforms off the coast of Colombia in just five hours and fifteen minutes from time of requisition to receipt."

"And make twice as much as your counterpart at FedEx doing so," Knox added between sips of coffee.

Danzig winked. "Yes, sir. DGT's the place to be."

"You should be in recruitment."

Danzig grinned and left to check on the Gulfstream.

Luci blew the steam off her coffee. "What's next?"

"We fly back to D.C. and I take you to Mr. Dwyer's house, where I'm to watch over you until further notice," Knox replied.

"Who's Mr. Dwyer?"

"He's the man who owns DGT, which owns this place, the Gulfstream outside, and at least one billion dollars in other assets."

"Sounds important. Why's he doing all of this for me?"

"Mike didn't tell you?" Knox asked.

"He's not big on explanations. He only told me his name a couple of hours ago."

"He and Dan Dwyer started the company. They go back."

Luci sensed an opportunity. "I see. So what's Mike's deal?"

"What do you mean?"

"Come on." Luci chuckled. "There's something about you guys. You, Danzig, Garin. Especially Garin. What's he all about?"

Knox hesitated, then shrugged. "Dude's different. First you got that whole Russian fatalism thing going. Imperturbable. Implacable. Then there's the fact that he doesn't know limits. At least physical limits."

Luci's brow knotted in concern. "I noticed. One day he's going to push a little too hard."

"Everyone has a wall," Knox continued. "Marathon runners, extreme athletes. He doesn't. At least none that I've seen yet. Hard to figure. Must be some kind of chemistry or biology experiment. Seriously."

"Well, he's in amazing shape," Luci explained.

"No, it's more than that. And then there's his patriotism. Duty, honor, country. They stopped making the prototype around 1990. Maybe 1890. Believes in good and evil. Dwyer calls him a Boy Scout."

"Do you agree?"

I once saw him pray the Rosary after killing four people, Knox said to himself. "Yeah, I think that fits. But he's still cool. I've seen him be . . . almost suave, even."

"What do you mean by 'Russian fatalism'?"

"You know those characters in Russian literature who are always resigned to a miserable fate? Mike sometimes seems like that. I think it rubbed off from his grandfather."

"His grandfather's from Russia, then?" Luci asked, intrigued.

"Somebody told me he escaped from the NKVD. Supposed to be a remarkable story. Like right out of a movie or something. I haven't had a chance to ask Mike about it yet."

"What's the NKVD?"

"Soviet secret police around World War II. Seriously nasty dudes," Knox explained. "Predecessor to the KGB."

"I've heard of the KGB," Luci acknowledged. "So Mike's still with DGT too?"

"He left years ago."

Luci sensed she was finally getting somewhere. "To do what?"

"Can't say."

Another roadblock. "Can't say or won't say?"

Knox took a sip of coffee. "A little of both, I guess."

Luci shifted tactics. "Well, then, what do you do?"

Knox smiled. "I work for DGT."

"C'mon," Luci pled, laughing. "It's like pulling teeth with you guys. What does DGT do?"

"We provide security, soup to nuts. Executive security, cybersecurity, infrastructure security, diplomatic security—you name it. And we provide gap support to the military and intelligence services."

"How long have you worked for DGT?"

"You'd make a good trial lawyer, Luci," Knox observed. "Pretty good at cross-examination."

"Answer the question."

"Just started a month ago."

"And before that?"

"I was in the service, Counselor."

"What branch?"

"Army."

"You weren't like in the"—Luci searched for the correct term—"regular Army or whatever it's called, were you?"

"Everything is regular in the Army. *Nothing* is regular in the Army."

"You know what I mean," Luci insisted. "You were one of those commando types, weren't you?"

He was beginning to like Luci. "We really don't refer to ourselves as commandos," Knox noted.

"What do you prefer to call yourselves, then?"

"Operators, Counselor."

"That's it. Operators. Special operators. Special forces, right?" Luci said excitedly. "Like Navy SEALs, right?"

"That's the Navy. I was Army."

"Before he started DGT was Mike Garin an operator, too?"

Knox looked stumped. "Tell you the truth," Knox said, stroking his goatee, "I'm not sure anyone really knows what Mike was doing before DGT. Not even Dan Dwyer. There's, like, two, three years where no one knows anything about Mike. Seriously spooky stuff."

"You know, you say 'seriously' a lot," Luci needled. "Seriously."

Danzig poked his head in the door. "Your crew says they plan to be wheels up in the next fifteen."

As they rose to leave, Luci noted that she barely reached Knox's imposing chest. She felt safe with him too, and she liked his smile.

CHAPTER 15

The buzzer stirred Dan Dwyer from his slumber in the captain's chair of his communications room. During his time in the teams he had perfected the art of falling asleep anywhere at any time. It didn't hurt that the chair was almost obscenely plush and reclined to the precise angle most likely to induce sleep.

His eyes closed, Dwyer grasped for the speakerphone button on the armrest console.

"Dwyer."

"Need more help."

Now familiar with Garin's voice, Bear and Diesel perked up along with Max.

"Geez Louise. If we're going to be fighting Big Bad Bor again, I'm going to need some sleep. Where are you now?"

"Northbound on I-45, near Corsicana."

Dwyer sat up in the chair and opened his eyes, focusing on the digital clock that displayed central daylight time. "That's about sixty miles south of Dallas. Hate to tell you this, but you're heading in the wrong direction, Mikey."

"Need a favor."

"You said that."

"Can you send a team to check on Katy and her family? Maybe have them sit in a car outside her house?" Garin was referring to his older sister. Garin's enemies had once tried to get to him by threatening Katy, her husband, and their three small children.

"Absolutely. Hold on."

Dwyer placed Garin on hold, punched another button, and gave instructions to his operations center in Quantico to send a protective detail to the home of Joe and Katy Burns in Brecksville, Ohio, a suburb of Cleveland. Dwyer then returned to Garin's call.

"Will be there within the half hour."

"Thanks much. Luci's secure?"

"She and Congo Knox should be northeast bound at thirty-eight thousand feet somewhere over Tennessee right now."

"Thanks again. What about Olivia? Were you able to reach her?"

Dwyer sighed and rubbed his eyes. Diesel yawned loudly.

"What was that?" Garin asked.

"Diesel yawned."

"What?"

"Never mind," Dwyer said. "Her phone is off. Didn't want to leave a voice mail. It's eleven o'clock, Mike. She's probably asleep. I'll call first thing. Why are you headed back to Dallas?"

"The only reason I left Dallas was to get Luci to safety. And to avoid any backup shooters or being linked to the bodies of the dead shooters," Garin explained. "Now that Luci's safe and we suspect Bor's involved, I need to find him, and the best way of doing that is through his backup teams."

Dwyer's voice became uncommonly sober. "Not a good move in my opinion, Mike. Last time we encountered Bor, he was using Iranian Quds Force operatives as surrogates; they were pretty good, but no match for you. He won't make that mistake again. I'm surprised he made that mistake in the first place."

"Are you saying he'd deploy Spetsnaz this time?" Garin scoffed, referring to Russian special operators. "Russians—the Soviets before them—never used Spetsnaz to kill Americans on American soil."

"No, Mike. Not Spetsnaz."

"Then who?"

"Zaslon."

Silence. He had Garin's attention. After several seconds Garin spoke again.

"Zaslon Unit operators?"

"That's right, Mike."

There was another pause and then he heard Garin exhale. He spoke tentatively.

"That would be a concern," Garin acknowledged. "But we've never really had confirmation of Zaslon's existence. It's all been conjecture."

"Pretty impressive for conjecture, wouldn't you say?"

"Are you referring to London? Crimea? Syria? No one—not CIA, not DIA, not MI6—has nailed down with any degree of certainty that those operations were the work of the Zaslon Unit. For all we know Zaslon is pure fiction. Classic Russian misdirection," Garin replied.

"Mike, I've never heard you engage in denial before. Don't start now. I saw their work firsthand in 2003 when I was with Task Force 121 hunting down Saddam Hussein. And even though you've never acknowledged it, all the Batman stories I heard point to you having been there too. So, you've seen their work."

"I saw *outcomes*," Garin countered. "Impressive, I agree. But that doesn't prove the existence of Zaslon."

"What was it that Clint Laws drilled into you?" Dwyer asked, referring to the special operations legend who was Garin's mentor. "'If there's any doubt, it's certain.' And what's the other? 'There are no coincidences in this business'? Mike, the mere fact that we're wondering about Zaslon all but confirms its existence. Zaslon," declared Dwyer, "is the Russian Omega."

There were several more seconds of silence. Nonetheless, the former SEAL thought it unlikely he had dissuaded Garin. Dwyer said, "All I'm saying is, be careful, Mike. Speaking of which, I assume you've got a new phone?"

"Several. From a sketchy all-night place outside of Sugar Land."

"And the vehicle?" Dwyer asked.

"Ditched it outside Sugar Land Regional. Avis won't be happy, but I've taken care of it."

Dwyer rolled his eyes. "Money in the glove box again?"

"It will more than cover the cost of shuttling it back to the rental office," Garin assured him. "Your man Danzig lent me a DGT fleet car."

"Nice of him to be so generous with my property. Please don't do anything with it that exceeds the insurance coverage, Mike."

"I won't," Garin assured him, and terminated the call. *But I can't speak for Zaslon.*

CHAPTER 16

Allie Nichols had prepared omelets and hash browns and taken them out to the volunteers in the barn, who gratefully consumed them. She had prepared the same breakfast for Bor, who had slept in the den. When he came into the kitchen, his plate was warming on the stove and a grocery bag with about a dozen brown paper bags containing sandwiches for lunch was on the kitchen table.

Bor, seeming somewhat groggy, picked up the plate, dropping the fork behind the stove. He cursed under his breath, fumbled behind the stove for the fork, and, upon retrieving it, rinsed it in the sink before moving to the kitchen table, where he made fast work of the meal. He planned to be on the road in ten minutes.

Bor placed the dish and silverware in the sink and thanked Allie for her hospitality.

"Where's George?" Bor asked.

"He went into the den. He's going to sand and putty the floor where he dropped the door to the cellar last night. It left a little dent. I think he should just put a rug over it and be done with it. But he likes to fix things."

Bor picked up the grocery bag from the counter and proceeded toward the door.

"Thank George for me."

"Good luck," Allie replied perfunctorily.

Bor stopped for a moment next to the door, turned, and nodded. Then he walked briskly onto the porch and saw that the volunteers had retaken their respective seats in the two vehicles. He looked at his watch, then scanned the countryside. Not another house, vehicle, or person in sight. They would make good progress today.

He rode in the passenger seat of the van again as it led the LaCrosse down the long driveway and onto the two-lane country road, heading north. They drove for a minute or so before they heard something that sounded like a rumble of thunder, but the skies were clear. Bor heard murmuring coming from the rear seats, followed by excited whispers. He glanced over his shoulder and saw the volunteers looking wide-eyed out the right window and slightly to the rear.

Rising above the tree line was a plume of thick black smoke in the general vicinity of the Nichols farmhouse. With no wind to disturb it, it billowed gently into a mushroom before the outer edges dissipated into a formless, ash-colored cloud.

The magnesium incendiaries had worked a bit faster than he'd expected, but not by much. From the time he flipped the thirty-second timer switch next to the front door to the time of the explosion, approximately two and a half minutes had elapsed. As expected, the extreme heat from the incendiaries was sufficient not only to incinerate the cellar, but to set the house ablaze also. In hindsight, tampering with the gas line behind the stove was probably superfluous and a bit of a risk. The couple might have smelled the odor of the tagging agent in the natural gas and attempted to escape. Besides, with some of the windows open on this warm morning, the volume of gas might not have built to a combustible critical mass. Regardless, the natural gas would lead any local fire investigators down a rabbit hole, causing them to conclude it was at least a contributing factor.

But Bor knew something the elderly couple and any local fire officials did not. Regardless of the natural gas or the open windows, the house was doomed the moment Bor initiated the thirty-second timer.

Inside the container with the stenciled markings were several kilograms of pentaerythritol tetranitrate, enough to level the entire farmhouse and leave a sizable crater. The searing heat from the magnesium incendiaries was more than seven times hotter than the ignition temperature of the white crystalline substance inside that stenciled container. The container would protect its contents against the heat of the incendiaries for a brief interval, but combustion was inevitable.

Bor knew this because the stenciled markings were the letters and numbers signifying the chemical formula for the explosive, an explosive with which the assassin was well familiar. His innocent farmhouse hosts were not. The container had likely been delivered for an operation that never received a green light, never transpired. No agents had come to collect it. Consequently, it sat unused and forgotten along with all of the other relics in the cellar.

So whatever remained of the pulverized and cremated bodies of Oleg Nikolin of Leningrad and Aleksandra Ivanova of Moscow was likely part of the ash-gray cloud hovering over the well-tended farm in a land that had become their home. It was a land upon which their assassin would soon visit execrable horror.

CHAPTER 17

The buzzing in Olivia's ears had returned.

It was the visit to the National Geospatial-Intelligence Agency and the satellite images Laura Casini had put up on the screen in her office. The buzzing was an insistent reminder to tend to an unsolved puzzle, a signal that something was amiss. It harried her to acquire more information and to examine the information she did have from another angle.

The last time the buzzing had irritated her was approximately a month ago. Then it had been even more aggravating than now, perhaps because at the time the informational vacuum had been greater and the threat more palpable. It had stopped when Michael Garin had acquired the last pieces of the puzzle, establishing that the curious anomalies at Russian industrial sites were in preparation for a massive EMP strike against the United States. Once Garin had provided the pieces, the puzzle was complete and the buzzing stopped. The threat had been eliminated.

But had it? The Allied bombing campaign had devastated Iran's nuclear and ICBM programs. The threat of an EMP attack from Iran had been eliminated. The standard electrical equipment warehoused in such abundance in anticipation of the EMP was now superfluous. There was no market for it.

So why did it seem as if suspicious activity at the Russian warehouses and industrial sites had resumed?

Sure, the satellite images weren't unequivocal. The activity at the warehouses wasn't nearly as frenzied as it had been in the weeks prior to the planned EMP strike. In fact, it was arguable that the activity level was lower, far lower than that of ordinary warehouses and plants.

But the activity level had been zero in the weeks immediately following the onset of the bombing campaign and the warning to Russia to stand down. And since the equipment was standard and unremarkable—in some cases generations old—Olivia believed the activity level should have remained near zero.

She needed to advise Brandt, her famously unflappable boss. He would soberly consider the information, factor it into other strategic developments around the world, and determine whether it should be brought to the president's attention.

Olivia logged out and turned off the desktop before leaving her office in the Old Executive Office Building for the White House. The buzzing persisted as the clack of her heels echoed down the hall. It continued as she exited the massive structure. It persisted as she maneuvered between the camps of reporters and their broadcast crews, fixtures on the west lawn of the White House.

By the time she was in the White House and just outside Brandt's office, she was convinced that the increase in activity revealed in the satellite images was deserving of further inquiry, maybe even worthy of mention to the president.

The buzzing in her ears was supplanted by groaning, groaning so exaggerated as to be comical. Groaning she recognized in an instant.

As she turned into Brandt's office she saw the source of the groaning lying on his back, Brandt's foot rubbing his chest. Arlo, Brandt's long-time German shepherd service dog, enjoying a massage, leapt up upon seeing Olivia and offered his muzzle for stroking. Olivia and Arlo went back several years to when Brandt was Olivia's mentor at Stanford. Brandt had already gained the sobriquet "the Oracle" because of his prescience regarding global affairs. For nearly a quarter of a century he had been predicting the unpredictable: the collapse of the Soviet Union; the rapid economic emergence of China; the rise of radical Islam to supplant communism as the chief threat to the West. He often was years ahead of the other analysts in assessing and knitting together the implications of isolated geopolitical developments.

The nickname had almost as much to do with his regal appearance as his intellect. Sightless from birth, his blue eyes were framed by thick white eyebrows that matched the shade of the hair atop his head, brushed in the style favored by nineteenth-century British aristocracy. The perpetual upward tilt of his chin suggested confidence, sagacity. No one could recall ever seeing him rattled, regardless of the circumstances.

Many of Brandt's colleagues, both at Stanford and within the administration, believed that in Olivia, Brandt had met his intellectual equal. In fact, during their six-month collaboration in the White House, Olivia's analyses had bested Brandt's.

"That's got to drive the Secret Service nuts," Olivia said, referring to Arlo's sound effects. "It sounds like an administration official's being tortured."

"Some of the newer ones do poke their heads in from time to time," Brandt confirmed. "I think they just want to be absolutely sure that no one slipped through security and is trying to extract classified information from me."

"I'm afraid I've got some more for you, courtesy of KH-13."

"Go ahead."

"Yesterday, Laura Casini showed me a series—"

"No, wait," Brandt interrupted. "Before you do that, how are things with Senator Braxton?"

Brandt had long taken somewhat of a paternal interest in Olivia's social life. Despite looks that surpassed those of most runway models, Olivia had been painfully shy and had dated infrequently at Stanford. Brandt had made it his mission to get her to have some fun.

"He's a senator," Olivia explained.

"Pompous, arrogant, sophomoric . . ."

"That's being charitable, Professor."

"So, not going well?"

"I'm sure he thinks he's charming, witty, and loads of fun."

"I understand he's been written up in all the social columns. 'Best-Looking Bachelor on the Hill.' 'Most Eligible Senator.' He's supposed to be the best-looking politician in Washington," Brandt continued.

"I'm sure he agrees."

"Whatever happened with our daring action hero, Mr. Garin? I thought I detected something there, Ms. Perry. You finally met your match. And before you deny it, remember my one superpower."

Olivia cast her eyes to the ceiling. "Detecting bull."

"That's right. I could practically hear you panting whenever his name was mentioned."

"That was fear, Professor. He *kills* people."

"Is that all?" Brandt said innocently. "I take it killing people is a deal breaker, then?"

"Can we talk about what I came here to talk about?"

Brandt chuckled softly. His true superpower was getting under his protégé's skin. "What's on your mind?"

"Russia."

"They've been behaving since the bombing campaign began. Compliant, obsequious even," Brandt noted.

"KH-13 satellite images show activity at the same warehouses and plants that drew our attention prior to discovery of the EMP plot. They're moving the supplies and electrical equipment. Not at the rate or in the quantities that they were moving them before the EMP planned strike, but product definitely has resumed moving."

"At what rate, precisely?" Brandt asked, steepling his fingers beneath his chin.

Olivia shifted slightly in her seat. "More slowly than before. But the point is, they are moving it again."

"I understand. But can you estimate? Would you say, for example, it's eighty percent of the pre-EMP pace? Seventy percent? Sixty percent?"

"It's difficult to measure, Professor."

"I can't see the satellite images, Olivia . . ."

"Twenty percent of the previous rate. Perhaps fifteen."

"That's nothing, Olivia."

"But the equipment is standard grade. Some of it's a generation behind—"

"The type of equipment often sold to emerging or poor markets," Brandt observed. "The spike in oil prices due to the Iranian bombing campaign has affected everyone, but none more so than third world economies. Cheap, standard-grade equipment that's affordable is just what the doctor ordered. It would make sense for the Russians to try to sell it, and for those countries to buy it."

A simple explanation and, Olivia conceded to herself, the most plausible one. But when it came to the Russians, both Olivia and Brandt distrusted simple explanations.

"Then it might not hurt to let the president know. He can verify what's going on with Mikhailov, who, as you noted, has been compliant."

Brandt thought for a moment. "This isn't something that rises to that level. This is something for NSA or NGA to continue to look at. If there's a radical increase, we may revisit the issue. Okay?"

Olivia nodded. "Yes."

"I have a meeting with Iris," Brandt said, referring to the president's chief of staff, Iris Cho. "Just some housekeeping. Anything else?"

"There's still the matter of the Senate Intelligence hearing."

"We can do that later. You handled McCoy well, although you were surprisingly combative."

"I'm sorry. I didn't mean to embarrass you."

"You're very protective of Mr. Garin, Ms. Perry." Brandt grinned mischievously. "But, of course, even killers need protection. Nothing more than that, I'm sure."

Mildly annoyed, Olivia rose from her chair. "I'll touch base with NSA and NGA."

"Say hello to Senator Braxton for me."

Olivia headed back to her office at OEOB, reassured by Brandt's assessment of the satellite images' relative insignificance. The reassurance was short-lived.

Before she entered the OEOB, her cell phone vibrated. It was Dan Dwyer.

"Dan!" she said in a tone a brainy little sister would use to a protective older brother. "It's been weeks. How have you been?"

"Bor's back in play."

And just like that, the buzzing returned.

CHAPTER 18

Piotr Egorshin had arrived fifteen minutes before his appointment with Aleksandr Stetchkin. One of Stetchkin's aides led him to an immense room at the south end of the Senate Building in the Kremlin.

Egorshin was relieved. Not only had the meeting been pushed back to a more civilized hour, but what he had believed was to be a private meeting with his new boss in the latter's office—a prospect that would have frightened nearly any sentient being within the borders of Russia—appeared instead to be a gathering of nearly everyone in a command position in Russian cyberwarfare.

Egorshin could see his reflection in the highly polished floors and the countless gold-framed mirrors that hung along the walls between the floor-to-ceiling windows bordered by thick velvet drapes. Eight enormous chandeliers hung from the twenty-foot ceilings, adorned with frescoes of Russian military victories and gold-leaf borders.

Approximately fifty chairs ringed the room, each occupied by an officer, every single one of whom sat bolt upright, including Egorshin, who was seated along the middle of the left wall as one entered the room through massive double doors made of carved wood. At the end of the room opposite the doors sat a single large chair, almost resembling a throne, thought Egorshin. No doubt reserved for Stetchkin.

The room's occupants sat silently for several minutes. At precisely four thirty P.M., the double doors opened and Stetchkin appeared, tall—nearly six foot six—and very lean. His eyes were blue-gray and the stubble of hair that covered his skull silver. His face, Egorshin thought, looked naked without a monocle. His gait was long, fluid, and unhurried, a man used to having others wait for him and on him. An aide followed two steps behind and to his left side.

Stetchkin sat in the chair at the head of the room and gazed back at the entrance, which remained open. The room was nearly silent for several minutes, the faint tapping of footsteps slowly approaching in the distance echoing in the room. Egorshin's eyes flitted about, noting that none of the others present dared look at Stetchkin. Most looked straight ahead, a few others downward, and one or two glanced toward the doorway.

The approaching footfalls gradually grew louder. Egorshin marveled that someone would have the temerity to approach so slowly while the tyrant waited. For a moment Egorshin wondered whether it might be President Mikhailov himself who would be making his entrance.

Seconds later, Egorshin was startled to see his former boss, Ivan Uganov, enter the room. Judging by the faint gasp, others in the room also had heard the rumors of Uganov's supposed banishment to Black Dolphin for questioning Stetchkin's intelligence.

Yet there he was, staring uncowed at the tyrant Stetchkin. Uganov entered the room, his pace more casual than even Stetchkin's. Though not nearly as tall as Stetchkin, he was much heavier. A smaller man followed close behind. A confrontation was about to occur. Two gunfighters from a scene in an old American Western.

Uganov's steps were painfully slow, ponderous, and a bit unsteady. Egorshin thought he might be inebriated, not an unexpected condition for a man about to lock horns with the tyrant.

But as Uganov continued his steady approach, his pace seemed more of a shuffle than a confident stride. And as he passed, Egorshin observed that his former boss's eyes weren't vengeful or even purposeful, but glazed and vacant. His facial muscles were slack and his complexion chalky. Two fresh red scars dashed his temples. The body was ambulatory, but there was no animating intelligence within.

The small man Egorshin had presumed was Uganov's aide guided him to the front of the room only a few feet from Stetchkin. The tyrant glared at the husk of a man contemptuously for several seconds and then waved for the smaller man to turn Uganov around to face the assembly.

Silence enveloped the room. Everyone present stared at the general with emotions ranging from pity to terror. Then the small man turned Uganov back to Stetchkin, who sat ramrod straight in his chair, a cruel sneer covering his face.

"Who's the idiot now?" Stetchkin bellowed.

There was not a person present who did not absorb the message. Stetchkin was invincible. Stetchkin was supreme. And Stetchkin would suffer no apostasies.

And Piotr Egorshin knew that from that moment forward fear would govern every aspect of his life.

CHAPTER 19

G arin left as many bread crumbs as he could.

He ran a stop sign in full view of a Dallas police officer, then dutifully provided the officer with his actual driver's license. He explained that the car was a loaner from DGT and was pleased when, as expected, the officer radioed various entities throughout the Southwest attempting to verify the explanation from a Michael Garin, currently of Dale City, Virginia.

Shortly after the traffic stop, Garin returned to the Omni Hotel, where he checked in once again, using a credit card that had expired. When it was rejected, he apologized and provided a current one—again with his actual name.

Once registered, he proceeded not to the floor of the room assignment, but to the fourth floor, where hours ago he had killed the two shooters. He walked to the emergency door leading to the stairwell where he'd placed the bodies, opened it, and confirmed that the bodies were no longer there. Had the bodies been discovered by anyone other than Bor's associates, the area would have been cordoned off as a crime scene and police would be everywhere. Thus, Garin knew Bor's people were somewhere in the vicinity.

Garin returned to the front desk and checked out with an apology that he'd been summoned to an important appointment in Cleveland, Ohio. He left the hotel, returned to the DGT loaner, and parked a block away. He waited for about a half hour, smoking an Arturo Fuente and presuming it unlikely anything would happen. His presumption proving correct, he drove to DFW, where he parked the car in the long-term parking lot.

Garin entered the terminal, making sure to afford each and every surveillance camera he could find an unobstructed view of his face. He purchased a ticket for an American Airlines flight to Cleveland, Ohio, using yet a third credit card that bore his actual name. Before leaving the ticket counter he apologized to the agent and asked to change his flight to the earlier flight to Cleveland, using a different credit card. The agent happily complied. Garin then cleared passenger screening at the TSA checkpoint and proceeded to the gate.

Garin sat in the waiting area facing the concourse, observing the crush of passengers flowing through the terminal. He was confident he had triggered enough alarms in the last couple of hours for Bor's highly placed confidant or confidants within the US government to alert the assassin and his team as to Garin's whereabouts. If anything, the alarms had been so obvious, so blatant, that even marginally so-phisticated trackers would immediately suspect Garin was triggering them intentionally. Garin was unconcerned. Regardless of whether Bor's confederates thought the alarms were inadvertent or intentional, they would be coming after him.

Optimally, Bor would prefer one team to accompany Garin on the flight and another to be waiting for his arrival in Cleveland. If Dan Dwyer's speculation that the team was comprised of Zaslon operators was correct, they would be tactically proficient. Garin, however, had little doubt he would be able to detect them. Men who kill know the look of men who kill.

Garin scanned the immediate vicinity and saw no one who appeared even remotely capable of posing a threat. The adjacent seating areas were populated by business travelers, vacationers, and students. Some looked pleasant, others serious, most merely preoccupied. None had the telltale hardness in their eyes.

On the other side of the concourse, however, was a man browsing in a bookstore. He wore casual business attire like many in the gate area and was too far away for Garin to discern any particular look in his eyes. But his movements gave him away. He stood with his weight on the balls of his feet rather than on his heels. His stance was shoulder-width, like that of an athlete prepared to pivot.

Garin stared at the man for several minutes. He moved slowly from bookshelf to magazine shelf to knickknack shelf. He opened a paperback, read the jacket of a hardcover, and spoke to the cashier. At no time did he cast even a glance in Garin's direction or speak into his cell phone to report contact with Garin. A professional. Probably elite. Possibly even Zaslon level.

If, of course, there was such a thing.

CHAPTER 20

Mike Garin's credit card transactions, the electronic log of the radio call the Dallas police officer had made regarding Garin's traffic violation, as well as millions of other bits of electronic communications were intercepted and processed by one of Spetssvyaz's Inter-Ghost Surveillance Program's supercomputers located in a massive underground facility beneath the buildings that housed Piotr Egorshin's nameless enterprise. An algorithm flagged the transactions and displayed them on a wall-to-wall, floor-to-ceiling screen in a room on the fourth floor of the facility. Seated at a desk before that screen was Major Valeri Volkov, who, upon viewing the data, typed a series of commands on his keyboard prompting the screen to display a satellite image of the city of Dallas, Texas, USA. A series of red arrows pointed to the locations from which the transactions emanated. Beneath the locations were rectangular boxes containing text descriptions of the various locations, along with the times of the transactions.

Volkov picked up the phone, paused, and then put it down again. This was important enough for a personal visit with his boss. An opportunity to ingratiate himself with the rising star.

Volkov strode out the door, past the guards, and took the elevator to the eleventh floor. The doors opened, revealing a large bullpen-style area filled with scores of analysts seated before banks of computer screens. Volkov approached Colonel Piotr Egorshin, who was standing near one of the screens, hunched over to get a closer look.

"Sir, he has been located."

Egorshin turned to Volkov, a momentary look of incomprehension

on his face. Egorshin remained a bit rattled from the Stetchkin demonstration.

"Michael Garin, Colonel," Volkov said helpfully. "He is in the Dallas
Fort Worth airport. He has purchased a ticket for an American Airlines
flight with an eleven A.M. central departure to Cleveland, Ohio."

"Yes. Very good," Egorshin replied. In addition to being rattled, he
was irritated. The event would occur within three days and all of his
energies were concentrated on its execution. This was a distraction.

"Would you like me to inform Stetchkin so that he may inform Mr.
Bor?" Volkov asked eagerly.

"No one contacts Bor but Vasiliev," Egorshin said, referring to President Mikhailov's chief of staff. "Not even Stetchkin."

"Do you prefer to inform Stetchkin yourself, sir?"

Egorshin preferred to avoid contact with Stetchkin under any circumstance. "You have my permission to do so, Major. He is in General
Maximov's office."

Volkov, like most Spetssvyaz, was aware of Stetchkin's reputation
but had never had personal experience with him. The major's eyes
gleamed as if he were being given a promotion, or at least a coveted
opportunity to earn a promotion. *Idiot,* thought Egorshin.

Volkov excused himself and practically ran to General Maximov's
provisional office down the corridor. Through the glass door, Volkov
could see both Stetchkin and Maximov standing next to Maximov's
desk, engaged in conversation. Maximov saw Volkov and waved him in.

"Yes. What is it?" Maximov asked curtly.

Volkov looked at Stetchkin. "I have information regarding the location of Mr. Garin, sir. He is in the Dallas Fort Worth airport, and based
on the fact that he purchased an American Airlines ticket for an eleven
A.M. departure which has been delayed slightly, he will be at the gate
for only a few more minutes."

Volkov was pleased with himself. He had conveyed vital information
to the president's closest ally. Stetchkin, however, did not appear pleased.

"Egorshin sends you to give me this information? A major? A major
to speak to me? Does he consider such a task beneath him?"

The gleam faded from Volkov's eyes. Egorshin had sent him into a buzz saw.

"Mr. Stetchkin," Volkov sputtered. "Garin presently is at DFW Airport. He will be at the gate for American Airlines Flight 1212 for the next five to ten minutes."

"And why was it so difficult for Egorshin to tell me this, Major?" Without waiting for a reply, Stetchkin turned and pointed at General Maximov. "Contact Vasiliev. Tell him." Then he looked back at Volkov. "Where is the colonel?"

"In the main room, sir."

Stetchkin brushed past Volkov in search of Egorshin. The colonel spotted Stetchkin before the tyrant could locate Egorshin among the scores of bodies in the room. Egorshin knew immediately that sending Volkov was a mistake, the impact of which he sought to lessen by quickly walking toward Stetchkin.

"May I help you, sir?"

"Come with me, Colonel Egorshin."

The two men walked down the hall out of earshot of the analysts in the main room and Egorshin's subordinates. When they were out of sight of the analysts, Stetchkin turned to Egorshin.

"Colonel Piotr Egorshin. Ivan Uganov thought very highly of you. He thought one day you would be his successor. He *wanted* you to be his successor." Stetchkin paused for several moments, looking malevolently at Egorshin's eyes. "Do you think you will be?"

"I have not thought about it," Egorshin lied. "I suppose it is up to you."

"Everything that transpires in this building is up to me, Colonel. Whether or not you have dinner tonight is up to me. Whether or not you defecate afterward is up to me."

"Yes, sir."

"Shut your mouth," Stetchkin said softly. "I know everything there is to know about you, Colonel. I know how smart you think you are. I know your family. I know, for instance, of your uncle, who provides you with information that has contributed to your rapid advancement. I know that you've used the vast resources of this unit to gather compromising

The intense physical competition was compounded by the events of the last several hours and lack of sleep. Despite Luci's rubdown, his muscles were tight and his joints ached. He needed to be alert and mobile after his plane touched down in Cleveland.

When his flight began boarding, Garin walked to the end of the line, examining every face he passed. He couldn't identify anyone as a possible member of Bor's team.

Garin entered the cabin and was cheerfully greeted by two flight attendants, one about ten years older than the other, both attractive.

"Ma'am, I have a special request," Garin said politely to the senior attendant. "I'm going to be dead asleep during the flight and prefer not to be disturbed during the beverage service." Garin scanned the cabin and saw a college-age male seated in the window seat of Row 17, next to a young woman with an infant. "I'm in Row 17."

"Not a problem." She smiled.

"But I'll need a boatload of caffeine when we land."

"I'm afraid we have to secure the beverage tray before landing. That includes the coffeepots." She wore a pained expression. "For the safety of passengers and crew."

"Could you put some coffee in the fridge until we come to a stop at the gate in Cleveland?"

"It'll be cold."

"Just how I like it." Garin nodded. "When everyone's deplaned I'll inhale it and be on my way."

She examined him with a quizzical grin. Garin caught her furtive glance at his ring finger.

"There are restaurants in the terminal." She chuckled, shaking her head. "But all right. I don't see why we can't accommodate you."

"Thanks so much. A full pot, okay?"

"It will cost you a bundle."

"I'm good for it," Garin said as he continued down the aisle.

"I'll bet he is," the junior flight attendant whispered.

Garin examined the faces of the passengers one last time before proceeding to Row 17. No one stood out. He excused himself to the woman with the infant and, extending a wad of cash, addressed the college student. "I'll give you a hundred dollars to switch seats with me. I'm in the middle seat in Row 6. Prefer a window seat." The guy simply grinned, took the cash, and made his way forward. Garin squeezed into the window seat, placed his gym bag under the seat in front of him, and fastened his safety belt. It was unlikely the woman next to him with the infant was a Bor associate.

He was dead asleep before the flight attendants had finished reciting the safety instructions.

CHAPTER 22

MOUNT VERNON, VIRGINIA, AUGUST 15, 2:28 P.M. EDT

For Luci Saldana, the last twenty hours were as if she had gone through the looking glass. She was sitting in a house easily five times larger than any she'd been in before, and someone she'd seen on television in background shots of White House briefings had just walked into the room escorted by Dan Dwyer. Both Luci and Congo Knox rose to greet her.

"Olivia, this is Luci Saldana," Dwyer said. "You know Congo, of course."

Olivia took Luci's hand. "Pleased to meet you, Ms. Saldana. I'm Olivia Perry."

"I recognize you from the news, Ms. Perry. Please call me Luci."

"Then it's agreed we're all on a first-name basis here," Olivia said.

At five foot three, Luci was accustomed to being one of the smaller persons in the room, but it seemed she had just landed in Brobdingnag. To her left, Congo Knox was more than a foot taller and more than twice as heavy; in front of her, Dan Dwyer stood at least six foot five and was at least thirty pounds heavier than Knox, although not quite as fit. With his thick hair—so blond it looked almost white—he resembled a Viking warrior. And Olivia Perry appeared to be about five-ten—maybe taller.

Olivia had a bronze complexion and an impossible abundance of jet-black hair that fell in lustrous cascades to the small of her back. Her features were delicate, her ethnicity indeterminate. Despite her looks, or maybe because of them, Luci sensed in Olivia a modesty Luci found inviting, even endearing. Olivia seemed as introverted as Luci was extroverted.

Dan gestured and they sat in chairs arrayed around a circular glass coffee table. "Luci, tell Olivia what you saw last night in Dallas."

"Where do you want me to begin?"

"From when you were about to go to dinner," Dwyer replied.

"Okay. Well, I was at the Omni Hotel with a man whose participation in a competition known as the Crucible I was supporting—Mike Garin." Luci paused. "Do you know him?"

Olivia nodded. "I know Mr. Garin." Luci wondered how well.

"It was close to seven o'clock. We were about to go to dinner. I opened the door to the room and I saw two men standing there with guns. They had silencers on them; Mike called them 'suppressors.'"

"What did the men look like?" Olivia asked.

"It all happened really fast. As soon as I opened the door, Mike, who was behind me, pulled me backward and I fell to the floor. They looked almost like clones of one another. They were white; short dark hair. Both around six feet tall, maybe two hundred pounds. I thought they looked like cops—they had white shirts and sport coats—professional.

"I didn't see all of what happened next because I was on the floor, and, I have to say, pretty scared. Stunned more than scared. But I heard a shot. Mike was right—those things aren't silencers. The sound was kind of like a metallic popping. But it was pretty loud. And one of the guys goes down. Then, somehow, Mike's got one of the guns and shoots the other guy."

"Were there any other people with them?" Olivia asked.

"No. Nobody. It was weird. I mean, these guys looked like real pros, right? Like they knew what they were doing? And they had surprised us, had their guns raised like they were ready to rock. Yet Mike overwhelmed them, like they were just speed bumps to him. Like they had no chance."

A knowing smile crept over Dwyer's face. He waved toward Olivia and Congo. "We've all seen it firsthand."

"So then Mike hauls the bodies away. I didn't see where. And then he comes back and tells me to pack up everything because we're getting out of Dodge."

"Did the shooters look like they were Slavic? Russian? Or would you say that they maybe looked Middle Eastern, Persian?" Olivia asked.

"I really didn't get a good look. I can't say if they were Russian. But if I had to guess I'd say they weren't Middle Eastern."

"What else do you remember?"

"That's about it. We barreled down the highway to Sugar Land. Mike said we couldn't go to the cops or we'd end up dead—I got the impression the bad guys might be in league with the authorities or something. Then, I'm on a jet here."

Perry, Dwyer, and Knox nodded.

"Luci, you need to excuse us. Dan and I need to discuss something," Olivia said.

"I understand."

"Are you hungry?" Dwyer asked.

Luci gave a shrug signaling something between indifference and interest.

"Congo, can you take Luci to the kitchen? You'll find almost anything you might want in there, Luci."

Dwyer watched Knox lead Luci out of the room and then turned to Olivia.

"Well, what do you think?"

"Disturbing, no doubt. From Michael's standpoint, I can see why he'd be concerned that this may be a reprise of the Omega assassinations. But there's nothing that suggests Bor's involvement. More precisely, there's nothing that justifies me going to James Brandt and suggesting Bor's operating on American soil again. And even if I did go to him, he'd never go to the president with a story this inconclusive."

Dwyer fixed Olivia with a hard look. "Last night three Georgia State Patrol officers and two civilians were found shot along a highway northeast of Atlanta. I know—unfortunately, that's not necessarily an extraordinary story these days. Sounds like just a local crime story. Each of the victims was shot multiple times. But each had one gunshot wound in exactly the same place: in the forehead, at the ridgeline above the bridge of the nose."

Olivia exhaled. "Michael's signature shot. The one Bor replicated to frame Michael for the Omega assassinations."

"Exactly."

"But that shot's not unique to Michael. Or, for that matter, Bor," Olivia said. "Besides, the Omega assassinations, the EMP operation, were barely a month ago. The Russians were seriously sanctioned for their involvement. I can't imagine a scenario where they would even think about engaging in the slightest mischief or provocation against the US."

"It's not as if Mike and I haven't gone through the same thought process, Olivia. The Russians should be, and have been, on their knees groveling since the EMP operation. But both Mike and I instantly thought of Bor when we heard about Georgia. How could we not? Alarm bells went off, big-time."

Just like the buzzing returned when I saw the satellite images of Arkhangelsk, thought Olivia. *And got louder when you called.*

"I get it, Dan. Bor's an alarming person. Remember, I was face-to-face with him."

"Mike thinks Brandt should be made aware. So do I."

Olivia pursed her lips. "Don't misunderstand, Dan. This has got my attention. But these are disparate bits of information. They don't rise to the level of James Brandt's involvement," she said, virtually repeating what James Brandt had said to her a short time ago about the satellite images. "This is something for law enforcement to monitor. If something else happens—depending on its nature—maybe then it will rise to national security advisor level."

"I couldn't disagree more, Olivia. When it comes to Bor, time is always of the essence. And we've got to suspect the worst. There are no coincidences in this business."

"Dan, if I went to James Brandt every time there was a coincidence, I'd have to set up camp outside his office. We'd be in constant crisis mode, playing perpetual Chicken Little. I'm afraid the office of the national security advisor would lose all credibility."

"Don't you mean you're afraid you'd lose all credibility?"

"Dan, this isn't about—"

"Congratulations, Olivia," Dwyer interrupted. "You really are a whiz kid. You've been in Washington less than six months and yet you've already perfected the fine art of covering your ass." Dwyer's tone became increasingly strident. "You're not some bureaucrat at the EPA or IRS, whose job description is making life miserable for your fellow citizens. You're an aide to the damn national security advisor. National security, Olivia. Not wetlands management or paperwork reduction. Your job goes to the essence of what the government's supposed to do and increasingly refuses to do. Six months, Olivia. Is that all it took for you to become an inside-the-Beltway hack? A political-class drone?"

The words stung. Especially coming from the good-natured Dwyer, who had become almost like a big brother in the short time they'd known each other. And because Olivia felt the words rang true. Earlier she'd felt somewhat chastened when Brandt facilely dismissed her concern about the satellite images. She felt she'd overreacted, embarrassing herself before her boss and mentor. "This isn't something that rises to that level," he'd said. She was reluctant to approach him again with something so attenuated.

"Dan—"

"No effin' bull crap, Olivia. You give me bull crap and I'll make sure you'll have to answer to Mike himself."

Olivia grinned in spite of herself. The two toughest men she knew rarely cursed. And one of them had just threatened to report her to the other.

"Okay. I'll go to Jim with this. In fact, in addition to Georgia—" She halted abruptly. She was about to relate her observations from the satellite images, but even the very existence of the KH-13 was highly classified and compartmentalized. She knew from the EMP operation that Dwyer was party to a classified information nondisclosure agreement but was uncertain if it covered the satellite images.

"What?" Dwyer asked.

The hell with it, Olivia thought. Half the politicians in this town leaked classified information as if it were tabloid gossip. Dwyer was more responsible and reliable than all of them together. "In addition to Georgia and Dallas," she continued, "there may be something going on at those Russian industrial sites again."

"When in doubt . . . ," Dwyer began.

". . . suspect the worst from the Russians."

"Remember, Olivia, it was you, not the Oracle, who connected the pivotal dots unraveling the EMP operation. Your opinion matters."

"Actually, the credit belongs to Michael."

The pair rose from their chairs.

"Bor was assisted by Quds Force operatives during the last operation, Olivia. My guess is they were imposed on him for political reasons. He'll have the best working for him this time."

"Michael seemed to make short work of their best."

"Those weren't their best, Olivia. I bet Bor, if that was him in Georgia, didn't even have operational authority over them. But having gotten their clocks cleaned by Mike twice already, you can be sure that the serious Russians are in charge now."

"I'll convey your assessment to Jim," Olivia assured him. "Can I get a ride back to the District?"

"Matt will take you." Dwyer grasped Olivia's arm. "Remember, last time Bor worked on a very tight schedule. We have to assume time's of the essence."

"Always."

CHAPTER 23

The murmuring had continued almost incessantly since the Nicholses had been vaporized.

Nonetheless, Bor was pleased with their progress. They were making good time. They had made only one stop for five minutes at a convenience store to purchase Gatorade for the trip. If they maintained their current pace, they'd be well ahead of schedule. Time to spare. Time for contingencies.

The traffic had been light all morning—or so it seemed to Bor. They hadn't passed a single speed trap or patrol vehicle. The sky was clear and the sun was bright.

But a pall hung over the van and Bor presumed one hung over the trailing LaCrosse as well. It was apparent from the whispers floating from the volunteers in the rear seats. They had a singsong rhythm—call-and-response. Their tones betrayed the mood: a whisper of concern, then a whisper of reassurance. A whisper of doubt met by a whisper of encouragement.

The pervading tone, however, was one of fear.

Fear, Bor knew, was the dominant factor whenever stakes were high. Fear seemed to be in the background whenever the matter involved Bor. It was an environment in which he felt comfortable, in which he thrived and succeeded.

As much as an environment, fear was an instrument, a tool few, if any, wielded as deftly as Bor. It might, he thought, be time to wield it again.

For most of their acquaintance Bor had been a guide and mentor to the volunteers. The relationship had been more that of a kindly uncle and his eager nephews than that of a commander and his troops. They referred to him as "Teacher" and believed him to be Chechen. In reality, he'd once been known as the "Terror of Tbilisi."

It had taken nearly two years to find and assemble them. Most of the work had been done by Piotr Egorshin's unit. In fact, Bor had had no involvement in the recruitment.

An ambitious young major by the name of Volkov had created websites inspired by ISIS, al-Qaeda, Boko Haram—one more radical than the next. They featured lectures from scholars and exhortations from jihadists. Slickly produced videos were posted depicting the glories of jihad and the establishment of the caliphate. History lessons were presented, always with an abundance of maps and graphs, showing the incursions by the infidels over the centuries into lands not their own.

But the primary attraction of the websites, by far the principal driver of traffic, was their gruesome videos. Not just the standard fare offered by other radical sites, but scenes of depravity and evil incomprehensible to most in the West, particularly their supine elite. There were beheadings of Syrian and Iraqi soldiers. There were crucifixions of women and children, who writhed until death under the blistering sun. There were ghastly disembowelments that took hours, the victims kept conscious and their pain made more acute by repeated injections of stimulants. There were impalements on sharp stakes, the piercings creatively arranged like displays of fine art. And there were immolations, an attraction favored by the site's visitors because of its multiple and varied camera angles.

Interspersed throughout the videos were reminders of the infidels' degradations as well as invitations to join the fight against the West. Visitors to the site could enter encrypted chat rooms to discover how they might help the cause. There, unbeknownst to them, their conversations were processed through psychological evaluation programs to determine fitness for service and to weed out possible infiltration by agents of the CIA, MI6, DGSE, and other Western intelligence agencies.

Tens of thousands applied. They hailed from nearly every nation;

men and women, young and old. Some fit the stereotypical profile of such applicants presented by Western politicians and the media— young, disturbed, estranged, or disaffected losers searching for purpose in life. But many were relatively successful, seemingly stable teachers, accountants, landscapers, clerks, physicians, pilots, students, and homemakers. Multitudes of them. The Western public would be astonished and alarmed by their number and diversity. Neighbors, friends, coworkers, and acquaintances—all aspiring combatants in the holy war.

The selection process had been arduous and time-consuming. Egorshin's unit wasn't simply looking for bodies. The main qualification was brains—more specifically, a proficiency with computers.

An applicant pool of thousands was winnowed to fifty the psych programs had identified as the most promising. Those fifty were the subjects of months of round-the-clock SVR surveillance and detailed background checks. From that number, a selection committee consisting of computer specialists, psychologists, and intelligence agents culled twenty-five semifinalists. Among them were Brits, Americans, Canadians, Belgians, and French. Some were Muslim; some were not. Each had indicated a willingness to sacrifice himself for the cause. More importantly, their psychological profiles confirmed the same. Each of the semifinalists was contacted in person by an SVR agent posing as a recruiter for ISIS or a similar terrorist group. Arrangements were made for travel to a Middle Eastern destination—one of two sites in Syria or Libya—for training.

The travel to the training sites was arranged to replicate that employed by terrorist recruiters. Drivers, escorts, and logicians emulated those from ISIS or its brethren. Nothing about the process gave the semifinalists even a hint that it was run from beginning to end by the SVR.

The training lasted several weeks. To the disappointment of some, there was no firearms training, no instruction in IEDs. There was a moderate amount of training regarding surveillance detection and evasion. But almost all of their time was devoted to computers and electronics.

Naturally, there was some attrition. Some disillusioned semifinalists asked to return home. Others sought to join different terrorist groups. And a few simply couldn't make the cut and were sent packing. To ensure operational security, each of them was executed within minutes of their departure from the training sites. The remaining volunteers, numbering ten finalists, all male, all between nineteen and twenty-eight years of age, were completely unaware of their comrades' fate.

Now they were in the land of the Great Satan on the cusp of fulfilling a great and historic mission. And yet there was murmuring in the rear of the van.

Bor knew that all of the training, psychological profiles, and computer simulations in the world couldn't predict with certainty how recruits would act when actually in the field. Allowed to continue and perhaps escalate, the murmuring would lead to dissent, which could negatively affect, if not jeopardize, the mission.

That was unacceptable.

Most of the backseat discussion appeared driven by Rasul Baslaev. He was the eldest and had emerged as the unofficial leader of the volunteers. He was originally from Dagestan in the Caucasus, just north of Azerbaijan, where his family still resided. He had moved to London and was a university graduate, but after a series of short-lived jobs, he'd been unemployed for almost three years.

Their jitters were understandable. They were close to the time of execution. They had seen Bor kill several people in the last twenty-four hours. That was done to ensure obedience.

But Bor believed it would be helpful to give them some encouragement also. It would be most effective if he focused such encouragement on Baslaev, the leader, and let it trickle down from him to the others.

Bor turned sideways in his seat to address Baslaev. The whispers stopped and the volunteers looked on with apprehension.

"Are you getting nervous, Rasul? Having misgivings, second thoughts?"

"No, Teacher." Several of the other volunteers also shook their heads in denial.

"There's no shame in it, Rasul. It happens to all of us. You wouldn't be human if you weren't more than a little anxious."

"Who were the old couple?" Baslaev asked.

"I see." Bor nodded. "What you see as the unnecessary expenditure of life troubles you. I assure you, I wouldn't have done it if it wasn't necessary."

"They were infidels?"

"In a manner of speaking," Bor replied.

"You killed them?"

"The house caught fire."

"But they provided assistance to us."

"I made a judgment, Rasul. Perhaps it was in error, but I did what I thought was best. It might have been better had I first talked to you about it."

"We were surprised, Teacher. That's all." The others nodded agreement.

Bor looked at his watch. They were still ahead of schedule and making good time. He scanned the road ahead.

"You've worked hard. You deserve an explanation." He looked to the driver and pointed ahead. "Pull off on that road up ahead. Let's take a break and discuss this."

A faint smile crossed Baslaev's face. The other volunteers broke out in grins.

CHAPTER 24

MOSCOW,
AUGUST 15, 11:18 P.M. MSK

Egorshin took the encrypted call while seated at his desk drinking tea and reviewing information in preparation for the event. The enormity of the undertaking was overwhelming. Petabytes of data were involved. They had run countless simulations over several months. Recalibrated, tweaked, and refined their calculations. For the last month every simulation yielded the same results. Save for inconsequential deviations to account for uncontrollable atmospheric variables, every simulation was a success. Most gratifying was the success of yesterday's dry run for the secondary plan, involving a flight from Salt Lake City to Seattle.

Egorshin sat up straight as he placed the receiver to his ear. The call came on the line reserved for one purpose, and just a short time ago Aleksandr Stetchkin had made clear he expected Egorshin to accommodate the caller.

"Yes?"

"We need simultaneous satellite feeds for all of the families."

"Of course," Egorshin replied.

"With full audio and encryption."

"Understood."

"When can you establish connections?"

"When do you need them?"

"It will take a few minutes for us to set up each of the locations."

"Ten minutes?" Egorshin asked.

"Excellent. Would it be possible to display the images on the screen as a grid?"

"That is how I understood your request."

"Very good," said the Zaslon Unit operator and terminated the call.

Egorshin punched the button for Major Volkov. When his subordinate picked up, Egorshin tersely directed him to satisfy the Zaslon operator's request while emphasizing the imperative that it be done immediately. Egorshin didn't want any complaints to be made to the tyrant.

Then he resumed scrutinizing the data.

CHAPTER 25

Olivia decided to get right to it.

"Professor, there was a disturbing incident that occurred last night in northern Georgia. Three highway patrol officers and two civilians were shot by an unknown assailant. Perhaps you heard it on the news?"

Brandt was sitting in the same chair as when they had met earlier, and again, Arlo was, literally, underfoot. "No, I don't think I've heard anything about it, but go on."

"The five victims were each shot several times, including one shot above the bridge of the nose. You will remember that Taras Bor used just such a placement in an attempt to cast suspicion on Michael Garin for the Omega assassinations."

"Yes. I remember that well." The Oracle leapt ahead at light speed. "I suspect you've concluded that Bor was, therefore, involved in the Georgia killings. Bor's involvement in the killings then demands greater scrutiny of the activity at Russian industrial sites, which heightened activity you do not believe is coincidental."

"Yes." Olivia shrugged. "In a nutshell, that's precisely what I think."

"And you also think that we should bring this to the attention of President Marshall."

"That's your call, Professor." As soon as she said it, Olivia chastised herself. She was punting, avoiding making a firm recommendation. Covering her ass, as Dwyer had said.

"Then my call is to thank you for the information and take it under advisement. There are other matters requiring immediate attention.

The previous administration left us strategic chaos: China, North Korea, ISIS. And of course Iran. Those messes aren't speculative."

"Professor—"

"This still doesn't even remotely rise to the level of presidential concern. Look, Olivia, I know the EMP operation was a traumatic experience for you. You were new on the job, new in D.C., and you're thrown literally into the middle of the biggest national security threat since the Cuban Missile Crisis. It's understandable that Bor would loom large in your mind. But sometimes coincidences are just coincidences." Brandt waved his hand dismissively. "A couple more forklifts at a Russian warehouse coupled with a drive-by shooting in Georgia doesn't command a National Security Council briefing in the Situation Room."

Brandt's belittling sarcasm, so unlike him and so alien to their long relationship, angered Olivia, but she remained calm.

"Professor, those satellite images might have shown a modest uptick in activity, but respectfully, any uptick in the sort of activity that presaged what would've been the most catastrophic attack in American history should be taken seriously. And, yes, when coupled with the slaughter of five people in the same way Omega was slaughtered during the EMP operation, it should, without doubt, be brought to the attention of the president. And, for what it's worth, Bor doesn't just loom large in my mind. He also looms large in the minds of Michael Garin and Dan Dwyer. They're worried it's Bor and that something's afoot."

The normally unflappable Brandt was somewhat taken aback by Olivia's adamancy. Several seconds passed before he responded, his tone conciliatory.

"Olivia, in all the time I've known you, I've always respected your judgment, and I do so now. It's precisely this kind of alertness that makes you invaluable. The president himself was grateful for your alertness and analysis in helping prevent the EMP attack." Brandt paused, choosing his words with precision.

"You've done your job by telling me of this. And I'm convinced it should be taken seriously. As national security advisor, however, my job isn't merely to relay important information to the president. It's to weigh that information, consider it in context, integrate it with other information, and advise the president accordingly. In that respect, I'm also something of a gatekeeper, not simply a conduit. So you've done your job and now I must do mine. Thank you."

Olivia rose and walked out of Brandt's office. She was irritated. Brandt's attempt to mollify her had come off as patronizing, a posture he'd not taken before.

Even so, while she disagreed, she understood his position. It made perfect sense.

But the irritation persisted along with the buzzing in her ears.

By the time she'd exited the White House, her phone began vibrating. It was Laura Casini. Olivia answered it.

"Every time I talk to you, my boss ends up thinking I should be fitted for a tinfoil hat. Tell me why I should talk to you this time," Olivia said, slightly exasperated.

"Because you're very good at solving puzzles and I have another piece for you to play with."

"I don't need any more puzzles, Laura. I need answers."

"Can't help you there. In fact, if you come for another visit I'm sure what you see will raise even more questions than before."

Olivia groaned. "Same subject matter?"

"No. Same country. But different subject altogether. And, to my mind at least, utterly nonsensical."

Olivia was no longer irritated. She was worried. "I'm on my way."

"Bring your imagination."

CHAPTER 26

NORTH CAROLINA,
AUGUST 15, 3:37 P.M. EDT

Bor had directed the driver to turn right at the gravel road approximately a mile from where they had first turned off. The LaCrosse followed. He spotted a small clearing where there stood a wooden picnic table near the kind of outhouse often found in older parks and recreation areas. There was no traffic, there were no nearby residences, and the area looked as if it hadn't been used in years, since back before traffic had abandoned the gravel road for newer, larger paved roads.

They drove into the meadow and parked the two vehicles near the picnic table. Doors opened on all sides and the occupants got out stiffly and stretched and meandered about, each taking a turn using the toilet facilities.

Bor placed the bag of sandwiches prepared by the now atomized Allie Nichols on the picnic table along with his gym bag and the bottles of Gatorade. A light breeze sifted through nearby pines, which provided shade against the sun. It was a quiet, comfortable, secluded setting—perfect for bucking up the troops, providing encouragement to the team.

Presently, everyone gathered around the picnic table, most sitting, a few standing, including Bor, who stood at one end as if he were about to propose a toast with Gatorade. He waited while they ate their sandwiches. There was a smattering of quiet chatter, a low chuckle, but mainly they ate in silence.

Finally, Bor spoke, instantly commanding everyone's attention.

"We're only seventy-two hours away and soon you all will forever have a place in history. And when it's written, it will describe how you changed the course of the world. What you are doing is momentous, but it's understandable even at this stage—maybe especially at this stage—to have anxiety or misgivings or doubt. Unfortunately," Bor said, tilting his head toward Baslaev, "it took one of you to remind me of all this, and of what an extraordinary decision you've all made."

Bor paused as the others glanced at Baslaev, the unofficial leader, impressed that he had prompted Bor to address them in this fashion. Baslaev nodded almost imperceptibly in acknowledgment.

"For those of you who are following in the car, I told Rasul his second thoughts were understandable. It's natural to feel anxious at this stage. But merely saying that is not enough, I realize. Considering the nature and scope of your undertaking, you deserve much more. Even though your journey's almost complete, you still need more than a simple pat on the back. You need assurances, motivation, encouragement."

Bor produced a tablet computer from his gym bag and tapped its screen. After examining its face for a few moments, he turned it around so the volunteers could see its display.

It took several seconds for their eyes to adjust, to locate the relevant images, for their brains to process what they were looking at and its import. But upon grasping its import, the face of each volunteer became frozen with terror and each body grew rigid with fear.

Displayed on Bor's tablet was a grid of ten images. Each image was different yet each was the same. Because of their size, each volunteer strained to identify everything depicted in the image most pertinent to him, and doing so only heightened the impact.

Each panel on the grid showed a live feed of the family members of the respective volunteers. Most showed one or both parents. Some also showed siblings. There were eight-year-old sisters and twenty-year-old brothers. Grandmothers shared the screen with beloved uncles and aunts. There even was a cousin or two. Every single face held an expression of horror. Each appeared to be pleading, praying, begging. Each was painful to watch.

Behind the family members were men wearing balaclavas and

holding firearms trained at the hostages' heads. It was impossible to tell the locations of the images, but it was clear they were all different.

Bor held the tablet before the volunteers for several seconds. Then he turned the screen back to himself and tapped his index finger twice on one of the images.

"Rasul, pay close attention. Relax. This will encourage you. I'm sure it will encourage you all."

Bor turned the screen around and held it closer to Baslaev's face but made sure everyone could see also. The screen now held a single image: that of Rasul's mother, father, and fifteen-year-old brother sitting in wooden chairs before two men holding some type of submachine guns trained at their heads. Baslaev could see his mother was weeping.

Bor leaned close to the tablet's mic.

"Please cut to the second incentive."

The image blurred momentarily as the camera shifted away from Baslaev's family and rested upon what appeared to be an open cigar box containing two fleshy red orbs. A collective gasp came from the volunteers when the camera became still and the focus sharpened.

"Those," Bor said coldly, "are your uncle Umar's testicles, Rasul. I gave instructions that he not be killed, so I assume he's still alive and somewhere in the vicinity of this shot. Please understand that we have the ability—and intent—to perform the same type of surgery on the male relatives of everyone gathered around this picnic table. Truthfully, however, because the men you see in the background holding firearms are professionals, they are likely to dispense with cheap theatrics and simply shoot everyone. I will not object if they do so. It's more efficient that way.

"Here's the good news, Rasul." Bor momentarily turned the screen back to himself, tapped it twice again, and flipped it back toward Baslaev and the others. The only image on the screen was a briefcase of cash. Lots of cash.

"You're looking at five million in cash. American dollars. Your family, each of your families, will receive five million dollars upon completion of the mission. Considering that each of you contacted us and volunteered for the mission without the expectation of any compensation whatsoever, that's an extraordinary bonus and incentive. I'm sure you'll agree—that's encouragement."

Bor tapped the screen once more and the image reverted to Baslaev's family. In addition to his mother, his brother was now weeping.

"The choice is clear, Rasul. In fact, it's not even a choice. It's a mandate. I expect in the remaining hours before the event, you will embrace the mission enthusiastically. Five million dollars for your family, glory for you, and a mighty victory for the cause. Far more than you'd ever dreamed of when you first entered the chat room. So no more doubts, no more whispers. All right?"

The eyes of every volunteer were riveted to the images on the screen. The expression on Baslaev's face hadn't changed for two full minutes, not a twitch of an eyebrow, not so much as a quiver of his lips. It was a mask frozen in horror.

"So, I'm confident all of you now are extremely encouraged by what you've just seen and heard." Bor looked at Baslaev. "Are you encouraged, Rasul?"

Baslaev continued staring at the screen and did not answer. Bor waited expectantly for a beat, then again leaned toward the tablet and spoke into its mic.

"Dagestan. Execute."

On the tablet's screen the bodies of the Baslaev family pitched violently forward and their heads exploded as they were riddled with gunfire from the submachine guns held by the hooded men behind them. The upper left corner of the image was obscured by tissue that had sprayed from one of the victims.

The volunteers recoiled and flinched at the sight. Baslaev's piercing shriek drowned their gasps. Bor pulled the Glock 43 from his waistband and fired a single shot into Baslaev's throat, silencing him.

"Too late," Bor said, returning the weapon to his waistband and covering it with his shirt. "He who hesitates . . ."

Baslaev's body toppled backward onto the grass. The serial shocks of the last several minutes seemed to have rendered the other volunteers nearly catatonic. They remained stationary, staring wide-eyed at the corpse lying in the meadow.

Notwithstanding Baslaev's death, Bor had sufficient volunteers to discharge the mission. Looking at the faces of the remaining volunteers, he was certain those numbers wouldn't change. Their initial zealotry was now magnified by uncompromising pragmatism.

"Take the body into the woods," Bor said to no one in particular. Immediately, several volunteers lifted Baslaev's corpse by the arms and legs and disappeared into the pines. The other volunteers collected all the trash, placed it into the shopping bag, and stored it in the trunk of the LaCrosse.

Within a minute everyone had retaken their seats in the two vehicles.

The picnic was over. Suitably encouraged, they were prepared to resume the journey.

Bor glanced at his watch. Still on time.

CHAPTER 27

CLEVELAND, OHIO,
AUGUST 15, 4:02 P.M. EDT

Garin awoke slightly disoriented as the plane taxied toward Gate C29 at Cleveland Hopkins Airport. The two and a half hours of sleep hadn't been nearly enough, and he was sore and stiffer than when he'd boarded the plane.

Garin remained seated as the other passengers gathered their items from the overhead bins and moved toward the exit. He took one last opportunity to survey as many of the passengers as he could, although most had their backs to him.

Garin trailed the last passenger up the aisle to the galley, where the senior flight attendant, as promised, had an extra-large cup of coffee waiting for him. Garin downed the cold coffee in a couple of gulps, grateful for the infusion of caffeine. He thanked her and proceeded up the Jetway to the terminal.

Foot traffic along the concourse was moderate, permitting Garin a relatively unobstructed view of those who populated it. Although he put nothing past Bor, who was capable of the most brazen of acts, Garin knew it was extraordinarily unlikely anything would happen within the terminal. As Garin walked in the direction of the parking garage, he pulled out yet another burner and called Dan Dwyer, who picked up immediately.

"What's the latest?" Garin asked.

"Luci's here with Congo. She told Olivia about your dance in Dallas, and I told her about the party in Georgia. Olivia was hesitant to go to her boss with just that, but she did anyway. I haven't heard from her since she left, but she should've spoken to him by now."

"Why was she hesitant?"

"CYA syndrome. In her defense, it's not exactly conclusive evidence."

"Of all people, she should know what we're up against. Who we're up against."

"She does," Dwyer assured him. "Remember, she's still a civilian. For a civilian she's a good soldier. Cut her some slack."

"No one gets any slack, Dan. No one."

Dwyer sighed. "What are we up against, anyway?"

"I hope to find out very soon," Garin replied.

"Who are we up against? Beyond our scary friend?"

"That's not for this call, Dan. No markers."

"You're using a throwaway and my system's as secure as it gets."

"Not for this call."

"That bad?"

"Think about it."

Dwyer sighed again. "What's next?"

"I'm pretty sure I'll know soon. Very soon," Garin said. "Am I all set?"

"All set. Keep me posted. I'll do the same."

Garin terminated the call as he passed Gate C3. In the window overlooking the tarmac he caught the reflection of a woman walking a few steps behind him. It was a woman who had been seated four rows before him on the flight. Her lips were moving—just barely—as if she were whispering to herself. And he caught the glint of a small device in her ear.

CHAPTER 28

Once again, Laura, I have no idea what I'm looking at."

"You're looking at a wide-angle shot of the Caucasus to provide perspective, not detail," said Laura Casini. "It's helpful to orient yourself to the geography first."

"Southwestern Russia."

"Right. Black Sea to the west, Caspian to the east. This shot is just north of the Caucasus from Sochi to Grozny. You can also see part of the eastern shore of the Caspian in Kazakhstan."

"I'm oriented," Olivia said.

"Okay, now I'm going in for a tight shot—the highway between Grozny and Makhachkala."

Casini manipulated the mouse, and the image on the big screen dissolved, reconstituted, then sharpened.

"T-14 tanks, APCs, trucks, self-propelled Msta-Ss, and troops," Olivia said, puzzled. "Lots and lots of them. I'd say two divisions at least. I haven't heard anything about this. Does DIA know?"

"This is from just a few hours ago. I went back in time to see when the movement began, but we don't have any recent images. If I had to guess, I'd say this all happened in the last forty-eight hours. And that's not all . . ."

Casini manipulated the mouse again. "This is a closer shot of the northeastern shore of the Caspian. Kazakhstan."

"Are those Russian troops?"

"See for yourself." A closer shot appeared.

"Another division," Olivia said, confusion in her voice. "Russians in Kazakhstan?"

"They're moving south."

"Toward Syria?"

"Nope," Casini said. "They're too far east. If the western division continues in the present direction, they'll go through Georgia, and then Azerbaijan, to Iran. The eastern division will go through Kazakhstan, then Turkmenistan, to Iran."

Olivia stared at the screen, her brow furrowed. The puzzle still was missing several pieces.

"Laura, do you have any shots of the area south of Saint Petersburg?"

"I know what you're thinking, and we do."

The screen showed troops and equipment near Estonia and Latvia.

"At least three tank battalions from the Western Military District within miles of the Latvian border. Two more with lots of artillery near Estonia," Olivia observed. "In total that's far more than we've seen in recent maneuvers. They could easily overwhelm NATO forces. We have Abrams tanks and Bradleys at Grafenwoehr. But by the time we could deploy them the game would already be over."

"They're not moving at all, though," Casini said. "They seem to just be parked there. No activity."

"They don't have to be moving to be concerning. Within hours of getting the order from Mikhailov, they'd be halfway inside the Baltics," Olivia explained. "What really concerns me are the divisions near the Caspian. They *are* moving. And their movement is, frankly, incomprehensible."

"What's incomprehensible about it?"

"The Russians know that, eventually, we'd notice these buildups, these movements. You don't need KH-13 to see that. Concentrations of troops and matériel of this size are going to be spotted in the ordinary course," Olivia explained. "And given everything that's happened in the last month, they know NATO would read them the riot act if there was any inkling that mischief was afoot.

"But apparently, that doesn't bother them. They're massing and moving as if they're unconcerned about NATO reaction, like these exercises are completely innocent and nonthreatening. And like we know they're innocent and so we aren't going to react."

"Aren't they?" Casini asked. "I mean, after the failed EMP operation, they wouldn't provoke another crisis, right?"

Olivia examined the screens for several seconds in silence.

"You're not going to disappear again on me, are you, Olivia? That was rude."

"Laura, do you have images from Baltiysk and Kronshtadt?"

"The Baltic Fleet." Casini nodded matter-of-factly.

Seconds later the split-screen images of naval bases appeared. The two women studied the screen for anomalies.

"I don't see anything out of the ordinary," Olivia said tentatively.

"That's because you're not a super-sharp-eyed spy-satellite sleuth," Casini countered. "There's absolutely no sign of the Nakhimov Missile Ship Brigade."

"Are you sure?"

"Your job is analysis. My job is surveillance."

"Do you see anything else missing?" Olivia asked.

"Not immediately."

"Laura, I need you to examine any and all available satellite surveillance of Russian naval bases in the near abroad." Olivia paused. "No, make that Russian military bases in the near abroad, especially Georgia, Kazakhstan, and Tajikistan—and let me know what you find."

"What do you expect me to find?"

"Nothing out of the ordinary," Olivia replied. "I hope."

CHAPTER 29

Garin took the escalator from the terminal to the people mover that led to the parking garage. There were few people along the way.

By the time he reached the elevator to the upper floor of the parking garage, he was alone. The woman who was seated four rows ahead of him had faded into the foot traffic somewhere within the terminal.

When the elevator arrived, he pressed the button for the top floor of the garage, where a DGT fleet vehicle positioned by one of Dwyer's men would be waiting. The vehicle, likely a Crown Victoria, would be unlocked, with the key hidden, unimaginatively, in the front driver's-side wheel well. Garin thought the probability that assassins also would be waiting was fairly good.

The elevator doors opened and he proceeded to the top deck of the garage. The area was virtually empty—only two vehicles on the entire floor—one of them a Crown Victoria parked just a few feet away. Garin retrieved the keys from the wheel well, opened the trunk, threw in his bag, and retrieved the SIG Sauer P226—Garin's weapon of choice—just as a spray of suppressed gunfire shattered the driver's-side windows.

Garin dove behind the passenger side of the car as it was riddled by several additional rounds of semiautomatic gunfire. Garin dropped to the concrete floor of the garage and peered under the vehicle in the direction of the shots, spotting the thick cylindrical shapes of suppressors attached to what appeared to be HK MP5s protruding from behind concrete pillars approximately thirty yards away. He rose to one knee and fired two covering rounds at the pillars, the gunshots reverberating throughout the garage.

Barely a second later, return fire struck the body of the driver's side, providing cover for one of the shooters to advance to a pillar closer to Garin. He fired a round at the pillar, the echo of the shot followed by the sound of a nearby police siren. By its direction, Garin guessed it was that of the Cleveland Police patrol car stationed near the passenger pickup area a few floors below. Garin estimated it would take the police about a minute and a half to negotiate through the drop-off-zone drive-way, circle around the Sheraton Hotel, and arrive at the entrance to the garage. It would take another thirty seconds to maneuver up the ramps and around the turns of the garage to the top floor.

Two minutes. The shooters had less than that to kill Garin. It wasn't a mistake on their part. No doubt they believed Garin would be unarmed coming off the flight, so they wouldn't have anticipated that the sound of unsuppressed gunfire would summon the police.

The imminent arrival of the police complicated matters for Garin. He'd hoped to flush out and apprehend a Bor agent for questioning. The woman had been the most appealing prospect, but she had disappeared. The shooters now were his best option. Even assuming he could survive until then, he couldn't afford the delay of being placed into custody.

Two more suppressed shots glanced off the concrete pavement. Garin saw one of the shooters sprinting toward a Ford Explorer. He fired three rounds, one of which, to Garin's astonishment, struck the sprinter in the left temple, dropping him dead. Garin ducked his head as the other shooter fired two three-round bursts as he moved toward the Explorer. Before Garin could return fire he heard another three-round burst followed by an agonized grunt and the slamming of a vehicle door.

Garin popped his head above the Crown Victoria's hood. Twenty feet from the Explorer lay the body of a diligent parking garage security guard, next to which was a gelatinous red blob that had once been his head. The Explorer jolted forward, bounced over the security guard's remains, and sped down the ramp toward the lower levels.

Garin swung around the hood of the Crown Vic to the driver's door, climbed in, and started the car. Seconds later the screeching of tires from the two vehicles mixed with the wails of the approaching police sirens. As Garin drove down the ramp to the fourth floor, he could see the Explorer to his right descending the ramp to the third floor. Another minute, maybe less, before Cleveland's finest arrived at the garage entrance. At that point, the variables would become unmanageable. Both Garin and the shooter had few, if any, good options.

Garin needed to seize any option, for better or worse. The Explorer, having just spun around the landing at the top of the second-floor ramp, was facing him and beginning its descent one level below. Garin braced his arms against the steering wheel and yanked it hard right, driving through the wire barriers separating the ramps and plunging the Crown Vic downward several feet and into the passenger side of the Explorer, wedging it against a concrete pylon.

Jarred, Garin attempted to get his bearings as he heard sirens closing in. The front of his car had caved in the Explorer's passenger door, pinning the shooter between it and the driver's-side door, which was, in turn, pinned against a pylon. Through the clouds of steam surrounding the vehicles and past the airbag, Garin could see the shooter struggling to free himself, blood rushing from his nose and mouth. He appeared to be reaching toward the seat. *The MP5,* thought Garin.

Garin located the SIG on the passenger-side floor, grasped it, and sprang from the car. Veins bulged on the shooter's forehead as he strained to free himself. Garin lunged for the rear passenger-side door, the only door not obstructed by metal or concrete.

Through the door's window he could see the end of the suppressor pointing from the floor and upward toward the shooter, his right hand reaching for the trigger. Garin wrenched the door open just as the top of the shooter's skull exploded against the roof of the vehicle.

Garin cursed, stuck the SIG in his waistband, and reached across the back seat toward the body. He frisked the torso, retrieved a phone from the right hip pocket, and placed it in his own. Then he levered himself out of the Explorer and popped the trunk of the Crown Victoria to grab his bag. The sound of the sirens began to echo, indicating that the police vehicles had entered the parking garage.

Bag in hand, Garin bolted toward the opposite end of the garage and through the metal door to the stairwell. Behind him he could hear the screeching of tires drawing closer to the wreck. He descended the stairs, taking two steps at a time until he came to the ground level, where he composed himself for a moment before opening the metal door to the exterior of the garage. Behind him the sirens and screeching tires halted abruptly.

Garin walked calmly past the parking attendant kiosks and toward the Sheraton Hotel, casting a couple of befuddled glances over his shoulder as he went, an arriving traveler curious about the commotion somewhere inside the concrete structure. He crossed the access road separating the outdoor parking area from the hotel and proceeded toward the row of taxis at the hotel's front entrance.

Garin nodded at the tall, lanky driver who was leaning against the cab at the front of the queue. The driver opened the door for Garin, shut it behind him, and then settled behind the wheel.

Through the back window Garin could see the strobe-like reflections of flashing lights in the recesses of the parking garage. The sound of several more sirens approached from Interstate 71 to the north.

"What's going on?" Garin asked.

"Don't know," the driver replied with a midwestern accent. "There was a bunch of noise coming from the garage a couple of minutes ago." The driver glanced in the rearview mirror. "Where to?"

"Downtown."

Garin glimpsed himself in the rearview mirror. His heart rate was elevated from the caffeine and exertion, but his appearance was unremarkable, almost serene. He pulled one of the burners from the gym bag and placed a call.

"Dwyer."

"In a cab heading toward downtown Cleveland."

"And?"

"I made contact with our friends and associates," Garin informed him.

Dwyer understood from experience that Garin's innocuous statement suggested such associates were no longer responsive. "Were you able to learn anything?"

"I have one of their phones," Garin said, his tone suggesting he didn't expect that phone to provide any useful information.

"What's next?"

Garin thought briefly about checking on his sister, who lived twenty minutes southeast, but knew he couldn't spare the time. "I'm at a dead end."

"Why not go loud? They'll be certain to come for you."

"I just did that. I can't stay here, though."

"Last go-round most of the action was in the D.C. area. Why not come back?"

"I can't fly out of here. And it would take six hours to drive."

"Where are you right now?" Dwyer asked.

"About to take the I-71 to downtown Cleveland."

"Go to Cuyahoga County Airport instead. In anticipation of your causing your usual mess, I've positioned one of our Bell 429s there, prepped, fueled, and ready to go."

Garin shook his head slightly. "Either you're getting very good at this or I'm getting very bad."

"We'll get you here in under two hours."

"Good."

"Nothing's gonna happen before then, anyway."

Garin wasn't so sure.

CHAPTER 30

R uth Ponder was beside herself.

In forty-four years of marriage she and Amos had been apart only two nights. Once when she had attended a cousin's funeral in Columbus that Amos couldn't attend because he had the flu. And another twelve years ago when his truck broke down in Savannah and he stayed overnight in a motel until the mechanic could finish his repairs.

He hadn't called. By ten last night she'd already called their two daughters, who lived within twenty miles, as well as their son, who lived in Atlanta. None had heard from him.

She'd called the sheriff's office, but they wouldn't take a missing persons report unless twenty-four hours had elapsed. She didn't care. She kept calling every hour and the last time made sure they took down the make and license number of his car. She called Amos's best friend, Bob Lampley, but he hadn't heard from him since the weekend. She called the local hospital, but since last night they had admitted only twin ten-year-olds with food poisoning.

Ruth hadn't slept since the previous night. When she wasn't pacing the kitchen floor she was sitting at the kitchen table wringing her hands, which she was doing at this very moment.

She looked at the clock above the sink. Something was wrong. Something was very wrong.

CHAPTER 31

B or knew they needed to abandon the vehicles and obtain new ones. No one would be actively looking for them this far from northern Georgia, but it was likely someone had reported the young man and the old man missing and provided license numbers and descriptions of their respective vehicles.

Bor suspected the old man would be the first to be reported missing. The young man, likely a college student, probably had several previous escapades during which he couldn't be reached; his short-term disappearance wouldn't be unusual.

The volunteers, if not exactly encouraged by what they had recently witnessed, were scrupulously obedient. Baslaev's death might not have been necessary, but it guaranteed their compliance and, therefore, the mission's success.

Provided, of course, that the possible impediment—Mike Garin—was removed. Bor remained somewhat skeptical that Garin would be neutralized before the event. He knew the capabilities of his former Omega leader better than almost anyone, which was why he had insisted to Moscow that Garin be at least held in check, preferably permanently, while Bor executed his mission. The last mission, executed perfectly in every respect, had failed because Moscow had directed Bor to use Quds Force to handle Garin. Bor had objected strenuously to Stetchkin, but it was Mikhailov who was ultimately unmoved. It was part of the Russian president's misdirection; he wanted the Iranians to believe they were full partners in the operation, not just pawns. In theory, the misdirection was brilliant. In practice, pitting the overmatched Quds Force against Garin proved a disaster.

The failure, however, was short-lived. In fact, the EMP operation was itself part of an elaborate misdirection. And now that Russian special operators were involved, the odds that Garin would at least be kept in check were good. Or better.

They were approaching the outskirts of another small town, crisscrossed by an interstate exchange. In America, Bor knew, these areas often were dedicated to all things automotive: auto-parts stores, auto-repair shops, and car dealerships. Sure enough, a mile later a used-car lot appeared on the right.

Bor directed the van's driver to drive past the lot to the truck stop approximately an eighth of a mile down the road and park behind the diner. The LaCrosse followed suit.

Bor turned to Talib Nadir, one of the volunteers who had a driver's license, seated behind him.

"You, come with me," Bor commanded. "We have to switch vehicles. The rest of you wait here. We'll return shortly."

He had no concern they wouldn't do exactly as ordered.

Bor pulled back the slide on the Glock to check the chamber, returned it to his waistband, and covered it with his shirt. The act was not lost on anyone in the van. All of them recognized it as the precursor to some poor soul's imminent demise.

Bor got out of the van and motioned to the occupants of the LaCrosse to remain put. Talib in tow, Bor jogged the two hundred yards to the used-car lot, which, Bor quickly determined, held a variety of adequate vehicles. In a minute Bor identified a red 2000 Dodge Durango and a gray 2002 Chevy Tahoe as the group's next transports. In the same time, a laconic salesman in jeans and a gray poplin jacket approached. Before he could say hello, Bor pointed to his selections.

"We'd like these two."

The desultory salesman's face broke into a broad grin. Bor had just made his day.

"Would you like to take them for a ride?"

"Nope. They look good to me. If we have a problem, I'll just come back and shoot you."

The salesman chuckled. "Sounds fair enough."

"How much?"

"The price on the windshield. Twenty-five hundred for the Durango and seventeen eighty for the Tahoe."

"No," Bor said. "How much?"

"Thirty-five hundred for both?"

Bor nodded.

The salesman motioned toward a trailer in the front corner of the lot. "Follow me. We'll take care of the paperwork and get you on your way in no time."

The salesman led them to the trailer and up the two stairs to the sales office. It contained two desks, two filing cabinets, a desktop computer, and a coffeemaker. Behind the desk to the right was a pegboard from which scores of keys hung. The salesman swung behind the desk and took two sets of keys off the board. He slapped them atop the desk and extended his hand toward Bor.

"I'm Randy, by the way."

Bor ignored the extended hand and glanced at the keys. Then back at the salesman. Talib saw a look of calculation in Bor's eyes. The volunteer held his breath in anticipation as Bor reached behind his back. The salesman continued to stand with his hand extended as Bor took his wallet from his back pocket and pulled out a sheaf of bills.

"Skip the paperwork," Bor said. "Five thousand cash for title and registration to both. Write it up any way you want to."

The salesman laughed and winked. "In a hurry, huh? Listen, bud. I'd like to help you out there, but if I don't do this proper, the owner of this joint, who happens to be my sister's husband, is gonna be mighty pissed at me. Last time I did it we got into a world of hurt. DMV, insurance. Woulda been fired or worse if not for my sister."

Bor stared at the salesman in silence. The salesman began to feel uncomfortable. Talib moved back a step.

"But just a couple doors down from here, Rob Brock's got a couple of his old wrecks he's been trying to sell for months. No takers, but they're not in bad shape. Even tried to sell them to us, but my brother-in-law's a cheap cuss and Rob's stubborn and they couldn't agree on a price."

Bor continued staring. Then: "Where's Brock's place?"

Talib exhaled.

Bor found Brock neither stubborn nor unreasonable. He sold Bor a forest-green 1996 Ford Windstar minivan and a Chevy Caprice of indeterminate vintage for the five thousand dollars Bor had offered the salesman. Paperwork wasn't necessary.

Minutes later, Bor and Talib arrived behind the diner driving the minivan and Caprice, respectively. The faces of several volunteers bore expressions of apprehension until Talib subtly shook his head, answering the question on everyone's mind.

The volunteers transferred to the new vehicles. Bor didn't bother to wipe down the old ones for fingerprints. By the time someone noticed the Econoline and LaCrosse and reported them to the authorities, the plates were run, and forensics were completed, the mission would be complete.

By that point fingerprints wouldn't matter. Not much would.

CHAPTER 32

Egorshin hadn't slept in nearly thirty hours before dozing for forty-five minutes in the recliner by the window of his girlfriend's apartment. He knew it was unlikely he'd sleep anytime in the next seventy-two.

The view outside the window was magnificent. Popular media portrayed cities such as Paris, Vienna, and Saint Petersburg as some of the most beautiful on earth, at least parts of them. But to Egorshin, there were portions of Moscow unrivaled in magnificence and majesty.

Aside from high-level officials and oligarchs, few could boast of access to such views from their residences. Tatiana Palinieva could afford it. She had been one of the top models in Europe for nearly a decade and now cohosted one of the more popular news talk shows in Moscow. She and Egorshin had been seeing each other for nearly two years. In the last two months their conversations had sometimes flitted toward the possibility of marriage.

Marriage, let alone the magnificent view from the apartment, was in the back of his mind. At the forefront was what he had witnessed on the secure link Volkov had established for the special operations unit. It was horrific. It emphasized what men were capable of, especially Stetchkin.

Tatiana was in the bathroom and preparing to shower. That was an enterprise likely to take at least thirty minutes. Egorshin had arranged for his guest to arrive during that operation so they could speak in private. Sure enough, at the moment he heard the rush of water from the showerhead, there was a light rap at the apartment door.

Egorshin opened the door to find a short, balding, average-built man in his late sixties standing in the hallway. He wore a modest, finely tailored blue suit and black-framed glasses. It was Sergei Morosov of the SVR, Egorshin's favorite uncle, his only uncle, who had entertained him as a child with magic tricks and tales of epic adventures.

"Thank you for coming," Egorshin said, stepping aside and waving Morosov in.

"Of course."

The two went into the dining room, where Egorshin sat on one side of the dining room table and Morosov on the other. Morosov had a look of concern on his face. He and his nephew rarely met in person these days and never at this apartment. He surmised his nephew must be in trouble. Instincts honed by thirty years in the KGB and SVR told him it was the type of trouble that could get one killed.

"Should we talk here, Piotr?"

"It is all right, Uncle. Do not be concerned."

"You forget who I work for. I am always concerned. Someone could be watching. Listening."

Egorshin smiled. "You forget who I work for. I *am* the watcher. I *am* the listener."

"You are not the only one," Morosov countered.

"But I am the best one," Egorshin said. "This apartment is completely sterile. Redundant surveillance countermeasures are in place."

"Installed by your unit?"

"Installed by me."

Morosov smiled and nodded. His nephew had no peer when it came to such matters.

"I have not seen you in weeks. Neither has your mother."

"I have a problem. I need your advice."

"My personal advice or my professional advice?"

"This is personal, Uncle Sergei."

"What kind of personal problem requires the assistance of an agent of the SVR?"

"Aleksandr Stetchkin."

Morosov's facial muscles tightened visibly and he drew back his head.

Egorshin continued. "I am telling you this because, to be honest, I am frightened. You may have heard Stetchkin had my former boss, Uganov, removed . . ."

"Yes." Morosov nodded.

"And you know what he did to him?"

"I suspect I knew before you did."

Egorshin's shoulders drooped. "I think he plans to do something similar to me."

"Even if he would like to, he cannot," Morosov assured him. "You are too valuable to Mikhailov."

"You know what I am doing?" Egorshin asked, surprised.

"No. I do not. Not specifically." Morosov shrugged and held out his hands. "I am SVR. I know you are doing something of unique importance and that it is a special project of Yuri Mikhailov. Even Stetchkin would not dare touch you—at least until your project is complete."

"That is precisely my concern. The 'special project,' as you called it, is ready to go. All that needs to be done, really, is press a button, figuratively speaking. Then I am no longer essential. He can dispose of me like Uganov."

"Stetchkin and Uganov were rivals, Piotr. They had a long, unpleasant history, going back to before the collapse. You have no such history with him, and you are not a threat to his power or position."

"He hates me. He hates weakness. He thinks I am soft," Egorshin said.

Morosov smiled again. "But you *are* soft, Piotr. Most of you young people are. Not like the Americans or Western Europeans, perhaps. Their institutions are actually training them to be soft. And they will reap the consequences. But our young people are not far behind."

"Why did he do that to Uganov? Why not simply remove him from his office?"

"Again, Piotr," Morosov said patiently. "They had a history. If you are still concerned, however, I can have a word with Alexei Vasiliev."

"The president's chief of staff? You know him?"

"Our families, Piotr, go back together to before the revolution. I would wager we even share a relative or two. We were *dvoryane;* Stetchkin's family were peasants.

"Is that why he hates me?"

"No," Morosov said, shaking his head. "How should I put this?" He looked to the ceiling, searching for the right word. "Stetchkin is *evil.*"

"You mean psychopathic."

"No. That is merely a clinical term to deflect accountability," Morosov said. "Understand, Stetchkin is evil. He and I served together thirty-five years ago in Afghanistan. We went in alongside the 103rd Guards Airborne Division. We were Zenith. Our job was to demoralize and suppress the resistance. Stetchkin excelled at it. He killed indiscriminately. Not just the mujahedin, but men, women, and children who were not involved in the fighting. If the mujahedin killed one of our soldiers, he would not simply kill one of theirs in retaliation. He would kill ten. To start. The mujahedin would torture our captured soldiers. But even they could not compete with Stetchkin in terms of sheer brutality. He would bring women and children to the center of the village, torture them for days, until they were dead. At night, the valleys rang with their screams. Stetchkin reveled in it. He invented new and extreme methods and trained others in the techniques he had perfected. When our group left Kunar Province, he left behind one of his pupils, called Lucifer. When we left Panjshir Valley, he left another disciple—the Butcher. But he was the master."

"That is the fate that awaits me? The same as Uganov? That is why you are telling me this?"

"Piotr, once again, Uganov was a rival." Morosov saw that his nephew was not mollified. "I will speak with Vasiliev so you may rest assured."

"Thank you, Uncle Sergei. I do not mean to burden you, but the matter of Uganov and Stetchkin's evident dislike for me makes me anxious."

"I can see."

The men heard Tatiana turn off the shower. The SVR agent stood. "I will be on my way," Morosov said. He patted Egorshin's shoulder. "Do not be concerned. Mikhailov needs you."

Egorshin walked Morosov to the door and gave him a hug. Morosov walked into the hallway and waved good-bye as Egorshin's phone vibrated. He waved as his uncle entered the elevator, closed the door, and took the call.

"Colonel?"

"Yes," replied Egorshin as he watched Tatiana, her hair wet, emerge from the bathroom in search of a robe.

"Colonel, this is Major Volkov."

"I know, Major. What can I do for you?"

"Colonel, Mr. Stetchkin is looking for you."

Egorshin felt a bolt of anxiety.

"And?"

"Colonel, he asked why you did not arrange the video link earlier."

"I did arrange the video link. I instructed you to do it. That is your function, and the link was established."

"Colonel, to be clear," Volkov said nervously. "He asked why you did not personally set up the link."

Anxiety mixed with bewilderment in Egorshin's mind. Setting up the link was a task for someone several levels below Egorshin's rank. No one could possibly expect Egorshin to perform such a task. It would be akin to expecting the regional vice president of Exxon to pump gas at a filling station.

"What does he want?" Egorshin asked, looking blankly about the apartment, oblivious even to the undressed form of Tatiana Palinieva.

"Colonel, he directed me to find you and tell you to report to his office at six A.M."

Egorshin stared at a smiling Tatiana, standing naked in the middle of the living room with a hand just above the curve of her hip, her legs shoulder-width apart. But in his head, all Egorshin could see was the image of a husk of a human being that had once been Ivan Uganov shuffling obediently down the aisle toward his master.

CHAPTER 33

Olivia had attempted to reach James Brandt upon leaving the National Geospatial-Intelligence Agency, but his secretary said he was still in a meeting with Iris Cho, President Marshall's chief of staff. Olivia took a cab back to her office at the OEOB, where she searched for any and all reports she could find that might shed some light on the troop movements on Laura Casini's screen.

James Brandt, exercising his best judgment, could discount the importance of a slight increase in activity at Russian industrial sites. He could dismiss the possibility of any correlation between such increased activity and the shootings in Georgia that bore a familiar, if not unique, signature. But with the addition of Russian troop movements, Olivia was confident Brandt would bring the matter to the president's attention.

None of the intelligence summaries spanning the last week, however, revealed anything out of the ordinary, nothing that would shed light on what was going on in the satellite images on Laura Casini's screen. In fact, the summaries contained no mention of any unusual or unexpected Russian military maneuvers. According to the reports, it appeared everything in Russia was business as usual.

No matter, thought Olivia. Russian troops near the borders of Baltic nations might not be unusual; Russian troops moving southward along the Caspian was strange, to say the least. From the outset of their collaboration, dating back to her undergrad days at Stanford, James Brandt had taught Olivia to take seriously any strange or unusual Russian behavior. There was rarely, if ever, an innocuous explanation for such behavior.

Olivia was prepared to log off her computer and call Brandt's secretary again when a footnote in one of the summaries caught her eye. But for the satellite images Olivia had just seen, the footnote might otherwise be anodyne. In the last week there had been increased Russian naval presence at Bandar Abbas, the Iranian Persian Gulf port on the northern coast of the Strait of Hormuz. There was no description of the Russian vessels other than they appeared to be part of the Russian Pacific fleet out of Vladivostok.

Olivia dialed Laura Casini's number.

"Casini."

"Laura, take a look at Bandar Abbas for me, will you? Time lapse the last week. Let me know what you see, okay?"

"On it."

Olivia hung up. "There are no coincidences in this business," Dwyer had said. The coincidences were piling up. She looked at the time on the lower right corner of her computer screen. Brandt's meeting with Cho had to be over by now. Iris was famous for terseness and time management.

Olivia called Brandt's cell. It went to voice mail. Olivia terminated the call and dialed Brandt's secretary, Jess, who picked up on the first ring.

"Jess, it's Olivia. Is he available?"

"He wasn't feeling well and cut short the meeting with Iris, Olivia. He left a while ago and is probably over the bridge by now. Did you try his mobile?"

"Straight to voice mail."

"Oh, well, is there anything I can help you with?"

"If he calls in, please ask him to call me. Tell him I think I have some new information that he'll find interesting." Olivia thought for a moment. "Information that's important."

"He may not be in tomorrow. I have a feeling he may be working from home. It will be a while before he gets there, though."

"I'll try him there a bit later. Thank you, Jess."

Frustrated at being unable to reach Brandt, she dialed Dan Dwyer's number. Although she had to be circumspect talking with a civilian, even one privy to certain classified information, she had to talk to someone. The new information on the Russian movements was beginning to instill in her a vague sense of urgency. And the buzzing in her ears persisted.

CHAPTER 34

BETHANY BEACH, DELAWARE,
AUGUST 15, 8:25 P.M. EDT

The patrician took the assassin's call while standing on the balcony of the beach house. Again, as always, he spoke sterilely.

"Yes."

"We have arrived," Bor said. "We will complete preparations shortly."

"Good."

"But I have not heard from Trident's runner. I assume, therefore, that the impediment remains."

"I received a report a short time ago," the patrician said. "The impediment does, indeed, remain."

"The impediment must be removed. No compromises."

"Unfortunately, the assets have been eliminated and we do not have capable substitutes in place."

There was a short silence. "There are capable substitutes here. Perhaps not at the level of the assets, but they can compensate with numbers."

"I see." The patrician took a long drag on his Winston and exhaled slowly. "To whom do they belong?"

"One of our friends from Georgia," Bor replied.

"Yes, I know our friend. In the past he has been reliable. Somewhat expensive, if I recall. How much do you estimate?"

"Does it matter?" Bor asked.

The patrician took another drag and exhaled. "No. Just curious. But we will need to assemble the compensation, nonetheless."

"Considering the difficulty in removing the impediment, and considering the removal will occur here . . ." Bor calculated. "Five. US."

"It will be available in the hour."

The patrician terminated the call and went inside.

B or was disappointed but not especially surprised that Garin had been able to defeat the two Zaslon operators. His ability to do so underscored why he remained a threat to the operation. The patrician, who was well familiar with Garin's capabilities, knew it as well. That was why he didn't hesitate to approve the payment of five million dollars.

Bor stood on the rear lawn of the house that would serve as a base of operations for the foreseeable future. The volunteers were inside, under the supervision of an SVR agent from the consulate. The friend to whom Bor had referred on the call was resident not of the state of Georgia, but of the Republic of Georgia. He was Nikoloz Abkashvili, the billionaire head of a Georgian Mafia group whose interests spanned parts of Russia, Western Europe, and North America. Abkashvili occasionally provided certain services requiring Russian deniability to the FSB and SVR, both at home and abroad. In return, the SVR refrained from killing him and permitted him to conduct his affairs with minimal interference. The SVR also compensated Abkashvili, not lavishly but appropriately. Five million dollars was appropriate for the elimination of Mike Garin on US soil.

Bor keyed the number for the man who likely would be handling the assignment, Levan Bulkvadze, Abkashvili's captain in the northeastern United States. Bulkvadze, a former member of the First Special Operations Group of the Georgian Armed Forces, was tough and smart—smart enough to assemble a sufficient number of men with the requisite skills to take out a man like Garin.

"Who is this?" Bulkvadze's voice was steeped in hostility.

"It is I, Levan."

"My friend." The tenor of Bulkvadze's voice changed from hostile to obsequious. "It is good to hear from you. You are well?"

Bulkvadze, who was engaged in enterprises ranging from arms

trafficking to industrial espionage, knew enough not to mention names or other information useful to electronic eavesdroppers. For that reason, Bor would tolerate a sentence or two of inane chatter.

"I am well. And you?"

"Well also," Bulkvadze said, knowing the brief exchange was the limit of Bor's patience.

"Meet me at our usual place at nine P.M."

"I will not be late," Bulkvadze said superfluously. No one displeased Bor by being late.

Bor ended the call. He went inside to inform the SVR minder that he would be gone for a while and then drove the Caprice to the Russian embassy on Wisconsin Avenue to retrieve the five million dollars in cash before meeting Bulkvadze at the Mayflower.

Garin would soon be on his way. Bor was sure of it. Even if Bulkvadze's men couldn't kill Garin, they would at least delay him long enough for Bor and the volunteers to accomplish their mission.

The traffic along Wisconsin Avenue was light. Bor arrived at the consulate and was met by two attractive and efficient-looking women who had no idea who he was but who had been told to provide him with everything and anything he needed, and more specifically, to be sure he was given a large leather satchel in the office of the resident.

The two women escorted Bor to a conference room where a short, thin, severe-looking man with ice-blue eyes sat next to a mahogany desk on top of which lay the satchel. Upon seeing Bor, the man rose to his feet.

"Taras," he said, one of the few people in the world who knew Bor's first name, and one of the fewer still who dared call him by it. "It has been quite a long time."

"Vadim," Bor said, embracing the smaller man. "I am happy to see you here, someone I can count on."

"I am also."

Vadim Stepulev was a former Spetsnaz comrade of Bor's, now a high-ranking SVR agent. Though one of the smallest operators, he had impressed Bor as one of the more proficient. On a cold, rainy night several years previously, the two had been trapped on a hilltop in Chechnya, surrounded by two dozen Chechen rebels. They had emerged from the hilltop after a harrowing firefight in which they had suffered grievous wounds but had slaughtered all of the Chechen fighters. They emerged having forged a lifelong bond.

Bor pointed to the satchel.

"Yes. That is it," Stepulev confirmed. "I counted it myself."

Bor turned to the efficient-looking women. "Would you please excuse us?"

The women smiled and vanished from the room. Bor turned to Stepulev and said quietly, "I would like to catch up a bit."

Stepulev understood. Every room in the embassy had a camera and a highly sensitive microphone that recorded everything 24/7. Stepulev produced two Macanudos from the breast pocket of his suit jacket. "Let us go for a stroll."

Minutes later, the two men were walking casually down Tunlaw Road out of range of the embassy's video and audio devices. Neither was under the illusion that they were not, however, being watched— either by long-range surveillance equipment or by agents somewhere along the street—probably both. When either spoke, he did so quietly with a hand holding a cigar obscuring his face.

"What do you know of the operation, Vadim?" Bor asked.

"Very little, other than my limited role and that the operation is very important."

"It is." Bor nodded. "Yet it is being handled amateurishly."

"But *you* are involved, Taras. If you are involved, it will succeed. I was briefed throughout the first part of the operation. That was not your fault, Taras. Political considerations produced bad judgments. We should not have given any role to the Iranians regarding Omega. From what I have seen, you performed your part brilliantly."

"Bad judgments are being made again and they will jeopardize the mission. I informed them at the outset that an impediment needed to be removed before we embarked on the second phase of the operation. That impediment still remains."

"Garin," Stepulev said flatly.

"Yes, Garin."

"Formidable," Stepulev acknowledged. "Where is he now?"

"On his way here. If he is not here already."

"How do you know?"

"I know, Vadim. I am certain."

"You have beaten him before. For nearly two years you were an Omega operator and he never discovered who you were until it was too late."

"I deceived him; I did not beat him."

"Do not take this the wrong way, but you and he are remarkably alike, my friend."

"That is what I have been told," Bor replied with a grimace.

Stepulev chuckled darkly. "Then perhaps we should be worried after all. I presume arrangements have been made to eliminate him?"

"They were unsuccessful. He killed two Zaslon Unit men hours ago."

"By himself?"

"By himself."

Stepulev was silent. The two men turned onto Fulton and walked to the next block.

"What is the next step?"

"The five million dollars is for Abkashvili's man," Bor replied. "I am meeting Bulkvadze shortly."

"I figured as much. How many of his men do you think it will take to eliminate Garin?"

Bor contemplated the question. "Enough," he said simply.

"More than two; that is clear."

"I will *insist* he uses more than two."

"You are not confident they can do the job."

"They must do the job," Bor stressed. "If they do not, I assure you, Vadim, the mission will fail."

"Nothing is guaranteed in this business, especially when the stakes are so high. But if you desire near certainty, may I make a suggestion?"

"We have no more Zaslon operators here right now, Vadim. That is why I'm using Bulkvadze."

"Let me show you something," Stepulev said as they returned to the embassy.

Stepulev led Bor through the foyer and down two flights of steps to a dimly lit room with a bar and several small tables and chairs.

Except for a figure seated at a table in the far corner, the room was empty.

The man appeared to be in his late fifties and of average height and weight. Even in the dim light, he was one of the most grotesque-looking men Bor had ever seen. His eyes were rheumy, the left bulging slightly from its socket. A deep scar stretched from the left corner of his mouth to his ear. His nose was crooked and flat, as if it had been broken numerous times, and his mostly bald scalp was covered with an assortment of welts and knots separated by wispy tufts of white hair. Bor could imagine him perched on a ledge at Notre-Dame Cathedral.

"Who is he?" Bor asked.

"I do not know his name. No one in the embassy knows his name. His file simply, albeit somewhat theatrically, refers to him as the Butcher. He refers to himself as the Butcher."

"I have heard the name."

"If Bulkvadze fails, the Butcher will not."

"Two Zaslon men failed," Bor said quietly. "But this old man will not? Forgive me, Vadim, but that is utterly ridiculous. Garin is a predator at the top of the food chain. Why should I believe this pathetic creature will be successful when Zaslon was not?"

"Read his file, Taras," Stepulev replied. "But preferably, not before bedtime."

CHAPTER 35

D an Dwyer stood from his chair on the east patio of his home as he watched the black Ford Explorer navigate the quarter-mile drive and come to a stop at the bottom of the steps. The rear door opened and Mike Garin, carrying a black gym bag, emerged, jogged up the steps to the patio, and shook Dwyer's hand.

"Good flight?" Dwyer asked.

Garin nodded. "Where's Luci?"

"She's fine. Watching movies with Congo in the living room. Another woman smitten by the Great and Powerful Garin. I swear, I don't get it. But I think you may be getting competition from Congo now."

"What does Brandt think about all of this?"

"You can ask Olivia when she gets here. And don't act like you're not looking forward to seeing her. I swear, she gets better-looking every day. You know she's seeing some bozo senator? They were in the Style section of the *Post* last week. Some event at the Kennedy Center."

"Good to know. Who do we have for third-period geometry?"

"Play it off all you want, Mikey. I know better."

"You also know Bor is back."

"Geez, Mikey, can't you ever put it in neutral?"

Max, followed by Bear and Diesel, bounded from the French doors behind Dwyer to greet Garin. Diesel immediately began tearing at Garin's pant leg.

"When did you get the pups?" Garin asked, petting Max.

"Couple of weeks ago from SecDef Merritt. He's been breeding German shepherds for decades. Not for show. He says they don't have hip problems." Dwyer pointed at Diesel nipping furiously at Garin's shoes. "Well, look at that. Finally, someone who's not scared of you. Must be a sign, Mikey."

Garin squatted to pet Diesel, the expression on the man's face the closest approximation of a smile Dwyer had seen in months. Dwyer shouted over his shoulder toward the French doors. "Matt! Quick, take a picture and send it to the wire services. 'Garin Displays Sign of Affection. Apocalypse Approaching.'"

Matt Colton, Dwyer's chief of security, appeared through the doors a few moments later, a large grin on his face. He was as gregarious as Garin was taciturn. Matt extended a hand toward Garin, who rose to shake it as a Red Top cab came up the drive.

"I just buzzed the cab in," Matt said. "That's Olivia."

The taxi stopped next to the Ford Explorer. Olivia alighted and ascended the stairs. Seeing Garin for the first time since shortly after the conclusion of the EMP affair, she slowed her pace as she approached the top.

"Hello, Michael," she said.

Garin nodded in return.

Dwyer watched with amusement. Even the dogs, he thought, could sense the attraction, but Olivia and Garin would go to their respective graves vehemently denying its existence.

"Let's go inside and get caught up," Dwyer suggested.

The group went through the French doors into the library, the dogs following closely behind. Almost simultaneously, Congo Knox and Luci Saldana entered the room from the other end. Upon seeing Garin, Luci rushed to him and embraced him tightly for several seconds. The questions came in rapid succession.

"Are you okay? I was worried about you going back to Dallas. Why didn't you call me? Did you call the cops, finally?"

"I'm sorry for all of this," Garin said. "I'm grateful to Congo for stepping up on short notice. You okay?"

"Me? I'll probably end up with PTSD, but the last twenty-four hours have been the most amazing in my life. It feels like I'm in a movie. The near-death experience, then a getaway, then a private jet, this mansion, meeting Ms. Perry. Not to mention Mr. Sunshine over there," Luci said, pointing at Congo Knox.

Olivia's reaction to Luci wasn't lost on Dwyer, observing the scene from just inside the doors. Olivia, he thought, was scrutinizing Luci with the same intensity she likely devoted to classified intelligence assessments. Dwyer cleared his throat.

"Congo, Matt . . ."

"It's okay, Dan," Luci interjected. "I'll leave you guys to talk. I just thought I heard Mike's voice and ran in to check." She turned to Knox and hooked her arm in his. "Come on, let's finish the movie."

Dwyer waited for Knox and Luci to leave. He gestured to the couches and chairs. "Have a seat, everybody."

Garin got directly to the point. "Olivia, without compromising any confidences, is Brandt going to act on Bor?"

"That would be impossible to answer *without* disclosing confidences, Michael."

"What can you tell us, then?"

"That for now, you're on your own."

Garin stared in frustration. As far as he was concerned, the mere mention of Bor's name should prompt some kind of response.

"When did you last speak to him?"

"At approximately three thirty."

"There have been some developments since then that might change his perspective," Garin said. "Earlier, I flew from Dallas to Cleveland. No real reason to go to Cleveland other than it's my hometown—I wanted to leave a trail of bread crumbs to flush out Bor's men to get information from them. I succeeded, in part.

"In the airport parking lot two shooters almost took me out." Garin leaned forward in his chair. "Please understand, Olivia, these men were extremely skilled—the way they moved, their reactions." Garin turned to Dwyer. "Dan, you're probably right. I think they were Zaslon Unit."

"What's Zaslon Unit?" Olivia asked.

"A hyperelite unit of Spetsnaz operators," Dwyer answered. "At least that's how our media would describe them. To my knowledge, there's never been confirmation by our intelligence services that Zaslon exists, but in my estimation, enough evidence points in that direction. There was evidence of them in Iraq. Now in Crimea, Ukraine, Syria. Russian black operations have always made ours look tame in comparison, but even for the Russians, Zaslon takes it to another level. Present company excepted, they're the baddest of badasses."

"Then how did two of them fail?" Olivia asked.

"They missed. I didn't. Simple as that," Garin replied. "It was sheer luck, Olivia. I should be dead."

Olivia fought to suppress a shudder. She'd known Michael Garin for barely a month, and in almost every encounter death and violence followed him as closely as Dwyer's dogs followed him. Even if the men who attempted to kill Garin were not from some elite unit, the effort to kill him, she thought, was uncomfortably similar to the prelude to the EMP operation. It was implausible that the rapidly accumulating events of the last twenty-four hours were mere coincidence. "You don't need to convince me, Michael."

"Olivia," Garin said, "Bor is going to do something seriously bad. You know that from previous experience. And he doesn't do small stuff. I'm an operator without a home right now. I have no authority to go after him. Hell, the airport incident might have the FBI looking for me again at this very moment. I need authority and I need resources—the resources only our military and intelligence can provide. I need them right now. Brandt could facilitate green-lighting them."

"Even if James Brandt agreed, where would you get the manpower?"

"Reconstitute Omega," Garin said emphatically.

"I'm sorry, but that won't happen, Michael. Just yesterday, Senator McCoy made it plain that Omega will never be resurrected as long as he's chair of Senate Intelligence."

"What an idiot," Dwyer said. "Didn't that airhead learn anything from the near miss with the EMP? His freakin' counsel was the one providing intel to the Russians, for God's sake."

"And that's why he doesn't want to reconstitute Omega. Doing so would highlight just that. It would be not only embarrassing, but politically catastrophic for him," Olivia said.

"What about the best interests of the country? Doesn't anyone put country above self-interest anymore?" Dwyer practically shouted.

"Dan, with all due respect, where have you been lately?" Olivia asked.

Garin rubbed the stubble on his face pensively. "If we can't reconstitute an Omega team, can we commission and finance the functional equivalent?"

"What are you saying, Michael?"

"I'm saying that Omega need not be part of the US military or intelligence apparatus. Instead, the functional equivalent of the Omega team could be financed under the CIA's Title 50 authority. And it could operate as a contractor under JSOC direction."

"I don't want to be party to a plan to deceive Congress," Olivia said.

"We're not deceiving Congress," Garin explained. "We're accommodating them. At least one of them. If McCoy doesn't want to reconstitute Omega—if he doesn't want direct oversight responsibility for Omega—then let's give him what he wants."

"But if Omega is not part of DOD or the CIA or any other governmental entity, where do you get the personnel?"

"Omega was comprised of a select group of tier-one operators trained by Clint Laws," Garin responded, turning to Dwyer. "*This* man happens to employ a number of former tier-one operators—people like Congo Knox, for example. Even Matt over there, if you consider the sorry slugs from Australian SAS tier-one."

"Watch it, mate," Matt warned amiably.

"I'm not sure that will fly, Michael," Olivia said.

"What about me?" Dwyer protested. "Don't I get a say?"

"Run it by Brandt, Olivia. He'll see the merits of this given what we're up against. We need to get a team of the best together—immediately—to counter Bor." Garin pointed at Dwyer. "And you will be well compensated for providing a crucial service to the country. Win-win. But it has to happen now. We've got to be given authority and resources to go after Bor."

"Can do," Dwyer said.

"I can't speak for James Brandt, but I'm willing to bring it to him," Olivia said.

"Good." Garin fished in one of the side compartments of his gym bag, pulled out a cell phone, and tossed it to Dwyer. "I got that off one of the guys we presume were Zaslon. It's fully intact but no doubt heavily encrypted. No redial or recents. Can you have your tech guys pull all the information they can from it? If the guy was in communication with Bor, and if we're lucky, we might be able to track Bor's location."

Dwyer extended the phone to Colton. "Matt?"

"On it."

Dwyer looked back to Garin. "What else?"

Garin turned to Olivia. "Please call Brandt and see if he's on board." To Dwyer, he said, "Pick several of your best men who can be ready to go once Brandt gives us the green light.

"As for me, just in case the tech guys can't get anything from the phone, I'm going to drop some more bread crumbs."

CHAPTER 36

Bor spotted Levan Bulkvadze sitting alone at a far corner table of the Edgar, the restaurant-bar at the Mayflower Hotel.

Spotting Bulkvadze was a task only slightly more difficult than spotting an elephant in a phone booth. At six foot seven, he weighed well over three hundred pounds and was built like a power lifter. The thick black beard that covered much of his face matched the color of eyes that projected constant hostility. As he sat among the politicians, congressional staffers, and lobbyists who frequented the establishment, his overall appearance suggested a reversion in the evolutionary spectrum. Yet his frame was draped in an impeccably tailored twenty-five-hundred-dollar suit that somehow rendered him not merely civilized, but cultured.

Bulkvadze rose and smiled as the assassin approached. Bor placed a leather satchel on the floor next to the table and grasped Bulkvadze's outstretched hand. With his other hand the big man gestured for the waiter.

"I'm pleased to see you again, my friend," Bulkvadze lied. "What brings you to Washington?"

"Business," Bor replied tersely.

The waiter appeared at Bulkvadze's elbow. The big man nodded toward Bor. "Bring my friend whatever he wishes and another vodka for me."

"Nothing for me," Bor said.

The waiter retreated toward the bar. Bor pulled a mobile device from his hip pocket and tapped the screen, upon which a photo appeared. He turned it toward Bulkvadze.

"This man," Bor said.

"Who is he?"

"His name is Mike Garin. I will provide his location shortly. Upon receiving that information, you must eliminate him. Immediately."

"Tell me something about him."

"He is an American soldier. I worked with him once. He will be very difficult to kill. That's all you need to know other than where to find him."

"We have not agreed upon a price," Bulkvadze said. "Yet you have brought a bag I assume is filled with cash. How much have you brought, if I may ask?"

"Five million US. You will, however, receive an advance of one million only. The balance will be delivered upon proof of death."

"Very generous. But I'm afraid Nikoloz will demand ten."

"Five million. That is the price," Bor said with finality. "I expect you will skim one million off that total and tell Nikoloz that the price was four million. Regardless, how much you keep for yourself is your affair. What is of concern to me is results. If you fail, I will kill you and every one of your associates involved in such failure, including Nikoloz himself."

"Have we ever failed before? There will be no failure now," Bulkvadze said with all of the confidence he could muster. He was frightened of Bor. He knew of no one who wasn't.

"How many men do you plan to use?" Bor asked.

"You say it will be difficult to kill him." Bulkvadze thought for a moment. He held up three fingers. "Then I will use three."

"More."

The big man raised his eyebrows. "More than three, you say?" He tilted his head and looked at Garin's photo again. "Then I will use five."

"How many would you use to kill me?" Bor asked.

"Kill you, my friend? I would never think of such a thing. Why kill you?"

"Humor me. How many men would you use to kill me?"

Bulkvadze frowned. "But there are few, if any, like you. I say this not to flatter you, but for a man of your capabilities I would use two primary, two secondary, and three for a perimeter. So"—he rubbed the back of his neck—"to be absolutely certain, I would use seven."

"Bring ten."

CHAPTER 37

The walls of the waiting room to Stetchkin's suite of offices were covered with paintings depicting Napoléon's retreat from Moscow. Blood, agony, cold, snow. A metaphor, Egorshin thought, for the fate awaiting those who've incurred Stetchkin's wrath.

Immediately after the phone call informing him to report to Stetchkin, Egorshin had placed several calls to his uncle. There was no answer and there was no voice mail function. He wanted to impress upon his uncle the urgency of contacting the president's chief of staff immediately. Make sure the tyrant Stetchkin didn't do anything insane.

The event was only sixty-six hours away. He should be at his station making calculations, verifying previous calculations. It was inconceivable that a man in Stetchkin's position would compromise its success by taking some rash action out of personal pique.

Almost inconceivable. The image of Uganov, moving past him with eyes vacant, rendered all manner of horror conceivable. Evil. That was how Egorshin's uncle had described Stetchkin. An active malevolence.

An aide to Stetchkin sat rigidly at a large, neat desk adjacent to the wooden double doors leading to Stetchkin's office. He had pale skin, gray eyes, and bloodless lips resembling those of a cadaver. The eyes were pitiless, like the eyes of the man behind the doors. Eyes, Egorshin imagined, that had seen countless individuals walk through those doors and walk out minutes later, their lives shattered, bodies soon to be broken.

Egorshin keyed his uncle's number one last time, but before the cell could make the connection, the intercom on the aide's desk came to life. It was Stetchkin's voice, quiet and calm.

"Send him in."

The aide simply rose from his desk without a word and gestured toward the door. Egorshin stood and walked slowly, pausing to glance at the aide, who flicked his eyes toward the door, signaling him to enter.

Egorshin turned the brass handle and opened the door into an anteroom containing a French provincial couch and chairs. A credenza to the left held an assortment of handguns and knives and a grenade, which Egorshin guessed to be souvenirs from the Afghan war. A credenza on the right held a glass case the size of a bread box in which lay an assortment of campaign ribbons and medals. The wall separating the anteroom from the office was made entirely of glass, an archway in the middle serving as the entrance to Stetchkin's office.

Egorshin stepped through the archway and scanned the room. It was large, neat, but otherwise unremarkable and, in fact, somewhat utilitarian. A desk, two chairs, a conference table, more chairs, and a bookshelf. Stetchkin was nowhere in sight.

Moments later, a door on the right side of the room opened and the tyrant emerged from a bathroom. He strode to his desk, the pace as slow as when he had walked down the aisle in the Kremlin. He pressed a button that activated a speakerphone.

"Have my car ready in ten minutes."

He disconnected, turned, and gazed out the window behind the desk for several seconds, his hands clasped behind his back. Then he turned and looked at Egorshin for the first time.

"Sit."

Egorshin proceeded to the chair opposite the desk and sat on the edge of the seat. Stetchkin remained standing, staring at the young colonel for several seconds in silence. Egorshin could hear the ticking of an unseen clock somewhere behind him.

"You have defied me twice, Egorshin. Your defiance perplexes me, particularly since it is evident that you are a coward."

"Mr. Stetchkin, I did not defy—"

"Did I tell you to speak?" Stetchkin asked calmly, in almost a whisper.

"No, I just—"

"Then do not speak unless I give you permission to speak," the tyrant said softly.

Stetchkin walked from behind the desk to Egorshin's immediate right and stood directly over him. Egorshin continued to look at the space just vacated by Stetchkin, awaiting permission to look elsewhere. Stetchkin didn't speak for several uncomfortable seconds.

"I made it quite clear to you that if I needed your services for Zaslon Unit, I expected you to provide them. I was under the impression you understood me perfectly. You did not ask me to repeat myself. You did not ask for clarification. It was a simple instruction that anyone could process."

Stetchkin put his left hand on Egorshin's right shoulder, sending a charge through him. Stetchkin bent and spoke into Egorshin's ear.

"Tell me, Colonel, did I say that when Zaslon needs your services you should delegate the requested services to someone else?"

Egorshin sat mute, awaiting permission to answer.

"Speak," Stetchkin said.

"You did not."

"That is my recollection, also."

Stetchkin straightened and walked slowly back behind the desk. He tapped the surface with his index finger.

"Did Zaslon Unit contact you? Speak."

"Yes."

Stetchkin walked back around the desk and stood next to Egorshin again. Egorshin continued to stare forward.

"Did Zaslon Unit request a service? Speak."

"They did."

Stetchkin paced slowly back behind his desk and resumed tapping the surface with his index finger.

"Did Zaslon Unit request someone besides you to perform the service? Speak."

"They did not request anyone specifically."

"That answer is not responsive to the question I asked, Colonel. Did they request someone *else* perform the service? Speak."

"They did not."

Stetchkin's tapping became progressively slower. He tapped for a full thirty seconds without uttering a word. The only other sound in the room was the ticking of the clock.

The tapping stopped. Egorshin's heart raced.

"So," Stetchkin said in a whisper Egorshin strained to hear, "you understood that you were to provide services to Zaslon Unit upon request. Such request was made of you. It was made of no one else. You did not provide such service." Stetchkin paused, then paced back to Egorshin's side and once again placed his left hand on Egorshin's right shoulder and bent to speak into his ear. "How, then, is that not defiance? Speak."

"It was a misunderstanding."

"A misunderstanding, you say."

Egorshin did not respond.

"A misunderstanding," Stetchkin repeated, pacing contemplatively toward his desk and then back to Egorshin. "That puzzles me. This was a simple matter. A very simple matter. I instructed that you provide services to Zaslon Unit; I instructed no one else to provide such services; yet you did not provide the requested services. You are alleged to be brilliant. You have studied at Harvard and Oxford. Clearly, such a simple matter was easily understood by you. You could not have possibly misunderstood my instructions, so the misunderstanding must have been on my part." Stetchkin stopped pacing somewhere behind Egorshin. "Are you saying, therefore, that I am stupid?"

"Respectfully, I do not—"

Stetchkin slapped the back of Egorshin's head sharply. "Quiet," the tyrant whispered. "I did not direct you to speak. Or have I misunderstood our arrangement?"

Egorshin sat still, bewildered. What was this madman doing? Why was he tormenting him like this? They barely knew each other. Before now, they'd had hardly more than a couple of minutes of conversation. Why had he singled Egorshin out? What could possibly have sparked his wrath?

The voice came from behind. "Speak."

"Respectfully, I misunderstood your initial instructions to mean that I should *effectuate* Zaslon Unit's request for services. I sought to do so with the most efficient allocation of resources. Accordingly, I delegated the duty to the person within my unit charged with performing such services directly."

"Here is my dilemma, Colonel," Stetchkin said from somewhere behind Egorshin. "You have already defied me once. You have conceded that I gave you and no one else the instruction to accommodate Zaslon Unit. You are very bright. You do not misunderstand small things. All of that militates against this being a misunderstanding. Rather, it supports the conclusion that you intentionally disregarded my instructions out of spite. Or perhaps you thought such instruction was beneath you." Stetchkin's voice seemed to proceed farther behind Egorshin. "Either way," he continued, "it was another act of defiance."

The tyrant's voice seemed to be coming from several feet behind Egorshin, who dared not turn around for confirmation. There was a brief sound of metal against wood. Then, for several seconds, just the ticking of the clock. When Stetchkin spoke again, his voice was louder— to project from wherever he was standing. Egorshin calculated it was the archway.

"Your behavior was not mere insubordination. I gave you a clear and unequivocal instruction, which you did not simply ignore, but which you expressly disobeyed only a short time after receiving it. It was a rebuke. A slap in the face. It was defiance."

Egorshin heard the unmistakable sound of the slide on a semiautomatic pistol being pulled back to chamber a round. The Makarov from the credenza.

Multiple thoughts ran together in Egorshin's mind like a high-speed pileup, too many to sort out. This was lunacy. It could not be. He'd done nothing to deserve this.

Egorshin felt a vague sensation of pressure on the back of his head, anticipating the explosion of his head caused by a 9×18mm round slamming into his cranium at 1,370 feet per second, tumbling through his brain before bursting from his forehead. He became nauseous and closed his eyes, considering the sad possibility that the bile currently in his mouth would be the last thing he'd ever taste.

"Defiance is an interesting matter," Stetchkin said, his voice drawing nearer. "It lies on a continuum of acts. Some noble, some dishonorable. Toward the dishonorable end of the scale lies disloyalty, treachery, treason. Treason, of course, is punishable by death. Do you believe your defiance was an act of treason, Egorshin?" A pause. "Speak."

"No."

"It might relieve you to know that I agree with you," Stetchkin concurred. "It was not an act of treason. Although I note that your answer conceded your defiance. Therefore, you still remain in jeopardy, for there are acts of defiance below the level of treason that may still merit death. The question is whether your latest act of defiance qualifies. Do you think it qualifies?" Stetchkin pressed the muzzle of the Makarov against the base of Egorshin's skull. "Speak."

The noise that came from Egorshin's mouth was thin and raspy. It only vaguely sounded like "no."

"Tell me why your defiance does not merit death. Speak."

"Because, respectfully, it was not a conscious act of defiance. It was not intentional. It was not disrespectful." Egorshin swallowed. "Respectfully, it was not an act of defiance."

"So, it was an inadvertent act that could be perceived as defiance?"

Egorshin remained silent and motionless.

"Speak," Stetchkin commanded with a whisper and a poke of the Makarov.

"Yes."

"Plausible. Do you know why I consider your response plausible? Speak."

"Because I am being truthful."

"No. I give no credence whatsoever to your veracity. Under the circumstances, I believe you would lie about your mother's chasteness if you thought it would benefit you. No, I believe you were not defiant because you are too much of a coward to defy me. Do you know why I am certain you are a coward? Speak."

"No."

"Because you believe in nothing. Other than yourself and your own brilliance and superiority, of course. Since you are aware, however, of your true frailty and mortality, you are frightened. You have nothing beyond your own wretched self to provide ballast. You are empty. No true purpose. Without purpose there can be no courage. That is why you are such a coward, Egorshin. There is nothing inside." A pause. "You may speak if you wish."

Egorshin didn't know what to say. He remained silent for several moments, then: "Respectfully, I am not a coward."

Stetchkin snorted. "You are a sniveling, mewling coward. You would confess secrets to an enemy. You would retreat against an onslaught. You would beg for mercy. You would not die for a person or a cause. You are weak and worthless." Stetchkin walked slowly back behind his desk. "Do you wish to speak? Speak."

"Yes."

"Speak."

"I am not a coward. I am a true Russian. I have never failed, nor will I in the future. Respectfully, you are wrong."

"A true Russian," Stetchkin spat derisively. "Very nice. Are you finished? Speak."

"Yes."

"Then we are done here," the tyrant said, startling Egorshin. "Remember everything I have said. You will not get another opportunity to disappoint me. Do you have anything else you wish to tell me? Speak."

Egorshin rose to be dismissed. "I am not a coward," he said firmly.

Stetchkin looked Egorshin up and down in disgust. "Go home and change, Colonel. It appears you have soiled yourself."

CHAPTER 38

Ruth Ponder had persisted. Looking for Amos, she had ramped up her calls to the sheriff's office from every hour on the hour to every half hour. She'd enlisted Bob Lampley to call his friends at Georgia State Patrol. She'd repeatedly called the local newspaper, local hospital, local news radio station, and investigative reporter for the local TV station.

And because of her persistence, she received the worst news of her life. A deputy sheriff who had gone to elementary school with her kids was so sorry to have to give her the news over the phone instead of in person as would be proper. But she had persisted, so he told her.

Amos's body was among those that had been recovered in the big massacre that had been in all the news stories. Somehow, she'd already suspected as much. Forty-four years together and it was the first time she couldn't account for Amos's whereabouts at the same time a big massacre occurs in an area where the biggest crime story is an outbreak of mailbox vandalism. She knew it wringing her hands at the kitchen table and pacing the kitchen floor. She knew it when she kept calling Bob Lampley—heard it in his voice. He'd known Amos for more than fifty years and when he heard about the slaughter and that Amos was missing, well, in his experience, coincidences had a way of producing bad news.

Despite the distances that separated folks in this rural community, Ruth was soon standing in the kitchen with her three kids and seven grandkids. Bob Lampley and his wife were there, too. About a dozen neighbors were out on the front porch grumbling about how the country had gone to hell and nobody was doing anything about it except spending money on everything and everybody but America and Americans. Another dozen or so folks from church were scattered throughout the house, mainly in the living room, ready to cook, clean, and console as needed. Already, enough food for two or three large Thanksgiving dinners had appeared and was scattered on every available space atop Ruth's furniture.

A reporter from Atlanta had shown up and was quickly surrounded by a cordon of Ruth's friends and neighbors determined not to let the muckraker exploit the tragedy just to sell some more advertising space. Besides, it seemed whenever reporters from the big papers or TV stations did any kind of story about folks like Ruth and Amos, they made them look like backward and ignorant hayseeds, usually made fun of them even when the subject was a sad one. And with all the church folk in and around the house, several carrying family Bibles and a few wearing crucifixes, they'd no doubt be portrayed as intolerant ignoramuses and bigots. Nope, this wasn't an occasion for confirming stereotypes and prejudices for smug big-city folks.

But Ruth wasn't done. She had continued to make call after call to confirm Amos's personal effects, to determine whether anything was missing or stolen. And where was their car? That was a really nice LaCrosse. All kinds of features. The grandbaby's car seat was found in the woods near Amos. Why would they do that? There must have been more than one of them. More than two. They must've needed the back seat, said Ruth.

Pretty soon, Bob Lampley and some of Ruth's friends and neighbors were calling around also. What do you know? What do you hear? And the people on the other end of those calls reached out to their friends, neighbors, and contacts. Decades of friendships and bonds were put to use to get answers. Ruth and Amos deserved it.

Ruth persisted. Between calls she received condolences and served coffee and pie. She smiled and sometimes even chuckled at anecdotes about Amos's habits and foibles.

But she persisted. And in short order the dominoes falling from all of the calls that came out of the Ponder house produced results. According to Amy Randall from the church choir, whose sister was an insurance adjuster in Kannapolis, North Carolina, police in Albemarle had found a LaCrosse next to an Econoline behind a truck stop along Route 52. No damage. It still had plenty of gas. A patron in the diner adjacent to the truck stop saw about a dozen men get out of the LaCrosse and the van. Most of them were foreign-looking, but then it seemed just about everyone was foreign-looking these days.

But one of the guys stood out. The patron hadn't provided a very good description other than to say the guy—even from fifty yards away—gave the patron chills. Couldn't put his finger on it. Maybe it was the way the guy walked or how he appeared to interact with the others. But the patron was glad when the guy drove off in a minivan instead of coming into the diner.

The Albemarle police were reviewing the video from the security cameras atop the fuel islands at the truck stop. Because of the distance between the islands and the lot where the LaCrosse was parked, the video was blurry, and the angles were poor. But the FBI was coming down and they would run the feed through their equipment to clarify and enhance it.

Ruth wasn't done. She had found Amos. She had found the car. But she wanted the man who had killed her husband. And she knew in her bones it was the guy who had given the diner patron chills.

Ruth didn't know anything about forensics. But she knew one thing for sure. The man who had killed Amos headed north with all those foreign-looking men, probably to a big city where they could blend in. Probably, Ruth thought, to Washington, where it seemed there were hardly any Americans left, including those born here.

So Ruth would persist. So would more than a dozen of her friends and family. Because that's what friends and family did. You couldn't depend on the government. You certainly couldn't wait on them. They had one million other things going on that seemed to have absolutely nothing to do with anything important—or even remotely relevant—to you, your family, or your friends. So Ruth and a small army surrounding her would make pests of themselves until that scary man in the video was found. He had destroyed the best thing in Ruth's life and deprived Catoosa County of one of its best, and she was determined to make him pay.

CHAPTER 39

Five hundred sixty miles to the north, another group of individuals with their own network also was searching for the scary man in the video.

Shortly after Dan Dwyer had sensed the massacre in Georgia might be the work of Taras Bor, he had directed a team of DGT investigators to monitor the developments on the news and make inquiries with local law enforcement. Professional acquaintances and former colleagues were queried, extending even to a few people located at Pope Field at Fort Bragg.

Random bits of information were gleaned and analyzed. Pins were placed on points on a map. The team discussed the various scenarios and probabilities among themselves.

And they had come to the same conclusion as Ruth Ponder, although nearly an hour later. The scary man in the video taken by cameras stationed on the fuel islands of the truck stop was likely the perpetrator of the massacre in northern Georgia. But by virtue of their boss's previous experience with the likely perpetrator, the team had something Ruth did not: a name. Taras Bor.

The DGT team also had powerful computers and a platoon of extremely skilled experts to operate them and analyze their output. Even before the FBI got its hands on the video, it had been streamed to DGT's cybersecurity division just outside Quantico, Virginia, where it had been blown up and enhanced, its resolution sharpened. Hundreds of media reports were collated, sifted, and entered into various programs for analysis, including a report of a peculiar farmhouse explosion in rural western South Carolina and a report of shots fired near the North Carolina border.

For the most part, the adage "garbage in, garbage out" prevailed. But with the help of innovative computer programs and decades of investigative experience, the DGT team came to a conclusion similar to Ruth's: Taras Bor was headed to Washington, D.C. More ominous, their analysis showed that Bor had already arrived in the District.

As soon as the team arrived at their preliminary conclusions, the lead analyst called Dwyer, who transferred the call to the secure communications room. Dwyer sat in the captain's chair and put the call on speaker.

"What do you have?"

"Sir, it appears Taras Bor may be in Washington, D.C., right now."

"Crap."

"We have a very poor-quality video from a truck stop near Albemarle. We enhanced it, ran it through facial recognition, but the results are inconclusive. Could be Bor; might not be. But considering all of the ancillary facts—especially the style of execution—our operating premise is that it's Bor."

"What's the probability on facial recognition?"

"Between fifty-five and sixty percent. Usually we don't score it as a hit unless we get eighty percent or more."

"Can you pull the image up right now?" Dwyer asked.

"I'm looking at a magnification of a still on the big screen as we speak, sir."

"Can you see a J-shaped scar along the right jawline ending at the earlobe?"

"Not really, sir. The most we can see is a light shadow. Beyond a certain point, enhancement gets counterproductive. It just dissolves into spots and splotches. It could be a scar. Could just as well be the lighting."

"Understood. What feeds your operating premise besides the style of execution?"

"Well, it seems a reach, unless you at least consider that it may be

Bor," the lead replied. "But we inputted every police, fire, and EMS report in a two-hundred-mile radius of the massacre site from the time of execution to just a short time ago. The program spit back almost everything except an explosion and fire in rural western South Carolina. The program snagged that report because a preliminary arson investigator's assessment indicates the presence of accelerants. Plural. Magnesium, smokeless powder, possibly penta."

"Right. *Everyone* expects to find penta in a farmhouse in South Carolina."

"Exactly. There's some evidence of a munitions cache. The program took that and a couple of other data points, including the video, and plotted a path toward Washington, northward on I-95."

"Were you able to glean anything else?" Dwyer asked. "Makes and models? Plates?"

"Not yet. It appears as if Bor—presuming it's him—got into a green van behind the truck stop. Most of the vehicle was obscured behind vacuum pumps and the like, but we're working on it based on a partial configuration of the body. We've narrowed it down to Ford products. As far as plates are concerned—wrong angles. Nothing. We're looking at images during that period of any green vehicles from any traffic or security cameras within a five-mile radius of the truck stop. Not many cameras in that area, so no luck so far. Our best shot is satellite data. But we're limited in that regard, unless you can convince someone to enlist NSA, NGA, or the kind folks at the OGA, boss. Even then, I wouldn't hold my breath."

"Okay. Good job," Dwyer said. "You and the team keep working your magic. Keep me informed."

Dwyer disconnected, then punched the number for Mike Garin. He needed to know his former teammate and current nemesis was probably even closer than he thought.

CHAPTER 40

Garin figured he'd left at least a couple of loaves' worth of bread crumbs for Bor's compatriots to follow.

Garin had borrowed one of DGT's fleet of black Ford Explorers and circumnavigated much of the Beltway before parking at the short-term lot at Reagan National to deposit a few dozen crumbs within the terminal. Garin was unconcerned that whoever was watching on Bor's behalf would unquestionably conclude that Garin was leaving the crumbs on purpose. Bor was certain to send someone nonetheless. He had to. The personal special operator for President Yuri Mikhailov was involved in nothing but matters of geopolitical consequence. Garin knew him well, knew his history, his methods, his thought processes. He'd worked with Bor for nearly two years on Omega, back when Garin knew him as John Gates. He'd watched him move, seen him react.

It was like looking in a mirror.

To predict what Bor would do—tactically at least—Garin needed only to think of what he himself would do. The predictions wouldn't be perfect, of course, but Bor understood this also. So he would throw in the random counterintuitive, hoping that it might throw off Garin's timing or conclusions.

To ensure the success of Mikhailov's plan, whatever that plan might be, Bor would allow no room for Garin's possible intervention.

Garin knew this. Bor knew Garin knew this. Like Woody Hayes versus Bo Schembechler. No mystery. You know we're going to run off left tackle. You have to stop us to win.

Garin had meandered about Reagan National, entering the terminal at the United ticket counter, descending the escalator toward the concourses, and strolling past the shops and restaurants. A dozen cameras, seen and unseen, had captured his image. Using the same credit card he had used at DFW, he made a couple of purchases—a paperback and a water bottle. Electronic blips from the transactions would ricochet through cyberspace and alert Bor's watchers, and from somewhere in the highest reaches of the US government a traitor would transmit a message to Bor: Garin is at Qdoba on the main level of Reagan National, proceeding toward the baggage claim level opposite the taxi stand.

Garin spent fifteen minutes at the airport before climbing back into the Explorer, lowering the windows, lighting a Partagás, and streaming Jimi Hendrix at maximum volume. "All Along the Watchtower" reverberated throughout the parking garage. Signature Michael Garin, clandestine warrior, in plain sight for any and all to behold.

M oments ago Garin had pulled into the parking lot of a sprawling series of low-rise apartment buildings off Minnieville Road in Dale City. The units were occupied by low-income residents, a significant number of whom were day laborers for contractors in the area.

Garin had an apartment in the basement level of Building C, under the name Tom Lofton. However, he had not slept there since the Quds Force operators had attempted to assassinate him at the outset of the EMP operation. They had failed—Garin had killed them both. That unpleasantness, along with the commotion from the related police and FBI investigations, had, to put it mildly, set the complex's management on edge concerning lessee Lofton. Garin smoothed matters by compensating management for the cleaning bill and presenting them with a bonus of six months' rent. The bonus resolved any issues as far as management was concerned. As for the other residents—those who knew Lofton liked him, especially the younger kids, who viewed Lofton as an exciting enigma. Besides, it wasn't as if the complex was wholly unfamiliar with unpleasantness.

Garin spotted ten-year-old Emilio Val Buena in the window of his family's unit two floors above Garin's. Emilio seemed to nearly jump out of his skin upon spying Lofton through the SUV's driver's-side window and waved ecstatically. Emilio occupied an elevated status in the complex due to the fact that he was the only kid to have had an actual conversation with the legend. Emilio had massaged the conversation into tales of Lofton's epic adventures, which seemingly improbable tales gained instant legitimacy after the two bodies were removed from Lofton's apartment.

Garin waved back, and although it was one of the rare occasions when he felt the onset of a smile, he suppressed it—for Emilio's benefit: The enigma understood that a taciturn Lofton was far more mysterious, and therefore useful, to Emilio's continuing narrative for his friends.

Garin wasn't there to move back into the apartment. Not because he eschewed its Spartan appointments: Although he had earned a considerable sum several years ago cashing out of DGT, he preferred to live frugally and efficiently, and the apartment had satisfied both criteria. No, he was there to drop another bread crumb. Bor's people would eventually check the apartment, if they hadn't done so already.

Before Garin opened the door, his mobile vibrated. He put the device to his ear without checking the screen.

"Yes."

"Matt here. Dan told me to get this to you: The tech guys did the analysis you asked for. Do you want me to tell you what we found over the phone or do you want to come here?"

Garin appreciated Matt's caution. They had to assume Garin's conversation could be intercepted and monitored. Given Bor's likely presence in the area, this wasn't a bread crumb he wanted to drop.

"I'll be there in twenty minutes."

CHAPTER 41

The soft breeze off the ocean was largely ineffective against the stifling August heat. Nonetheless, the patrician found the balcony comfortable enough to work from.

Garin was an irritant. No, that wasn't quite right, thought the patrician. Garin clearly was much more than that. He was, after all, responsible for thwarting the EMP attack. He needed to be eliminated quickly.

The patrician was very pleased with the progression of all phases of the operation, but Garin persisted in complicating matters, getting uncomfortably close to the functional levers of the plan. The man was more than a soldier taking orders. Indeed, he was taking no orders now. He was initiating action, independent of the US government, which remained oblivious to what was about to happen.

It remained highly unlikely that Garin could disrupt the plan. There were too many layers and contingencies. As significant as the EMP plot had been, it was but the opening stage of a series of feints, decoys, and misdirections, each of which had the capacity to accomplish the ultimate aim.

As expected, having halted a black swan—an unprecedented event—had lulled the West into a sense of security, of disaster averted. Not Garin. He behaved as if black swans were an everyday occurrence.

He had to go.

The patrician lit a Winston and drew long and deep from it before expelling its blue smoke in a long trail. With his other hand he pressed a key on his phone and waited.

"Yes." Bor answered flatly.

"Your friend has been waving his arms frantically, trying to get us to notice him. He's been on the Beltway, at Reagan National, and in several places in between. It's rude that we haven't responded."

"We just need a location."

"We're monitoring in real time. We have eyes on. I'm forwarding the information now."

The patrician terminated the call and pressed a series of keys. The irritant, the danger, would soon be no more.

CHAPTER 42

Garin steered the Explorer off Jefferson Davis Highway, down a long, blacktopped driveway, and descended the ramp to the underground parking garage of DGT's Quantico facility—a futuristic-looking two-story glass, steel, and granite building surrounded by fifteen acres of forest not far from the Marine base.

The two black-uniformed guards with MP5s slung across their chests standing at a kiosk next to the entrance recognized the SUV but, according to protocol, raised their weapons and tracked the vehicle as it approached the lift gate. Garin lowered the window to identify himself.

Garin parked the Explorer in the spot reserved for Dan Dwyer and took a garage elevator to the cybersecurity division, located in a space the size of a basketball court just outside Dwyer's office. He spotted Matt sitting on a desk at the far end of the room talking with one of the tech assistants. Matt saw Garin approach and waved him toward a room enclosed from floor to ceiling in glass. A rolling murmur trailed Garin as he walked down the aisle, the techies regarding one of the firm's founding operators with something between curiosity and awe.

Matt pointed Garin toward a chair in front of a fifty-seven-inch monitor and pushed a swivel chair next to him.

"Every so often we get lucky." Matt smiled.

"No such thing. There's only life's intersection with favorable events and unfavorable events."

"Then consider this an intersection with a favorable event," Matt said. His Aussie accent made it seem as if he took nothing seriously. "We began the arduous process of pulling any possible clues we could find from the impenetrably encrypted phone you took off your would-be assassin in Cleveland. We devoted our best minds and tons of computing power to the task; the cybersleuth equivalent of the Manhattan Project; the Apollo space program of decryption. Vats of caffeine were consumed, incense was burned, virgins were sacrificed . . ."

"Matt." The gravedigger's voice.

"Well, mate, it's like this: The phone's not encrypted."

"How is that possible?"

"We think what you took off the guy wasn't his service device. That device, most likely, was in another pocket or somewhere else in the vehicle when you pulled this one from him," Matt said, holding the phone. "No doubt, the device issued to him was super-duper encrypted, and he made all duty-related communications with that phone. But they were also strictly monitored. SVR, Zaslon, never had a record, however, of any communication he made or received on *this* phone. They didn't even know it existed."

"So he kept this one for personal matters that he didn't want his superiors to know about."

"Even badass operators like their personal privacy. Bad breach of security, but even Zaslon's human."

"These guys don't make mistakes." Garin paused. "So anything that might possibly interest us, anything useful, would be on the encrypted device," Garin said. "Not this one."

"Probably."

"So how does that make us lucky?"

Matt shrugged amiably. "Maybe it does; maybe it doesn't. That's for you to determine."

"Show me."

Matt manipulated a mouse and metadata began scrolling on the monitor for several seconds, followed by a library of text messages and phone numbers. "We tracked all of the senders and receivers. For the most part, it's disappointingly mundane. Takeout orders, Jiffy Lube, cable company. Would you believe the guy's into fantasy football?"

"He was an assassin, not a monk," Garin said.

"Truer words were never spoken. Appears this gent was quite popular with the ladies too. Looks like you broke at least half a dozen hearts when you stopped his, Mike."

"He stopped his own."

"Well, we followed up on all of them. One in New York, another in Pensacola. He must've operated mainly out of D.C. because we found four of his honeys in and around the District. All of them checked out as ordinary civilians," Matt said, still scrolling. "Except one number."

"Who does it belong to?"

"No one," Matt said. He scrolled until he reached the number in question—a northern Virginia area code. "We traced this number. It's a hard line to a duplex in Lorton."

"All right," Garin asked impatiently, "who does the house belong to?"

"A dead guy."

"It's empty?"

"Don't know. The owner died four months ago. He lived by himself, so it should be vacant. We've got a guy surveilling the place but the drapes and curtains are all closed and there's no sign of activity. The executor is an attorney in Arlington. He's filed papers with the probate court but doesn't seem to be in a hurry to sell. The property hasn't been listed yet."

"When was the call made?"

"Yesterday."

"The Zaslon guy called the dead guy's house?"

"Yes. And apparently the dead guy picked up." Matt pointed to the monitor. "See? The call only lasted twenty-three seconds. Not unusual in my experience. Dead guys aren't too chatty."

"Peculiar," Garin said. "Zaslon calls a number for an unsecure phone using an unsecure phone."

"And talks to a dead guy. Don't forget that."

"Why would he do that?"

"Maybe he slipped up."

"Again, these guys don't make mistakes, Matt."

"Maybe he was in a hurry. Maybe he didn't have his service device handy. Not necessarily a big deal. The call only lasted twenty-three seconds and he could've talked in a way that would sound innocent to anyone listening."

"How good is the guy on surveillance?"

"Good enough," Matt replied. "Once upon a time he was in SAD."

Garin nodded approval. "Do me a favor, just in case. Ask Dan to send three more people to support the guy. Just before I came here Dan told me Bor was probably in the District. If he shows up at the house, I want sufficient resources deployed so we don't lose him. But if he does show, surveil only. No one engages until I get there."

"We'll handle it, Mike."

"No one engages." Garin rose. "I don't care if your guys are former Special Activities Division, Delta, or Six. Got it?"

"Don't worry. I'm well aware of Bor's capabilities. Where are you going?"

"Shower and a change of clothes."

"So you finally noticed."

CHAPTER 43

Dan Dwyer had provided Olivia with use of his communications room to place a secure call to James Brandt.

Olivia had placed several calls to Brandt since he left the White House. She'd grown increasingly frustrated as each one went to voice mail. In Olivia's mind, the commander in chief needed to be briefed.

Now, according to Dan Dwyer, DGT analysts had concluded that Taras Bor was in the nation's capital. The president needed to be advised as soon as possible. The confluence of increased activity at Russian industrial sites, unusual troop movements, and Bor's presence in Washington was not merely alarming, but a matter of urgency. Olivia was convinced something bad was coming, and, with Bor in the mix, it was coming soon.

Brandt picked up. "Hello, Olivia."

"Apologies for disturbing you, Professor. Jess told me you weren't feeling well."

"That's all right, Olivia. I'm not so infirm that I can't speak on the phone. And I trust your judgment whether to contact me. I suspect there have been developments pertaining to the Russians?"

"There's been a rather unusual pattern of movement of Russian troops and matériel."

"Baltics?"

"Yes, but not just the Baltics, Professor. There's been movement of Russian troops southward on either side of the Caspian. Russian naval presence also has increased in the Persian Gulf."

"When did this happen?"

"I can't say precisely. Very recently," Olivia stressed. "But there's more, Professor. Taras Bor likely is in Washington. Right now."

The silence from the other end gave Olivia hope that Brandt now might be of the same mind.

"Do we know definitively that Bor's in Washington? Has he been identified?"

"Not definitively."

"No witness IDs? No photos?"

"No. But in addition to the signature shootings in Georgia, there have been other odd occurrences. DGT's analysts have fed a ton of data into their computers. Police and fire reports; vectors. Admittedly, they're operating from the premise that it's Bor, but they conclude he's most likely in Washington. I'm not sure we can afford not to operate from the same premise."

"I think it's time to brief the president, Olivia," Brandt said to Olivia's relief. "There are a lot of moving parts. The more moving parts, the more likely the Russians are up to no good."

"Since you're not feeling well, would you like me to brief him in your stead?"

Brandt laughed. "I'm impressed, Olivia. A bold offer from my pain-fully shy and retiring aide. But I fear I might end up like Wally Pipp. Seriously, I appreciate your consideration, but I think I can manage."

"There's another matter you may wish to take up with the president, Professor."

"What might that be?"

"We've had a significant void in our national security apparatus since the assassination of the Omega team. We need to address that void."

"Barely a month ago we didn't even know of Omega's existence. No one did. Especially our adversaries, so we thought," Brandt said. "So first things first. Let's meet in my office so you can brief me on every-thing on which I need to brief the president. Then, at the appropriate time, you and I can discuss Omega."

"Professor, we didn't know about Omega because, thankfully, they did their jobs. Based on what we've seen since we've come into office, it's clear Omega was, and remains, essential to our national security. Especially in the present environment."

"Essential, yes. But not indispensable," Brandt countered. "Delta and SEAL Team Six can fill the void for now."

"Professor, I spoke with Mike Garin . . ."

"And what did our intrepid hero have to say?"

"Professor, you have to acknowledge he knows what he's doing and what he's talking about," Olivia prefaced.

"That I do," Brandt acknowledged.

"He's adamant that Omega needs to be reconstituted immediately. He insists America is naked in the present threat environment, especially considering the possibility that Bor is back in the country. A team tried to kill Garin just a short time ago. Remember: The same thing occurred only a few weeks ago—just before he averted Armageddon. His judgment on these matters should be taken with the utmost seriousness."

"Point taken. But how does Garin propose reconstituting Omega with Senator McCoy's likely opposition? And even if McCoy approved, it would take months to stand up."

"He just needs sanction and resources."

"Is that all?" Brandt said with a hint of sarcasm.

"He needs authority from the president and access to intelligence resources."

"What about operators, support personnel?"

"He says he'll get former tier-one operators. DGT can provide some logistical support. The rest, mainly intelligence, would be provided by CIA, NSA—and others. And that's only if needed. The main thing he needs is not to be arrested and prosecuted for doing things civilians aren't supposed to do."

"That's still a pretty heavy lift, Olivia."

"An Omega team is necessary, Professor. You know that, as does President Marshall. Either an Omega team attached to JSOC, Title 50 of the CIA, or an Omega team of limited sanction."

"The president does like having Omega," Brandt conceded. "And, although he'd never admit it, during the EMP crisis he was absolutely fascinated by Garin—kept asking questions about him."

"Then maybe it's not such a heavy lift."

"Make no mistake," Brandt emphasized. "I think the president would favor the immediate re-creation of an Omega team. But he didn't become president by being a political idiot. If he does this without at least some congressional input, McCoy and everyone on his side of the aisle will go nuclear—no pun intended. And so will their media allies. It's their opportunity to redirect attention from the acute embarrassment—not to mention damage—caused by counsel for Senate Intelligence working with the Russians. The headlines are all too predictable: 'President Bypasses Congress, Authorizes Secret Kill Teams.'"

"He's the commander in chief. This is about the best interests of the country. Not about his best political interests. He can reconfigure military units as he deems fit."

"That's the point, Olivia. Military units *in* the Defense Department, *within* the government. Not nongovernmental operations."

"Then make them part of the government," Olivia retorted. "Whatever works, whatever he's comfortable with. But Omega needs to be reestablished. Now."

"Proximity to Michael Garin seems to have had an effect on you, Olivia. Since the EMP crisis you've gone from meek postdoc to bold national security hawk. Stanford meets Coronado." Brandt paused. "All right. I'll stress immediate authorization of Omega with the president," Brandt said. "I'll make sure he knows it was your idea so he doesn't blame me when it inevitably becomes a political nightmare."

CHAPTER 44

This time Garin's excursion to his apartment was not to drop bread crumbs but to stay awake. Primarily. Scrubbing off the last twenty-four hours in the shower and putting on some fresh clothes would help. So would another cup of coffee—then, back to the fray.

The apartment was substantially as he'd left it—sans a couple of dead Quds Force assassins. And the carpet had been cleaned.

The apartment was utilitarian. A mattress lay on the floor of the living room, which merged into a tiny kitchenette. There was a small bathroom and an even smaller walk-in closet. Other than the mattress, the only furnishing in the unit was a folding metal chair Garin pulled next to the counter to eat his meals. "Spartan" would be a wildly lavish description of the unit.

Garin turned on the coffeemaker before getting into the shower and doing his best to return to resembling a member of the human race. Sheets of hot, almost scalding water, followed by cold. He toweled off briskly, taking inventory of the nicks and bruises accumulated from the Crucible and the incident in the airport parking garage in Cleveland. Minor and unconcerning.

He looked more closely in the mirror. His eyes were somewhat bloodshot, though not as crimson as he'd seen them numerous times before. For some, gazing in the mirror soon after being responsible for the deaths of several human beings, even in self-defense, was a time for introspection. It had never been so for Garin. As far as he was concerned, conflict and soul-searching were trite literary and cinematic conventions. The killings were necessary, justified. He would kill more soon. If he didn't, innocents would perish. Simple equation. At some point, he'd pray the Rosary. But his conscience carried no burdens.

He dispensed with a shave. He wasn't going to a job interview; he was trying to remain alert and something less than repellent.

But the shower helped. He was feeling pretty good, all things considered. He put on some jeans and a gray T-shirt and poured himself a large cup of coffee, plopping in a couple of ice cubes so he could down it almost as quickly as he had the pot on the plane.

Reaching atop the refrigerator, where he kept an array of nutritional supplements, Garin pulled down powdered turmeric, ginger, and a container of creatine. Turmeric and ginger to relieve muscle soreness, creatine for muscles depleted by the Crucible. He put a teaspoon of each in a glass of water and swallowed the concoction in two gulps. He chased that with another cup of iced coffee.

From his black gym bag Garin pulled a SIG Sauer P226. Dwyer had given it to him along with several spare magazines. Garin placed the handgun in a holster at the small of his back and the spare magazines in his hip pockets.

He placed a call on one of the burners. It was answered on the first ring.

"Dwyer."

"Matt tell you about the dead man's house?"

"He did. Some of my men are there right now. Haven't seen them this jacked since they left the teams. But they're under orders not to do anything without you."

"Good. I'm on my way. Send me a Google map of where they'll be positioned."

"We should let the FBI know at some point," Dwyer said.

"Know what? That a dead guy answered his phone?"

"If Russian agents are using a dead man's residence as a safe house, the FBI needs to know—especially if one of them's Bor. We have no authority to go blasting in there by ourselves. If the stuff hits the fan, we'll be in big trouble," Dwyer said. "Mikey?"

"I hear you."

"Then say something."

"This is just surveillance. That's all."

"Bull. You don't do surveillance. You do death and destruction," Dwyer countered. "And that's fine. But my men can't be part of it. We have no authority. We'll all go to prison."

"Dan, I'm not suicidal," Garin assured him. "Do you actually believe I would go into a house Bor might be in without an army surrounding the place?"

"Damn right you would. Remember who you're talking to, buddy. I know you. I trained you. You think you're freakin' indestructible. That's why you keep entering these nutty competitions. Daring someone or something to prove you're not invincible. So far, you've never lost. But guess what, buddy? First time for everything. So promise me, before you move, we call the FBI. In fact, I'm calling them right now."

"Don't," Garin said sharply. "Think about it, Dan. We know Bor was being helped by someone very high up in our government. So high up that they had the FBI after me during the EMP deal. Somehow, they even managed to get Delta after me. On American soil. In violation of about four thousand different statutes. That person or persons has never been captured or identified. Nothing's changed. We call the FBI, Bor will know about it. The only people we can trust are the ones who proved trustworthy before: Olivia, Brandt, and the president. That's it."

Dwyer exhaled. "All right. I won't call. But just surveillance. I'm telling my men, no matter what Garin does, they're to stand down. No engagement whatsoever."

"Good. I'm on my way."

CHAPTER 45

DALE CITY, VIRGINIA,
AUGUST 16, 12:55 P.M. EDT

Bulkvadze brought five men.

Ten. That's how many Bor had told him to bring. Against one man. Ridiculous. Bulkvadze felt foolish while composing the team. Each looked at him as if he were crazed when he told them there would be five of them. To kill one man. It was insulting.

Bulkvadze couldn't blame them. They were professionals. They'd proven their capabilities and worth. None were novices. Each had several kills to his credit—some even in the United States.

They were promised fifty thousand dollars apiece, ten thousand in advance. The amount quelled any grumbling. Bor had advanced one million dollars, with the balance of four million to be delivered upon verification of Garin's death. The shooters' share plus Bulkvadze's hundred-thousand-dollar finder's fee would come entirely from Abkashvili's four million. Of course, Abkashvili would know nothing about the one million Bulkvadze kept for himself.

Bulkvadze had a clear view of where the action would occur. He was comfortably seated in his black Mercedes S600 with tinted windows in the parking lot of the B complex. The entrance to Garin's basement unit in C complex was directly in front of him, down a gradual decline seventy yards away. His seat was racked all the way back to accommodate his large frame. It was as if he were in a movie theater. Only the popcorn was missing.

From his vantage point Bulkvadze could see each of his five shooters. Two of three primary shooters were deployed behind SUVs at forty-five-degree angles to Garin's door. The third primary shooter was deployed behind a large Dumpster directly in front of and fifty feet away from Garin's door.

The two secondary shooters were behind a row of hedges that separated the B and C parking lots. They were standing almost equidistant from Bulkvadze's car and Garin's front door. From their relaxed stances it was clear they had concluded, quite reasonably, that they would soon go home forty thousand dollars richer for doing nothing more than driving out to Dale City, Virginia.

There was no foot traffic in the vicinity. The stifling heat and humidity had chased the residents into their air-conditioned apartments.

The five men were visible to any B Complex residents who might happen to look out their windows, but Bulkvadze was unconcerned. People generally didn't look out their windows unless there was a loud noise or a bright light or they were expecting someone. Most were looking at TVs, computer screens, phones, kids, or stoves. A parking lot and hedgerow couldn't compete.

The five had, nonetheless, assumed poses of nonchalance, feigning scrolling through their mobile devices. A bit irritated, Bulkvadze thought their poses appeared somewhat less than random. Then again, he'd been on a number of crowded city streets where it seemed everyone was walking with their heads angled down toward their phone screens.

Bulkvadze's own phone rested on the seat next to him. He would record Garin's death and provide the recording to Bor for verification.

Although he was in no particular hurry, Bulkvadze preferred to get the matter over with. The longer Garin remained inside, the greater the probability that a patrol car would make a run past the complex or someone might pay Garin a visit. According to Bor, Garin rarely stayed in one place for long, but Bulkvadze was prepared to stay in place for as long as it took.

And it didn't take long. The heads of all three primary shooters jerked upward from their screens simultaneously. They must've heard a noise in Garin's apartment, Bulkvadze thought, or the sound of a doorknob turning. They placed their phones in their respective pockets and almost in unison pulled out their weapons and aimed them at the door. The secondary shooters pulled out their weapons also, holding them at their sides.

Bulkvadze saw the door beginning to open and the primary shooters tensing, weapons held at eye level. The doorway was black for a beat; then the blackness was broken by a gray T-shirt.

Bulkvadze raised his cell phone above the dash of his car and began to record the imminent demise of Michael Garin. The primary shooters each edged out from behind their respective hides in preparation for taking their shots. Natural human competitiveness made each want to claim credit for the decisive shot.

A second later, Bulkvadze saw the face from Bor's phone appear in the doorframe. What followed was a blizzard of gunfire and movement Bulkvadze's brain found impossible to process.

Before any of the primary shooters had even squeezed their triggers, Bulkvadze saw the bodies of the two who were at forty-five-degree angles to Garin's door quake and their heads repeatedly whiplash, as if struck several times by a heavy object—the impact of multiple semi-automatic rounds to the torso. A fraction of a second later both collapsed to the ground. A fraction after that the back of the third primary shooter's neck exploded outward, expelling a mass of blood, tissue, and bone displaced by a 9mm round to the throat from Garin's SIG.

Bulkvadze could see the raised pistols of the secondary shooters shift sharply from left to right, searching frantically for Garin. The search by the shooter to the left ended when the lower half of his face was blown away by a powerful round from an unknown direction. By the time Bulkvadze turned his attention to the last remaining shooter he was already falling to the ground. At least his body was falling to the ground; Bulkvadze saw no evidence of a head.

The elimination of Bulkvadze's kill team had consumed all of six seconds. He sat frozen in disbelief for several more. Then his chest began to heave. As he tried to catch his breath, he noticed that he had dropped his phone.

Bulkvadze scanned the scene in front of him, looking for Garin. The apartment door was still open. He wasn't standing in the entrance. Nor was he anywhere in the C Complex parking lot or on the expanse of grass adjacent to it.

Bulkvadze's nerves felt like exposed electrical wire. He put his car in gear, his head swiveling about searching for the target, half expecting his windshield to shatter in a hail of gunfire. He fought the urge to go screeching down the drive, out of range of any weapons. Instead, he drove away at the posted speed, past the bodies strewn about the parking lot, and turned onto Minnieville Road, where he accelerated gradually until the complex shrank and vanished in his rearview mirror.

"Bring ten." That's what Bor had commanded. "If you fail, I will kill you." Bulkvadze had taken Bor's money, disregarded his command, and failed to kill Garin. That had to be rectified. Right away. Or soon Bulkvadze's massive body would be lying in a parking lot with his head somewhere nearby.

CHAPTER 46

Garin watched the Mercedes turn onto Minnieville and disappear into traffic before he rose from the ground and ran toward the cover of the Dumpster. There, in a crouch, he ejected a nearly spent magazine from the SIG and seated a fresh one. He had fired at least ten rounds. He didn't want to have to change magazines in the middle of a fight if he had to confront several more assailants.

Garin knew he had killed the three shooters closest to him. As soon as he'd opened his door he'd noticed the three adult white males partially shielded by vehicles and a Dumpster, as well as the Mercedes idling a short distance beyond. None belonged, to put it gently. So when the male to his left made a sharp movement, Garin's instincts engaged and he pulled out the SIG, dropped to the ground, rolled to his right, and sighted the shooter. Upon seeing the weapon in the shooter's hands, Garin fired three rounds in rapid succession, rolled to his right, sighted the shooter to the right, and fired three more rounds. Shoot and roll. Then he swiveled his torso leftward and fired at least four more rounds at the shooter near the Dumpster.

Garin had not, however, shot the two shooters near the hedges.

So Garin scanned the perimeter of the complex, SIG at the low—ready. He checked the roofs, parked cars, trees, shrubs, windows, and doorways. Then he heard a voice.

"Mike."

Garin recognized the voice.

"Mike. At your ten." It was the calm baritone of Congo Knox, perhaps the most lethal sniper in the Western Hemisphere. "Coming out in three, two, one . . ."

Knox emerged from behind the nearest corner of B Complex holding an M110 above his head. Relieved, Garin dropped the SIG to his side and motioned for Knox to lower his weapon also.

"Where did you come from?" Garin asked.

"Dan Dwyer asked me to provide overwatch." Knox turned and pointed toward D Complex, sixty yards to the south. "I've been on that roof since you first arrived and then left abruptly. Dan said I should stay put because you were dropping bread crumbs and someone would show sooner or later. Said you think you're invincible, so might not be as careful as you should be. His words, not mine."

Still invincible, Garin thought.

"Thanks." Garin nodded. "That's twice now you've come to my rescue. Don't get any ideas this makes up for trying to kill me, though."

"That wasn't my idea. That order came from somewhere outside Delta. Besides, I never even took a shot."

"Finding out whose idea it was is the key to all of this," Garin said. "Right now we need to make ourselves scarce. Cops will be here any minute. How did you get here?"

Knox pointed to a DGT Ford Explorer in the D Complex parking lot.

"Let's go," Garin said.

As they walked toward the Explorer, Garin took a peek at the surrounding apartment windows. To areas familiar with the sound of gunshots, it wasn't unusual for no one to be at the windows. No one wanted to be a witness. No one wanted to be involved. No one wanted to be a victim.

No one was visible at any of the surrounding windows but one: that of the unit occupied by the Val Buena family. Emilio was front and center for a half second before he disappeared. As Garin and Knox opened the doors to the Explorer, the front entrance to C Complex burst open and Emilio came sprinting toward them. He skidded to a stop a few feet away.

"MC4J58," he gasped.

"What?"

"MC4J58, Señor Lofton. The license number of the black car. MC4J58. I memorized it. I knew you'd need it." Emilio, of course, had witnessed everything.

Garin bent and patted Emilio on the head. "MC4J58. Got it. Thanks."

Emilio turned and sprinted back to the building, punching the air in victory as he went. He was now undisputed king of the complex.

The doors of the Explorer slammed shut. "Where to, Mike?"

"Head toward I-95. Before all the excitement I was planning to go to a house in Lorton. But I want to think about that now."

"The dead guy's house?"

"News travels fast."

"Dan told me he might want me to go there also. To make sure you conduct surveillance only."

"Or what? You're supposed to shoot me?"

"I think the general idea was that I reason with you to keep your promise to Dan."

Knox turned right onto Dale Boulevard. The sound of multiple sirens could be heard in the distance.

"Five bodies, Mike. Think we should stick around for the cops? They're sure to trace it to us. We're fugitives."

"Self-defense. They'll soon find out those five guys weren't selling Girl Scout cookies."

"We left a crime scene."

"Had we stayed, they'd have us tied up for hours. By the time they'd cleared us, Bor would be telling his grandkids about how he saved Russia from America."

"No real argument, Mike. Just pointing out, we're in trouble."

"Perpetually." Garin nodded. "We'll deal with it once we've dealt with Bor. Dale City's a firecracker. Bor's an H-bomb."

"My mom won't be happy to see my face on the ten o'clock news."

Garin nearly smiled. "No security cameras at the apartment complex and any cell video would be too far away, so Mrs. Knox won't get to see her baby boy on TV."

"Too bad. She always says I'm so handsome, I should be on TV. Not for having shot up part of northern Virginia, though."

Two patrol cars sped past in the opposite direction.

"Who's providing security for Luci while you're watching me?" Garin asked.

"There are about a half dozen DGT personnel at Dwyer's place right now. They're on rotation."

"I appreciate you going to Sugar Land to escort her back. I feel terrible putting her in this spot. It's probably not necessary to sequester her like that, but until we get a handle on the situation I'm not taking any chances."

"What's your deal with Luci, Mike?"

"She was my support for the Crucible. She's really good. Getting a degree in exercise physiology. Couldn't ask for anyone better."

"That's it?"

"I like her a lot."

"She thinks you're some mysterious superhero."

"Look, Congo, it's not like we're rival cocaptains on the high school football team and she's homecoming queen. I have no designs on Luci. Besides, Dan tells me she likes you. You're a badass operator. Do what comes naturally."

"Ms. Perry seems more your type anyway," Knox observed. "Just saying."

"Ms. Perry isn't into badass operators. I think she's more into the intellectual type."

"Yeah, well, down at the Green Beret Parachute Club they say you're a freakin' genius or something."

"Everything's relative. From the standpoint of a bunch of drunk Delta boys, I probably qualify. Low bar."

"Not buying it, Mike. Remember, I had you in my sights for a while—I saw you outsmart everybody. Except Bor."

"Pretty big exception."

"Killing him's a tall order." Knox nodded. "Almost as tall an order as impressing Olivia Perry."

"Smooth transition, Congo."

"Dan tells me her father played at Alabama? One of the first black players under Bear Bryant?"

"Probably where she gets her height from."

"And her mother's from India?"

"Both parents were math teachers. Her father died when she was a girl. She was a math prodigy but switched to international relations at Stanford under Brandt."

"She's out of my league."

"She's out of everybody's league."

Knox turned onto the I-95 on-ramp. As usual, traffic was slow.

"What do you think Bor's up to, Mike? Assuming it's Bor."

"It's Bor."

"So?"

"Your guess is as good as mine. If we find him at the dead guy's house, you can ask him."

"No going in, Mike. Just surveillance."

"Right."

They drove along I-95 in silence for a while, Knox thinking and Garin checking his phone to see if Dwyer had sent a map of where his men were located around the dead guy's house. He had. A map of the block on which the house was situated displayed digital arrows where each member of the DGT surveillance team was positioned. The text accompanying the map advised Garin to approach along Gunston and park in an elementary school lot approximately two blocks away. Garin should call the team leader, who would meet them there. A link to the team leader's number appeared below the text.

Knox took the ramp off I-95 to Route 1. He turned onto the road and slowed.

Knox asked, "Do you think Bor's at the house?"

"The Zaslon guy called the house. Someone picked up."

"Zaslon," Knox said clinically. "The Russians deny their existence."

"Rule of thumb: If the Russians deny the existence of something, it's already in your basement."

Garin pointed Knox toward the elementary school parking lot where the team leader would meet them. The lot was empty.

"Do you know Dave Crane?" Garin asked. "He's who we're meeting."

"Haven't had the pleasure. I've only been with DGT a few weeks."

"Go to the back of the lot," Garin instructed. "He's about fifty feet into the woods, a hundred feet from the back door. I'll try to call him."

Garin's call went to voice mail.

Knox parked and they got out and proceeded into the woods. Once there, Garin drew his SIG and Knox produced a Browning .45. Both crept slowly and silently through the woods. Within a few seconds they could see the back lawn of the house. The executor must have engaged a lawn service, because the grass looked recently mowed.

Garin and Knox advanced a few more feet and stopped, looking for Crane. Knox located him first. He lay on his stomach behind a rotted tree stump, watching the rear of the residence. Just as Dwyer had reported, the drapes were drawn and there was no sign of activity. No sounds were coming from the place. No other signs of life.

Garin advanced a few more feet and then called softly to Crane, not wanting to startle him. "Two coming up on your six, Dave."

Crane remained still.

"Garin and Knox behind you, Dave."

No reaction.

Knox looked at the team leader. "Dave," he said simply, not expecting a response.

Garin and Knox trained their weapons on Crane. Knox circled in front of him and examined Crane's lifeless face, eyes still staring at the back of the house.

Garin and Knox dropped deep in a crouch, weapons at eye level. Knox moved closer to the body and examined a small entrance wound in the rear of Crane's head.

"Not a sniper," Knox informed Garin quietly. "Looks like a .22. Good for close quarters."

The two operators did a slow three-sixty, scanning the woods for human presence. They saw only trees. Garin pulled out his phone and examined the map for the locations of the other three watchers. Locating them, he motioned Knox toward the next closest.

They walked east—to Crane's left—down a shallow dip and across a small creek. Garin pointed in the direction indicated on the map. Seconds later, they saw the body of the second watcher in a pose identical to Crane's, a .22 wound in the back of the head.

Garin motioned in the direction of the third watcher, both Knox and Garin expecting to find a similar scene. Thirty seconds later they did, and a minute after that they found the last of the watchers lying dead on his right side. Four highly experienced men. Four men dead from a single shot to the head, killed by an assassin or assassins with unusual skill.

Garin and Knox stood over the body of the fourth watcher. Knox pointed to the dead man's head. "Very close range," he whispered. "Same with the others. Had to have used a suppressor. A ghost. Creeps up on four guys."

"Impressive work."

"Bor?" Knox asked.

"I'm not sure," Garin replied with a shake of his head. "Bor prefers a larger caliber."

"Could you do that?"

"I'm pretty sure I couldn't."

The two men did another three-sixty before retreating in the direction of the Explorer. They moved very slowly, once again scanning for any evidence of human presence, ready to fire at the slightest hint of it. To their relief, the two men, who between them had months of experience operating in some of the densest forests and jungles in the world, detected no sign of anyone in the vicinity.

Garin and Knox climbed into the Explorer and began pulling out of the lot. Less than one hundred feet away, shrouded by a canopy of oak leaves, a grotesque-looking man with a deep scar running from the corner of his mouth to his ear watched through rheumy, bloodshot eyes as the SUV turned right and headed toward I-95.

CHAPTER 47

It was the call he had dreaded and it came sooner than he'd expected. The phone vibration sounded angry, as if somehow trying to convey the attitude of the caller. It seemed impatient, insistent.

Bulkvadze did not answer. He knew of no one who voluntarily answered a call from their executioner.

"Bring ten."

What explanation would he give for failing to do so? He had been given sufficient funds to pay ten. He'd simply disregarded the command. Now, in the quiet of his Mercedes gliding along I-495, he wondered what in his makeup caused him to blithely disregard a command so easily fulfilled. He had the money. He had access to personnel. Why not simply follow the directive? Why did he have to second-guess it?

Bulkvadze suspected he'd never get an opportunity to provide an explanation. Bor wasn't a man who listened patiently to explanations, to rationalizations, to excuses. Bulkvadze could only hope that Bor did listen to pleas and assurances. Pleas for another opportunity, assurances that it would be done right. Bulkvadze was doubtful that Bor would, but it was the Georgian's only chance.

The phone stopped vibrating and he continued driving at the posted speed in the right lane. He didn't have a destination. He just wanted time. Eventually he would have to answer the phone. Sooner rather than later. He didn't want to make a plea to Bor after angering him still further by making him wait.

But he wanted a bit more time. Not to figure out how to craft his plea, but to procrastinate. Blessed procrastination. Procrastination,

Bulkvadze thought, was an underrated exercise. Procrastination expanded the range of possibilities: A solution might present itself; maybe Garin would be struck by a bus; maybe Bor would have a heart attack; maybe Bulkvadze would wake up from a dream. Maybe.

Procrastination prolonged the opportunity for fantasy and delayed the prospect of reality. And the reality was Bor was going to kill him.

Bulkvadze had but two alternatives: disappear so completely that Bor couldn't find him, or kill Garin as soon as possible. Both alternatives appeared impossible. There was no place on the planet Bulkvadze could go and not be found by Bor. Within the *vory* community rumors of Bor's assassinations had circulated for some time. No one in the community wanted to get on his bad side. Not only was he indefatigable, but he had the resources of the entire Russian intelligence apparatus at his disposal.

As for killing Garin, that was similarly problematic. Bulkvadze had no idea where Garin might be. The Washington, D.C., metropolitan area had more than six million people. Bulkvadze wasn't without resources, but finding one person among millions would take time, and Bor had made it clear Garin was to be eliminated immediately.

Even if Garin could be located right away, killing him was another matter entirely. Bulkvadze had had a front row seat for the last attempt. Garin had made short work of five assassins, and Bulkvadze didn't have time to assemble a new team, assuming ten were even available.

The insistent vibrating resumed. Indulging in the vice of procrastination only prolonged the anxiety and aggravated Bor. Bulkvadze picked up and tried to make his voice sound calm.

"Yes."

"You have been thinking about how and when I am going to fulfill my promise to you," Bor said. "It will be a bullet to the back of the head. Imminently. If you prefer to avoid the suspense, you may present yourself at an agreed location."

"There is an alternative."

"Alternatives are usually less satisfactory. And I do not have time to accommodate another failure."

"I can do it before you can get someone else. You would save time."

"You have already lost me time."

"I will forgo the balance of the payment. Keep the four million."

"I would be interested in hearing how you explain that to Abkashvili."

"I will handle Abkashvili."

"I don't like giving second chances. Failure should not be rewarded. It should be punished."

"With all due respect, failure is what you will have again if you employ someone else," Bulkvadze pled. "I have seen Garin. I now have a full appreciation of his capabilities. A new team would not. And they would meet with the same fate as my first team."

Bulkvadze paused but Bor remained silent. Bulkvadze pressed. "Also, assembling a new team would take more time and more money."

For several seconds Bulkvadze heard only his own breathing, then: "The last location I have for Garin is near Lorton along Route 1, likely toward I-95. That was a few minutes ago. He is in a black Ford Explorer. Partial Virginia license plate VY72."

A wave of relief and gratitude came over Bulkvadze, but he tried to keep his voice measured and businesslike. "Do you know his destination?"

"Yes. He may be proceeding along I-95, but he will be returning to the location from which he recently left, if he hasn't returned already."

"How do you know he will return?"

"I know how he thinks."

"What is the location to which he will return?"

"I will forward the exact address by text," Bor replied. "He will not, however, be at that precise location. He will be somewhere in the immediate vicinity, obscured or partially hidden. He will be watching the house at the address you will receive momentarily. Approach accordingly."

"I will."

Bor said, "Report immediately upon completion of the assignment with proof of death. You understand what will happen if you don't succeed."

Bor terminated the call. A few seconds later Bulkvadze received the text with the address. The wave of relief and gratitude began to recede, to be replaced by concern. He knew he couldn't assemble another kill team any more quickly than anyone who would've replaced him. In fact, since word of the first kill team's fate would spread rapidly, it was highly likely he couldn't assemble a kill team at all. Five dead bodies were a powerful deterrent to anyone asked to finish the job.

Bulkvadze would have to complete the task himself. He would've preferred otherwise, but now that he had Garin's location it was feasible. He was experienced. He was a good shot. He was tough. He was strong. And he was intensely motivated.

Bulkvadze took the next exit and drove toward the address in the text. He was in the most elemental of circumstances. Kill or be killed. The simplicity of it all focused his mind. He had but one objective, and every other thing in the world was irrelevant. He found it strangely liberating.

CHAPTER 48

The black Ford Explorer passed the dead man's house and proceeded to the end of the block before turning right.

"Drop me off at that playground up ahead," Garin said. "When you get back to Dan's place make sure to call the FBI and tell them about the bodies in the woods."

"What about the mole?"

"It's pretty clear the mole knows about the bodies. Bor or someone associated with Bor killed those men. So it's not like we're letting the cat out of the bag."

"Right."

"Besides, we can't just let those bodies lie in the woods. They need to be treated appropriately. Next of kin will have to be notified, arrangements made."

"Do you want me to come back? Maybe bring some more personnel?"

"I'll let you know if I need help."

Knox stopped the vehicle near the playground beyond the view of the dead man's house. Garin got out and waved Knox onward.

The playground was far from the best vantage point to observe the house. It was nearly two hundred feet from the front and afforded a view of only the front and west sides of the edifice. It would have to do.

The playground did have the benefit of providing a six-foot-high wooden fence that surrounded a collection of trash receptacles. Garin could lean against the fence and be hidden from view from any of the house's windows. And that's what he did.

There was no sign of activity. The drapes remained drawn. But for the four dead bodies in the woods behind the house, Garin would've concluded that the house had no connection to Bor. A reasonable person would think Bor would abandon the house for fear the four bodies would be discovered nearby. Therefore, reasonable people wouldn't look for Bor at the house, which was precisely why it was a good place for Bor to be.

Garin settled against the fence and called Dwyer's cell.

"Dwyer."

"Congo call you?"

"He did. Those were good men. All my people are good people. They survived Fallujah and Ramadi only to die in tranquil northern Virginia."

"I'm very sorry for you and their families."

"Where are you?"

"At the dead guy's house."

"Don't go in."

"I won't. But we need to keep eyes on. The execution of your four watchers proves the house is related to our old friend."

"I'm all in, Mikey. Need anything from us?"

"Is Olivia still there?"

"Right across from me."

"Can you forward this call to one of your secure phones? I need to give her some information."

"Hold on."

The line seemed to go dead for nearly a minute; then Olivia spoke from Dwyer's communications room. "Michael?"

"Have you spoken to Brandt?"

"I have, and he's going to brief the president. Not just about Bor, Michael. The Russians are doing peculiar things."

"What kind of things?"

"There's been considerable military movement. The Baltics, of course. Some of it appears to be staging movements. But there are Russian troops moving southward near the Caspian also, and Russian naval presence has increased significantly around the Persian Gulf."

"You told Brandt this?"

"Yes. And he's going to communicate his concerns to the president."

"What are his concerns?"

Olivia was embarrassed. "Well, to be honest, I'm not really sure. I've told him that Bor's possible presence in the US at the same time the Russians are involved in large-scale military maneuvers is something the president should be told about. He agreed."

"There's more, Olivia. Did Dan tell you about the suspected safe house and the four DGT men who were killed surveilling the house?"

"He did."

"Also, earlier today five men tried to kill me."

Garin heard a sharp intake of breath.

"Are you all right?"

Garin tried not to read into Olivia's reaction, though the gasp made him pause.

"They're dead. But that puts the exclamation point on everything to date. Not only has there been more than one attempt on my life, but there have been nine related killings in northern Virginia in a span of just a few hours. If there is any doubt something very serious is about to occur, it's been completely erased."

"I'll let Jim know everything. I'm sure he'll recommend to the president that the full resources of the intelligence community be applied to this." She hesitated. "Are you all right?"

An expression of concern. Although it might not be anything more than simple courtesy. After all, most people don't often talk with someone who's been the subject of multiple assassination attempts. "I'm fine."

"We have no idea what they're planning, either here or in Russia, do we?"

"We can probably rule out an EMP attack."

"But do you think it's possible it's something of similar magnitude?"

"I think it's a mistake to underestimate the Russians and a mistake to underestimate Taras Bor."

"I'm not sure we've ever underestimated him, Michael. He just seems always to stay one step ahead."

"He's more than just one step ahead now. He's been invisible. But he's here. There's evidence of his presence from Dallas to Cleveland, from Atlanta to D.C."

"Do you think he's in the house?"

"Can't say. Bor likes to move. If there's anyone in the house, they're part of his team. He might, however, drop in at some point."

"You're only there to perform surveillance, right?"

His subconscious registered the question as another possible expression of concern. "Just surveillance. We need to enlist the cavalry, Olivia. So impress upon Brandt the urgency of this. I need sanction and I need a reconstituted Omega, and I need them last month."

"I will."

"Good."

"Just surveillance, Michael."

"Just surveillance."

CHAPTER 49

Egorshin couldn't very well return to Tatiana's apartment with soiled trousers. So after the degradation and humiliation at the hands of Stetchkin, he went to his own apartment, showered, and put on some fresh clothes.

He sat morosely at his kitchen table with a glass of vodka. He didn't drink it; he rarely drank. It was just a security blanket.

Stetchkin was insane. He was also powerful and cunning—a terrifying combination of qualities in an enemy.

Stetchkin's hatred for him was baffling, but Egorshin no longer dwelt on it. Regardless of the reason or lack thereof, Stetchkin had identified Egorshin as someone to torment, and there was nothing he could do about it. The important thing was survival. Egorshin was certain the reprieve he'd gotten earlier was fleeting and Stetchkin was determined to kill him.

He spun the glass slowly on the table. His immediate objective was to survive the next twenty-four hours with his prefrontal lobes still intact. The only person he knew who might help him achieve that objective was his uncle, whom he hadn't been able to reach since leaving Stetchkin's office. Morosov, he hoped, had spoken to President Mikhailov's senior aide, Alexei Vasiliev. Mikhailov would stop this lunacy. Mikhailov needed Egorshin.

Or did he?

CHAPTER 50

Yuri Mikhailov was as tall as Stetchkin but nearly ninety pounds heavier. He'd been a discus thrower on the 1984 Soviet Olympic team, after which he'd spent a brief stint in the KGB. Before becoming the Russian president he'd amassed a small fortune in the energy sector, in no small part due to his position and contacts in the KGB.

Mikhailov was one of the few men in Russia not fearful of Stetchkin. In fact, Mikhailov found Stetchkin barely tolerable. More than once he'd considered getting rid of the man. But Stetchkin was efficient, effective, and useful. Once he ceased being all three, however, Mikhailov would cast him aside like a rotten apple core.

Mikhailov had reluctantly granted Stetchkin an audience. The man might be useful, but his presence was grating and bearable only in small doses, with appreciable intervals in between.

The pair had just sat a few feet apart on matching leather chairs in a large Baroque anteroom in Mikhailov's office. Two small tables next to each held glasses of water. A massive chandelier hung overhead. They were alone.

"Chao-Li sends his regards, Aleksandr," Mikhailov said, referring to the Chinese president. "He asked me to tell you how much he enjoyed your visit to Beijing last year during the joint exercises."

"He is a good man," Stetchkin said.

"He is better than his predecessor," Mikhailov conceded. "But I do not trust him. His trade delegations have made repeated inquiries about traveling throughout lower Siberia, ostensibly to boost commerce to the benefit of both countries."

"Given the current state of our economy in that region, I would say that may redound to our benefit, particularly the mining sector."

"They are not interested in mining, Aleksandr. They are not interested in commerce."

"Then where lies their interest?"

"Lebensraum."

"I have seen no aggressive actions on their part."

"Merely because there have been no aggressive actions does not foreclose the certainty that they are being planned. I am a bit concerned you seem not to have considered this."

"It is, in fact, something my staff has evaluated in great detail," Stetchkin lied.

Mikhailov was not fooled. He hadn't been fooled by any underling in his entire professional career. That, combined with sheer ruthlessness, was how he became, and remained, president of Russia.

"Then why haven't you reported your staff's evaluations to me, Aleksandr?"

"They are not yet complete."

"Then you should get better staff. Your current staff is a collection of idiots. There is no evaluation to be done, Aleksandr. It is common sense and simple math. China is a nation of 1.5 billion people on 3.7 million square miles of land. Siberia, on the other hand, is more than five million square miles of land inhabited by barely forty million people—less than three percent of China's population on twenty-five percent more land. Lebensraum."

"We have enjoyed good cooperation regarding disputes with the West," Stetchkin countered.

"Of course. Nations have no permanent allies or enemies, only interests."

"Kissinger."

"Lord Palmerston said it more than one hundred years earlier," Mikhailov informed him. "We will cooperate with the Chinese when it is in our mutual interest to do so. But they have an overriding concern that cannot be obviated: too many people on too small a landmass.

And just north of them is vacant land as far as the eye can see. The largest expanse on the planet. They are building artificial islands in the South China Sea to claim those waters. The Americans were too stupid and feckless to even raise an eyebrow about it. We will not be so stupid. If we permit the Chinese a foothold on our territory—whether it is a plant or refinery or farm or weather station—they will use that in the same fashion they are using the islands in the South China Sea. We, however, are not the Americans, Aleksandr." Mikhailov took a sip of water before changing subjects. "You have absorbed Uganov's operations?"

"Yes."

"How has the absorption improved operations?"

Stetchkin began speaking and stopped. He began again and stopped once more. He really couldn't say how operations had been improved. "The operations are streamlined," he offered weakly.

"You turned a good man into a walking vegetable to streamline operations with no identifiable improvement in performance?"

"Uganov was troublesome and unreliable. We could not depend on him."

Mikhailov, his eyes hooded, stared at Stetchkin. "Understand something, Aleksandr. I give you latitude because you produce results, not because I am fond of you. If you do not produce results, not only will you receive no latitude; you will be useless to me." Mikhailov picked a piece of lint from the leg of his trousers. "You should endeavor never to become useless to me."

"I shall."

"If you cannot tell me of any improvement in the operations, tell me the status of the operations."

"We remain on schedule. All simulations have been successful."

"Timing is important, Aleksandr. As you know, we have several components to the plan that must mesh."

"I understand. Out of curiosity, has NATO given any indication they are even aware of our various movements?"

"NATO has been silent, as expected. They have undertaken a

simulation similar to Locked Shields recently, but it appears the timing was mere happenstance."

Stetchkin chuckled derisively. "They behave as raccoons. They believe if they put their hands over their eyes, the predator will not see them and will leave them alone."

"The West remains preoccupied with the EMP issue, with the bombing campaign against Iran. They cannot conceive of a second potential cataclysm following so soon after averting the EMP. In this, I do not fault them. It is a rational conclusion driven by human nature. And even though our history is one that instructs us that one cataclysm can certainly follow soon after another, we, too, would likely be lulled into complacency, a sense of security."

"But we do not think in one-dimensional terms as they do," Stetchkin noted. "Even some of their leaders have acknowledged that they play checkers while we play chess."

"Even so, Aleksandr, we likely would never envision such a deceptive maneuver." Another sip of water. "Do any contingencies remain at your end?"

Stetchkin saw an opening. "Our preparations are complete. It is just a matter of initiating the procedure. For that reason, Colonel Egorshin is no longer integral to the operation."

Mikhailov could barely restrain rolling his eyes. Stetchkin had little capacity for subtlety. "You are saying he is unnecessary?"

"Yes."

"And you wish to remove him?"

"That is correct."

"In the same fashion you removed Uganov?"

"Not exactly," Stetchkin replied slowly.

"So you wish to kill him."

"He is useless now."

Mikhailov examined the crease on his pant leg, running an index finger along its crest. He remained silent for several moments. "You wish to kill a brilliant young man because he has successfully completed an enormously complex task so all that remains, essentially, is to push a button, so to speak . . ." Mikhailov looked up. "Are you completely deranged, Aleksandr?"

Stetchkin stammered, at a loss for how to respond.

Mikhailov continued. "You worry me. I have given you enormous authority to ensure our objectives are met. I am growing concerned I may have made an error of judgment. I have long been aware of your . . . eccentricities. Your accomplishments, however, outweighed the eccentricities, and so I tolerated them. But there are limits to my tolerance. This is one of them."

"It is merely that he is an affront—"

"Listen to me," Mikhailov interrupted. "You acted on Uganov without checking with me. Although somewhat pedestrian, Uganov was competent. I did not object because Egorshin was the true center of the operation." Mikhailov leaned forward, eyes narrowed. "That did not mean I approved, and I *must* approve. Do I make myself absolutely clear?"

Stetchkin nodded.

"I understand your reputation. I helped create your reputation. But you are not free to simply eliminate essential personnel without seeking my approval beforehand. That is unacceptable."

"I understand fully."

"Then understand this also: Only when you can certify to me that the event can proceed with one hundred percent certainty without Egorshin may you act as you wish. If you act without so certifying, you will be fortunate to suffer the same fate as Uganov. Am I clear?"

Stetchkin swallowed nervously. "Yes."

CHAPTER 51

After dismissing Stetchkin, Mikhailov retreated to his study and spent several minutes looking out the window at Kremlin Park, thinking about what the world was about to look like. Of one thing he was certain: No matter how it looked, he would be regarded as the most consequential Russian leader since Peter the Great.

A light rap at the door preceded the entry of Mikhailov's senior aide, Alexei Vasiliev. Like most competent aides, Vasiliev had a good understanding of his boss's thought processes and tried to anticipate what he would need or do next. Without a prefatory greeting, Vasiliev said, "Stetchkin planned to kill Egorshin?"

"Yes." Mikhailov turned from the window. "Make a note, Alexei. When this matter is concluded, we must reevaluate Stetchkin. He's proved valuable. A man with his qualities usually is. But he strikes me as increasingly . . . odious. The issue of Uganov, for example. That advanced nothing except Stetchkin's own preferences."

"Morosov—Egorshin's uncle—contacted me again a short time ago. He is a sober individual. He provided details of Egorshin's encounter in Stetchkin's office. From what Morosov described, Stetchkin is either a peculiar motivator of personnel or dangerously unhinged."

"Since I have known him he has been both. It seems lately his behavior leans increasingly toward the latter."

"The Uganov episode was something of a retrogression."

"Yes, it certainly was. Stetchkin seems to imagine himself a modern-day Beria. If he is not careful, he will come to a similar end."

"Everyone can use a Beria."

"Perhaps. Until he becomes a liability. Stetchkin is balancing pre- cariously close to the edge."

"Morosov agrees."

"I directed Stetchkin he may take no action unless he is able to certify to me with one hundred percent certainty that the event can proceed without Egorshin. He cannot objectively make such certification."

Vasiliev nodded. "Egorshin is the architect and the engineer. With- out him, the most Stetchkin can guarantee is a ninety percent probabil- ity of success."

"Egorshin is the future. Stetchkin is the past. You may tell your friend Morosov that Stetchkin will not move against Egorshin."

Vasiliev began to leave but paused at the door and turned to Mikhailov. "May I ask, Mr. President, what the consequences would be if Stetchkin continues to act . . . odiously?"

A wry smile crossed Mikhailov's face, as if he were enjoying the prospect. "Then Stetchkin will receive a visit from Taras Bor."

CHAPTER 52

GEORGIA,
AUGUST 16, 8:30 P.M. EDT

Ruth Ponder continued to persist, inspiring others to rally around her. The kids had reclaimed their childhood bedrooms, and sleeping bags and air mattresses were laid down for the grandkids. Bob and Sue Lampley were, of course, fixtures in the living room and kitchen, respectively, Bob making phone calls to every law enforcement contact he knew and Sue keeping food warm and serving the other folks in the house. Amy Randall of the church choir, whose sister was the insurance adjuster, was sitting on a couch in the living room charging her cell phone in the wall outlet nearby. She had made dozens of calls to anyone and everyone who might possibly have information on the people responsible for Amos Ponder's murder, and she had been invaluable—primarily because her calls prompted other people to make their own calls, which in turn kept the authorities from relaxing even one little bit.

According to Amy's sister, the LaCrosse had been impounded and was being examined for evidence. Amos's body was also being examined by the Cobb County coroner, after which it would be prepared for transport back home. Everyone in the house prevailed upon Ruth to stay put and not go up there—Amos's body would be back soon enough.

Ruth's persistence had turned the investigation of the massacre along I-85 into a juggernaut. Most of the folks busy calling, texting, and e-mailing in Ruth Ponder's home were no more than high school graduates. Most were blue-collar. Ordinary, decent, hardworking folks. The kind of folks whom the young reporter from the big-city newspaper, who had given up and left, would consider backward and unsophisticated.

But they knew how to think and they had faith that Ruth's persistence and their own diligence would yield answers. Rev. Broussard had led them in prayer to produce such answers.

And sure enough, answers started coming. In little disparate bits. Seemingly unconnected. But not burdened by the traps of superficial sophistication, the folks in Ruth Ponder's home began to piece together leads.

The most important lead came from one of Ruth's commonsense questions: "How did the scary man who had given the diner patron chills, along with his foreign-looking friends, leave the truck stop where they had parked Amos's LaCrosse?" They didn't just abandon it and proceed on foot. They had to have taken another vehicle. So where did that vehicle come from? Unless they'd stolen another one, they must've bought or rented it. And since there were no reports of stolen vehicles in the vicinity during that timeframe, they must've rented or bought another vehicle. Maybe two. And since it appeared the scary man and his friends left the area in relatively short order, they must've bought or rented the replacement vehicles from someplace close.

Not too complicated.

So Ruth asked Amy Randall if she could find out if there were any car rental places or sales lots nearby the truck stop. Amy brought up the satellite view of the area from Google Maps, and she zoomed in until Ruth could see what looked like trees and roads and roofs of buildings with the names of streets and businesses printed on top.

Ruth peered over Amy's shoulder and bent down to get a better look. She took the glasses that were hanging on the little chain around her neck and slipped them on and could see the truck stop with its islands and pumps. Right behind was the diner where the patron had gotten the chills.

Across the street was a regular Shell gas station and next to that was something called Adam's Professional Services. On the other side was the Rookwood Head Start Academy. No car sales or rental places.

Amy took her index finger and swiped it slowly across the screen.

Ruth could see the buildings and creeks and roads move a little, and different buildings appeared. Next to the truck stop was Kirk's Automotive Parts Store, and across the street next to Adam's Professional Services was a Subway sandwich shop, and next to that on the other side of Five Mile Creek was Good Shepherd Baptist Church. No car sales or rental places.

So Ruth bent down a little more and swiped her own finger across the screen in the other direction, and the image moved slowly in that direction. On the opposite side of the truck stop was Carol's Beauty and Braiding Shop, then Holy Redeemer Church, and then Roberts Car and Truck Sales.

Bingo.

Amy tapped the screen and the image changed to Street View. It looked to Ruth like the place was filled predominantly with used cars and pickup trucks. *Probably easy in, easy out,* Ruth thought. *Less likely to need bank financing. Fewer calls, fewer hassles, less paperwork.*

"Amy, can you find me the telephone number for Roberts Car and Truck Sales?"

A few minutes later Ruth was talking to Randy, who had been getting ready to go home and who at first was helpful because he thought he might make one last sale, then became guarded when Ruth started asking questions about a scary-looking guy who might be with foreign-looking friends.

But then Ruth told Randy about Amos and the massacre and the LaCrosse, and Randy had seen the stories on TV and it started to make some kind of sense. The guy who had been interested in the Durango and Tahoe was built like a mixed-martial-arts champ or maybe even an NFL running back, and Randy could easily see how he could be scary when he wasn't friendly. And he was with a little guy who did look kind of foreign-looking. And he was ready to pay cash and was in a hurry.

So Randy weighed it and balanced it and turned it over in his head and decided that it was better to help Ruth than to help a possible bad guy get away. Besides, Randy wasn't sure but he might be aiding and abetting or something or other if he didn't tell Ruth what she needed to know. And it was the right thing to do. Heck, a widow calling for help so soon after her longtime husband got murdered.

Randy told Ruth that the scary/friendly guy didn't buy from Roberts but may have gone to see Rob Brock. No, he didn't have Rob Brock's number, but he gave her a description of the scary/friendly guy, as best as he could remember. Randy felt good about it, even felt a little proud of himself.

Ruth thanked him politely and ended the call and looked at the piece of paper on which she'd written all of Randy's information. Rev. Broussard saw the look on her face, came over, and patted her shoulder. Ruth looked up. "I don't know what else to do. The car lot didn't sell to the man I believe killed Amos, Reverend."

Rev. Broussard glanced at Amy's computer screen and bent to get a closer look. He pointed at the map depicting Roberts Car and Truck Sales. "Is this the dealership?"

"Yes, it is. But they sent Amos's killer to someone else."

Rev. Broussard continued gazing at the screen. "That's Holy Redeemer there."

Ruth looked at the icon to which the reverend was pointing.

"That's Pastor Luke Quinn's church. We were in seminary together. I see him at retreats pretty regularly and we stay in touch."

Rev. Broussard nodded pensively. "Ruth, may I use your phone?"

Ruth pointed to the wall phone in the kitchen, and moments later Rev. Broussard was in conversation. Ruth saw him brace the receiver between his ear and shoulder as he wrote on the notepad hanging next to the phone. Then he hung up, redialed, and a minute later was writing again. A minute after that he came back to Ruth.

"Pastor Luke's parishioner Rob Brock's been trying to sell a Windstar and a Caprice for the longest. He finally got a buyer."

Rev. Broussard handed Ruth a page from the notebook.

That scary-looking man was going to jail if Ruth Ponder had anything to say about it. That was for sure.

CHAPTER 53

Bulkvadze had been Abkashvili's man on the East Coast for nearly a decade. During that time he had lived in Boston, New York City, Newark, and Washington, D.C. He hated the latter's weather most.

He stood next to his Mercedes on a short dead-end drive bounded mostly by wooded lots with a sprinkling of residences at the far end. The developer had seen promise in the location, but financing had run out after a few houses had been constructed.

The drive was two blocks from the safe house that Mike Garin was probably watching at this very moment.

Bulkvadze had done a light reconnaissance of the perimeter of the area before parking his car at the isolated, wooded end of the drive. Although he hadn't seen Garin in the area—he'd stayed well outside of the sight lines of the safe house to avoid being seen by him—he had a fair idea of where Garin might position himself. There were only two decent vantage points for surveillance: the woods behind the house—and Bulkvadze concluded that for obvious reasons Garin would avoid that area—and a playground in front of the house. He planned to approach the playground from the rear; uninspired, but success, not creativity, was his primary concern. Optimally, he'd spot Garin, advance from behind to within firing range, shoot him as many times as necessary, and photograph the corpse with his cell. Then he'd send the photo to Bor.

The humidity had risen over the last few hours and the heat remained oppressive. Bulkvadze took off his black sport coat and laid it on the passenger seat of his car before locking it. He pulled his T-shirt, also black, over the Taurus stuck in his waistband and walked slowly in the direction of the playground.

By the time he reached the portion of the drive with residences, his plan immediately got more complicated. The owners of the house on the right side of the drive nearest the rear of the playground were host-ing a gathering of some sort. Whatever it was, there were at least fifty people in the backyard and the chatter was low and the music tranquil, low and tranquil enough that the sound of gunfire from the nearby playground would easily be heard. Worse, parked among the guests' cars were two police patrol cars. Clearly, they weren't there to address a noise complaint. They were probably friends of the family, briefly dropping by to wish whomever well.

And Bulkvadze had no suppressor to attach to the Taurus. He hadn't planned on being a shooter. He'd had five men to do just that. If only he'd brought ten.

But Bulkvadze had to kill Garin. Right away. Or Bor would kill Bulkvadze. He wouldn't get another opportunity; that was clear. He had to locate Garin and do it now.

If he shot Garin, the people at the gathering, including the police officers, would hear the sounds crack through the still, humid air. He couldn't then run back past the house to his car. Nor was there any way for a man of his massive dimensions to hide or look inconspicuous. He'd be caught or shot almost immediately.

Bulkvadze had to find Garin and kill him by hand. The decision was simple. The act might not be.

Bulkvadze, however, had the advantage. He was expecting to find Garin; Garin wasn't expecting Bulkvadze. Bulkvadze had killed before by hand, and fairly adeptly. He dwarfed Garin and undoubtedly was far stronger.

And Bulkvadze was motivated.

Bulkvadze moved past the house with the gathering and past two more before coming to where the drive turned to the right and pro-ceeded westward. Bulkvadze continued straight to a row of pines that bordered the rear of the playground.

The giant stopped behind one of the pines and looked about the playground for signs of his quarry. To Bulkvadze's left was a baseball diamond, the backstop almost fifty feet from where he stood. To his right was another field—probably for football or soccer, although there were no goals. Along the right sideline of the field was a row of low-rise bleachers no more than six feet high. High enough, however, to obscure an advance to the far end of the playground, where there stood an array of standard playground equipment and what appeared to be a very wide sandbox. About three feet to the right of the sandbox was a wooden fence, the kind Bulkvadze had seen surrounding trash receptacles next to the drive-through at fast-food places. Standing behind the fence, at its right-hand edge, was a figure with its back to Bulkvadze.

Garin. Even in the gloom of the evening and from nearly one hundred yards Bulkvadze recognized the wide shoulders tapering to a narrow waist. One hundred pounds lighter than Bulkvadze. Five inches shorter. Focused on the house some distance beyond. Oblivious to the big man's presence.

Bulkvadze moved farther to the right, until he was behind the bleachers. Were Garin to look back for some reason, the stands would shield Bulkvadze from view. He could walk the length of the field behind the stands and it would take him fifteen to twenty feet behind Garin. That would take a minute. Closing the remaining distance and snapping Garin's neck would take a few seconds more. After a quick series of photos, he'd hit send and then walk back to his car. All that would remain would be dealing with Abkashvili. Not a problem. He knew Abkashvili, given a choice, would gratefully accept nearly one million dollars rather than deal with Bor.

Bulkvadze walked behind the stands in a slight crouch, pausing every ten yards or so to check Garin's position. Bulkvadze could feel his heart begin to beat more rapidly and his muscles tense and flex involuntarily, much like a power lifter preparing for a maximum dead lift. An intense, brutal move—all the strength in his body summoned and channeled toward a single effort.

Bulkvadze came to the end of the bleachers. He was close enough to see the movement of the gun stuck in Garin's back as his lungs expanded and contracted with each breath. Bulkvadze paused, gathered himself, and crept to within five feet of his target. Then he burst forward with his right hand outstretched, ripped the gun from Garin's trousers, and flung it out of reach. Simultaneously, he clamped his left arm around Garin's neck in a choke hold, nearly lifting the smaller man off the ground in the process.

Garin had begun to turn before Bulkvadze was able to close the choke hold, but not fast enough. Garin could feel his windpipe cinch, cutting off the air to his lungs. Blood rushed to his skull with such force that his eyes bulged from their sockets and his eardrums felt as if they would burst. His chest heaved as his lungs tried to suck in any available oxygen, but there was none. Garin sensed the cartilage in his neck compress and heard the internal acoustics of bone beginning to separate from bone.

Garin frantically pumped his right leg backward—as if kickstarting a motorbike—in search of his attacker's knee. His aim was off-center, the heel of his shoe catching the outer portion of the man's kneecap— not nearly enough force to collapse the huge joint, but enough to cause acute pain.

Yet it wasn't enough to cause the giant to release his choke hold. It was only enough to cause a slight and momentary relaxation of the muscles in the man's arm. Garin twisted hard to his right with his elbow raised, striking his attacker in the ribs, but he wasn't able to generate sufficient torque for the blow to be of consequence. He immediately whipped his body in the other direction, other elbow raised, and struck the attacker's left side. This time he was able to generate a bit more force and felt his attacker cave slightly to the left. Once more Garin spun to his right and dug the sharp point of his elbow into the man's ribs.

The choke hold loosened, not much, but enough for Garin to make a quarter turn and jam the heel of his right hand under the man's chin, snapping his head backward and causing him to bite off the tip of his tongue.

Blood spurted from the man's mouth, but he refused to release his grip. It did, however, loosen. Just a few millimeters, but enough for Garin to twist and thrust the heel of his right hand once more, this time catching Bulkvadze under the nose and driving upward into his skull.

Garin had once killed a man with a similar blow, driving bone and cartilage into his brain. It merely stunned Bulkvadze.

But that gave Garin an opening. The choke hold loosened a bit more, allowing Garin to turn his head sideways, drop under the man's arm, and collapse to the ground. Garin crabbed backward out of reach but butted up against the wooden fence. He began to raise himself upright when Bulkvadze's left forearm slammed into Garin's chest, knocking what little wind he had out of him and driving him against the fence.

Time then inched to a crawl.

Garin could feel the fence give and bend slightly against his back and he caught the scent of linseed oil covering its wood. As the fence bucked and rebounded, Garin used its force to propel himself, head cast slightly downward, toward the big man.

The top of Garin's head struck Bulkvadze midway between his throat and chin, crushing both. Still, it wasn't enough to drop him. Bulkvadze staggered backward two steps before regaining his balance and pulled his right hand back to throw a roundhouse.

Garin was quicker. He threw a right hook to Bulkvadze's left temple, followed by a left cross to Bulkvadze's right temple, followed by a knee to Bulkvadze's groin.

Bulkvadze's head whipsawed right and left from the punches and he doubled over as the air was forced from his lungs.

Though hunched over, he remained on his feet, almost as an act of defiance. Garin could hear his own gasps for air, rapid from exertion and ragged from the choke hold. He heard similar sounds from Bulkvadze, blood now gushing from his nose as well as his mouth. There was a glazed look in his eyes, and a ropelike artery pulsed in his right temple. In one motion, Garin spun behind the big man and with his right arm enveloped Bulkvadze's neck and fell backward to the ground, using both of their body weights to violently snap the big man's head backward at its base. The sound was that of a dry tree branch breaking. Garin lay on the ground with Bulkvadze on top of him and with all of his strength continued to apply pressure to the man's neck. It was unnecessary. All of the tension in the giant's body was gone. There was no beat against Garin's arm from the pulse in the man's neck. No breathing. Nothing.

Speed beats size. Speed kills.

Garin lay on the ground with Bulkvadze on top of him for several seconds, trying to catch his breath. Then he squirmed and shoved and pulled himself from under the corpse, got to one knee, and stood erect.

Garin took a deep breath and exhaled slowly. He could feel the endorphin rush of extreme exertion begin to flow through his body. The twin exhilarations of victory and narrowly escaping death washed over him.

And then everything went black.

CHAPTER 54

You have an outside call, Mr. Colton," the DGT operator said. "Mrs. Ruth Ponder."

"I don't know a Ruth Ponder. Who is she?"

"She says she's from Catoosa County, Georgia, and that she thinks you're looking for the same person. She has information about him."

Matt sat straight in his chair. "Connect her."

A second later Ruth Ponder said, "Hello? Mr. Colton?"

"This is Matt Colton. How may I help you?"

"I thought we might help each other, Mr. Colton. My husband, Amos, was killed in that mass shooting you may have heard about? It was on all the news channels?"

Ruth Ponder had Matt's undivided attention.

"Yes, Mrs. Ponder, I'm aware of the shooting. I'm very sorry to hear about your husband."

"Well, thank you, sir. I'll try to make this simple, Mr. Colton, since I believe I can anticipate most of your questions."

Matt was anxious to get to the point, but Ruth Ponder's gracious manner and deliberate cadence reminded him of his maternal grandmother. Urgency did not trump courtesy. "Go ahead, ma'am."

"I've been trying to find the man or men who killed Amos and those other unfortunate individuals. So, along with several friends, we've spent some time calling around. Now, please understand, I've got no complaint against the law enforcement folks. They've got a tough job and their hands are full. We just thought we could help a bit."

"Yes, ma'am. I understand."

"Well, two of my friends noticed that the name 'DGT' had come up more than a few times in our conversations with law enforcement and the like. And then we realized that we were asking some of the same questions as DGT. That got me curious, so my friend Amy was kind enough to look you folks up and she found your website. Am I right that you're military contractors?"

"Yes, ma'am."

"And you sometimes help the government or military when they're stretched kind of thin?"

"That's correct."

"Now, I've been told that folks like you all sometimes can move faster and can find out things that maybe the police can't find out, because of the way they have to do things."

"On occasion that may be true."

"We understand you were asking about a scary-looking man who had with him some foreigners or some foreign-looking people who got in a vehicle at a truck stop near Albemarle."

"We were indeed."

"And you were very interested in a green vehicle that looked like it was made by Ford because—and here I may be jumping to conclusions—the scary-looking guy had abandoned Amos's LaCrosse."

"Yes, Mrs. Ponder. We are looking for a green vehicle, but so far we haven't been able to identify it. The video we have is inconclusive and from what we understand the FBI hasn't been able to make much progress yet either."

"Well, that's where we maybe can help each other out, Mr. Colton. We figured the scary man with the foreign-looking friends wasn't from around there. So if he just dropped off Amos's LaCrosse, he would've had to steal another car—meaning the green vehicle—or he had to have bought or rented that car, right?"

"I suppose that's true, Mrs. Ponder."

"You know, Mr. Colton, Amos was very fond of that LaCrosse. It was the nicest car we ever had. He was very proud of it, too. He kept it clean, polished, and in perfect running condition. We—"

Matt heard unintelligible chatter on the other end. Then Ruth Ponder's melodic voice came back on the line.

"I apologize, Mr. Colton. My daughter tells me that I'm rambling and I need to get to the point. You're a very busy man, no doubt."

"No apologies necessary, Mrs. Ponder. You've just lost your husband. Please, take your time."

"Thank you for being such a gentleman, Mr. Colton. It still hasn't hit me, I suppose, and when it does I'll probably shut up and stop talking for days. Anyway, here's my point: The scary-looking guy bought two vehicles, cash, from Mr. Rob Brock less than a quarter mile from the truck stop. He bought a 1996 forest-green Ford Windstar minivan and a 2001 or 2002 white Chevy Caprice. The Windstar had a small dent in the passenger door. They still have their original tags. The state of North Carolina tag number for the Windstar is WYF2312 and for the Chevy Caprice the number is MTR7213 . . ."

"This is enormously helpful, ma'am."

"Will you be able to find the scary-looking man?"

"We'll run this through our systems and forward it to all of the appropriate law enforcement agencies, Mrs. Ponder."

"But do you think you'll get him?"

"Ma'am, we have a pretty good idea who this man is. He's not an ordinary criminal. For that matter, he's not an ordinary person. Honestly, I can't make any promises because getting him will be very, very tough. I can tell you this: The very best people in the country are looking for him, and we will do our very, very best to get him and his foreign-looking friends. And your information helps. A lot."

"Well, Mr. Colton . . . May I call you Matt?"

"Always, Mrs. Ponder."

"Thank you, Matt. That's all one can ask. Will you do me one favor, though?"

"What's that, ma'am?"

"When you do find him and his foreign-looking friends, would you please call me to let me know? I left my number with your answering lady."

"You can bet on it, Mrs. Ponder."

"Thank you, Matt. And good luck."

Matt disconnected and instantly made another call.

"Dwyer."

"I have the license numbers for the vehicles Bor's driving."

"Outstanding. Alert our folks, starting with Garin. Then law enforcement, starting with the FBI. Olivia's right here. She'll get them to Brandt. How in the world did you find him?"

"I didn't. Mrs. Ponder did."

CHAPTER 55

Major Valeri Volkov was appropriately terrified.

Seated outside the tyrant's office for the last fifteen minutes, he'd searched his memory for every possible mistake, offense, or indiscretion he may have committed in his career. The problem with conducting such a search was that it was nearly impossible to determine what Aleksandr Stetchkin considered a mistake, offense, or indiscretion. As far as the tyrant was concerned, Volkov having been born to his parents might qualify as a mistake, having coffee instead of tea could be an offense, and saying hello to the doorman may have been an indiscretion.

The face of the aide who sat at the desk revealed nothing. He simply looked at Volkov impassively. Maybe the aide gazed that way at everyone who entered the office. Or maybe the look was reserved only for the doomed. Volkov resisted the urge to ask, afraid the question itself might be the very thing that would tip the scales against him.

The phone on the aide's desk buzzed and he lifted the receiver to his ear. After replacing the receiver in the cradle, he stood and motioned for Volkov to enter Stetchkin's office.

Volkov took a breath to compose himself and proceeded through the door and into an anteroom beyond which Stetchkin was standing at his desk with his hands clasped behind his back.

"Major Volkov. Please sit down."

Volkov did as told. Stetchkin strode slowly from behind the desk and stood to Volkov's right, towering over him.

"Thank you for coming, Major. It is most considerate of you."

The comment bewildered Volkov. Of course Volkov was going to come. He had been commanded to come. No doubt he'd have been shot if he hadn't come. "Thank you, sir."

"Your file is quite interesting. Impressive. Consistently at the top of your class at university. Exceptional evaluations. When you substitute for Colonel Egorshin the unit appears to function at least as efficiently."

"Thank you, sir."

"Your career path was not as smooth as Colonel Egorshin's. Whereas he seems to have had to overcome comparatively few obstacles, you have had to work hard for your attainments." Stetchkin strode back behind his desk. Volkov exhaled quietly.

"What are your ambitions, Major?"

"Sir?"

"Your personal ambitions, Major. Someone with your talents often seeks a specific command."

Volkov grew more uncomfortable. Discussing personal ambitions with any superior was risky. With Stetchkin, it was treacherous. Volkov felt as if he were being lured into a trap. When in doubt, Volkov thought, be obsequious.

"My ambition at this point is to do my job as well as I can, sir. Where that may take me is up to others. And ultimately, you, sir."

The answer pleased Stetchkin. "Tell me about Colonel Egorshin, Major. How do you assess his performance?"

"Outstanding, sir. Colonel Egorshin's knowledge and capabilities are unsurpassed. He is the primary reason we are about to achieve a great success. Those under his command aspire to be as accomplished."

Stetchkin strode around his desk and stood next to Volkov again.

"Your loyalty to your superior is noted, Major. And admirable. Yet I hear differently."

Volkov looked straight ahead. He had no idea where Stetchkin was going and didn't want to say something wrong. He waited for Stetchkin to continue.

"He seems to prevail upon you whenever something important must be done. He is rather impudent whenever I give a directive. I note that he often delegates matters to you. This causes me concern about his competence, not to mention his loyalty." Stetchkin rubbed the back of his neck in a display of deliberation. "It strikes me as prudent to consider a reorganization of the unit. Understand, this is no slight to Colonel Egorshin, for whom it is clear you have a great deal of regard. But going forward—especially given the continuing importance of the unit—I think it wise that someone with unimpeachable dedication and loyalty take command. Most importantly, someone who does not equivocate."

Volkov remained silent. Was he actually suggesting Volkov would be given command? Was this a test to judge Volkov's loyalty to his superior? A response, any response, could be a misstep.

Again Stetchkin strode to the other side of his desk. He stood behind the high-backed leather chair, resting his forearms across the top.

"I need your frank assessment on a very specific matter, Major. This is critical. It reflects not only on Colonel Egorshin, but on your entire unit, including yourself, since you have had such an instrumental role. The operation is scheduled to begin shortly and President Mikhailov expects that it be flawless. In fact, he insists he be provided one hundred percent certainty that it move forward as scheduled. I gather from what you have just told me that it will move forward as scheduled—that your unit has completed all preparations and needs only to initiate the process. Correct?"

Volkov felt as if he were in a vise. No one could guarantee one hundred percent success of the operation, and he didn't want to be held responsible should it not achieve that goal. But he had just touted its imminent success. And, in truth, the preparations were one hundred percent complete. There was nothing left to be done. Colonel Egorshin had covered every contingency and the unit's work was astonishingly good.

Stetchkin added, "Of course, I understand no one can guarantee with one hundred percent certainty that all aspects of the operation will conclude successfully. But am I correct that you believe it is one hundred percent ready to proceed?"

"Yes, all preparations are, indeed, complete and it is one hundred percent ready to proceed."

"Good. Very good. It is that type of straightforwardness that is the hallmark of a leader ready to command." Stetchkin smiled. "And you will certify such?"

"Absolutely."

"Outstanding, Major Volkov. President Mikhailov will be pleased." Stetchkin again walked to Volkov's side, placing a hand on the major's shoulder. "Your clarity is refreshing, a departure from the temerity and obfuscation I get from Egorshin. I do not mean to be overly critical of him. By your own account, he has done a good job. Clearly, the pressure of the impending event has taken a toll. But he seems unduly distracted. Tired. I'm not sure he is budgeting his time well. Is he, to your knowledge, preoccupied with something?"

"Not to my knowledge, sir."

"Perhaps he is having financial problems; problems with a woman? I am told he has been seeing Tatiana Palinieva, the television hostess, for some time now. Has he expressed any problems with their relationship?"

"Not to me, sir."

"Has he discussed her at all with you?"

"Our relationship is professional, sir. Colonel Egorshin does not discuss his social life with me."

"Have you met Palinieva?"

"I have spoken to her a few times at official functions, sir."

"And what are your observations regarding her?"

"She is very pleasant. She seems to be interested and even knowledgeable about a range of matters—from politics to science to sports."

"Did you discern any dissatisfaction with her personal affairs? Any signs of frustration, discontent?"

"No, sir, I did not."

Stetchkin nodded and walked behind his desk again. "You have been very helpful, once again, Major. You have a bright future. You are dismissed."

Volkov rose and walked out of Stetchkin's office more than relieved. He was almost ebullient.

CHAPTER 56

He knew the signs of frostbite and he was fairly certain two toes on his left foot were gone; the rims of his ears too. He needed treatment before gangrene set in.

Lieutenant Nikolai Garin had been walking—sometimes jogging—almost nonstop in the sixty hours since he'd overpowered the guard and slipped under the barbed wire of the detention camp located in the Soviet sector of postwar Germany. The NKVD had identified him as an apostate, a nonbeliever in the communist state. As such, he was destined for death or a labor camp, but only after brutal interrogation by the sledovatels who had dismembered or otherwise disfigured most of his cellmates.

He hadn't eaten in nearly three days. He was lightheaded and concerned that after walking through near-whiteout conditions for long stretches he was disoriented and might be headed back to the Soviet sector. He had no guideposts or landmarks for direction. But he'd already evaded two patrols. Since the patrols likely would become more frequent the closer he got to the American sector, he surmised he was headed in the right direction.

This was the critical time. The next few hours would determine whether he would live free or die. Because no matter what, he wasn't going back. Nikolai Garin's children and grandchildren would never be told what to think or what to say. His progeny would grow up in America. Hobbled, starving, exhausted, and frostbitten, Garin was prepared to kill anyone who stood in his way.

As would his grandson.

The very first thing Garin registered was that he was restrained. Something was restricting his movement. But he couldn't identify it, couldn't even see it. He didn't even know if it was real.

His mind was floating in a zone somewhere between consciousness and unconsciousness. His senses were scrambled. He heard sounds, but they were muffled and unintelligible. He saw lights and shades, but they were formless and ethereal. He smelled air that was cool and damp with an odor of cardboard and mildew. The taste in his mouth was acidic and artificial.

His head hurt. It was not the pain of an external blow but of internal discomfort. And he was mildly nauseous.

He tried to focus, to discern something from the lights and shadows. But everything before him appeared as if he were looking up from the bottom of a swimming pool in late evening—vague, distorted, and shifting.

For a moment he thought he heard a voice. It was slow, deep, and ponderous. But he wasn't sure. Maybe he was imagining it.

He was somewhat certain, however, that the restraints were real. Something was tight on his wrists, tight enough to cause discomfort, if not pain. But then, he couldn't even be sure of that, because when he tried to move his arms his muscles failed to respond. Same with his legs. His brain was giving orders but the electrical impulses never made it to his extremities. Maybe he wasn't restrained, after all. Maybe he was paralyzed.

Strangely, the thought of paralysis generated no emotion. Not fear, not anxiety, not even depression or sadness. It was as if he was completely detached from his body, viewing it from a different plane, examining it like a test tube specimen.

He had no concept of time. The random thoughts traversing his brain might be occupying seconds, minutes, or hours. His brain attempted to analyze the situation, but it did so without any urgency, which confused him. He knew his present state was abnormal—perhaps even dangerous—yet his brain was in no rush to provide answers or solutions.

Some part of him, something far above the medulla, tried to get the rest of him to concentrate, to at least focus his eyes, penetrate the fog of blurry lights and undulating shadows. The more he did so, the more his head hurt and the nausea increased.

Then there was a loud crack. It sounded like a heavy object striking stone or concrete. The noise brought a fleeting moment of clarity, but within a short time—he couldn't gauge how long—he began to recede back into a mist.

Another sound. This one not as loud but more identifiable. It was the sound of a chair scraping across the floor. The floor was stone or concrete. He saw movement or, more precisely, a shadow shifting laterally. But once again, he began to recede into a mist.

He sensed a subtle change in air pressure. It seemed to have accompanied the shifting shadow. Then he heard a voice; at least he thought it was a voice. No, he was certain it was a voice.

There was more shifting of shadows, which yielded to larger expanses of light. The shadows were assuming shapes, though the shapes were fluid and indistinct.

He felt a twitch. His right quadriceps had moved involuntarily; he wasn't paralyzed after all. He tried to move his legs but there was no response. He tried to move his arms. Still no response.

The fog before him was lifting a bit more and the nausea was gone. But his head hurt worse and now he was feeling pain in his hands and around his neck. He must've struck something hard with his fists. He was beginning to sense the passage of time more accurately. He was gradually becoming more self-aware.

There was a voice. He didn't understand what it was saying. Whatever it was saying was barely a sentence long. Its tone was declarative.

The voice spoke again. This time it's tone was imperative. After a pause, he felt a sting on the right side of his face. He had been struck by something. His thinking became sharper, on the cusp of lucidity.

His face was stung by something again. He identified it as skin, the palm of a hand.

He heard the voice again. A declarative sentence followed by an imperative sentence. Then there was a different voice followed by footsteps. Yes, footsteps. He was able to discern the sound. The footsteps faded and then there was another loud noise like the first one he'd heard. A heavy object striking an immovable object.

He became aware of his hands clenching. His knuckles hurt. He'd felt that type of pain before. He'd recently struck someone.

His hands now were obeying his commands. His legs too. His legs strained against restraints that were, in fact, tied around his ankles. He was tied to a chair. The armrests were metal, not cushioned. They felt wide and thick and substantial.

He could hear himself breathe. Shallow and ragged. He'd been hurt. He was beginning to feel anxious, no longer detached.

Yet another declarative sentence. Then a question followed by a slap to the face. And another. And another.

He could hear the echo of the slaps in the room and almost immediately the fog dissipated and his brain went from addled to alert. His eyes began to adjust rapidly. The shadows turned into identifiable objects. A cinder-block wall, a thick metal door, a heavy metal table, a metal toolbox on top of the table, a concrete floor, cardboard boxes stacked to his left, and a heavy metal chair right in front of him, no more than three feet away.

All of the things in the room, even the cardboard boxes, were gunmetal gray except one. Seated on the chair three feet away was a man in his fifties with rheumy, bloodshot eyes, a scar running from the left side of his mouth to his ear, and a knotted scalp covered with tufts of white hair. He was one of the most grotesque-looking men Mike Garin had ever seen.

And he was smiling.

CHAPTER 57

R ussians."

President John Allen Marshall shook his head, the tone of his voice a mixture of exasperation and frustration. He suspected he'd said the word just as FDR had after learning of the Molotov-Ribbentrop Pact, JFK had after learning the Soviets were moving ballistic missiles into Cuba, and Reagan had after learning the Soviets had shot down Korean Air Lines Flight 007.

Marshall rapped his knuckles on the Resolute desk in the Oval Office. It occurred to him he'd used a similar tone just a few weeks ago upon learning of the EMP plot, although at that time his voice was infused with more alarm.

Marshall had confronted Mikhailov and threatened to form a nearly worldwide coalition to impose crippling sanctions on the Russian government for its involvement in the plot. Mikhailov conceded that some Russians were involved in the matter but that such involvement was not sanctioned by the Russian government. It was true, Mikhailov said, that a Russian physicist named Dmitri Chernin had provided technical assistance to the Iranian nuclear weapons and ballistic missile programs, but Chernin was acting without the Russian government's knowledge, let alone approval. Indeed, upon learning of Chernin's role, the SVR had immediately located and assassinated the physicist—going so far as to provide photos of the corpse to CIA deputy director John Kessler as proof. An act of penance.

Marshall wasn't wholly convinced by Mikhailov's explanations, but he was hamstrung by the reluctance of most Western nations to take any action more punitive than mild to moderate sanctions. The French pointed out—correctly—that it was the North Koreans who had provided hundreds of scientists and technicians to help Iran build a crude nuke and improve the range of its Shahab missiles so it could strike the continental United States. Germany, embarrassed that some of the advanced equipment used by the Iranians had been obtained from German manufacturers, noted that there were few, if any, Russian fingerprints on either the Iranian nuke program or the EMP plot. Indeed, most of the G8 powers argued that if anything, sanctions should be imposed on North Korea, not Russia.

It was mere coincidence that most of the G8 powers depended on Russia for natural gas and other critical resources but were dependent on the hermit kingdom for absolutely nothing.

Marshall wasn't persuaded of Russian innocence, but the Russians had plausible deniability. Mikhailov shrewdly preempted stiff sanctions by boosting Gazprom's sales of natural gas to Europe by thirty billion cubic meters and lowering the price of such gas by a full ten percent. That, combined with the lack of stomach among Western powers for any form of confrontation, resulted in the geopolitical equivalent of a slap on the wrist.

To be fair, the Russians did nothing militarily, economically, or diplomatically to distract from or impede the bombing campaign against Iran. Mikhailov even allowed Allied aircraft to coordinate logistics and stage some bombing runs using the Mozdok Air Base in North Ossetia.

Still, Marshall believed there was more to Russian involvement in the EMP plot than met the eye, and he remained wary of Mikhailov and his ambitions.

James Brandt had just informed Marshall that the Russians were moving troops and matériel, movements that were baffling, prompting Marshall's exasperation.

"Whatever they're doing, they're up to no good, Jim. That's a constant. What's your take?"

"I'm a bit mystified, Mr. President."

"This wasn't in the President's Daily Brief. When was this discovered and by whom?"

"It wasn't anyone in the intelligence community, per se. My assistant, Ms. Perry, happened upon it and alerted me."

"I might just get rid of you and make her national security advisor. All the good stuff comes from her. Come to think of it, the increased Russian naval presence in the Persian Gulf *was* noted in the PDB a couple of days ago. But no correlation was made with the troop movements in southern Russia. Or the activity around the Baltics. Or the industrial sites."

"Ms. Perry agrees with you that the Russians are up to no good."

"She gets that from you, Jim. It's practically your mantra."

"I'm not sure I agree in this case. There's nothing especially unusual in these movements. Plus, they've been on their best behavior since the Iranian EMP affair and it's been barely a month since then."

"Movements around the Caspian are strange."

"Not really. They've conducted exercises nearby in the past, particularly when they've had issues with the likes of the Chechens."

"Then why bring this to my attention?"

"To be honest, sir? Because Ms. Perry has been hectoring me."

Marshall smiled.

"She insisted I tell you one more thing. Several attempts have been made on Mike Garin's life in the last couple of days. She believes the Russians may have something to do with it."

Brandt had Marshall's attention. From the beginning of the EMP operation, Marshall had been intrigued by all things Garin. "Several attempts on Garin's life? Seriously?"

"According to Ms. Perry."

"What does Garin say?"

"He told Ms. Perry he thinks it's that Russian operator from the EMP affair."

Marshall leaned back in his chair. "What do you think?"

"Garin is not somebody who makes mistakes, and he doesn't jump to conclusions."

Marshall nodded. "Serious as a heart attack. But that Russian was running circles around our law enforcement and intelligence guys last time. If there were several *unsuccessful* attempts on Garin's life, it doesn't sound like that Russian."

"True. But we are talking about Garin."

Marshall chuckled. "We're fortunate we still produce men like that, Jim, though he may be one of a kind."

"Ms. Perry believes the combination of these things indicates some type of Russian strike against US interests is imminent or under way."

"Imminent or under way? Based on what, precisely?"

"Everything we've just discussed plus our experience from the EMP affair. That unfolded at light speed. We stopped it only hours from execution."

"What do you propose we do this time?"

"I propose we devote more intelligence assets and resources to this matter to determine what's going on."

"And Ms. Perry?"

"She believes, Mr. President, that time's of the essence. She proposes we reconstitute Omega to deal with any potential threat that may emerge."

"Reconstituting Omega—selection, training—would take as much as a year. That doesn't make much sense if time's of the essence."

"I take it Garin has in mind a provisional Omega consisting of former tier-one operators."

"Even if I thought that was a good idea, a certain faction of the Senate—not to mention the press—would be up in arms if I moved to re-create Omega like that. It would be labeled as a cadre of hired assassins, mercenaries."

"I don't disagree."

Marshall drummed his fingers on his desk. "Before we take any action, I'd like to speak to Garin directly. Then I want to discuss this with the NSC."

"Wise decision."

Marshall stopped drumming his fingers, turned, and gazed at the Rose Garden.

"Russians."

CHAPTER 58

The Butcher slowly arranged his instruments of torture on the table before the subject, believing from long experience that the revelation of each was torture in and of itself, the subject's mind conjuring horrors nearly as awful as the physical pain to come. The Butcher was a master, taking great pride in his craft. He had done this scores of times before over nearly two dozen years. He knew the human body as well as any surgeon or physiologist. He had tweaked and adjusted his repertoire to inspire maximum dread, unbearable agony. And an irresistible compulsion on the part of the subject to cooperate.

The instruments varied slightly from subject to subject. The Butcher had an instinct regarding such things, refined by experience. Judging from the subject's appearance and what the Butcher had been told about the man, the Butcher suspected he might require more than one session, each fairly protracted. But he was confident he'd extract any information, however useless it might be, before the event was scheduled to occur.

The subject was fit and densely muscled, thick cords of veins bulging in his neck and arms. Pounding and pulverizing implements such as mallets, vises, and hammers would be less effective than piercing or slicing instruments. Accordingly, the Butcher selected a nine-inch-long stainless steel needle and placed it on the table. Its slow insertion in the ear canal or eyeball could, obviously, inflict horrible pain, the shock of which often resulted in unconsciousness—counterproductive to the objective. Consequently, the Butcher employed the needle as a primer. He would prick the ear canal or eyelid enough to elicit a shriek and a pearl of blood, but immediately withdraw it, the promise of worse pain to come.

To the right of the needle, the Butcher placed a finely honed, slightly parabolic six-inch razor with which he would peel off the subject's epidermis, an endeavor that required skill as well as patience.

His mentor had insisted that for maximum pain the razor should first be applied to the scalp at the front hairline, scaling the skin backward over the skull. But the Butcher found this to cause too much blood to stream into the subject's eyes, producing a disorientation that impeded eliciting useful information. Instead, the Butcher preferred slicing across the back of the subject's hand at the knuckles and slowly pulling the skin toward the elbow, pausing every few centimeters to use the third object he'd placed on the table—a simple propane torch.

The appearance of the torch almost invariably generated panic in his subject, but its actual purpose was to cauterize the area from which the skin was pulled back: slice, pull, pause, torch; slice, pull, pause, torch. Effective, even if the acrid smell of seared flesh, blood, and bone sometimes made him wretch.

The Butcher would need no other instruments. He sat a few feet away from and opposite the subject, whose ankles, waist, and wrists were strapped respectively to the legs, back, and arms of a high-backed metal chair. He observed the subject almost clinically for a few moments, somewhat fascinated by his taciturn expression. Probably catatonic from fear, thought the Butcher. Unsurprising.

He wondered how long the subject would live.

The smile had been fleeting, so much so that Garin couldn't be sure it had actually been there.

The smile—if it had been there—had been replaced by an analytical expression, that of a predator assessing the vulnerabilities of its prey.

Garin conducted his own analysis: He was in trouble. His hands and feet were bound to a heavy iron chair by multiple swaths of heavy-grade duct tape. His torso was bound upright against the back of the chair.

Save for the implements the grotesque-looking man had just arrayed on the metal table, the room was empty of anything Garin could possibly use as a weapon, and there was no possibility of reaching such implements. The room itself was approximately eight feet by twelve, consisting of cinder-block walls and poured concrete. The door was metal and looked several inches thick. The concrete floor was covered with a sheet of plastic.

The fog that had enshrouded his brain had lifted quickly, but he still had a vague, unsettled feeling throughout much of his body. The last thing he could remember was lying on the ground with his arm around Bulkvadze's neck, the giant's weight suddenly becoming inert. Garin had no recollection of confronting or even seeing the grotesque-looking man, and he was sure if he had he wouldn't have forgotten him.

"You killed Bulkvadze," the Butcher informed him in a voice that surprised Garin. It was urbane and cultured, with perfect diction. Incongruous, coming from a face that brutal. It was tinged with a Russian accent so slight that only someone who heard the language regularly would catch it. "Unexpected given the substantial size disparity and his initial tactical advantage. Normally, I would have given him four-to-one odds of defeating you within ten seconds."

Garin's expression remained taciturn, inscrutable.

"You should be dead, not Bulkvadze."

"Speed kills," Garin said, his voice low and quiet.

"That has been my experience as well. But there are times when death can come slowly and deliberately. This shall be one of those occasions."

Garin's face remained inscrutable.

"I suspect you think that my purpose is to pry information from you, to employ the judicious application of pain to determine what you and your government know about what we are doing and how you plan to deal with it." The Butcher picked up the needle from the table. "That is a bit theatrical. Although I will secure information from you, my charge is simply to kill you if Bulkvadze failed. How I do so is up to me."

Garin knew the purpose for the grotesque-looking man picking up the needle was to foreshadow pain, to instill fear and apprehension. Garin kept his gaze focused on the man's eyes.

"You have no information useful to us," the Butcher continued. He paused and cocked his head slightly in reconsideration. "Perhaps that is an overstatement. You may have some information, but it is likely to be of marginal consequence. Nonetheless, to be thorough I will extract it before we are done here."

The Butcher tapped the tip of the needle with his thumb. A bead of blood appeared. Garin kept his eyes focused on the grotesque-looking man's face but saw the needle in the periphery of his field of vision.

"What shall I call you?" Garin asked.

"Why do you care?"

"Decency," Garin replied softly. "It's only proper to know the name of someone you're going to kill."

"Delightful," the Butcher responded, though his voice contained not even a hint of mirth. "We've already met in a manner of speaking. I believe you were introduced to some of my artwork in the nuclear facility at Yongbyon. We knew you were coming. We know what you are going to do before you do. So I was charged with eliminating any evidence of Russian assistance to the regime's nuclear program." A pause. "I have no name, Garin, although I suspect somewhere in the vast databases of your intelligence services there is a rather unimaginative reference to someone known as 'the Butcher.'"

"Quite unimaginative," Garin agreed. "But it will make for an interesting gravestone. A conversation starter."

"Your attempt at bravado is understandable but misplaced. It will not change the futility of your circumstance. I assume by now you've determined that you are in the house you were watching. We are in a subbasement. This room was specially constructed to be soundproof. Steel-reinforced walls. Did you know that for years Saddam Hussein maintained such a room in the basement of the Iraqi consulate in the middle of New York City? His agents would torture Iraqi expatriates in that room, those with relatives still in Iraq. A superb way to control the population back home. It was only discovered after your country's invasion of Iraq in 2003. The floor of the room was covered with thick plastic to catch the blood, intestines, and other body parts of the subjects."

The Butcher caught the slight flick of Garin's eyes toward the floor.

"You expect that your law enforcement will, eventually, come to the house because you've alerted them to my handiwork in the woods in back. They will not detect the entrance to this room. Regardless, we will be finished before they step foot in the house." The Butcher shook his head. "No one will hear your screams, Garin."

"Nor yours."

The Butcher sighed. "Dispense with shows of insolence. I've been briefed about you. Primarily by Bor. You are a gifted operator. Tough. But the evidence shows Bor outwitted you. He is at least as talented and tough as you."

"But you are not."

"I have been around much longer than Bor. I have seen things neither of you have. I know toughness. I suspect you envision yourself as tough as Lieutenant Nikolai Garin. You are not."

The Butcher noted a slight quiver of Garin's mouth.

"You revere your grandfather. He exhibited insolence of a different kind. Insolence toward the communist state. That is hazardous even when you are not an officer in the Red Army. So he was detained by the NKVD at the end of the war in Germany. But he escaped through the barbed wire and past the guard dogs. I am told he evaded search teams, traveling nearly one hundred miles by foot through the snow and arriving in the American sector near death. You see him as heroic and you wish to emulate him."

"Not really. I much prefer to emulate a braying jackass like you. More entertaining."

"I confess I am unfamiliar with the colloquialism. But I, of course, recognize sarcasm when I hear it." The Butcher drew his mangled face to within inches of Garin's. "Nikolai Garin was a coward. He fled his country for a false promise of freedom. How ironic he came to this country. Every day your leaders erode those freedoms. You are like a frog in a pot on the stove; that is a colloquialism I do know."

"You should also know that here in the US, mouthwash comes in a variety of delicious flavors."

The Butcher pressed the tip of the needle directly on Garin's throat. Not enough to draw blood.

"American politicians make vapid statements about torture to appease certain constituencies. Some assert torture is ineffective. Those in our business know better. Of course, as with everything in life, it must be done correctly. But used correctly, it is nearly foolproof."

Garin remained absolutely still.

"Although, in honesty, definitions are important. What you Americans define as torture would be considered discomfort in my world. Discomfort is not foolproof. You are not about to experience discomfort, Garin. You are about to experience hell. Delayed retribution for your grandfather's treason."

"He was a greater patriot, a better Russian, than you. But he died an American."

Finally, the Butcher thought, *a reaction*. Emotion. Now was the time for pain.

"There are more than one hundred major clusters of nerves in the average human body. Medical journals reciting research into pain management maintain that these clusters are the body's primary locus of physical pain. They are incorrect. I have studied pain for forty years. In my experience pain is largely psychological. But in terms of inflicting maximum physical pain, the most vulnerable areas are not nerve clusters but locations adjacent thereto. It is as if the chemical reactions that produce the pain signal send the electrical impulse toward the cluster, where it is whipped toward the various nerve tributaries, accelerated and magnified in the process, like a comet whipping around a star, gathering debris, growing and quickening . . ."

"I gather your droning is part of the torture."

The Butcher pressed the needle a millimeter into Garin's throat, just perforating the skin. The location almost universally generated a spike of fear in the subject.

Garin didn't flinch. The Butcher raised his eyebrows, somewhat impressed.

"Stoicism is a virtue indeed, but it is useless in this regard. That was, literally, a pinprick. A small preview of coming attractions. Soon your limbs and organs will be strewn about the floor. You will scream despite your best efforts."

"Music to your ears, no doubt."

The Butcher nodded. "A rhapsody. I wager I can inflict pain in such a manner that your screams will come in different notes and chords. Allegro and adagio. Once I made a Pashtun tribesman unwittingly perform an aria. So, a piece of advice: Holding back the screams is futile, and will only amplify the pain."

Garin resolved to ignore that advice to his last breath. The Butcher watched as an unsettling look came over Garin's face. It was a look the Butcher couldn't remember having seen in a subject before. Beyond determination. Ferocity. As if the subject was the one inflicting the pain.

Let's see how quickly that look turns to terror, the Butcher thought.

The Butcher withdrew the needle and glanced at the propane tank, as if giving brief consideration to dispensing with preliminaries and escalating the proceedings. He caught Garin noticing the glance. That should be sufficient.

Yet the unsettling look remained.

The Butcher repositioned the needle just outside Garin's right ear and held it there for several moments. He saw Garin wince slightly. Anticipation was part of the torture. In those few moments the subject's mind would imagine the precise quality and extent of the pain. The muscles would tense, particularly in the neck and jaw; breathing would become rapid and shallow. The heart would pound and blood would rush to the site of the impending perforation.

Garin gazed steadily at his tormentor's face. The Butcher moved the needle a few millimeters closer, enough that Garin would notice the movement of the arm holding the implement. Garin blinked once slowly and clenched his jaws hard, resolved to suppress any scream, however involuntary, and keep it buried deep in his lungs. *Don't give the son of a bitch the satisfaction. Show him what Pop showed the monsters of the NKVD. Not just courage, defiance.*

The Butcher slowly inserted the needle into Garin's ear canal, being careful not to touch any portion of the skin and cartilage of its surrounding walls to heighten the trepidation. He manipulated the implement with the care and deftness of a neurosurgeon. The metal generated a ringing whine in Garin's ear, so soft and ephemeral he was unsure if it was real or imaginary, but his mind fixated upon it defensively, a distraction from imminent agony.

Garin disciplined himself to continue staring at the Butcher's face. His jaw was rigid but the remainder of his facial muscles revealed nothing to the Butcher, who concluded he would not prevail in a purely psychological battle, at least not this one. Garin was implacable. Severe physical pain was required.

So the Butcher inserted the tip of the long needle deeper into the auditory canal, slightly upward past the acoustic meatus and piercing the tympanic membrane, causing a shrieking burst of noise that shot through the auditory tube and was conveyed by the auditory nerve to Garin's brain.

Garin couldn't know whether he had successfully suppressed a scream. He lost consciousness when the needle traversed the middle ear and skirted just above the eustachian tube on its way to the cochlea.

CHAPTER 59

**MOUNT VERNON, VIRGINIA,
AUGUST 17, 10:30 A.M. EDT**

Olivia was seated in the captain's chair of the communications room in Dan Dwyer's subbasement.

She had tried to reach Brandt several times, anxious to know what action the president would take. Brandt hadn't picked up, which Olivia took as a sign that he was still in the Oval Office.

Between calls she ruminated over the satellite images. The mind, she knew, often resists making the logical progressions toward unpleasant conclusions, however obvious they may be. Although they denied official involvement, the Russians were on their best behavior after the EMP affair. It was implausible that they would be engaged in any form of questionable activity so soon after that affair. But Brandt had continually emphasized to her to always expect the unexpected from the Russians, and to anticipate the worst.

So she analyzed the images in her mind over and over. She considered the speed of the Russian movements. More importantly, she considered their trajectory. The Baltic movements were relatively unremarkable. They'd seen such movements in the past.

But the southward thrusts were different. Nothing about them suggested mere training maneuvers. They followed no previously observed pattern. They fit none of the myriad war-game models with which she was familiar. In short, they served none of the standard strategic imperatives Western powers had ascribed to either the Soviets or the Russians.

But the vectors were plain. The southward thrusts were headed toward Iran. Russian naval presence had increased markedly in the

Persian Gulf. This, clearly, was about Iran. Iran, whose nuclear program had been obliterated by weeks of devastating Allied bombing runs. The logical progression led to the unpleasant conclusion that the Russians were coming to Iran's assistance.

But why so late? There was little left of the nuclear program to salvage. The various enrichment facilities, missile sites, and nuclear plants had been all but destroyed. Iran's nuclear capacity had been reduced to rubble.

Or had it?

Olivia heard the electronic locks on the communications room door slide open, and Dwyer entered the room.

"You need to be fed."

"Not that hungry, Dan. But thanks."

"Nonsense, young lady. You're eating. I read somewhere that the brain uses up something like a gazillion watts of energy. That means short of hooking you up to a power plant, that big brain of yours needs about six thousand pounds of beef. We'll force-feed you if necessary."

"I'm anxious to talk to Jim."

"I'm anxious to talk to Angelina Jolie. Both of us may be in for a wait."

"What do you think the Russians are up to, Dan?"

"Same thing as you. Nothing good. Hope for the best, plan for the worst."

"What's the worst?"

"From a country with seven thousand nukes?"

"Realistically."

"Taras Bor is involved, Olivia. You tell me."

"Have you heard from Michael?"

"Not in a while."

"Bor won't stop trying to kill him, will he?"

"Is your concern personal or professional?"

"My concern is immediate. Things seem to be moving faster than we can keep up with. I'm concerned, Dan, that the endgame is approaching, that it will arrive before we have an inkling of what's really going on."

"I admit having the same concern," Dwyer agreed. "But the good news, Olivia, is that your hero and mine, Mike Garin, Defender of the Free World and Guardian of the Realm, is chewing gum, kicking butt, and taking names out there."

Olivia rolled her eyes.

"But seriously," Dwyer said, turning sober, "he always wins. Every single time. Without fail. I've seen it. Even you've seen some of it. And that means right now, as we speak, this very moment, the bad guys are losing, and losing really, really bad."

CHAPTER 60

There was a loud noise and a flash of light. Then he remembered a dull pain. Next came his older sister Katy's voice, strong and demanding.

He opened his eyes in a hospital bed, monitors arranged about him. Katy was at the foot of the bed talking to a doctor who was holding a clipboard with papers attached. She had a serious look on her face, like all Garins. They noted that he was awake and came to his side. Katy stroked his hair. She had a sad smile. Garin remembered and knew why.

"How do you feel?" she asked.

"Good. Are you okay?"

Katy's laugh was almost a cry. No matter what his condition, her little brother would always respond like that.

"Mom and Dad are dead," Katy said. Direct, no preliminaries, no softness. The family way. Take care of business, grieve when time allowed.

Garin nodded. It came back in a rush. The family was returning from an awards banquet. Garin had been named an all-state running back. A drunk driver hit them head-on. Garin's parents were killed instantly. Garin had been knocked unconscious. Katy had barely a scratch.

"Michael, I'm Dr. Lee." Garin saw a man in his early sixties, tall and lean with a look of confidence. "I'm very sorry for your loss."

Dr. Lee raised the clipboard and scanned the charts. He waited a few beats before continuing. "You have a concussion and some contusions.

No broken bones. Because of the concussion, we'll want to keep you under observation for twenty-four hours before discharging you."

Dr. Lee glanced at Katy before continuing. "When you were brought in we did the typical preliminary scans. The radiologist caught something, so we did a few more scans and tests."

Dr. Lee continued with a lengthy but not overly technical explanation. Something about valves and chambers. All that Garin remembered was the phrase "congenital heart defect." Dr. Lee tried to be optimistic, but it was likely Garin would not see his fortieth birthday, maybe not even his thirty-fifth.

A lone tear streaked down Katy's cheek; otherwise, she was composed. So much so that she followed Dr. Lee out of Garin's room, ostensibly to go to the hospital chapel, and when Dr. Lee deposited Garin's exam results at the vacant nurses' station and proceeded on his rounds, Katy retrieved the results and placed them in her purse. Then she quickly checked the station's desktop computer to confirm that the results hadn't yet been entered into the system. All record of Garin's condition was wiped from the face of the Earth.

Several months later, their grandfather, Nikolai Garin, arrived from Europe to care for them. With his death a few years back, Katy and Dr. Lee were the only ones who knew of Garin's condition. With passage of time and thousands of exams, Dr. Lee, if he was still alive, had probably long since forgotten.

Katy insisted Garin treat the heart anomaly as liberating. Knowing that he had only half the time he'd expected forced him to live life on fast-forward, compress eighty years of living into, at most, forty. So he held absolutely nothing back. He never paced himself. Although he wasn't irresponsible and avoided jeopardizing the safety of others, he took risks, confronted dangers, and overcame hazards that would cause others to shrink, flinch, and cower. He felt . . . invincible.

In some ways, he was tantamount to dead. The dead feel no pain; pain is irrelevant. The dead have no fear; fear is irrelevant.

The same is true for the doomed. Theoretically.

Garin wasn't dead yet.

The gash from the Butcher's mouth to his ear was the first thing that came into focus. Within seconds everything else did as well. He was back in the present.

Garin felt a sharp pain from his right ear to the sinus cavity under his right eye. It was the pain that had caused him to lose consciousness, but also roused him awake.

"You were out only a few minutes," the Butcher informed him. "And you did not scream. That will change."

Garin blinked several times and shook his head. His right cheek was wet and warm. Blood trickling from his ear.

"Your body's defense mechanisms are quite good," the Butcher continued. "Many subjects remain unconscious far longer. A few suffer heart failure. Your heart must be quite strong. But we're just getting started."

Garin realized he couldn't hear out of his right ear. He opened and closed his mouth and worked his jaw as if he had swimmer's ear. The sensation of pain changed from a sharpness to a dull ache.

The Butcher brought the needle to within inches of Garin's right eye. The act caused both of Garin's eyes to water.

"Tears from the indomitable Garin. I have caused the intrepid warrior to cry."

"Tears of joy, for your demise."

"Your continued bravado is, I freely admit, unusual. Past subjects have evacuated their bladders by this point, especially upon seeing the needle directed at an eye. The reaction is primal; the piercing of an eye is far more frightening than that of an ear."

"Do both," Garin pled. "It'll be a relief not to see your face any longer."

The Butcher tilted his head slightly, as an entomologist might upon observing a newly discovered insect species. The art of torture depended in large part on the ability to instill fear and dread in the subject. The Butcher was a master at choreographing the various steps of the process to bring such fear and dread to a crescendo. But Garin refused to dance.

"I do not take requests, Garin." The Butcher withdrew the needle, placed it on the metal table, and fired up the propane torch.

"Two thousand degrees, Garin," the Butcher said, adjusting the flow valve. "That is Celsius. Three thousand six hundred Fahrenheit. Enough to quickly cut through the meat of the thigh to the femur in a few seconds. Done correctly, there is little bleeding, as the heat cauterizes the wound. The emphasis is on 'correctly'; otherwise, there may be a mess."

The Butcher looked from the flame back to Garin's face. The unsettling look persisted.

"A more useful approach, however, is to apply the flame to an area that has comparatively little muscle or fat: The face, hands, and feet are ideal. Pain impulses normally travel at a slower rate than other nerve signals, usually no more than two to three feet per second. But the impulses seem to be conveyed much more quickly in these areas. And felt more acutely."

"Less talking, more doing," Garin said. "Otherwise you'll miss the big show."

"Although you have no idea what you are talking about, you have stumbled onto good counsel. The event is scheduled soon and I should be on my way shortly."

"Bor is central to the event," Garin said.

"This only confirms you know nothing of the event. The event consists of two stages and a backup. Bor is central to the backup."

"Thank you for the information. It'll come in handy."

The Butcher nodded. "In hell, perhaps. Bor insisted you be killed before the first stage was initiated. I am told he conveyed this insistence to Mikhailov himself."

"I'm flattered."

"You have a right to be, Garin. One person cannot stop the plan, yet Bor is sufficiently concerned that he made your elimination a prerequisite."

"Tell me about it so I have a sporting chance of stopping it."

"You may trust me, Garin. Since you are a dead man, I would tell you if I knew. But they do not entrust details to someone like me. I know little, other than you will be paralyzed."

"Then, what *do* you know?"

"The first stage only."

"What does it entail?"

"Again, I know little of it."

"As you said, I'm a dead man. Grant me my dying wish. Like a ciga-rette before a firing squad."

"The first stage consists of suicide bombers."

"Russia doesn't use suicide bombers."

"Russia does not use Russian suicide bombers, yes. As a means to an end, however, Russia will use suicide bombers who believe they are striking against the West on behalf of ISIS."

"Very cynical."

"Not really. The suicide bombers, with our assistance, are getting exactly what they want. It just happens to serve Russian interests also."

"Marginally clever. How many suicide bombers?"

"I do not know."

"When will they set off their bombs?"

"I do not know that either. Very soon."

"Where will they set off the bombs?"

"Again—"

"You don't know much, do you?"

"I know that it is a misdirection, to make you think the threat has passed, and to relax your guard."

"Then the real event, so to speak, occurs."

The Butcher nodded. "That is my understanding."

"And Bor's part of a backup plan."

"Nikolai Garin surely taught you that Russians play chess . . ."

"Yes."

"You are not even competent at checkers, Garin."

"What's the purpose? The endgame?"

"I do not know."

"Well, you're no help." Garin nodded toward the table where the Butcher had placed the torch. "Your torch is burning. Do your thing."

"Before I resume, it is your turn. Tell me what you know about the event."

"What you've just told me is the sum total of what I know about the event. May I offer an opinion, though?"

"What is that, Garin?"

"It's going to fail."

"Let us resume." The Butcher picked up the parabolic razor from the table and displayed it to Garin. "This is used to peel the skin. There is some disagreement over its most effective manner of use. My preference is to use it in tandem with the torch. An incision is made across the top of the hand at the knuckles. Because your wrists are secured to the armrest, however, in this instance, we will begin at the forearm. The skin is pulled back a few centimeters toward the elbow and beyond. Then the flame is used to cauterize the wound. The process is repeated until death. If you had any useful information to impart, there would be a pause after each cauterization to interrogate. Since you have no information, this will go rather quickly."

"Take your time. I don't have to be anywhere soon."

"You no longer need to convince me. Like Bor, your training has made you hard and tough. It is, however, irrelevant."

"No, Nikolai Garin made me hard and tough." *And I have nothing to lose,* Garin thought. *I never have.*

"I had to use quite a bit of duct tape to bind you to the chair, Garin. You are quite strong. Therefore, I will have to begin the incision just above the wrist."

Garin remained silent. He willed himself to resist screaming.

The Butcher scooted his chair a few inches closer to Garin to make it easier to wield the blade over Garin's right arm. Garin jacked backward to scoot his chair away, but the weight of the chair prevented him from moving more than a few inches.

"Futile, Garin."

The Butcher leaned closer to Garin. As he did so, Garin whipped his head backward, then forward, as hard and fast as he could. Garin's forehead slammed into the Butcher's forehead just above the bridge of his nose, driving him backward off his chair and onto the floor, where he lay stunned and barely conscious. Bound to the chair, Garin leaned forward and extended his legs and stood as high as he could, lifting the rear of the chair several inches off the floor. He shuffled rapidly toward the Butcher and positioned the right rear leg of the chair over the Butcher's head and neck as he lay prone on his back. Garin drove downward as hard as he could, impaling the center of the Butcher's throat with the heavy metal leg of the chair. Garin rose and drove back down again, this time impaling the lower portion of the throat. Garin rose and drove downward again. And again. And again. And again, until the Butcher's pulverized throat was an unrecognizable mass of blood, bone, and cartilage.

Garin assessed his options. The razor was useless in freeing him since both of his hands were bound to the arms of the chair. That left the propane torch sitting on the metal table. The problem was it was too far from the edge to be of use.

Garin shuffled to the table, lowered his shoulder, and rammed it into the apron. The torch wobbled but remained upright. He struck the table again and the torch toppled onto its side and rolled. He struck it again and the torch rolled off the other side of the table onto the floor.

Garin shuffled to where the torch was melting the plastic covering on the floor and awkwardly flipped himself onto his left side. For the next minute he wriggled and squirmed to slide closer to the torch and align his left wrist with the flame. He paused upon drawing to within a few inches of the torch and steeled himself. The only way to free himself was to make one final thrust to within an inch or two of the flame and burn the duct tape from his wrist. No sense hesitating. Pain was unavoidable. Get it over with.

He bit his lower lip and kicked and thrust himself to within centimeters of the flame, but he was misaligned. The acrid smell of the flesh burning his forearm arrived only milliseconds after the searing heat blistered much of the area around the brachialis.

He kept biting his lip as he kicked and swiveled to position the duct-taped wrist next to the flame. The flame caused the polyethylene to bubble and boil, exposing the rayon fabric, which flashed and quickly separated, but not before also burning a gash into the top of Garin's wrist. His lungs emitted a low, feral growl of agony as he tore his wrist from the arm of the chair and shunted himself away from the flame. He growled once more as he tore the duct tape from his right wrist, then from his torso and each ankle.

Garin stood slowly and conducted an inventory. The skin along the top of his left forearm to his wrist was a gash of scarlet and black, deformed like melted plastic. The Butcher lay dead on top of his chair, next to the metal table. The metal box, needles, razor, and torch were scattered across the plastic, a section of which had been liquefied by the propane torch.

Garin spotted a roll of duct tape still inside the metal toolbox. He tore a strip of cloth from the Butcher's shirt, wrapped it around the wound. Then, with his right hand, he placed the roll over his left wrist and wound the tape around his forearm from wrist to elbow. The pain produced yet another growl, and his eyes watered. In a perfect world, he would be either loaded with painkillers or—preferably—sedated when the tape was removed.

He picked up the torch and turned it off. Then he walked to the metal door, and even though the Butcher had told him the room was soundproof, he put his ear to it. He heard nothing.

He briefly considered picking up the razor as a weapon but decided it wasn't worth it. His hands were good enough.

Garin visualized the layout of the house. It was a modest ranch-style affair. From his surveillance, he estimated that it had seven rooms, probably consisting of a standard three bedrooms, bath, kitchen, living room, and dining room. There was an attached garage. He hadn't seen any signs the house was occupied, but, of course, the curtains had been drawn.

According to the Butcher, the entrance to the room Garin was in was undetectable. He surmised it was hidden behind a wall in the basement.

Garin opened the door slowly. The short passageway immediately outside was illuminated by a single low-wattage light bulb hanging from a low ceiling. There was a metal ladder at the far end leading to a trap-door. He climbed up a few rungs until he was hunched under the door, paused, and listened. Nothing. He burst upward through the trapdoor onto a concrete floor and spun around in a crouch, prepared to engage the Butcher's associates.

There was no one to engage. He'd emerged into an empty two-car garage.

The door leading into the house was at his left. He lowered the trap-door slowly and quietly until it was flush with the concrete garage floor. The Butcher was right. No one would've found the torture room, at least not right away.

Garin crossed to the door and listened. He heard nothing. He turned the knob and opened the door slowly. Standing a few feet away at a breakfast nook in the kitchen was a fit, military-age male about Garin's size with a look of astonishment on his face. Clearly, he'd been expect-ing the Butcher, not Garin.

Garin closed the space between the two in a blur and jammed the three middle fingers of his right hand into the man's throat. The man dropped to the floor retching, gagging, and reaching behind him for the handgun in a holster at the small of his back. Garin reached it first. The man continued to gag and his face turned from red to purple to blue. His windpipe was crushed.

A second man appeared in the doorway separating the kitchen from a small dining room. Garin shot him in the forehead just above the bridge of his nose. Then Garin did the same to the man gasping for air on the floor.

Garin released the magazine on the weapon and checked the am-munition. He had several rounds left. He reseated it and listened for movement in the house. Nothing. After a few seconds he moved to the dining room, weapon at the ready. He scanned it quickly before moving to the living room and then clearing each of the bedrooms and the bathroom. He then opened the doorway in the hall leading from the dining room to the bedrooms. Stairs led to a dark basement. He flipped the switch at the top of the stairs and waited. He saw and heard nothing. He began a quick cost-benefit analysis of descending the stairs, but the pain in his forearm and ear made him too angry and incautious not to proceed. If any of the Butcher's associates were down there, he was going to kill them.

Any associates in the basement had a tactical advantage. They could simply train their weapons at the bottom of the stairs, wait for Garin to come down, and open fire.

So Garin sprinted down the stairs, rolled onto the basement floor, and came up on one knee, scanning about a small rec room. No associates. He emitted another growl, having struck the burnt forearm during the fall. He took several deep breaths while he tried to mentally suppress the pain.

Other than Garin and the corpses he'd left, the house was empty. He looked about the basement for anything related to Bor, then went back upstairs and did the same, beginning with the bedrooms, followed by the bathroom, living room, dining room, and kitchen. The house was clear. No evidence, no clues about what Bor was up to. Except . . .

Garin rifled through the pockets of the dead man in the dining room. No wallet, no identification, not a shred of pocket litter.

The pockets of the dead man in the kitchen also contained no wallet, no identification, nor any other items. Except his right front pocket held one five-by-seven-inch piece of paper with ten lines of handwritten letters and numbers.

Garin studied the paper for several seconds before putting it in his pocket. He couldn't discern the meaning or import of the lines, but he planned to have Dwyer's people analyze them.

Assuming it wasn't too late.

CHAPTER 61

Egorshin answered the knock on the door of Tatiana Palinieva's apartment immediately. It was Sergei Morosov.

"Come in."

Egorshin led Morosov to the living room, where they sat in opposing chairs.

"Tatiana is at a production meeting. She will be gone for some time," Egorshin said, rubbing his hands nervously. "Stetchkin is going to kill me. I can feel it. His behavior toward me is incomprehensible. He hates me for no reason."

"I have spoken to Vasiliev, Piotr."

"You have? Thank you. Has he spoken to Mikhailov?"

"Yes." Morosov crossed his legs. "Piotr, what do you know of Tatiana's past relationships?"

Egorshin looked befuddled. "Why do you ask?"

"I should be more direct. I suspect you have absolutely no idea that a few years ago Tatiana spurned the advances of one Aleksandr Stetchkin?"

Egorshin sat straight with his hands on his knees, a look of surprise on his face. "What? How did you get this information?"

"I am SVR."

"What do you mean she spurned him?"

"From what I gather, Stetchkin became enamored . . ." Morosov paused. "No, enthralled with Tatiana when she was still in the fashion industry. He arranged to meet her. I am told—I do not know how my sources know this, but it is eminently believable—that he assisted her transition to television, that he is the reason she got the opportunity to host her program. She gladly took advantage of the opportunity. The story I was told is that she manipulated Stetchkin's affections quite adroitly until she was secure in her position and then ignored him. She did not take his calls. She refused to see him."

"Tatiana is the reason Stetchkin hates me?"

"It appears so."

"She never told me anything about this. She knows I have been experiencing difficulties with Stetchkin, but she never uttered a word."

"Perhaps she's not proud of her actions, but it is not as if her conduct was unique in history. And Stetchkin certainly hoped that Tatiana would accept his offer of assistance. Whether she reciprocated as he hoped was a gamble, not a contract."

"So Stetchkin wants me out of the way so he may pursue Tatiana."

"So to speak."

The look on Egorshin's face was that of near panic. Morosov leaned forward and patted his nephew's knee.

"Calm yourself, Piotr. Mikhailov is just as ruthless as Stetchkin, but smarter. More important, Mikhailov is president. He will not permit Stetchkin to harm you."

"Are you certain? I may only be of use to Mikhailov until . . ."

Egorshin fell silent.

"I know you are involved in something of importance to Mikhailov, Piotr. I am informed that Mikhailov considers you valuable even after the important thing is concluded, whatever it may be."

"That would give me comfort if I thought Stetchkin were rational. A rational person would not do anything to incur Mikhailov's displeasure, let alone his wrath. I remain concerned that Stetchkin will let his impulses overcome his intelligence."

"Vasiliev informs me that Mikhailov made clear to Stetchkin that he was to leave you alone. Stetchkin has been around too long to make the mistake of letting his interest in women negatively affect his fortunes—even a woman as attractive as Tatiana."

Egorshin shook his head. "All of this for Tatiana? Do not

misunderstand. Of course she is attractive. Spectacular. But it is crazy for a man as powerful as Stetchkin to jeopardize his position for her. And I believe he *is* crazy. Anyone who saw what he did to Uganov would concur."

Morosov smiled. "So, I suspect, since you are my sister's son and since my sister is insufferably prepared for any and every eventuality, that you have made plans to further protect yourself."

"I have not."

Morosov arched his eyebrows. "That is not like Svetlana."

"I have made preparations, but not to protect myself. Such preparations are futile. If Stetchkin is determined enough to try to kill me in defiance of Mikhailov, then I am a dead man. Nothing can save me. So I have made other preparations."

"To what end?"

"Revenge."

"Revenge? How does a dead man exact revenge?"

"Through his uncle, the magician."

"You are asking me to kill Stetchkin? Do you want our entire family killed?"

"I do not want you to kill Stetchkin. Mikhailov will do it."

"Then what would you have me do?"

Egorshin reached into his pocket, pulled out a small object, and pressed it into his uncle's palm. Morosov examined it with a quizzical expression. "And what is this?"

"Revenge."

CHAPTER 62

Bor reports that all assets are in place and they are ready to execute."
Mikhailov leaned back in his chair and steepled his fingers in
front of his chest. "Is he satisfied that the impediment has been removed?"

"He made no mention of the impediment. I gather, therefore, that in
his estimation he is no longer an issue," Vasiliev replied.

"No matter. The impediment was Bor's concern, not ours. The event
would take place regardless. Summon General Maximov, Stetchkin,
and Egorshin. Tell them to meet me for a final briefing before implementation."

Stetchkin sat alone in his office examining time-lapse aerial photographs of Russian troop movements in the Caucasus on his desktop
computer. There were dozens of photographs spanning the last three
days. The last series of six photographs showed no movements whatsoever. The troops had reached their penultimate destination. Now
they were merely staging, coordinating, and preparing.

Stetchkin tapped his keyboard and a completely unrelated image
appeared. It was a single document: the final assessment report from
Egorshin's unit, prepared by Egorshin himself. All simulations had been
concluded. The unit's preparations were complete.

Stetchkin manipulated the mouse and the screen displayed another
image pertaining to Egorshin's unit. It was a long list of categories and
names. Next to each was a small box. Every single box contained a

checkmark. In the upper-right-hand corner of the screen was a small digital clock, the numbers of which were declining. It was a countdown. Very little time remained before all of the digits reached zero.

Stetchkin tapped the speaker function on his desk phone and then pressed four keys. There was a brief buzzing sound before someone picked up.

"Yes, sir."

"It is time," Stetchkin said and disconnected.

CHAPTER 63

Local police arrived at the parking lot behind the woods in the rear of the dead man's house almost contemporaneously with Congo Knox picking Garin up from the front. Knox had waited, as Garin requested, for a time before placing an anonymous call to alert the police of the dead bodies to give Garin time to surveil the entire house.

Knox drove toward Dwyer's house, where Dwyer, Matt, Olivia, and additional DGT personnel were assembled.

"You look like hell," Knox observed.

"Thanks."

"Cut your arm?"

"Propane torch."

"My mom told me to be careful around open flames."

"I'll try to remember that."

"Why are you doing this, Mike?"

Garin looked sharply at Knox. "What do you mean, why am I doing this? Did you somehow forget the shootout in Dale City? Did you forget about the EMP? Forget Bor?"

"No, Mike. I mean why you? Why do you, as opposed to anyone and everyone else in our security apparatus, have to do this?"

"Because right now, who else is there? Besides you, Dan, Olivia, and Matt?"

"There's no Omega anymore. But even if the nation's security apparatus was involved, I bet you'd still be involved. So why you?"

"Why not? I'm an operator. I'm an American."

"Okay, then, how?"

"You lost me, Congo."

"You're . . ." Knox searched for a word. "Inexorable. You keep coming, like some genetic freak—if there's a gene for determination, that is. You act like you can't die."

Garin didn't respond. *I can't,* he thought. *I'm already dead.*

"So, did you get anything useful in there?"

"Maybe. How long until we get to Dwyer's?"

"With the traffic, about twenty-five minutes."

"I ran into four of Bor's associates but got very little from them."

"I assume they're all room temperature now." It was not a question.

"Whatever they've got planned, it's going to happen soon and it's going to 'paralyze' us. And it involves suicide bombers. At least in part. Supposedly, Bor's not part of the main event. He's part of a backup plan."

"You don't know who, how, where, what, etcetera?"

"I don't know jack, except . . ." Garin pulled out the piece of paper. "I found what looks like a to-do list. I don't know what it means, but part of it looks like times. Maybe for the suicide bombings."

"The president wants to talk to you."

"I take it Olivia talked to Brandt and Brandt talked to Marshall."

"Yes. You've got the president's attention now. What are you going to tell him?"

"What I just told you, Congo. That's all I've got. And I'm going to emphasize the need for Omega and authority."

"Think he'll do it?"

"Marshall's serious. He won't hesitate if he thinks it's necessary."

"He's also a politician."

"He's an American first."

"One of only three in Washington who is."

"It's not that bad, Congo."

"Worse."

"Very cynical, Congo."

"You think so? I was ordered to kill you, remember?"

"Point taken. And the person who gave that order is still out there. Do you think he or she acted alone?"

"Well, we know Julian Day was part of it."

"Besides him."

"Who knows, Mike? Regardless, it sure wasn't some GS-14 at the Department of Agriculture. It had to have been a big-time heavyweight. Really big-time." Knox paused while turning onto I-95. "What do you mean we're going to be paralyzed?"

"It's the word one of Bor's guys used. Paralyzed. If I take it literally, it might refer to immobilizing our transportation capabilities. Maybe communications."

"If you take it literally. But toward what end? Even if they could somehow immobilize our transportation or communications, how does that benefit the Russians? My guess is it's a figure of speech, not literal."

"That's the problem. We're guessing. We need more intel."

Knox snorted. "Who's going to give it to us?"

The pain in Garin's arm continued to anger him.

"Bor."

CHAPTER 64

The segment would go very well, she thought. Things were lining up nicely.

Tatiana Palinieva had finished preparations with her production team for a report on the recent massive increase in natural gas production by the Russian energy giant, Gazprom. The increase had significant ramifications, including a projected fifteen to eighteen percent decline in the price of natural gas sold to Europe. That decline assured European dependence on Russian natural gas for the foreseeable future, a major strategic coup for Mikhailov.

Now all Tatiana wanted to do was relax with a cup of tea and tell Piotr about the upcoming piece, yet another step on the seemingly endless ladder of her success. Only last month she'd received a sizable increase in her salary, including a bonus that, standing alone, constituted a year's rent on her unit in one of the most exclusive apartment buildings in Moscow. Her modeling income had been substantial, but early in her former career she began saving and making plans for when age would reduce her demand. Although in her late thirties, ancient by fashion industry standards, Tatiana was still youthful-looking enough to continue modeling, but she was shrewd enough to have made an early transition to television news, which was only somewhat less ruthless when it came to cosmetic considerations.

The apartment building was opulent, quiet, and stately. She saw her neighbors so rarely that it seemed as if she was one of only a handful of residents. On the rare occasions she shared an elevator with another occupant, they'd exchange only a brief, polite greeting. No one ever made a fuss about her celebrity status. It was a relief, although she found herself occasionally wishing someone did treat her like a star. But that was all right. Once she stepped out on the street, passersby would stare, point, and wave. Some would commend her for a particular story or recommend a topic for another.

Every person in the city recognized her face. Every woman envied her beauty and admired her attire. Most men didn't dare approach her, concluding they had no chance. Only the occasional oligarch or high government official would make a play.

She and Piotr had been together nearly two years. He was neither an oligarch nor a high governmental official, but it was clear he was a rocket headed to the stars. Piotr's looks were, at best, slightly above average. In fact, their public appearances together presented a visual contrast somewhat akin to Grace Kelly and Prince Rainier; not staggering, but notable.

Tatiana's income was far greater than Piotr's, but it was clear it was only a matter of time before that would change, and probably dramatically. Piotr had all the right contacts in all the right circles, not because of shrewd networking, but because he was valuable, almost indispensable. He was uncommonly smart and a tireless worker. He could figure things out. He could get things done.

Tatiana had started out liking Piotr. He was interesting, a polymath who could discuss a variety of topics. And not merely in a superficial or pedantic way, but with depth and a sly sense of humor. He was considerate and sported a charm that was a cross between old-world courtliness and new-world irreverence.

Tatiana grew to love Piotr—only the second man in her life after her father. She was sure he would ask her to marry him and was a bit impressed, if not mystified, that he hadn't already. Most past boyfriends had proposed marriage within months, if not weeks. Piotr, however, had more confidence.

He was working on something of some magnitude. That was plain.

It consumed most of his time, as well as attention that would otherwise be directed at her. But whatever it was, it appeared to be drawing to a conclusion. And after that he would propose.

It was the manner and venue of the proposal that occupied her mind when the doors of the elevator opened silently on the eighth floor. She considered a number of possibilities, but Piotr was so creative and unpredictable that she suspected the proposal would be different from anything she could envision.

But as she placed her card key next to the electronic pad of the door to her apartment, it came to her and she smiled. Piotr wouldn't propose to her. She wouldn't give him the chance. She would propose to him. Here. Right now. Why not?

She also was creative and occasionally unpredictable. It would be a wonderful surprise. The perfect way to celebrate the completion of Piotr's project and the success of her program. She knew she'd remember forever the look of surprise that would cover his face.

And Tatiana was right. When she opened the door and entered the foyer, she saw Piotr sitting on a lounge chair directly in front of her, staring at the ceiling. He had a look of surprise on his face. And a bullet hole in his forehead.

CHAPTER 65

They were waiting for Garin and Knox on the east patio: Dwyer, Olivia, Matt, Luci, and two others from DGT, Ty Wilson and Isaac Coe, the latter a former corpsman.

Knox had alerted Dwyer to the condition of Garin's arm, and Dwyer had summoned Coe to tend to Garin.

The six looked on anxiously as Garin and Knox climbed the steps. Dwyer motioned to Coe, who approached Garin to administer treatment, only to stop cold upon seeing the unamused look on his face.

"Later, Dan. I need to talk to the president."

"Michael, that can wait," Olivia said. "Have your arm taken care of first."

The statement was registered by the same region of Garin's brain that had stored Olivia's previous expressions of concern and interest. Thinking he had the green light, Coe approached Garin once again, only to be met by a look that had gone from cold to glacial.

Garin was silent. Dwyer simply led Garin through the French doors into the library and down to the communications room in the subbasement. Olivia followed, while Luci took Knox's hand and sat with him on the patio.

Dwyer punched the keypad next to the communications room door. The bolts slid open and the heavy steel door swung aside.

"I suspect I'm not cleared for this, so I'll leave you two alone. Please give the commander in chief my regards and tell him I voted for him last year. Once in the primary and twice in the general."

Dwyer withdrew. The door closed and the bolts locked into place.

Olivia caught Garin's eye and nodded at his arm. "What happened?"

"Small accident."

"It doesn't look small."

"I'll take care of it. First, the president."

Olivia moved to one side of the captain's chair, pressed the speaker-phone function, and keyed Brandt's office number. Garin stood next to the opposite arm rest.

Brandt himself answered. "Yes?"

"Professor, I have Michael Garin with me. He's calling for the president."

"Hold on. This will take a minute. I'll have the call patched to the Situation Room. The president, Kessler, and Secretary of Defense Merritt will be there momentarily, and I'm joining them."

There was a click and then silence.

"It will take Arlo and the Secret Service a few minutes to get him there," Olivia said. She looked Garin up and down. The incongruity in his appearance was ever present: intensity in a relaxed body.

"Can you tell me how that happened?" Olivia asked, nodding at his arm.

"Just an occupational hazard." The gravedigger's voice.

"You could always change occupations."

Garin didn't respond.

"Jim says the president thinks very highly of you. There's been some discussion of issuing a commendation to you for"—Olivia smiled—"well, averting a war. The president seems to want you in a policy position."

Garin's single shake of his head conveyed finality: no way.

"At some point you won't be able to do what you're doing now, at least not at the same level. The cumulative effect of the physical traumas will slow you down. I saw it among some of my father's friends in the NFL. They'd lose a half step, then a step—enough to lose their starting spots, then their spots on the team. Your job is more punishing by an order of magnitude. If you lose a step . . ."

"I'm dead," Garin acknowledged. *I'm dead anyway*, Garin thought.

"During the EMP crisis James Brandt had me research you. Dan gave me background, that you weren't expected to live at birth; your twin died in utero and you were infirm for much of your childhood."

"This sounds like a prelude to psychoanalysis."

"No." Olivia shook her head. "Just suggesting you might consider easing back a bit, enjoying life with less peril."

"Are you enjoying life as an aide to the NSA?"

"It's what I'm trained to do." A flick of her impossible abundance of hair off her left shoulder. "It's what I *want* to do."

"I'm doing what I want to do, Olivia."

She examined him for several seconds. "What you want to do may be fatal."

"Everyone dies."

"Very Homeric. But even Achilles, Hector, and Ajax didn't seek to expedite it, Michael. You're entitled to some enjoyment in life."

"As are you."

Olivia cocked her head, bemused. "You don't think I enjoy myself?"

"You work twenty-four/seven. Now *you're* forgetting Aurelius, Plutarch, and Goethe."

Olivia laughed. "You're mocking me."

"I can reference the classics too. Ivy League and all."

"Remember, I've seen what you do, Michael."

"And you disapprove."

"No. Well, admittedly, seeing you kill people was . . . I wasn't prepared for that. But you came close to being killed yourself. The odds will catch up to you, eventually."

"Thank you."

"For what?"

It was Garin's turn to appear bemused. "Very few people express concern about my well-being, let alone my career path."

"The Washington policy world needs a Michael Garin. Washington, in general, needs adults."

"I can't disagree with that."

"You just might find that your talents are even better suited for making policy rather than executing it. Washington needs more people who don't suffer fools gladly."

A whisper of a smile briefly crossed Garin's face. "A great American philosopher said, 'A man's got to know his limitations.'"

Olivia laughed. Garin found it musical.

"I love that movie. I love all the Dirty Harry movies."

"Even *The Dead Pool*?"

Another laugh, just as musical. "I'd like to binge-watch them sometime."

A not so subtle opening not lost on Garin. Before he could respond, a click came over the speakerphone.

"Mr. Garin, this is the president."

"Yes, Mr. President. Olivia Perry is with me, sir."

"Secretary of Defense Merritt, John Kessler, and Jim Brandt are with me. I understand you want to reconstitute Omega and want authority. Tell me what's going on."

"Sir, there have been a series of events that indicate that the Russians are about to strike us. It could be minutes, hours, or days—but it'll be a two-stage attack conducted somewhere on American soil. The first stage will consist of an unknown number of suicide bombers. The locations of the bombings also are unknown.

"The bombings are a feint, an attempt to lull us into complacency. Sometime after, another attack will occur, presumably of greater magnitude. I'm told it will 'paralyze' us. I have no further details on the main attack."

"Who told you the attack will paralyze us?"

"An associate of the Russian agent Taras Bor."

"Who is this man?"

"He has no name. He referred to himself as the Butcher."

"Where is he now?"

"He's dead, sir."

"I see."

"Sir, I was told there's a backup to the main attack. Taras Bor is expected to execute the secondary plan if the main attack is prevented. Again, no details on the backup plan either."

"Mike." It was Deputy Director Kessler. "Do you have any evidence with which we can confront the Russians about this?"

"There have been several attempts on my life. But I have captured no one and the men I've killed had no evidence on them signifying Russian involvement."

"How many men, Mr. Garin?" Marshall asked.

Garin hesitated, glancing at Olivia. "Several."

"How do we know the Butcher isn't some crazy man?" the president asked. "How do we know someone, say the Chinese, isn't trying to foment a conflict between the US and Russia? How can we be sure this isn't a false-flag operation?"

"Mr. President, we can't. We have nothing concrete. Obviously, nothing that would qualify as proof in a court of law."

"Or the court of public opinion," Marshall said. "Mr. Garin, even if I were to reconstitute Omega, it doesn't have authority to operate domestically, not without congressional approval or a finding of a nuclear threat. We have no evidence to support that."

"I understand completely, Mr. President. I cannot provide concrete evidence, but it's clear this is a Bor operation. You know what that means."

"I believe you. But belief is insufficient. Although we seem to be forgetting it with increasing frequency, we're still a democratic republic subject to the rule of law. There's a reason for those checks and balances. There's a reason for *posse comitatus*. This type of domestic situation calls for the FBI, not a special operations unit of the military."

"Sir, hard evidence or not, Bor is involved. And where Bor is involved, we need tier-one special operators."

"We can't stand up a functional tier-one unit with a snap of our fingers anyway."

"Mr. President, I have a number of former special operators ready to go right now."

"I know how smart you are. So I know that you know I can't sanction private citizens like that. Even if I somehow recommissioned them, it would set off an earthquake."

"We need specially trained people for Bor."

"Mr. Garin, the FBI has extraordinary SWAT capabilities, HRT."

"No argument. But, respectfully, this isn't a standard domestic operation. This is a hybrid. And remember, sir, we haven't discovered who the Russian mole is. Julian Day wasn't high enough. If we tell the FBI or Congress, the Russians will know and evade our every action."

Muffled sounds came over the speaker. Then: "Just a moment, Mr. Garin." The speaker was muted at the president's end.

Kessler said to the president, "Mr. President, we've seen what Bor can do, all too recently. He's on a different plane from everyone else. We've also seen what Garin can do. He's our best counter to Bor. He's asking to be put in the fight, with a little help. We could provide him with logistical assistance where necessary, drawn from our Title 50 funds. Even my people don't need to know what's happening. At least specifically. It would be opaque. Untraceable. Deniable."

"And unlawful," Marshall interjected.

"Mr. President, the Constitution is not a suicide pact. If we follow the letter of the law, we may not be able to protect the American people. The EMP plot, had it been successful, would have killed millions. The Founding Fathers couldn't possibly have envisioned something like an EMP attack."

"They didn't have to. The Constitution and the rule of law still apply regardless of technological developments."

Secretary of Defense Merritt said, "Mr. President, if you violate the law by authorizing special operations on US soil, you are, indeed, subject to the law. But, as I think you know, the Office of Legal Counsel of the attorney general twice in our history determined that a sitting president is not subject to criminal prosecution. Instead, the remedy would be impeachment and removal from office. If it became known that you authorized special operations on American soil to protect against an extraordinary threat to the American people—no Congress would ever move articles of impeachment."

"So you're saying I should knowingly violate the law because my actions will be popular?"

"No, not at all. I'm saying sometimes a commander in chief's got to bear the consequences of being between a rock and a hard place. Mr. President, it's the old question about exigent circumstances: If you know that a nuclear device is about to go off in an American city, would you violate the law to stop it? Or would you adhere to the rule of law and allow millions of Americans to die? For all we know, we may be facing that situation here. We saw just a few weeks ago that if Bor's involved, this isn't going to be some garden-variety attack." Merritt straightened. "Sir."

"What's your advice, Jim?" Marshall asked Brandt.

"You need to be very careful, sir."

"Mr. President," Merritt continued. "You've been in office less than a year. Your predecessor, with all due respect to him, left you a mess—pretending all the world was our friend. You shouldn't have had to face one such crisis in your first year, let alone two. But here we are. Your first duty is to protect America and the American people."

"My first duty, Doug, is to protect and defend the Constitution. There is no America without the Constitution."

"You can do both, Mr. President. Authorize Omega. Let Garin stop Bor. Then, afterward, let Congress know. If they determine you've committed an impeachable offense, and if they have the political will, they can impeach you, remove you from office, and you can stand for prosecution. Checks and balances. The system works."

"That's not how the system's supposed to work," Marshall said. "I want a meeting of the NSC here within the hour." He stood silently and rubbed the back of his neck for several moments; then he unmuted the speakerphone.

"Sorry, Mr. Garin. We've been talking Civics 101." Marshall sighed and paused several more moments, surveying the faces of the men surrounding him. "Do what you have to do, Mr. Garin. I'll have your back. That's all I can say."

"Understood, Mr. President."

The line went dead.

Olivia looked puzzled. "What in the world does that mean?"

"It means a good man has been put in an impossible position," Garin replied. "And I'm going to do my best to get him out of it."

CHAPTER 66

Yuri Mikhailov rose from the chair behind his desk and arched his back. Sitting for long periods of time occasionally produced lower-back spasms, a consequence of a weight-training injury during his days as an athlete. His physician had recommended surgery, but Mikhailov considered the pain a mere nuisance he could live with.

There was a short rap at the door and Vasiliev entered.

"Piotr Egorshin is dead."

Mikhailov showed no reaction. His face was impassive. Vasiliev had seen the look many times before. It wasn't indifference. It was cold, shrewd calculation. The ultimate poker face. Mikhailov's mind was assessing the implications and formulating a strategy. Several questions and commands would be forthcoming.

Vasiliev said, "He was found in Palinieva's apartment a short time ago. He'd been shot in the head."

"Stetchkin," Mikhailov said.

"Evidently."

"I want to know who Stetchkin commissioned to kill Egorshin and where that person is within the next thirty minutes. Direct FSB to send me transcripts of all of Stetchkin's communications—whether by land-lines, cell phones, laptop—for the last twenty-four hours. I want transcripts for the communications of all of his principal assistants also. Tell FSB Stetchkin is not to leave their sight. And then tell Stetchkin to be here at precisely 7:00 A.M."

"Anything else?"

"Does Egorshin's death affect our plans in any way?"

"Stetchkin was right. Everything is in place. Egorshin's death is immaterial to the success of the event."

"I told him he could take no action against Egorshin. I was clear about that." Mikhailov paused. "Where is Palinieva?"

"She was the one who found Egorshin's body in her apartment upon returning from a meeting. She placed the call to Moscow police. I assume she is still at the apartment."

"Make sure there is sufficient security with her at all times. She is to be kept perfectly safe. And Stetchkin must not be permitted anywhere near her."

Vasiliev nodded and began to leave.

"Wait."

Vasiliev stopped, turned, and nodded deferentially.

"Who will execute the event now that Egorshin is dead?"

"It is my understanding it is a Major Volkov, Egorshin's second."

"I assume he is highly competent; otherwise, he would not have been in such a position."

"All reports indicate he should be more than capable of handling the task. He is not in Egorshin's class, but Egorshin trained Volkov well. It is my understanding that Egorshin planned for such a contingency—not necessarily his death, of course, but some form of incapacity or circumstance preventing him from personally handling the matter. He was very thorough. In fact, Volkov is only one of three individuals Egorshin trained to act in case of an emergency."

"Very good. Have Volkov and the other two individuals Egorshin trained—what are their names?"

"Major Gennady Tokarsky and Major Igor Starpov."

"Have all three of them report here no later than 7:00 A.M."

"Very well, sir."

"Where is Bor at this moment?"

"I believe he is at the embassy in Washington."

"Contact him. If he is not at the embassy, find him—and have him contact me. No one, either here or at the embassy, must know. Alpha protocol."

her? She seems to have taken a liking to you. Not surprising. You're both unmanageable SOBs. In her case, almost literally."

"Dan, I might need help tracking and stopping Bor."

"So the president's not going to officially reconstitute Omega—at least not without Congress. That's not surprising. In fact, it would be astonishing if he did. Can you tell me what he *is* willing to do?"

"No."

"Vague assurances, at least?"

"I can't make any representations on his behalf."

Dwyer nodded. "I understand. Once again, if things go south, we're on our own."

"Not necessarily, Dan."

"Mike, I think the world of Marshall. He's a stand-up guy, unlike his predecessor. Hell, unlike most in this town. But you've been in this situation more than just about anyone. You know when the operation blows up, everyone on the White House staff is going to insist that the president plead ignorance. And for the greater good, he's got to. Because it's not about his character or honesty or commitment to you. It's about what's best for the country. The country can't afford to think that the president of the United States authorizes secret kill teams—and make no mistake, that's how it will be portrayed. So even though I believe Marshall's got the best of intentions, we're on our own. Again."

"You're such a cynic."

"But I'm way ahead of you, Mikey, as usual. I polled a few of our guys I know I can trust. Asked them whether anyone was interested in embarking on a kill-or-be-killed mission with the Myth, the Legend, the Man All Women Want and All Men Want to Be, to save democracy, the country, and the American way of life. And inexplicably, a bunch of them raised their hands." Dwyer sported a quizzical look. "Now that I think of it, it's pretty clear we need to do a better job vetting these guys for mental stability during the hiring process. Anyway, I picked Ike, Ty, and Congo before you even got here."

"Thank you."

"You know Congo's background, of course. Ike is former Six. He was a corpsman at one time. Ty was Delta and spent a little while with Special Activities. They're at your disposal. For liability purposes, they've consented to take a leave of absence, so this won't be a DGT matter. They'll be freelancing. If the operation succeeds without you blowing up half of D.C., I'll give them a nice bonus. Nothing in writing. Matt will coordinate any logistics you need."

"I owe you one."

"Lima Charlie. Although you did save my life once upon a time."

"Yes, I did."

"But you still owe me."

"Obviously. Your life isn't worth all that much."

"Now," Dwyer said. "Just one condition."

"Which is?"

"Bring them all back in good condition. These guys are superstars, the best of the best. But even they have never been pushed to Garin extremes. So be considerate."

"If you insist."

Dwyer turned toward the doorway and shouted, "Coe, the beast is ready!"

A startled Diesel sat up. Coe appeared seconds later carrying a small satchel.

Garin said, "Thanks for volunteering, Ike."

"Join the Navy, see the world."

Coe removed a syringe from the satchel. "I'll give you a local. This is going to hurt big-time."

"No."

He examined the wound. "Looks like it's third-degree, Mike. Some skin's going to come off with the tape. This is serious."

"No."

Coe looked to Dwyer. "Dan, say something. Talk some sense into him."

"I've been trying since BUD/S, champ. Not happening."

Coe looked back to Garin. He appeared intractable. Coe shook his head, returned the syringe to the satchel, and removed a pair of tape cutters. "Brace your forearm on the armrest, Mike. You may want something to bite on; otherwise, you'll scare the puppy."

Garin remained silent.

Coe shrugged and sighed. "Okay. Here we go."

He slipped the bottom edge of the tape cutter under the duct tape at the top of Garin's wrist and sliced through to the elbow.

"Okay. That was the easy part," Coe informed him. "Hold on."

Garin remained impassive.

"Stop that this instant," Luci demanded, having appeared at the door. "What do you think you're doing?"

Coe blinked uncomprehendingly at Luci.

"You're about to take off the duct tape, aren't you? And I bet he refused a local, right?"

"Well . . . yeah," Coe stammered.

"Not on my watch," Luci declared, striding toward Garin. "He gave you his executioner's look, didn't he? He does that when he's obstinate. You've got to ignore him. Step aside. I'll do this."

Coe looked to Garin, who nodded permission.

"Do you know what you're doing?" Coe asked.

"I'm his trainer. I'm not letting you or anyone else do this. He's going to be ready for CrossFit or Badwater if I have anything to say about it."

Dwyer looked exasperated. "Geez, Mikey. CrossFit or Badwater? You're still on that? Give it up already."

"He owes me," Luci said. She examined Garin's arm for a moment, then pulled the tape apart and unwound it from Garin's arm, not fast, not slow. Portions of the shirt fabric Garin had used as a dressing had melded into the burnt flesh and peeled off with the tape, causing blood to ooze from parts of the wound.

Luci looked at Garin's face. Other than a tightness in his jaws, he remained impassive.

"I'm going to debride and disinfect the wound now," Luci warned him.

Luci used a short, bladed implement from Coe's bag to scrape dead tissue and debris from the wound. Tiny beads of blood bubbled up from the deformed skin as she did so. Dwyer averted his gaze.

Luci blotted the affected area with an antibiotic cream and then applied a treated wrap that she secured with strips of adhesive. She observed Garin's stoic demeanor. "You are one serious badass. But you need to get to a hospital soon. In the meantime, we'll need to change the dressings regularly so you don't get an infection."

Garin flexed his arm a few times. "Thanks. It doesn't hurt much. Maybe the nerves are dead."

"Like the ones in your cranium." She leaned forward and kissed the top of his head.

Diesel took her place atop Garin's feet again, appearing at once both protected and protective.

"Chili time, Mikey," Dwyer said. "In the meantime, I'll send the list to Quantico for analysis. We'll figure out what Bor's up to and where. Then, you do death and destruction."

Garin looked up as Matt strode quickly into the room. He was almost breathless and had a look of urgency on his face. "We just got a hit on one of the license numbers Mrs. Ponder gave us," he said. "We think we might know where Bor is."

CHAPTER 68

"Tell me why I should not have you killed," Mikhailov demanded.

The blood drained from Aleksandr Stetchkin's face. He'd known Yuri Mikhailov for more than twenty years, serving as one of his most critical and trusted associates for the last six. The Russian president was one of the few people in the entire country not frightened or intimidated by Stetchkin, and Mikhailov was one of only two people in all of Russia who frightened or intimidated Stetchkin. The other was Mikhailov's personal assassin, Taras Bor.

"Yuri . . ."

"I am President Mikhailov."

"Yes, Mr. President. I assume you have concluded that Piotr Egorshin's death was my doing. I—"

"I have concluded, Stetchkin, that you acted in a stupid, irresponsible, and treasonous manner in defiance of explicit orders given you only a short time before. I have concluded you have compromised a strategic initiative of paramount importance to the future of this country. I have concluded you have done these things out of arrogance, idiocy, and recklessness—in part because you have never been disciplined or apprised of the limits of your authority. I have concluded that you must explain to me why the country would benefit more from your continued pathetic existence than from your elimination."

Stetchkin sat riveted to his chair in front of Mikhailov's massive desk. For the first time he felt small and powerless. For the first time since he'd known Mikhailov, Stetchkin conceded to himself that Mikhailov was at least as cunning and cutthroat as Stetchkin himself.

For the first time since he'd risen to head the Twelfth Directorate he felt vulnerable, that his life was truly in jeopardy.

"Yuri—"

"Mr. President," Mikhailov corrected sharply.

"Mr. President, it is true that I had Egorshin eliminated."

"You feckless idiot," Mikhailov said, his voice icy and low. "You did it for Palinieva. You did it because you are a wretched excuse for a man."

"I believed I had your authority, Mr. President."

"No one, not even you, is stupid enough to believe you had authority to kill someone on a whim, to satisfy some urge. You did it because you believed I gave you enough room to craft an excuse, to exploit a loophole. You believe you are clever."

"Mr. President—"

"Silence, Stetchkin. We are hours from the most ambitious maneuver of the twenty-first century and you are occupied with petty personal matters. You had someone murdered for reasons that do not advance Russian interests. Yet this is not solely about actions that advance Russian interests. You murdered someone for the most banal reason. It is no longer 1950."

"Mr. President," Stetchkin said plaintively, "I misunderstood—"

Mikhailov cut him off. "You misunderstood nothing."

"But I understood you to say—"

Mikhailov waved him off and pressed the intercom on his desk. "Send in Volkov."

The office door opened almost instantly and Major Valeri Volkov entered tentatively, unsure of the protocols related to meeting and addressing the president. Just a few hours ago he couldn't have imagined a private meeting with Aleksandr Stetchkin. Now here he was in the office of President Yuri Mikhailov, and Stetchkin was seated in front of him, a surprised look on his face. Volkov's distress was evident from his face, which was covered with a sheen of moisture. He saluted and remained in the doorway, eyes fixed forward.

Mikhailov pointed to an empty chair next to Stetchkin. Volkov entered on legs of rubber and sat ramrod straight on the edge of the chair.

Stetchkin spoke rapidly. "Mr. President, Major Volkov was the one who assured me the event can proceed in Egorshin's absence—"

"I am aware of what the major told you," Mikhailov said, his voice neutral. His displeasure with Stetchkin wasn't something he wished to reveal to the young officer. "I simply have a few questions for him." Mikhailov turned to Volkov. "You were Egorshin's second?"

"Yes, Mr. President." Volkov tried to project a military bearing, but his voice was tremulous.

"Egorshin is dead," Mikhailov informed him. Volkov looked stunned. "Can the event proceed without him?"

After a moment, Volkov replied, "Yes, Mr. President."

"You are one hundred percent certain?"

"I am, Mr. President."

"You informed Mr. Stetchkin of this earlier?"

Volkov froze. He suddenly felt like a defendant on trial. He had the sensation of Stetchkin staring at him.

"I did, Mr. President."

"Did Mr. Stetchkin offer any inducements to you to come to that conclusion?"

Volkov's head felt as if it were in a vise. He wasn't on trial, Stetchkin was, and the latter's welfare might depend on Volkov's response. He couldn't lie to the president, but then, the president would have no way of knowing it was a lie. On the other hand, if Volkov's response angered Stetchkin and he still retained authority over him, the tyrant would certainly retaliate, possibly with death.

"I did not provide the conclusions in response to an inducement."

It wasn't lost on Mikhailov that Volkov had elided, but he let it go. He glanced at Stetchkin, who couldn't mask his apprehension.

"Did Mr. Stetchkin make any threats to you to provide that conclusion?"

"He did not." Technically true, thought Volkov, although at the time he'd had absolutely no doubt what conclusion Stetchkin wanted from him.

Mikhailov stared at Volkov for several seconds, then glared at

Stetchkin for several more. Both were anxious. Although Volkov's anxiety was more pronounced, Stetchkin's was far more striking given his reputation and position. Mikhailov pressed the intercom button again. "Send in Majors Tokarsky and Starpov."

Seconds later the door opened to reveal Tokarsky and Starpov. They looked more composed than Volkov but appeared similarly unfamiliar with appropriate protocol. They stood motionless for a second, then saluted in unison. Mikhailov motioned for them to enter and they walked to the left of Volkov's chair, where they stood at attention.

"Majors Tokarsky and Starpov, I am told each of you is independently capable of overseeing the unit and executing the event if necessary. Is this correct?"

They spoke in tandem. "Yes, Mr. President."

Mikhailov nodded approvingly. "I am also informed that it is one hundred percent certain the event will be successful even without Egorshin's involvement. Major Tokarsky, do you agree with that assessment?"

Major Tokarsky glanced quickly at Major Starpov and said, "Yes, Mr. President."

"And you, Major Starpov?"

"I agree as well, Mr. President."

A look of relief came over the faces of Stetchkin and Volkov.

"Very good. Very good," Mikhailov said. "We are barely sixteen hours away. You understand how important it is to have effective redundancies for something of this magnitude. Thank you. You are dismissed."

Majors Tokarsky and Starpov saluted smartly, pivoted, and walked to the door.

Then Mikhailov called after them. "I have a final question, Majors, a hypothetical."

The two officers stopped and turned.

"Based on your previous responses, I gather it would be accurate to say that the event would proceed with one hundred percent success even if some tragedy were to befall Mr. Stetchkin and Mr. Volkov and they could not participate?"

The anxious looks instantly returned to the faces of Stetchkin and Volkov.

The two majors said, "Yes, Mr. President."

"Thank you. You are dismissed."

CHAPTER 69

Morosov passed through the scanner and retrieved his Makarov PMM, phone, and watch from one of the dour-faced, heavily armed security guards at the other end. Before placing the pistol in his holster, he released the magazine as if to inspect it and then reseated it. Just beyond the guards, the twin blast-proof doors slid open, revealing a seemingly endless brightly lit tunnel with mirrored walls. He stepped into a small electric cart that sat upon two rails and it automatically conveyed him approximately half a kilometer to a bank of glass elevators, scores of unseen cameras monitoring him the entire way.

The cart slowed to a stop. Its soft whine was replaced by a barely perceptible hum from massive arrays of supercomputers somewhere below. Morosov stepped off, held a proximity card next to a pad at the center of the elevator bank, and waited.

Only eight hours ago, Tatiana had informed him of his nephew's death. Immediately upon disconnecting he'd picked up his pistol and released the magazine. Then, as Piotr had instructed, he'd placed the device in the empty magazine and seated it, enabling him to clear the facility's multiple security scans.

The doors of the elevator to Morosov's left opened. He entered and was automatically conveyed to the twelfth floor, where the doors opened to an enormous workspace that seemed incongruously quiet despite the presence of scores of personnel. He was met seconds later by Leonid Gramov, a short, severe-looking man in his mid-thirties who was one of Egorshin's closest aides. He looked stunned. News of Egorshin's death had traveled rapidly throughout the unit.

"Leonid Gramov, Mr. Morosov. We met some time ago at a party thrown by Tatiana. We heard the news just a short time ago. I do not know what to say. Piotr was the heart of this unit. He was our leader. He had abilities none of us can match. Every member of the unit respected him and was fond of him. This is his unit and we were proud to serve under him. I am so very sorry."

"Thank you, Leonid. My nephew spoke highly of you. He was equally fond of the members of this unit. I understand he handpicked many of you."

"It was an honor to have been chosen by someone so gifted," Gramov said, his voice cracking. "We are at a loss. How could this have happened? Are you here to investigate?"

Morosov shook his head. "I'm here as a family member only, Leonid. Someone else will investigate. I came to gather any personal belongings. I assume his workstation has been inspected?"

Gramov nodded. "The rest of us found out when security impounded everything at his desk. They came in a swarm. They did not speak to us but, of course, we were alarmed. We are not permitted outside communication from this area, but you cannot keep such things quiet. It appears someone left to make a call, and soon, everyone knew."

Morosov looked about the room. At least half a dozen uniformed security personnel were stationed about the perimeter. He suspected there were others who had been embedded in the unit since its inception. In fact, as he surveyed the surroundings the old SVR agent was able to spot them without much difficulty. A few were observing him with furtive sidelong glances while ostensibly working on their desktop computers.

A tall, striking woman with short flame-red hair and a crestfallen expression walked briskly toward Morosov and extended her hand. "Elena Kolovskya. I apologize for being so forward. We met when Colonel Egorshin was in university. He and I were classmates. Honestly, *no one* was in his class. We were all simply admirers. Major Volkov was his second, officially. But I had the privilege of being Piotr's principal technical assistant. We worked closely. My condolences."

"Thank you, that means much to me," Morosov said genuinely. "I have no children, and as you may know, Piotr's father died when Piotr was young, so he was like a son to me."

Gramov and Kolovskya nodded sympathetically. Gramov said to Kolovskya, "Mr. Morosov's here to collect any personal effects."

"Security protocols were implemented as soon as the news became known," Kolovskya said. "They inspected Piotr's entire workspace and I presume they took everything of note with them. But you are welcome to look over his workspace and take whatever remains. Security, of course, will want to inspect whatever you take with you before you leave."

"Please show me the way," Morosov said.

Kolovskya led Morosov to a ten-by-ten glass-enclosed workspace at the front of the room facing the giant screen. The room contained only a plexiglass desk, a simple desktop computer, a phone, and a chair. The arrangement appeared no more complex or impressive than that of an average telemarketer. But it was the command and control for the entire operation, an almost incomprehensible amount of computing power. The computer screen displayed a whimsical screensaver. No doubt security had checked it.

Kolovskya and Gramov left Morosov alone. He scanned the area for any personal effects. A photo of Tatiana in a small wooden frame next to the computer screen was all that remained on Piotr's desk. She was smiling, the Eiffel Tower in the background.

Morosov leaned forward to inspect the photo. As he did so he placed his right hand flat on the desk on one side of the computer and his left hand on the other. He picked up the photo to gaze at it for a moment, then returned it to the desk, placing it on the left side of the computer. While continuing to gaze at the photo, he tapped his right index finger on the desk. The subtlest of misdirections. With a practically imperceptible movement of his left hand he inserted Piotr's device into a port in the side of the computer, obscured by the photo frame. The magician.

Morosov straightened, looked about, and left the space. Gramov and Kolovskya met him immediately.

"I suspect security took everything?" Kolovskya asked.

"Almost. They left a photo of Tatiana. Nothing else."

"Once security sifts through everything, they will release anything that does not relate to work. I can contact you if anything remains," Kolovskya offered.

"That is kind of you. Thank you," Morosov said as he conducted a mental countdown. "I suppose I will be on my way and leave you to your work."

Morosov shook their hands and walked to the exit. Halfway there he paused, looked at his watch a moment, then turned and walked back. Gramov and Kolovskya met him just outside Piotr's workspace.

"On reflection," Morosov said, "I suppose I should take the photo. Tatiana would want it, I believe. Do you mind?"

Gramov and Kolovskya moved aside deferentially. "Of course not," Kolovskya said, waving him in. "Please."

Morosov entered the workspace and once again leaned against the desktop, briefly assuming the same pose he'd held before. Another magic trick and Piotr's device was in his left palm. Morosov removed the photograph from the desk, nodded thanks toward Gramov and Kolovskya, and proceeded toward the elevators.

Several minutes later Piotr Egorshin's favorite uncle, his only uncle, was walking toward his car. His stride was long, almost triumphant, not that of a man on the verge of retirement.

Upon reaching his car he turned to look at the building where his nephew had worked. That building, and the cavernous spaces beneath, held more destructive power than had been unleashed by the entire Red Army during World War II. Although it was the tyrant Stetchkin's domain, it was Piotr, the gentlest of souls, who had made its power possible.

And Piotr, through his uncle Sergei the magician, would have his revenge.

CHAPTER 70

Several members of the National Security Council were waiting in the Situation Room for President Marshall. They had been summoned by White House Chief of Staff Iris Cho, who, contrary to standard practice, provided no reason for the meeting.

The assembled group consisted of Secretary of Defense Douglas Merritt, CIA Deputy Director John Kessler, Secretary of State Ted Lawrence, Secretary of Homeland Security Susan Cruz, Director of National Intelligence Joseph Antonetti, and Chairman of the Joint Chiefs Robert Taylor.

Their wait was brief. The door opened and President Marshall entered, followed by Iris Cho and James Brandt, who was led to his customary seat between Merritt and Cruz by Arlo. Marshall remained standing behind his chair, a practice he'd adopted since the EMP affair, partly out of superstition.

"Thank you for getting here on time with such short notice. I'm told the others are traveling and are unavailable for videoconference. I don't have a specific agenda. That's not my normal practice, I know, but this is not a normal meeting.

"What we learned from the EMP affair gave us all, I suspect, a PhD in vigilance and threat assessment. We also learned to pay attention to Mike Garin."

There was a faint rustle in the room. The mention of the name had the effect of an injection of caffeine.

"Jim and I spoke with Garin a short time ago. He believes the Russian agent Taras Bor is here to 'paralyze' us, whatever that means. But, apparently, the specific word 'paralyze' was used by a Bor associate to describe what Bor was planning to do."

Marshall paused to let everyone absorb what he said. He continued.

"The paralysis is to be preceded by a decoy attack consisting of suicide bombers. We have no further information about any of this, other than Bor is personally responsible for some sort of backup attack should the main attack fail.

"Now, before we go any further, keep in mind that for the time being nothing discussed here is to go beyond this room. Not even your deputies can know about this. Whoever was providing assistance to the Russians during the EMP affair is still operating. Since all of you were involved in stopping the EMP attack, I can entrust this information to you. But for now, only you. Unless, during the course of this meeting, we determine otherwise.

"There's another component to all of this. The Russians are engaged in military maneuvers along their western border—all the way from the Baltics southward. I received some inconclusive information about this in the PDB, but nothing to suggest the troop movements were anything out of the ordinary."

Kessler spoke up. "Mr. President, we've seen Russian troop presence along the borders of the Baltic states, but nothing beyond what's noted in the PDB. We haven't heard or seen anything that might confirm Garin's concerns."

Marshall looked about the room. "Anybody else?"

Secretary of State Ted Lawrence raised his hand tentatively. Regarded by many in the room as a self-promoting blowhard, even by Washington standards, he'd been chastened by his erroneous conclusions during the EMP affair. Many expected him to be replaced by Brandt after the midterm elections.

"Yes, Ted."

"Mr. President, the troop presence near the Baltics is unremarkable. They've been more aggressive in that region ever since the previous administration bent over backward to make friends with them." Lawrence struck a pedantic pose familiar to everyone who knew him.

"Besides, the EMP affair was only a month ago. They have been exemplary members of the international community since then, even assisting the Western allies in the campaign against Iran. And while we're skeptical that they were completely innocent in that affair, there really is little evidence that they did anything more than be indifferent to Iran's efforts to strike us."

Marshall nodded. "Thank you, Ted. But what do we make of Garin's encounter with what he believes to be a Russian agent—or at least an associate of Bor?"

"Mr. President, not to downplay Mr. Garin's information, but it's no secret the Russians have scores of agents in the area," Susan Cruz offered. "Yes, they're up to no good, if by that we mean they are operating with Russian, not American, interests in mind. But that's a pretty low bar. It's true of nearly every substantial foreign power, including some of our allies."

Several heads around the room nodded. Secretary of Defense Merritt's was not among them.

"Mr. President," Merritt said. "I respectfully submit that the prudent approach is to assume the worst, that the Russians are about to engage in hostile action and that such action affects the United States."

Marshall asked, "Any ideas what the agent may have meant by 'paralyze'?"

"Cyberattack," Brandt said bluntly.

The room remained silent, partly because Brandt was so often right and partly because of the weight Brandt's opinions carried with the president.

The Oracle's sightless ice-blue eyes were cast in the general direction of the president. He listened for a response from anyone in the room. When none came he continued. "Mr. President, we should consider the possibility that the Russians are preparing to launch a massive cyberattack. And if our operating premise, as suggested by Doug, is to assume the worst, then we should expect it to affect every critical sector of our economy and government."

"Upon what do you base this, Jim?"

"It's a guess, but a guess informed by logic and the progression of Russian asymmetrical warfare. Consider that the EMP plot was essentially asymmetrical, so much so that we hadn't developed a response doctrine in the event of an EMP."

Marshall's jaws tightened. He had been furious about learning during the EMP affair that the country had never developed a response doctrine to an EMP strike. "Please don't tell me we haven't developed a response doctrine to a massive cyberattack."

"We have, Mr. President," DHS secretary Cruz interjected. "My department, along with the Office of the DNI and the National Cyber Investigative Joint Task Force, has been hardening the National Cyber Incident Response Plan. We've prepared coordinated responses for various federal agencies, military, states, and local authorities."

Marshall exhaled. "Thank goodness."

"We've also had significant success in joint DOD and DHS Cyber Guard Exercises," Cruz added. "The last such exercise took place earlier this summer."

"So we're up to speed against a cyberattack, then?" Marshall asked.

"I believe so, Mr. President," Cruz replied.

"Ted," Marshall said, turning to Secretary of State Lawrence, "what about coordination with our allies? If Russia strikes us there's a good chance they'll do so against other Western nations, particularly NATO signatories."

"We've conferred with NATO allies on a regular basis, Mr. President. Many of them agree that we should do what we can to prevent cyberattacks, but the threat is somewhat overblown." Lawrence quickly raised his hand. "That's not to say it's not a concern, but we and our allies are ahead of the game."

Marshall turned to Brandt. "Why are you concerned about a cyberattack from the Russians, especially if—as it seems to be the case—we're fairly well prepared?"

"Mr. President, both Susan and Ted are correct that we've been coordinating both within our government and with allies to prevent or respond to any major incident of cyberwarfare. But most of that coordination is at the administrative level and is mostly responsive, not preventative. The efforts are focused primarily on what should be done to minimize the *effects* of a cyberattack and what agencies are responsible for addressing and remedying such effects."

"That's not quite accurate, Mr. President," Lawrence countered. "We have fairly robust defenses and countermeasures in place to deflect and thwart massive cyberattacks, not just at DHS and the Defense Department, but the CIA and NSA as well. Moreover, US Cyber Command has remarkable retaliatory capabilities that, among other things, act as a powerful deterrent.

"But more important, you may remember the NATO conference last spring on asymmetrical warfare where the consensus was that while we shouldn't understate the threat of cyberwarfare, the threat has been vastly overstated."

Marshall looked around the room. "Anyone else?"

"Mr. President," Secretary of Defense Merritt said, "I also was in attendance at the NATO conference this spring. No doubt the presenters were the best minds on the topic. But you may recall the dissenting opinion of Hans Richter from the German Federal Office for Information Security. His hair was on fire. He related that the Germans only by chance had discovered cyberattacks against them that had corrupted several of their best-defended systems. According to Richter, it was clear the attacks were mere probing forays to gauge the vulnerability of German systems, but had they been full-blown attacks, catastrophic damage would have been done to critical infrastructure."

"As I recall, Richter didn't assign blame to any particular state actor," Marshall said.

"He did not," Merritt acknowledged. "But the Russians are the most capable. From a defense perspective, I submit the most responsible course of action is to assume a massive cyberattack would be catastrophic, and that the Russians may be behind it."

Marshall turned to Brandt. "Jim?"

"I concur completely with Doug. Yes, the consensus is that a massive cyberattack might cause some problems but it wouldn't be catastrophic.

I respectfully submit this view, however well-considered, suffers from a profound lack of imagination."

Marshall's brow furrowed. "We just averted an EMP. Could it be as catastrophic as that would've been?"

"The word 'paralyze' was used," Brandt replied. "That's an apt description of what a major cyberattack could do to us. But only a partial description. It would also render us deaf, dumb, and blind."

"Wonderful." Marshall sighed. "I'm loving this job more every day. Elaborate, Jim."

"Senate Armed Services conducted a hearing on this just a couple of months ago. The Russians could disrupt our electrical power grid, industrial control systems, communications systems—almost any system that isn't air-gapped. We could be without lights, cell phones, computers. Financial data could crash and disappear—trillions upon trillions of dollars could evaporate. We would, indeed, be functionally paralyzed. We couldn't identify and respond to external threats. The economy would be in turmoil. In many respects, we'd become the functional equivalent of a third world country. We would be dangerously overmatched against any of our present or potential adversaries."

Lawrence bristled. "Not really, Mr. President. Our military and intelligence infrastructures are largely insulated. We've hardened most of our defense systems."

"But," Brandt countered, "the domestic disturbance would render any such hardening irrelevant. Because we'd be dealing with utter chaos at home. Lord of the Flies. Besides, there's some evidence Russia or China has already had success hacking our satellites and drones—so defense and intelligence *aren't* invulnerable."

"The dilemma, as I see it," Marshall said, "is that we have no demonstrable evidence that a cyberattack will occur, or if one occurs, where it will come from. We have nothing to confront the potential attacker. Our option, then, is to be vigilant and do whatever we can in the interim to prevent it."

"And prepare for the worst," Brandt muttered under his breath.

The small but ornate conference room adjacent to Yuri Mikhailov's office was quiet. No one spoke; there was barely any movement. Assembled within it were seven of the most powerful men in Russia, each in his own way formidable and intimidating. Each was used to being the most important person in the room, commanding attention, respect, and obedience merely by his presence.

Arranged around a rectangular marble-topped table were First Deputy Prime Minister Boris Novikov, Minister of Defense Igor Oblomov, Minister of External Affairs Grigory Goncharov, Minister of Emerging Situations Ivan Sorokin, Marshal Vitaly Brin, General Pavel Turgenev, and the head of the Twelfth Chief Directorate, Aleksandr Stetchkin. Although technically Stetchkin reported to Oblomov, the former, by virtue of his long-standing relationship with the Russian president, was the most influential person in the room.

There were two empty chairs at the table. Presently, the door leading to Mikhailov's office opened and Alexei Vasiliev entered and took a seat. The room remained silent for another minute. Then the door opened and Yuri Mikhailov entered, taking the seat at the head of the table without looking at anyone. To the others in the room he appeared to be studying the backs of his hands.

After a few more seconds of silence Mikhailov said, "Alexei."

Vasiliev, in turn, looked at Marshal Brin and General Turgenev. "Gentlemen?"

Brin said, "Elements of the Southern and Central Military Districts, consisting chiefly of the Fifty-eighth and Forty-ninth Armies, including the Twenty-second Spetsnaz Brigade, are staged approximately one hundred kilometers south of Makhachkala and two hundred fifty kilometers south of Aktau, respectively. We estimate they will enter Iranian territory to the west of Ardabil and to the east of Gorgan within two hours of the event. Intelligence estimates indicate we will meet minimal resistance until we are within the Tehran defense perimeter. Given the degradation of Iranian defenses by the Western bombing campaign, the resistance at the perimeter will be defeated within thirty-six hours." Brin looked at Turgenev. "General?"

"Thank you. We estimate, Mr. President, that within a timeframe similar to that outlined by Marshal Brin, the Baltic tank battalions will have secured much of the Latvian and Estonian countryside. The event will prevent meaningful NATO resistance, let alone retaliation. Within the following twelve hours Riga and Tallinn will be under control.

"Most of eastern Ukraine will be under the control of various elements of the Sixth Army within sixty hours of the event. We project our forces to dominate the area on a line southward from Zhytomyr to Vinnytsya to Odessa."

"What of Lithuania?" Vasiliev asked.

"NATO exercises in and around northeast Poland have caused us to recalculate the original timeframe regarding Lithuania. It is less than three hundred kilometers from Białystok to Vilnius. NATO, therefore, may be able to mount a response," Turgenev answered.

"Even if blind?"

"We assume worst case, Mr. Vasiliev."

"How long do you estimate before Lithuania is secured, General? Worst case?"

"Ninety-six hours."

"Acceptable," Vasiliev said, turning to Stetchkin. "What is the probability we will encounter a worst-case scenario?"

"Unlikely," Stetchkin replied. "The event will immobilize NATO for several weeks. Their civilian infrastructure will be completely paralyzed and we have been, frankly, astonished at the unexpected vulnerability of their military apparatus. Most of the European NATO signatories have expended meager sums to protect their systems from electronic warfare and could not have anticipated an attack even remotely as sophisticated as the event. They will be brought to a near standstill. They will be overwhelmed."

"What of the Americans?" Vasiliev asked.

"Their defenses are formidable but insufficient," Stetchkin replied. "The simulations show they will be blind and effectively paralyzed, unable to mount a timely response. Our annexation of Iran and much of the near abroad will be done before they have even begun restoring their cybercapabilities. They will have virtually no telecommunication capabilities. All cellular and Internet service will be out. Financial data will be erased. Their financial markets will go dark.

"For enhanced chaos we have targeted sluice gates at approximately two dozen of their largest dams. There will be massive flooding at these locations. Power grids in the thirty largest metropolitan areas—New York, Los Angeles, Chicago, Houston, Washington—will be shut down completely. No light or electricity whatsoever. That alone will be a cataclysm that will occupy all aspects of emergency response. Police, fire, and military will have to mobilize without telecommunications ability." Stetchkin paused. "SVR says the Americans believe their military and intelligence servers will be able to weather an attack, but they have underestimated our capabilities." Stetchkin looked at Mikhailov. "By the time they have even begun to assess the extent of their paralysis, we will have absorbed most of Greater Russia as well as Iran. And, if we so choose, much of Scandinavia and the Balkans would be ours."

Mikhailov did not react. Vasiliev spoke instead. "What is your estimate of the time from initiation of the event until reconstitution of Greater Russia?"

"I defer to Marshal Brin," Stetchkin answered.

"One hundred twenty hours," Brin said. "One hundred sixty-eight at the outside."

Vasiliev nodded, then looked to Grigory Goncharov. "Your previous estimate of the percentage of electrical equipment that would be moved as a result of the event remains the same?"

"Essentially, yes," Goncharov answered cautiously. "Demand will be appreciably less than if an electromagnetic pulse had struck the US mainland. But the event will affect far more territory. There will certainly be demand."

Mikhailov rose, drawing everyone's riveted attention. "We are getting ahead of ourselves. Discussion of markets can and will wait until control of Greater Russia is secure and we have seized Iran. Any discussion of Scandinavia, the Balkans, and other regions will wait, also. Should the event be successful, dominoes will fall of their own accord."

Everyone in the room nodded. Stetchkin did so with a smile of satisfaction, a smile that was short-lived. Mikhailov pointed at Stetchkin and said, "Be certain that the event succeeds."

The Russian president walked to the entrance to his office, opened the door, and shut it sharply behind him.

CHAPTER 71

Garin waited in Dwyer's communications room for a report from Coe and Wilson. He was seated in the captain's chair. Dwyer, Knox, and Olivia were with him, each in his or her own seat around the perimeter of the room. Diesel had followed them and was at Garin's feet.

The license number for the forest-green Ford Windstar was first captured by a traffic camera at Fourteenth and C in Washington. The vehicle had crossed C Street just as the light turned red. The information was picked up by DGT personnel, who tracked the minivan along Fourteenth Street using proprietary cameras and GPS until it stopped at 2641 Tunlaw, the address of the Russian consulate, where it had remained until now. It was unclear whether Bor was, in fact, in the vehicle, but Dwyer dispatched Coe and Wilson to the Russian embassy to keep watch and report back should they spot the Russian.

"Where's Luci?" Garin asked.

"She's upstairs," Knox answered. "In the— What do you call that room with the big screen and all the audio, Dan?"

"The room with the big screen and all the audio."

"I hope she doesn't feel like we're holding her hostage," Garin said.

"She's having the time of her life," Knox said. "Plus, she wants to keep an eye on her investment."

"She can and should stay here until we figure out what's going on," Dwyer added.

"Any update from Matt about the numbers and letters on the sheet of paper?" Garin asked.

"Not yet."

"What letters and numbers?" Olivia asked.

Garin handed her the sheet of paper. "These."

Olivia looked it over. "Flight information," she said instantly.

"What do you mean?" Dwyer asked.

"UA4272; MK9BRU; 01623190175961," Olivia said, reading one of the lines. "That's a United Airlines flight number followed by a confirmation number and ticket number." She recited another line. "DL5416; JNVG76; 0062332192690; Delta Airlines, probably a regional express jet if I had to guess."

"Unbelievable," Dwyer said. "How did we miss this?"

"It was simple. You were looking for something complex. Where did you get this?" Olivia asked.

"From someone I believe was working for Bor," Garin replied.

"What you have here"—Olivia counted to herself—"are ten separate flights. Based on the prefixes, it appears they're United, Delta, and American.

"Based on the flight numbers I would guess that the origin of the United flights might be Reagan National. But why guess? Just log on to the airlines' websites and input the data. One thing we do know is these flights were or are booked, because of the confirmation number. Maybe they've already been taken. But maybe they were booked in advance and remain to be taken."

"How many look like United flights out of Reagan?" Garin asked.

Olivia scanned the paper. "At least four."

"Could they be escape routes for Bor's men?" Knox asked.

Dwyer rose, walked to the captain's chair, and keyed a number on the console. Matt's voice came over the speaker.

"Yes, Dan?"

"Those numbers and letters I asked you to check?"

"Yes."

"Well, Ms. Perry here figured out that they're flight information. Check them against the various carriers and get me all the data you can: origins, destinations, times, etcetera. Pronto."

"Got it."

Knox came back to the purpose for the flights. "They may be escape routes, or maybe the suicide bombers will use the tickets."

"There are supposedly three parts to this," Garin said. "Diversionary suicide bombers, a paralyzing main attack, and a backup plan. Where do ten airline flights fit in?"

"Suicide bombers couldn't get on a plane with the ingredients for a bomb," Knox said. "And they sure as hell won't need a plane afterward."

"So, unless the bombers are flying to various destinations to pick up their suicide vests or whatever, the flight information doesn't have anything to do with them," Dwyer said.

"Right. But let's put part one of the plan on hold," Garin advised. "Let's go to part two—the main attack. What would ten flights have to do with that?"

"Maybe they're planning to hijack ten planes," Dwyer mused.

"Nearly impossible to do these days with the post-9/11 airline security protocols, hardened cockpits," Olivia said. "If they're extremely lucky, maybe they get one, two tops."

"Olivia's right," Garin concurred. "Besides, hijacking planes, though significant, isn't necessarily 'paralyzing.'"

"Mike, maybe you're putting too much significance on the term 'paralyze,'" Knox said. "Step back. Maybe the guy wasn't being literal. Maybe he just meant something big."

"Possible, but I don't think so. This guy was precise. He spoke excellent English, but like most foreigners he didn't use a lot of colloquialisms. I think he meant 'paralyze' as in 'cause us to come to a stop; freeze us in place.'"

"Okay," Dwyer said. "If it's not part of the main attack, maybe they're escape routes, like Congo said."

"Then they'd have to be escape routes for those involved in Bor's backup operation," Garin said. "Possible. But let's look at it from another angle. What if the flights *are* the backup operation?"

"Doesn't compute, Mikey," Dwyer said. "Just as you said about the suicide bombers or hijackers. The odds for success just aren't good enough."

"Back to square one," Knox concluded. "But this is good intel. If these flights are coming up, we tell the president or Brandt about them and they can put a ton of security around them, maybe pick up Bor's people."

"The problem with that is as soon as the FBI or anyone else is alerted, there's a good probability Bor's people will be alerted as well. Then they'll just make other arrangements and we'll miss them."

"The FBI is compromised?" Knox asked.

"We think so, yes. Even so, we've got to do something," Garin responded.

A buzz sounded over the speaker. Dwyer, standing next to the captain's chair, connected.

"We have eyes on Bor," Coe said.

"You sure?" Dwyer asked.

"The guy looks like he could induce cardiac arrest with a glance. Plus, he has a J-shaped scar along his right jawline."

Garin instantly rose from the captain's chair. He began to move toward the door but he felt unsteady and momentarily disoriented. Olivia was looking at him with alarm.

"Michael, you have *blood* flowing from your ear."

Garin dabbed at the wetness on his cheek. As he did so, he felt a piercing pain radiate throughout the right side of his head. He grasped the armrest of the chair, his vision distorted and blurred, and braced himself, struggling to remain upright.

"Dan, *help* him," Olivia demanded, stepping toward Garin.

"No," Garin ordered, his eyes blinking to orient himself.

Olivia ignored him and grabbed both of Garin's arms, forcing him to sit. "Michael, what's wrong? What happened to you?"

"Mikey, you look seriously messed up," Dwyer said. "All evidence to the contrary, you're not invincible. We need to get you some treatment. Now."

Garin continued blinking, attempting to gain focus. "No."

"Mike," Knox said. "You need to listen to Dan. You don't look right. I mean, something's very wrong."

Garin said nothing. He shook his head and squeezed his eyelids tight.

When he opened them the pain shot through to the other side of his head and a wave of nausea overcame him.

"I'm calling an ambulance," Dwyer said, pressing 911 on the console.

"No," Garin said in a voice that gave even Dwyer pause. "Bor . . ."

Dwyer cut him off. "To hell with Bor. You need a doctor."

A female voice came over the speaker. "Nine-one-one. What is the nature of your emergency?"

"None," Garin growled in his gravedigger's voice and disconnected. He fixed Dwyer and Knox with a withering gaze. "Do not do that again."

Olivia held on to his arms. "Michael, please listen to them. If anyone knows when someone is in serious need of medical help, they do. Please."

Garin grimaced and tried to stand, but his legs wouldn't support him. He collapsed back into the seat. He appeared drained.

"'I'll lay me down and bleed awhile. Then I'll rise and fight again,'" Dwyer recited. "Still good counsel, Mike."

"Sir Andrew had time to bleed," Garin retorted. "We don't."

"But you're bleeding *now*, Michael," Olivia said, continuing to hold his arms.

Dwyer said, "Let him go, Olivia. When he's like this there's no reasoning with him. Only his own body can stop him. And this time it will."

Olivia shook her head. "No. This is lunacy." She stared hard at Garin. "Michael, get medical help. You've got no obligation to do this. It's not your responsibility." She thought for a moment. "Nikolai Garin would tell you the same."

Garin focused. "Nice try," he growled. "Nikolai Garin would tell you to let go and let me do my job. Now."

"He—"

"Now."

Olivia hesitated but released her hold. Garin gathered himself, stood, and assessed his balance. Then he walked swiftly to the door and out of the room, Diesel following closely behind.

CHAPTER 72

RUSSIAN EMBASSY, WASHINGTON, D.C., AUGUST 18, 9:52 A.M. EDT

His cell vibrated. The caller ID said "unknown" but Bor recognized the voice instantly.

"He is impaired."

"How badly?" Bor asked.

"Enough."

"Unless he's dead it's not enough."

"Enough to give you the advantage if he finds you."

"You mean *when* he finds me," Bor corrected. "Details, please."

"Severe burns on his arm. It will limit his strength. He also suffered a head injury of some kind."

A pause as Bor processed the information. "How does the head injury manifest itself?"

"I'm unsure of the symptoms, other than severe pain, some disorientation."

"All right. Anything else?"

"That's all for now."

"Keep me apprised."

"When I can."

Bor terminated the call and exhaled. The information he'd just received was troubling. As far as he was concerned, a wounded Garin was a dangerous Garin.

Taras Bor and Vadim Stepulev examined the satellite photo of Washington, D.C., on the tablet provided by an aide to the *rezident*. Bor swiped the screen and the photo was replaced by a map with nearly a dozen digital pins stuck in various areas throughout the District.

Bor looked at Stepulev. "Ready?"

"Yes. The primaries should be easy enough. But if we encounter any obstacles, I am sure we can execute the secondaries."

"That does not mean you. Leave everything to your volunteers. You are merely the conveyance. Do not engage anyone. Period. You need not lose your life for a mere distraction."

Stepulev smiled broadly and clapped Bor's shoulder with his hand. "You do not sound like the committed lieutenant I first met years ago, Taras. Do you no longer believe in the cause? Is the fire extinguished?"

"I believe. But I do not believe in the state or its nonsense. I never have."

Stepulev laughed loudly, the sound muffled in the small office with soundproof walls. "Who among us ever did? Our parents did not believe in the state; they only mouthed the words because they were compelled to, my friend. Now the state is no longer supreme. But everyone must believe in something. What do you believe in?"

"Death."

"That is obvious. What comes after death?"

"For me, hell."

Stepulev looked at Bor quizzically. "The great Bor believes in hell?"

"Do you believe *this* is all there is?"

"I am no longer certain what I believe."

"That is the problem," Bor observed. "Your volunteers, what do they believe?"

"They believe they will be rewarded in paradise," Stepulev said.

"And you will help them test their faith," Bor said.

"I merely make it possible for them to fulfill their destinies. Just as you are doing with your volunteers."

"My volunteers, like yours, may not have the opportunity to fulfill their destinies," Bor said. "Garin is alive."

Stepulev frowned skeptically. "How do you know?"

"Bulkvadze failed once. I gave him a second chance. I have not heard from him since. But I *have* heard from a source that Garin is alive, but wounded."

"And you cannot reveal your source," Stepulev said. "But you believe Garin killed Bulkvadze?"

"I am certain of it."

"Then the Butcher will kill Garin," Stepulev assured him. "After having some fun with him."

"We have not heard from your Butcher either."

Stepulev contemplated the matter. "Regardless, it is too late. Garin knows nothing. He can stop nothing."

"He may not know anything now, but if he acquires any clues he will get up to speed very quickly," Bor said. "And when that happens, things will get complicated."

"Even so, we will be alerted of his plans and movements. We can stay one step ahead. That's all we need."

Bor shrugged. "Probably. Regardless, we may not even be in play. But if we are, we need to be vigilant and execute rapidly."

"My volunteers are ready," Stepulev said. "In fact, they are anxious."

"Mine as well. When this is over we will have achieved something very significant. But if not, thousands of individuals like the volunteers will remain. Then Russia will be their central focus. We will have to deal with them directly at some point."

"True," Stepulev acknowledged with a sigh. "But we do not have the same sensibilities as the West when it comes to dealing with adversaries. The West seems perpetually apologetic for defending themselves."

Bor rose from his chair and arched his back. "We could use a bit of self-reflection also, my friend."

"But not to the point of suicide."

"Speaking of which," Bor said. "How was the timing on your practice runs?"

"Good. We went through three exercises. I would have put them through more, but because of the locations I was concerned someone might notice our repeated presence. Also, the strike points undoubtedly are covered by redundant cameras. Not knowing whether the images are fed into algorithms to identify faces that make repeat appearances, I decided to limit our runs."

"Good."

"I will meet you shortly thereafter in Leesburg. My only detour will be to switch vehicles afterward. It won't take long for them to identify the original vehicle."

"Does the sequence still appear feasible?"

"Softest target to hardest. Unquestionably," Stepulev replied. "Union Station has considerable security, but nothing like the other two. Of course, after Union Station the other targets will be further hardened instantly."

Bor paced the small room slowly. "Have you considered reversing the order?"

"Several times, Taras. There are problems with any sequence we choose. As I have noted to my superiors, simultaneous strikes would be best."

"Yes, that would enhance the probabilities of success. What was their response?"

"They did not disagree. But they specifically wanted sequenced strikes for the psychological effect. It would be more devastating, more of a distraction. The US would anticipate yet more strikes, so it would occupy their attention in a way simultaneous strikes would not."

Bor cocked his head to the side, considering the rationale. "Perhaps. I am not sure that outweighs the logistical advantage to a simultaneous strike."

"Logistics are not their concern, Taras. They leave such considerations to us, no matter the feasibility. They simply come up with grand schemes and expect us to execute. From the comfort of their conference rooms their plans are infallible. If their schemes do not work, it is because we are incompetent."

"This does not sound like Mikhailov, Vadim. He is too shrewd. He would understand the need for logistical practicality to maximize the probability of success. This has the fingerprints of Aleksandr Stetchkin all over it."

"Stetchkin can be blamed for much," Stepulev said with disgust. "But in fairness, I do not think he was involved in these details. Mikhailov delegated this to Vasiliev. Mikhailov is focused on the main event. And your fail-safe. Are your volunteers ready?"

Bor continued to pace slowly. "My volunteers are not as hardened as yours, but they are motivated. They will be striking a powerful blow for ISIS, an historical one. Their names will be spoken with reverence for generations. And their families will become wealthy."

Stepulev noted the reservation in his friend's voice. "But . . . ?"

"Most of them went to university. They have the attitudes of many of those who go to university."

Stepulev grinned. "You mean they will defecate their pants at zero hour."

"Likely. But they will do their jobs. They are believers. In addition to fame, fortune ensures that they will do it. As does the safety of their families."

Stepulev nodded with understanding. "So they have all been treated to a demonstration of what misfortune could befall their family members should they fail?"

"They have no illusions about what will happen, Vadim."

"Even if one were to fail, the impact of the others will be more than sufficient, Taras. Have you considered that your fail-safe operation will be far more devastating than the main event?"

"I have," Bor said, running a hand through his hair. "But we are, as you have noted, on the logistics side of the equation, not the strategic side."

"It is a big risk."

"That is an understatement, my friend. They calculated that the EMP strike wouldn't trigger war. I am not so confident of that this time. Although I concede that they will have presented the West with an almost insuperable conundrum."

Stepulev's eyes narrowed. "They have indeed, Taras. Think about it. It is virtually no different from the conundrum presented by the EMP attack. The genius game theorists in the Kremlin have determined that the same calculus applies here."

"I fully understand, Vadim. They are employing misdirection once again, except this time it will appear as if ISIS, not Iran, has struck America." Bor stopped pacing. "But I fear game theory is about to crash into reality. I do not believe the Americans will fall for two false-flag operations in a row, especially when the previous one was barely a month ago. And especially when massive numbers of Americans will die."

"Massive numbers would have died after the EMP strike also—tens of millions."

Bor shook his head. "Not from the EMP itself—but from the aftermath. No buildings would have been destroyed, no apocalyptic fires would have raged, pulverized bodies would not have littered the streets. Those things *will* happen this time. And that, Vadim, is all the difference. The Kremlin's psychologists and game theorists should have spent some time pondering that."

"But they have," Stepulev insisted. "Americans have shown time and again they have no stomach for war, let alone appetite. And under no circumstances do they want to fight an equal. With time, they might find traces of our involvement. Especially considering our contemporaneous troop movements. But their politicians will gladly point to ISIS and tell the American people the jihadists were responsible."

"And vengeance is exacted on ISIS because to engage us would result in world war," Bor said.

"Exactly."

"Neatly done," Bor conceded. "But I remain unconvinced it will be so. As I said, theory is about to meet reality."

"We have our orders, Taras."

"Just so. This is not the first time we have questioned the wisdom of such orders."

"You sound like a cynic. Like a tired soldier."

"Nothing new."

"Not true, Taras. You have always been cynical. However, I have never seen you tired. That is new."

"Tbilisi, Vilnius, Sevastopol, Aleppo, Ramadi, and one hundred places in between. Yes, I am tired." Something close to a smile appeared on Bor's face. "But I have yet to reach my prime."

Stepulev rose and clapped Bor's shoulder again. "Now, there is a frightening thought."

The door to the room opened and the *rezident*'s aide stuck his head in. "I am to inform you to expect an encrypted call from Moscow in fifteen minutes. You are to take it in the secure facility I showed you earlier."

"Thank you," Bor replied. The aide closed the door.

The two operators were silent for several seconds while they contemplated the implications of what was about to occur.

"That will be it," Stepulev observed. "The order."

"Where are your volunteers now?"

"An apartment in College Park off Route 1. Denisov is with them. The vests are prepared. They were told to be ready to leave on five minutes' notice."

"Get to Leesburg airfield as quickly as possible after dropping off the last volunteer. Do not wait to observe the outcome. Switch vehicles and go. We cannot wait. There will be a period of confusion, of course. But they will mount a furious search almost immediately after the first strike occurs. You need to take off as quickly as possible."

"You are not coming also, Taras?"

"I will if the main event goes as planned, of course. But I'm the backup for a reason. If I have to execute the fail-safe, you will leave on your own. I will have to leave later. If possible."

Stepulev nodded. "Where did you move your volunteers?"

"A house in Lorton, a city in northern Virginia along I-95."

"Do you still plan to simply abandon them if the fail-safe is unnecessary?"

"No."

"What will you do with them?"

"Eliminate them."

"All?"

"Yes. They will be a liability."

"But they know nothing. They believe they are doing this on behalf of the caliphate."

"They came here expecting to die. I do not want them to be disappointed."

Stepulev smiled briefly. Then, with a solemn look on his face, he extended his hand to Bor. The assassin grasped it firmly and the two held the grip for several moments. Both came here expecting to die. Each wished the other didn't have to; each was proud the other was willing.

Bor released his grip and went to receive the order.

CHAPTER 73

General Maximov has confirmed all units are at full readiness," Vasiliev said.

Yuri Mikhailov nodded, saying nothing. Vasiliev, who was adept at reading his boss's moods, could discern nothing from his face. The eyes were hooded, masking the shrewd intellect behind them. To some he might appear inebriated, though contrary to his CIA profile, he almost never drank alcohol. The Russian president sat, quiet but formidable, his massive frame overwhelming the chair.

Mikhailov didn't feel formidable at the moment. He was surprised to find himself nervous, a feeling rare if not absent since his days in the KGB. A man vested with his power and authority had few, if any, occasions to feel truly anxious.

But Mikhailov had a sober appreciation for the scale of the endeavor he was about to initiate, as well as the implications. He was a student of history, and though he was not a military strategist, he was keenly aware of the need for all of the moving parts of the plan to fall into place—otherwise, not just failure, but possibly even disaster would ensue.

The plan, his plan, was bold. Its major components were simple— feint, distract, hold, and attack. Nothing that military strategists hadn't done for hundreds, if not thousands, of years. The tools were different, as well as the magnitude. But the principles remained the same.

Mikhailov read about and admired Frederick the Great, Stonewall Jackson, Patton, MacArthur, Rommel, von Rundstedt. Tactical audacity supported by meticulous planning and effectuated by lightning strikes. His plan was the equal of any of theirs, and he had the good fortune of facing a credulous opponent.

Nonetheless, should any of the moving parts falter—if there were a snag or a problem in timing—the plan could begin to unravel and his country could be imperiled in a way it hadn't been since Hitler's advance in 1942. The possibility would make anyone, even the formidable Mikhailov, nervous.

But the potential reward was worth the risk. The potential reward quelled the anxiety. Mikhailov would be assured of his place as one of the great men in history. He already possessed extraordinary power. Now he was on the brink of extraordinary glory.

Mikhailov examined his watch, a superfluous motion driven by nervous energy. He was aware of the time to the minute. "Everyone is to remain on standby until Stepulev notifies us. Then we will proceed in the planned sequence, at the planned intervals."

"Yes. Anything else, sir?"

"Stepulev is in motion?"

"He is."

"How much longer to the first strike?"

"Imminently."

The formidable frame remained motionless. "Inform me immediately."

"Of course," Vasiliev replied. "Anything else?"

Mikhailov paused, his hooded eyes gazing nowhere in particular. "Vodka."

CHAPTER 74

S tepulev drove the black Ford Explorer along Wisconsin Avenue, a volunteer in the passenger seat and two in the back. Their expressions were at once frightened and determined. Each wore a light poplin jacket under which were canvas vests into which was sewn enough explosive material to devastate nearly half a city block.

The legend among jihadists was that suicide bombers felt no pain; the explosion resulted in instantaneous death. They simply were, and then, they were not. There was insufficient time for the nerve impulses to register pain before the brain was pulverized and the jihadist was already in paradise. Of course, not all suicide bombers were fully convinced the legend was accurate, so they hedged their bets by ingesting their drug of choice to render them oblivious to the impending explosion. None of Stepulev's volunteers took that route.

Stepulev hadn't seen the four men located on the north end of Tunlaw as he drove from the Russian embassy minutes earlier. Ty Wilson and Ike Coe had been joined by Mike Garin and Congo Knox a short time earlier. Garin kept vigil at the embassy after Stepulev had driven away. Knox, Wilson, and Coe followed Stepulev in their own black Ford Explorer while Garin remained behind to wait for Bor. When Knox protested that sending three men after the Explorer was ridiculous, especially since Garin would be alone, the latter pointed out that the passengers in the vehicle were wearing jackets in August in Washington, D.C.

Knox understood. When he asked what instructions Garin had for the three DGT men if the men in the jackets acted suspiciously, Garin simply replied, "Shoot first and don't waste time asking questions later."

CHAPTER 75

The nearly four-hundred-person staff of the National Security Council dealt with a blizzard of information, much, if not most, of it of little consequence to national security. Indeed, the majority of the information was little more than background noise. It could sometimes yield useful information when tethered to a puzzling statement from a foreign leader or a peculiar incident seemingly unrelated to the safety of the populace.

James Brandt, the Oracle, had long developed a reputation for being able to divine the consequences of disparate bits of ostensibly unrelated information. He had surrounded himself with staff members who possessed similar, if far less profound, capabilities. Brandt, however, had seen in Olivia Perry capabilities at least as impressive as his own. Olivia might be the one person who could match Brandt in seeing answers where others saw only puzzles.

So it was when one of Olivia's NSC colleagues, Barry Brame, called her on her cell shortly after Garin had left Dwyer's house for the Russian embassy. Not that Brame had seen anything especially noteworthy about the information he was about to convey to Olivia, but as with most of the male staff of the NSC, he sought any excuse for contact with Olivia.

"Hi, Olivia. It's Barry. I know you've consulted with Professor Hammacher—Ryan Hammacher—about cyberattack issues."

"Hello, Barry. What's going on?"

"I just thought that since you know him and this is one of your issues, you should know that Hammacher was found dead in a men's room at Logan Airport."

"What? When?"

"About four days ago."

"What happened?"

"His girlfriend found him on the men's room floor just before they were to take a flight to Reagan. Airport security called Boston PD and paramedics. They pronounced him dead at the scene. Preliminary cause of death was listed as a heart attack and—"

Before Brame could finish, Olivia said, "Bull." Flat and unequivocal.

Startled, Brame asked, "Huh?"

"Nothing, Barry." Hammacher, someone Olivia knew to be relatively young and by all appearances healthy and fit, just happened to be found dead at the same time Bor had reemerged and satellite imagery showed peculiar Russian movements? Garin and Dwyer repeatedly said there were no coincidences in their business. "Did the police find any documents on him?"

"No. His girlfriend took them before they arrived on the scene."

"And she didn't turn them over? She's tampering with a potential crime scene."

"Tell that to her. She's a big-time lawyer. She must've figured they were important enough to take with her."

"Where are they now?"

"We have them."

"How?"

"The girlfriend—a Meagan Cahill—e-mailed them to Jess, to your attention."

"E-mailed? How . . ."

"iPhone."

"Jesus. I assume it wasn't secure?"

"You assume correctly. Anyone could have intercepted them."

"Okay. Well, we'll have to worry about that later." Olivia thought about asking Brame to have Jess forward the file to one of Dwyer's secure communications rooms, but if the information in the file pertained to national defense, such transmission would be illegal. She would follow protocol.

"Barry, I need to view that file as soon as possible. In a SCIF. Let Jess know I'm on my way to the OEOB."

CHAPTER 76

Bor would emerge from the embassy soon. Of that Garin was fairly certain. He had a better sense for how Bor operated than perhaps anyone. Garin had served with Bor for two years as Omega operators, Garin as the leader and Bor as one of his most trusted team members. Each had saved the other's life at some point—taking out a sniper before he got off a shot; providing cover while the other advanced. They'd slept shoulder to shoulder in rat holes, eaten rotted food, and dressed each other's wounds.

But it went beyond being teammates. More than one Omega member had noted the similarities between Garin and Bor. Both were indefatigable, even for special operators. Both were smart.

Both seemed to have a death wish.

So Garin waited for the man to show. Whatever Stepulev and his windbreakered crew were up to, whatever damage they were primed to cause, it was a sideshow. Bor was the main event. Bor was the danger. Bor was Yuri Mikhailov's Rider on a Pale Horse.

Bor had escaped last time. Barely. He'd been one step ahead of Garin throughout. This time, Garin had drawn almost even.

The traffic around Union Station was dense. A swarm of cabs flitted about its perimeter and a long queue had formed outside its entrance. Masses of commuters seeking various forms of conveyance were moving about the station's interior and exterior. Lobbyists taking the Acela along the eastern corridor, staffers taking the Metro, visitors and tourists taking Amtrak to Chicago and Atlanta. Hundreds of shoppers and diners milled about the densely packed main hall or sat in the various restaurants and cafés, passing time or waiting for a bus or a train.

Christine Brogan was one such commuter. Normally, she'd take the Metro from her office on Massachusetts back to her apartment in Woodbridge immediately after work. But her schedule was off, as was her concentration, having been earlier disrupted by a text from her boyfriend, Gabriel. A text telling her that he needed space. A text telling her he had been seeing someone else for several weeks. A text.

Christine hadn't seen it coming. Only a few days ago she and Gabriel had been sitting on a concrete bench near the Capitol Building planning to take a long weekend at a cabin in the Blue Ridge Mountains overlooking the Shenandoah. They'd been there before just a couple of months ago and had a marvelous time. When she'd told Barb Rankin, her college roommate, about the trip, Barb had shrieked that Gabriel was going to propose. Men didn't take two trips with a woman to a cabin in the Blue Ridge Mountains just for the ambience. The first trip had been for a purpose. It had been a scouting trip to determine whether the location was a suitable place to propose.

The two eagerly began planning Christine's future as a married woman. First an apartment, followed by a starter home somewhere in Prince George County, followed by two kids and an upgrade to a more substantial dwelling. Christine would take some time off from work when the kids were young but reenter the workforce when the kids were old enough for school. They had it all mapped out.

But then came the text. The coward's way of conveying bad news. He couldn't even tell her by way of a phone call, let alone in person. She'd read somewhere that today's young men had less testosterone than their fathers. Her own father was sure of it.

And just like that, all the best-laid plans of Barb and Christine went out the window.

Christine floated through the main hall of Union Station, her mind on the cruelty of Gabriel's cowardly text. Nearly three years of her life consumed by nothing more meaningful than a few dinners after work, the occasional weekend party or show, and every once in a while a trip to a nearby vacation spot. Nothing lasting, nothing to build on. Just treading water.

She wasn't angry or even sad. Mostly, she felt numb, blindsided. Scores of people passed her, jostling and purposeful. To Christine, they were just a blur of suits and ties and skirts and pantsuits, one no more noteworthy than the next.

Except for the short, thin man in the white windbreaker skirting about the main entrance near the taxi stand forty feet away. As she approached, Christine noticed the steady, intense look in his eyes, which was incompatible with his jittery body movements. He radiated . . . weirdness. Yet it appeared no one but Christine noticed.

If anyone had noticed, it wouldn't have mattered. It all happened before Christine took another step. The jittery man reached inside his windbreaker. A fraction of a second later a concussive blast lifted Christine off her feet and propelled her backward at the same time a fusillade of metal pellets and ball bearings tore through her limbs and torso, ripping off her left arm and leg and shredding her abdominal cavity. Strips of her flesh and shards of her bones mixed with those of scores of others and sprayed across the floor and walls of the edifice. Outside the main entrance the blast scythed the queue at the taxi stand, body parts covering the flagpoles and balustrade around Columbus Fountain at the center of Columbus Circle. Several limbs and heads were strewn along Massachusetts and Delaware Avenues, portions of which were smeared with blood and guts.

The blast knocked out windows more than a block away and could be heard throughout Capitol Hill. Within minutes NBC and Fox News had scrambled news crews from their nearby headquarters at North Capitol. The wail of multiple sirens drowned out all of the noise as multiple emergency vehicles were dispatched to the scene.

None of them would find any identifiable evidence of Christine Brogan, other than a fully intact cell phone on which Gabriel's text still remained.

CHAPTER 77

Congo Knox's ears were still ringing as he maneuvered the vehicle frantically down Massachusetts Avenue. Out of the corner of his eye he could see Isaac Coe shouting something unintelligible. The street ahead was filled with debris, smoke, and people running in different directions. He swerved, slowed, and swerved again to avoid them and proceed along New Jersey Avenue.

Just a few minutes earlier Knox, Coe, and Ty Wilson had been following the vehicle driven by Stepulev, who, after what appeared to be a number of surveillance detection maneuvers, eventually drove down Massachusetts Avenue toward Union Station. They had remained several cars behind, close enough to keep the vehicle in their sights. About a block before Union Station, their sight line had been blocked momentarily by a Metro bus. When they reacquired the car again they saw a jittery-looking man in a white windbreaker exiting the car and walking toward the main entrance. Ty Wilson immediately got out and followed, no more than a hundred feet behind.

Knox and Coe continued to trail Stepulev's vehicle down New Jersey, even after the blast. There had been no point in searching for Wilson. Both men knew from experience and simple calculation that he had been too close to the jittery man to have survived the explosion. All of their efforts now were directed at keeping Stepulev's vehicle in sight.

Five miles to the southeast, Mike Garin had heard the low roll of distant thunder followed by the sound of multiple sirens and instinctively knew the Russians had struck. He pulled his cell phone from his pocket and called Knox, who answered instantly.

"We're behind the vehicle, Mike, headed in a northwest direction," Knox informed. "One of the windbreakers got out and set off a suicide vest at the entrance to Union Station. Wilson's dead, along with lots of other folks."

"Don't interdict them unless you're certain they've arrived at their destination," Garin commanded. "They may be joining another crew, so we can't afford to intercept them until we're certain we have everyone. But once you're sure they've arrived at their next target location, look for any backup they may have and then take them all out immediately."

"Got it."

"Best guess, Congo. Where are they headed?"

"Northwest. We're heading in the general direction of Treasury, OEOB, and the White House."

"I'll tell Dan to alert Secret Service, FBI, and D.C. Metro. You'll have lots of company, so be careful. Under these circumstances Secret Service snipers will take out anything approaching the White House that looks even remotely suspicious. That includes you."

"They're too good for that, Mike."

"Good has nothing to do with it, Congo. Don't give them any reason to fire, but don't give the other windbreakers a chance to do anything. Use your best judgment. Then take them out."

Knox weaved between a stopped cab and an oncoming ambulance. "Mike, Dan says Olivia left for the OEOB a few minutes ago."

There was silence for a beat. "Stay focused. Make sure they don't have backup; make sure they don't set off another vest," Garin said. "And make sure you don't get waxed by Secret Service in the process."

CHAPTER 78

President Marshall watched and James Brandt listened to the chaos on the screen in the Situation Room.

First responders were massed throughout the entrance to Union Station and Columbus Circle performing triage operations, identifying and separating those victims likely to survive from those who would soon die. Dozens of stretchers were lined up on the pavement near Columbus Fountain awaiting patients. EMTs moved about swiftly, tending to the injured and carrying patients toward ambulances. Audio captured commands and screams and cries while handheld cameras bounced and swayed, displaying horrific scenes of agony and death.

Unofficial casualty estimates ranged from 120 to 150 dead and more than four hundred injured, but several reporters acknowledged that at this stage the figures were guesswork. Marshall had been told by Homeland Security that the numbers could easily triple by the end of the day.

The expression on the president's face shifted constantly between anger and anguish. A terrorist act that would claim scores of lives had occurred on his watch. Although his administration was barely six months old and the previous administration had been notoriously lax about matters of security, responsibility for this failure fell to the Marshall administration alone.

The newscasts were reporting that the blast appeared to be the work of a suicide bomber. There were few witnesses since most who could've provided useful information had been killed or maimed by the explosion. Most of the security cameras in the vicinity of the attack had been damaged or destroyed. DHS told Marshall, however, that one cabdriver fortunate to have somehow avoided serious injury reported seeing a jumpy guy with a white windbreaker near the entrance to Union Station seconds before the blast. According to the driver, the jumpy guy "looked like one of those folks beheading people on T.V."

Standing protocols were implemented almost instantly. Both government and private sector office workers were advised to remain where they were until further notice. Those people traveling about the District—whether workers, tourists, or errand runners—were asked to return to their headquarters, hotels, and homes. Off-duty members of the safety forces were summoned to assist and be ready to be deployed in case of further attacks.

There was a brief debate regarding the advisability of suspending ground transportation and air traffic in and out of the city. They settled upon temporary partial suspension, to be adjusted as developing circumstances warranted.

The security apparatus of the nation's capital operated smoothly, competently, and efficiently. All necessary resources moved swiftly into place. None of which provided Marshall any solace. In his mind, he had failed the American people. Whatever legacy the remainder of his term might produce—whether strong economic growth or foreign policy success—it would be marred by this day. What troubled Marshall the most was the sense that the day's events—the bad ones—weren't over. The commander in chief reassured himself, in part, with the thought that the best security personnel in the world were handling the matter. But he drew most comfort from the knowledge that he had given Mike Garin sanction to do what he did best.

CHAPTER 79

At that moment, Garin was doing nothing except continuing his surveillance of the Russian embassy. There were no signs of activity. The sounds of distant sirens had dissipated, but there was an energy, a tension in the air, as police and other government vehicles sped down nearby streets. Clearly, the authorities weren't sure the threat was over.

Garin was certain there was more to come. No matter how severe the attack had been, the true threat was still within the walls of the Russian embassy. The Butcher had said as much. There was to be a diversionary strike, then the main strike, to be backed up by Bor. Preventing the main strike was out of Garin's hands. But he found it interesting that there was a backup.

Olivia was the first to discover the backup plan.

Sitting in the SCIF, she was continuing to scan the Hammacher file, but the critical components of the plan had already coalesced in her mind. The plan was aggressive and bold, even hideous.

If Olivia's conclusions were correct, Russia was about to strike the United States in a way seemingly indifferent to the principle of mutually assured destruction. Mikhailov was taking an enormous gamble, a reckless gamble. Maybe she was wrong, maybe Mikhailov knew something she didn't, but Olivia believed the gamble was an uncharacteristic mistake by the Russian president, one that would have catastrophic consequences.

Olivia rapidly skimmed through the rest of the text. She found nothing that changed her original conclusion, but she wanted to be sure before she informed Brandt, who was next door, in the White House. For a moment she considered calling Garin with the information, then instantly rejected the thought. She'd seen him operate close-up. He could stop this. But she had no authority to pass on the information without clearance from either her boss or the president himself, even though the president said he had Garin's back.

Olivia walked quickly out of the room and through the OEOB and the plaza separating the OEOB from the White House.

O ne down, two to go.

Even if the last two segments of his mission failed, Stepulev believed he'd already accomplished the objective. The bombing at Union Station had exceeded their expectations. Although he had driven clear of Columbus Circle by the time of the blast, the roar of the explosion had been extraordinary and the radio news had already estimated deaths likely would be in the hundreds. An event of that magnitude at a transportation hub in the nation's capital easily would constitute the "distraction" desired by his superiors.

Stepulev hadn't, however, anticipated that the bombing would cause Washington traffic to so quickly come to a crawl. He had little experience driving in the city. He'd made several detours around his planned path and determined that dropping off a windbreaker at the second strike point would prolong the mission to the point of jeopardizing the third and most spectacular strike. He would be discovered and interdicted.

So Stepulev proceeded directly to the last strike point. Although he'd been given latitude to change the progression as circumstances dictated, he thought it best to give his superiors notice, so he palmed his cell and hit a preset.

Bor answered. "Congratulations. So far."

"Traffic congestion is greater than anticipated. As a result I am proceeding to the third strike point. Tell Moscow."

"I will," Bor said. "You should know Moscow had calculated you would complete two strikes at most. If you are able to execute the third target it will be an unanticipated bonus."

"You do not really think that surprises me, do you?"

Bor snorted. "Take care, my friend."

Before terminating the call, Stepulev noticed the Ford Explorer several car lengths to the rear. He recognized it as the same vehicle he'd seen a few minutes ago, the black man with the goatee driving.

"Prepare yourself, Ziad. You are next. We are being followed, so you will have to exit and get to the point as fast as possible. Remember to keep your hand on the detonator at all times. The White House snipers will be on high alert."

"I am prepared." The voice was frightened but determined.

Knox was becoming convinced that the car he was following was not going to meet any reinforcements, and its trajectory was in the general direction of the White House.

Isaac Coe apparently was thinking the same thing. "My vote is sooner rather than later, Congo."

"That makes it two to nothing. I'm going to overtake them and force them to the curb. Mike said shoot first and forget about the questions, so take out as many as you can. Fire at will."

Stepulev saw the car behind them increase in speed. He did the same, swerving around slower vehicles ahead of him. As they approached G Street, less than a hundred yards from the Old Executive Office Building, Stepulev pointed at the large gray building.

"I am going to stop up ahead, Ziad. Get out and run as fast as you can past that building and keep going toward the White House. You will see the press corps between that building and the White House. Get as close as you possibly can, just as we rehearsed it. Again, keep your hand on the trigger at all times."

Ziad's eyes met Stepulev's in the rearview mirror and he nodded.

The Russian pulled the steering wheel hard to the left and jumped the curb as pedestrians screamed and scrambled to get out of the way. The vehicle slammed into the steel barriers and Ziad sprang from the rear door of the car toward the OEOB at a full sprint, dodging startled office workers in his path.

Knox slammed on the brakes, stopping near the Renwick Gallery approximately forty yards behind Stepulev's car. "I'll cover, Ike. Go after the runner. Fire discipline, but get him."

Stepulev and the last windbreaker had gotten out of opposite sides of the vehicle, had shot two uniformed Secret Service agents, and were shielding themselves behind their respective car doors. Knox opened the driver's-side door and dove to the pavement, rolling twice before settling on his stomach in a prone position, his Glock 17 extended before him. He fired four rounds toward Stepulev's vehicle—two each slamming into the driver's- and passenger-side doors. Without turning to Coe, he shouted, "Go!" and fired four more rounds, the last two shattering Stepulev's passenger-side window and pulverizing the last windbreaker's head.

Coe shot forward, firing a burst of three rounds in the general direction of Stepulev, who was crouched behind the door of the car. Within a few seconds Coe was already past the car and gaining on Ziad, the weight of the vest slowing the suicide bomber considerably. The operator heard a pop as a round zinged past his head from Stepulev's weapon.

Panicked pedestrians ran in myriad directions, some diving to the pavement. Screams reverberated throughout the plaza as Coe chased the suicide bomber who was running toward the White House.

Coe could hear an exchange of gunfire between Stepulev and Knox behind him. Stepulev glanced behind him and saw that Ziad was in the detonation zone. The Russian pulled his cell phone from his pocket and pressed the key for Bor. "It is done," he said. Then Stepulev emptied his entire magazine toward Knox and smiled in satisfaction just as two rounds from Knox's pistol tore through the Russian's chest and throat.

It was clear Coe would be able to close to no more than thirty yards of the suicide bomber before the latter reached the perimeter of the White House grounds. If the explosives in the bomber's vest were as powerful as those set off by his compatriot at Union Station, lots of people were going to die in and around the most powerful edifice in the world.

O livia had emerged from the OEOB moments before two vehicles jumped the curb and havoc ensued. She was caught almost equidistant between the OEOB and the White House, cell phone in one hand and a sheaf of documents in the other. She sank to a defensive crouch as she heard the rounds of gunfire, people screaming, and glass shattering. A man in a white windbreaker ran past from left to right about forty yards in front of her, heading in the direction of the White House. Approximately forty yards behind the windbreaker she saw a man chasing him. Though bewildered, her mind registered that it was Isaac Coe.

She remained frozen in a crouch as Coe sped by in pursuit of the windbreaker, who a second later came to a jarring halt, as if he'd run into an invisible brick wall. A fraction of a second later Olivia heard the sharp crack of the rifle fired by the sniper atop the White House. She saw the windbreaker stagger and spin as a second report sounded, his right hand clutching the front of his jacket.

Before Olivia's brain realized that the atomized parts of the windbreaker had sprayed over her body, before she recognized that a small metal pellet traveling four hundred feet per second had torn through Isaac Coe's left biceps, nearly severing his arm from the shoulder, Olivia felt herself being lifted from her defensive crouch by the force of the suicide vest's massive blast.

The last thought she had before her body was violently deposited on the pavement nearly twenty feet away was that she'd always assumed she'd die on a cold winter's day, not a hot one in August.

CHAPTER 80

The distraction was complete.

Mikhailov had gotten the news directly from Bor only minutes after the bomb had exploded outside the White House. Vasiliev had also relayed reports from intelligence officers stationed near the blast. Although it was far too early for accurate estimates, the casualties were likely to be in the dozens, including members of the White House press corps. That fact alone ensured it would be a major story. But combined with the earlier bomb at Union Station, the story was already building to immense proportions—so immense that nearly every intelligence resource at America's disposal was being trained on the twin events, just as Mikhailov had expected. The media was already reporting the events as the work of jihadists.

Mikhailov hadn't touched the vodka Vasiliev had provided. As with Egorshin, the presence of the alcohol served as a security blanket. The plan was on pace and progressing nicely. He needed nothing but his own resolve to calm his nerves.

Mikhailov tapped a key on his phone, and moments later Vasiliev entered the room.

"It is almost time, Alexei. Tell Stetchkin to give Volkov the order."

"Yes, Mr. President."

"We should expect verification of the results almost immediately, correct?"

"Yes, Mr. President. It should be a matter of minutes."

"Upon receipt of verification, relay my authority to all responsible officers to proceed with their respective campaigns."

Vasiliev smiled. Finally it was under way. "Yes, Mr. President. Anything else?"

Mikhailov lifted the glass of vodka from the table next to him as if he were handling a used tissue. "And take this with you."

CHAPTER 81

Outwardly he appeared, as usual, unflappable, taciturn. But the sound of the distant sirens combined with the pain that radiated from his ear to his neck made Garin anxious. He wanted to act, not watch and wait.

His cell phone rang. It was Dwyer.

Garin answered with a question. "Any movement?"

"Knox called. They were tracking a bomber outside the OEOB. A White House sniper took out the bomber, but he was able to detonate before dying, or he had a dead man's trigger. Lots dead—I don't have a figure. Some press people included. Ike Coe was following close. He might lose an arm." Dwyer took a breath before continuing. "Mike, Olivia is down too. She's alive, but I don't know much else. She was almost as close to the bomber as Coe."

"Where is she now?" The gravedigger's voice.

"They were taking her to GW Hospital last I heard. If she's not there already, she will be soon."

There was silence.

Dwyer asked, "You're thinking about killing someone, aren't you?"

"No."

"The diversion's over, buddy. That means the main event's up next, and if that fails, Bor's up. So stay focused."

"I'm focused."

"I don't doubt it. Any more bleeding from your ear?"

As if prompted by the question, a piercing sensation shot from somewhere in the center of his skull to his jaw. "No."

"Are you going to be up to speed? Can you handle this?"

"Yes."

"I think we need to get the FBI and everyone else involved now, Mikey. Cat's out of the bag with the bombings."

"Wrong," Garin said harshly. "Bor still hasn't moved. If we tell the FBI all we know, it will get back to Bor and he'll compensate. We can't give him any advantage whatsoever. If he hears the FBI's about to intercept him, he'll set off whatever plan he has. He'll preempt them, or he'll evade them and then complete his plan."

"Then they just need to go into the embassy and grab him."

"That's Russian sovereign territory, Dan. If we do that, it's not just a violation of law; Mikhailov will say it was a provocation—a justification. But more importantly, Bor will see it coming and be long gone."

"I admire your newfound restraint, Mikey. Your usual approach is to kill the bastards and let God sort them out later."

"Usually works." The right side of Garin's face twitched as another sliver of pain skewered his ear. Garin's phone beeped. "I got another call, Dan. Send someone to GW to be with Olivia."

"Congo's already there."

"Good." Garin connected the other call.

"Michael?"

The voice was a whisper of pain and exhaustion. It was Olivia.

"How are you?" Garin asked urgently. "Where are you?"

"I just arrived at GW. They still haven't taken my cell, obviously."

Garin knew Olivia had something urgent to say; otherwise, she wouldn't be calling. "Take your time. What do you need to tell me?"

"They're going to take my cell any second."

"Don't let them. You're Brandt's chief aide and this is a matter of national security. If they can't process that, tell them to screw off. Is the phone secure?"

On the other end of the call, Olivia smiled weakly through the pain. "Yes, I'm using Congo's encrypted device. Michael, this so-called backup plan involving Bor; I'm pretty sure I know what it is. Ryan Hammacher, a professor at MIT, was killed. At least, I'm pretty sure he was killed. You guys always say there are no coincidences and this fits that pattern from before—"

"Olivia," Garin interjected gently, "save your strength. Tell me your conclusion."

"I'm sorry," Olivia said, her voice raspy. "I'm incoherent, I know."

"No worries. Take your time. Tell me what you know."

There was silence for a few seconds, followed by the sound of fabric rubbing against the phone. There was an officious voice in the background.

"Michael, the medical personnel are saying I have to turn off the phone because of the hospital equipment. I—"

"Put Congo on," Garin said.

Another pause, then, "Mike. Congo."

"Congo, tell the hospital people to back the hell off, now. Pull your Glock out if you have to. Intimidate them. Scare the *hell* out of them. I need to hear what Olivia has to say."

"No problem."

Garin heard indistinguishable noises coming over the phone. Then the sound of escalating voices followed by panicked voices followed by compliant voices. Knox had prevailed.

Olivia continued, "Michael, Hammacher was a professor at MIT. Computers, electrical engineering, or something. Maybe both. He testified before Congress a lot. Worked under contract with DARPA—the spooky kind of stuff." Olivia paused, her breathing labored. Garin could hear her fight the constriction in her vocal cords caused by pain. "He was about to board a flight to D.C. to testify again. They found him dead in a washroom at Boston Logan."

Garin heard a sharp command from Knox in the background. More compliant voices, retreating and fading. The sound of Olivia's breathing became more labored.

"Hammacher was working on systems for military and commercial aircraft, including drones," Olivia resumed, her voice enervated. Garin expected Olivia's lucidity to fade soon.

"Olivia," Garin interrupted. "What is Bor going to do?"

"I think Bor's backup is the kind of thing Ryan was working to prevent. Except Bor's plan is probably much larger than what Hammacher anticipated." Olivia exhaled and tried to summon the strength to continue.

"I'm listening," Garin said patiently. "Go ahead."

Several seconds passed. Garin heard the rustle of fabric and the voices of professionals discharging urgent functions. The voices were much closer than they had been seconds earlier.

"Mike?" It was Congo Knox, concern bordering on alarm in his voice. "Olivia just lost consciousness. Not good. Blood all over. I'll get back to you."

On the other end, the killer Boy Scout swore under his breath.

CHAPTER 82

Major Valeri Volkov had been a young man in a hurry for much of his adult life, and as with most such men, he'd rarely taken a moment to appreciate his accomplishments. He was always looking toward the next goal, his next opportunity to rise. All of his previous advancements had been the product of study, diligence, and sacrifice. He had no influential family members or connections to push him up the ladder.

To this point his station in life was based solely on merit. He was sufficiently introspective to acknowledge that he didn't possess nearly the natural talent of Piotr Egorshin. But he believed that once Egorshin advanced to bigger and better things, it would be Valeri Volkov, by virtue of endurance and determination, who would succeed him.

Volkov believed, however, that such succession would occur sometime far in the future. Yet here he was at the helm of the unnamed unit Egorshin had built and commanded with his brilliance, the unit that was central to Yuri Mikhailov's designs for Russian glory.

All Volkov had to do was give an order. The systems and programs had been devised and built by Egorshin. The unnamed unit's technicians had been trained by the prodigy, to whom Volkov had been loyal to the end.

At least that's what Volkov kept insisting to himself to brush away the stray threads of guilt he'd felt after the interrogation by Stetchkin. Volkov had been honest throughout. He hadn't trimmed or expanded his answers in service of his own ambitions. Nonetheless, upon learning of Egorshin's death, Volkov felt as if he'd advanced to the unit's leadership by stepping over a corpse.

While the feeling hadn't entirely dissipated, it had substantially receded behind feelings of pride and power. He'd ascended to one of the more important positions in Mikhailov's new Russia. His prospects now were almost as unlimited as those of the genius Egorshin had been. He allowed himself to think of a future of wealth, fame, and women.

All because of the tyrant Stetchkin's fixation on Tatiana Palinieva. Astonishingly foolish, if somewhat understandable. Palinieva was remarkably attractive. Perhaps now Volkov might draw her interest. After all, if Egorshin could, Volkov could too. And why not? He would possess all the accoutrements of power that he assumed a woman like Palinieva found attractive. He'd make sure to pay his respects at the funeral.

Volkov stood in his station on a low platform at the back of the large plexiglass-enclosed room. His eyes, like those of the dozens of analysts and technicians seated at the sleek ergonomic workstations before him, were fixed on the large digital clock set above the massive movie theater—like screen on the front wall. The screen flashed a blizzard of letters and characters arrayed about innumerable lighted dots on a world map separated into ninety-eight grids. Each member of the unit had been tasked with a specific grid, but all the work for each grid was complete. When all of the digits on the giant clock reached zero, it would be left to Volkov alone to press the command key to set the event in motion. A single key. The program could have self-executed at the appointed time, but Egorshin had wanted to engage the event manually.

Stetchkin was monitoring the proceedings from General Maximov's office down the long corridor on the same floor. Volkov was relieved that the tyrant wasn't standing behind his shoulder. As soon as the event had been engaged, Stetchkin would notify Mikhailov and take credit. Volkov had no problem with that. There was enough credit to go around.

As the enormous clock ticked down, a faint murmur spread through the room along with a feeling of anticipation akin to the countdown toward a New Year. Volkov saw slight turns of the head; sidelong glances and smiles proliferated among the unit members. They, too, felt the power of being part of shaping history.

Less than thirty seconds now. As the clock ticked downward, the murmur began to fade to silence. Volkov saw Ludmila Rutina, the attractive analyst from the cyberwarfare division, stare and smile brazenly at him. He returned it with a rakish grin.

Four, three, two . . . Volkov held his breath, his index finger over the key . . . Zero. He tapped the key.

The massive screen froze and went completely dark. Nothing. Not a flash or a flicker. Just black.

Bolts of bewilderment and anxiety lanced through Volkov. He pressed the command key again, harder. Nothing happened.

Zero plus two seconds.

He pressed it twice more. Again, no effect.

Zero plus four.

The heads of the personnel in front of him were swiveling back and forth, looking at their teammates, mouthing questions, scanning the screens on their desktops. Hands were shaking.

No answers.

Then, in rapid succession, the monitors on the desktops also froze and went dark. The sounds of confusion and panic rippled through the room. Technicians moved about urgently, looking over shoulders, asking questions, performing diagnostics.

Zero plus twelve, thirteen, fourteen . . .

Volkov cast about the room, frantically searching the faces of the unit members, looking for anything that might indicate the owner had an answer, a solution. All he found was confusion and disbelief. The best and brightest were stumped.

Volkov frantically pressed the other keys on the board.

Zero plus seventeen. The phone on his desk trilled.

Stetchkin.

Volkov's body froze, but his mind rocketed into overdrive. Fragments of explanations, images of Uganov and Egorshin, pleas for mercy, all careened and collided in his brain.

The phone trilled again and Volkov stared at the handset. He couldn't avoid or delay: Stetchkin demanded immediacy. He would expect a definitive explanation. He would want results.

Volkov reached for the handset, wincing in anticipation of the tyrant's unyielding questions and reproaches. But what he heard astonished him.

"Major, what is the problem? Can this be rectified immediately?"

Gone was the imperiousness and cruelty seemingly ever present in Stetchkin's tone. The voice on the other end was worried and plaintive. It threw Volkov momentarily off-balance. Nonetheless, so as not to aggravate the tyrant, his response was apologetic and deferential.

"Sir, staff is performing an analysis as we speak. It may take a few moments to determine the cause of the problem and remedy it."

"It is solvable, however? It is just a matter of time?"

The truth was Volkov had no idea. This should not have happened. Innumerable simulations had been run. All of the potential bugs had been worked out months ago. This was inexplicable, and the perplexed looks on the faces of the technicians scurrying about the room confirmed his belief.

"Without a doubt, sir. We will remedy this. I believe we can do so in short order."

"Can you give me an estimate of how long?"

"Not precisely, sir. We are working on that."

"A minute? Five minutes? An hour?"

"Very soon, sir," Volkov dodged.

"You are confident the event will proceed shortly?"

"I am confident, sir," Volkov lied.

"Is there anything your unit needs to ensure one hundred percent success?"

Volkov was struck by the servile, almost pleading quality in Stetchkin's voice. He wasn't just anxious; he was frightened. The sound was almost as incongruous as hearing a crocodile squeal.

And then Volkov remembered. He had represented to Stetchkin that the event could proceed without Egorshin with one hundred percent certainty. Under normal circumstances the failure of such representation would have doomed Volkov. Stetchkin, however, had made the very same representation to Yuri Mikhailov. Stetchkin, therefore, was no less terrified than Volkov. Thus, for the moment, Stetchkin and Volkov had common interests; they were allies.

Volkov replied, "Sir, we have everything we need. Thank you."

"Understand that all of the resources of the Russian Federation are at your disposal, Major."

"Thank you, sir."

"Good luck. Please notify me the instant the problem has been resolved."

"I will."

Volkov would not.

For unbeknownst to either of them, Egorshin had exacted his revenge from the grave, courtesy of his uncle Sergei the magician.

It was zero plus fifteen minutes. Not a significant delay, but enough to require adjustment of downstream timetables. Large numbers of troops with massive amounts of equipment and weaponry were poised for a highly coordinated strike. As with any military maneuver, the optimal window for such a strike would not remain open indefinitely. A decision would have to be made soon.

Alexei Vasiliev was the only person in the room with Mikhailov, who had preferred not to be surrounded by a herd of generals and advisors when the event was initiated, all jockeying for position and spewing advice and observations. Mikhailov preferred to drink from a straw rather than a firehose. At critical times, the quality of information was more important than its volume.

Vasiliev was Mikhailov's chief aide because he understood that principle. He didn't bother his boss with extraneous ruminations. He spoke sparingly and precisely, and only about things that advanced his boss's objective.

Mikhailov had sat alone in his office at the time scheduled for the event's initiation. He knew that any significant developments would be reported by Vasiliev, so he busied himself with a stack of mundane reports about natural gas production and related economic outputs.

Vasiliev had waited until zero plus five minutes before informing his boss that the event had not yet launched—there had been some type of catastrophic systems failure at the unit. Mikhailov received the news as if receiving a weather report. It was raining despite a forecast of a sunny day.

But, as always, the unflappable Mikhailov had packed an umbrella. So he invited Vasiliev to take a seat and the two talked hockey for several minutes, until there was a light knock at the door. Vasiliev rose and opened it to a tremulous aide, who whispered something before disappearing as fast as she could. Vasiliev turned to Mikhailov and simply shook his head once and retook his seat to await further instructions.

Mikhailov was deliberative. He had a bit of time. His contingency plan was in place and ready to proceed. All he had to do was give the order.

"We will give the unit another forty-five minutes."

Vasiliev nodded. "Realistically, Mr. President, if necessary we have more time than that."

"Yes, I know. But it is better to set a firm deadline; otherwise, we will find ourselves pushing the schedule back five more minutes, then ten, then ten more. Alert Bor." Mikhailov smiled, anticipating Vasiliev's response. It was his aide's unofficial duty to second-guess him.

"Mr. President, the Bor option presents enormous risk. Perhaps it would be advisable to wait."

"Either option presents enormous risk, Alexei."

"The Bor option, however, if executed with anything less than perfection, will assuredly precipitate war, and not merely regional skirmishes, but a major conflict. A world war, which could result in the use of nuclear weapons."

"Bor will execute with perfection. That is why we entrusted the backup operation to him."

"But he was thwarted in the EMP operation," Vasiliev noted. "There is no guarantee he will not be thwarted once more."

"Bor was not thwarted. The Iranians were. By Mr. Garin."

"Respectfully, Mr. President, I submit the risk is greater now. Garin—and for that matter, the Marshall administration—was placed on notice of our ambitions by the EMP operation. We cannot dismiss Garin—our file on him is substantial. Even Bor respects him."

"Alexei, we are cognizant of the risk. We have discussed the probabilities more times than I can count. Indeed, the Main Intelligence Directorate ran the probabilities through their supercomputers—what?—literally billions of times. The majority of outcomes show success. And if there is a failure—the possibility of which I do not discount—the Americans will assign blame to ISIS, because every single person Bor is running is inspired by, and believes himself to be working for, that group."

"This would dwarf the 9/11 attacks, Mr. President. The American people will expect and demand massive retaliation against anyone with any fingerprints on it."

"No, Alexei, they most assuredly will not. They will demand retribution, but not suicide. ISIS and the jihadists will be made to pay. And even then Marshall's hands will soon be tied. Half of the American populace believes Marshall to be a warmonger. They and the press will act as a restraint."

Vasiliev paused for a moment. "But what of NATO? When we move into Greater Russia, Article 5 will be triggered."

"Not one member of NATO will go to war over Latvia, Alexei. Or Estonia. Or even Ukraine. They are timid and dependent on our gas. And when we sweep through Iran, they will even cheer us for assisting them, for removing the chief state sponsor of terror. Again, keep in mind *probabilities*."

"Still, Mr. President, is it worth the risk?"

"We shall soon discover the answer, Alexei. But consider for a moment the potential rewards. Greater Russia, Iran, the Persian Gulf. No nation has conquered so much territory in more than seventy years.

None has done so successfully in more than one hundred. So"—Mikhailov smiled again—"having dutifully performed the role of court skeptic, kindly alert Bor to be prepared to receive final orders within the hour."

"And if the unit does not rectify the problem—a problem you were guaranteed would never occur—what shall we do with Stetchkin?"

The smile left Mikhailov's face. "Nothing. For now."

CHAPTER 83

All it took to fool the United States of America were glasses and a ball cap.

Vasiliev had alerted Bor to be prepared to deploy the volunteers. While it was still possible, even likely, that the event would proceed, he needed to leave the consulate and travel through the District to the house where the volunteers were waiting. Since they believed Bor was a jihadist, and to make sure the volunteers could never be connected to Russia, they were kept some distance away.

The Americans were credulous, but they weren't stupid. After the suicide bombings they would be on highest alert, and Garin was certain to have insisted to the powers that be that Bor was at the center of everything. Even if they weren't wholly convinced of his involvement, they would act out of an abundance of caution and check all surveillance videos for his image—presuming they knew what his image looked like.

Bor, always a step ahead of his adversaries, left nothing to chance. Both machines and man had biases. Those biases permitted Bor to evade detection by donning nothing more than heavy-framed glasses with one frame slightly smaller than the other and an Orioles cap pulled low over his brow. It was a matter of symmetry. Both human brains and facial-recognition algorithms were thrown off by subtle alterations. For humans, the alterations were magnified by stress. Chaos and pressure caused the closest of associates to misidentify one another. Even the most highly trained associates.

Even Garin.

He was somewhere nearby. Bor hadn't seen him. The consulate's ubiquitous surveillance cameras hadn't picked him up. But Garin was out there, waiting. Bor was sure of it. In the two years they'd been Omega teammates, Bor had watched Garin closely—observed his techniques, habits, and preferences. The man was relentless. Bor had never seen him fail. He made mistakes, as anyone would, but they were inconsequential and immediately rectified.

Bor slung a large black Adidas bag filled with handguns, ammunition, and an MP7 over his left shoulder and proceeded out of the door of the consulate surrounded by several visiting diplomats. He scanned the surroundings as he walked to Wisconsin Avenue and immediately hailed a cab. He saw no sign of Garin, nor did he expect to. If Garin identified Bor, he wouldn't intercept him here. Rather, Garin would lie back and observe Bor's movements, waiting for him to rendezvous with others. Then the fireworks would begin.

Garin anticipated that Bor wouldn't emerge alone from the consulate.

As clever and experienced as Bor was, when it came to evading detection, he had a significant handicap: his physique. Unless he was walking with a group of NFL running backs, his body would betray him.

And it did so only moments later when he left the consulate with several midlevel functionaries from the European Union. In contrast to their deskbound softness, his musculature had a rough, almost cartoonish quality. The minor alteration to his facial appearance would have been enough to throw off most people, but Garin spotted him just as he was entering the Red Top cab. Garin determined not to lose the cab in the traffic as he jogged to the black Explorer. He got in and followed several cars behind.

The traffic was sufficiently heavy that even if Bor looked back through the rear window it would be difficult for him to locate Garin. Given the events of the last couple of hours, Garin thought it likely Bor was now in play and would link up with whatever team might be supporting him.

They proceeded at a moderate speed down Memorial Parkway past

Arlington. Garin's phone vibrated and he answered, putting it on speaker. It was Olivia. Though she sounded weak, Garin was relieved. He demanded that she put Congo on.

"Listen to me, Michael. This can't wait. Hammacher was engaged by DARPA to design systems to prevent the hacking of aircraft—military, commercial, drones, anything."

Olivia paused to catch her breath. "There are vulnerabilities in the air traffic control system. The FAA and others are patching them, but as soon as they do, it seems new ones appear. There are up to three thousand commercial flights being monitored at any given time, so to some extent, it's like playing whack-a-mole."

"Olivia, I'm following Bor as we speak. Give me the CliffsNotes version."

"Before his death, Hammacher designed patches for vulnerabilities in GPS satellites, surveillance and broadband systems, and air traffic control centers, which the Department of Transportation implemented, in the main."

"In the main. You mean, not completely."

"Right. Congress had a battle over funding. I know, big surprise."

Garin shook his head. "Is Bor somehow going to exploit these remaining vulnerabilities?"

"Based on all of the evidence, I think he intends to hijack commercial airliners."

"By hacking air traffic control?"

"Yes and no. One attack could be directed at the air traffic control systems. Disrupting the routing of aircraft, creating havoc, possible crashes and midair collisions. Aircraft and air traffic controllers could be rendered blind. False images or locations of aircraft could appear or disappear on radar screens."

"You mean like that hack in Sweden last year?"

"Precisely. We believe Mikhailov used that as a test run. Swedish air traffic control systems went completely off-line. Thankfully, nothing serious happened, just some flight cancellations until the system came back online." Olivia was speaking rapidly.

"Why do you think Mikhailov, the Russians, were behind it? What evidence is there?"

"The lack of evidence is evidence. The Chinese, Iranians, usually leave some trace of their presence. The Russians, however, rarely, if ever, do. They're that good."

"So what's Bor's role in all of this? He's not a cyberwarrior."

"I think Bor is going to somehow attack aircraft directly."

Garin, absorbed in what Olivia was telling him, noticed that he was now only two cars behind the Red Top cab. If Bor looked back, he'd easily recognize Garin. He slowed into the right lane and let other cars overtake him, placing more distance between himself and the cab.

"What does that mean?"

"I think Bor's going to access the flight controls for individual aircraft."

"He can't, Olivia. No way. Cockpits are completely inaccessible these days. And protocols established since 9/11 prohibit pilots from opening the door in case, say, a terrorist threatens to kill a hostage."

"He doesn't *have* to get into the cockpit. He may be able to control the plane from the passenger compartment. That's what DARPA engaged Hammacher to prevent."

Garin slowed a bit and drifted farther behind Bor's cab. "You've got my attention."

"There's controversy as to whether a passenger can take over flight controls with a laptop, but apparently DARPA was sufficiently concerned that they were paying Hammacher a huge sum to make sure it could never happen."

"And you think Bor is capable of hacking flight controls? How would he do it?"

"From what I can gather it's done by scanning and accessing the plane's networks through the in-flight entertainment system. A passenger uses an Ethernet cable with a connection to a laptop or tablet computer. He removes the plastic cover to the seat electronic box that's located under some of the seats—usually the one located under the seat directly in front of him. It's easy to do—removing the cover, that is."

"Slow down."

She did, but barely. "Say he overwrites codes on the plane's thrust management computer. He can give it a command to descend or climb. Or maybe he issues a command to descend or climb to just *one* engine. The plane would pitch or roll. Theoretically, then, he could hijack or crash the plane."

The cab turned right. Garin sped up slightly to beat the changing traffic light and make the same turn. "It can't be that easy," he said. "Major airplane manufacturers leaving their systems so vulnerable some gamer could take over and fly the plane into Mount Whitney? They must have redundancies, interlocks, whatever you call it, to prevent someone from messing with a plane's software while it is in the sky."

"They do. But Hammacher says—said—they can be overridden."

Ahead, the cab slowed to a stop at a traffic light. Garin tensed momentarily in anticipation of the possibility of Bor getting out, but he remained in the vehicle. Garin stayed several vehicles to the rear, his attention split between the cab and Olivia.

"Even so," Garin argued, "wouldn't instruments in the cockpit signal that someone was attempting to tamper with the plane's network? I mean, wouldn't the plane's computer identify an attempted hack and counter it somehow?"

"Normally, yes. But if someone was sophisticated enough, he could create a virtual environment to evade the EICAS—to fool it. And this possibility had DARPA . . . I think the technical term is 'freaked.'"

Garin nodded to himself. "If it was possible, it *should* have them freaked. But that's just it. If someone could take over a plane by hacking its in-flight entertainment, DOT, FAA, and the airlines would also be freaked. But they're not . . ."

Garin stopped, realizing his error and anticipating Olivia's counter.

"And if they freaked it would be a disaster. Merely acknowledging the possibility would cause air travel to grind to a halt. No one would set foot on commercial aircraft. The Dow would crater. Commerce would be devastated."

Ahead, Bor turned to look back. Garin ducked his head toward the dash, not completely, but enough to obscure his face without appearing conspicuously evasive. He hesitated a few moments before straightening.

"Michael, can you still hear me?"

"I can. Okay, even if I'm not completely persuaded by the Hammacher file, we now know with certainty that Bor is involved in something, as if we needed two suicide bombers to prove it. And the guy who made my ear ring said Bor would discharge a backup operation." Garin followed the cab through a left turn. "I suppose you think he's going to hijack a plane?"

"Yes."

"Admittedly, that's bad."

"It gets worse."

"Figures. Go ahead."

"Commandeering a plane is bad enough, but that's just the means to an end," Olivia said, her cadence slowing. "Remember the sheet with the flight numbers?"

"He's hijacking all ten?"

"Even worse. I checked the flight paths of all ten. Bor does only big things, right?"

"How bad is it?"

"This is a leap on my part, but I think Bor's confederates are going to crash the airliners into critical infrastructure."

"Like another 9/11?"

"No. He's not just going to fly into buildings, as bad as that was and is. He's going to fly them into nuclear power plants, oil refineries, and hydroelectric dams. Just a dip of the wings, a slight detour, and they're there before fighters can be scrambled to intercept. Tens of thousands will be killed immediately. Ten times more eventually."

Garin's jaw clenched. His grip on the steering wheel tightened.

"And that's just a distraction to keep us preoccupied," Olivia continued. "The Russians have been engaged in movement of troops and a buildup of matériel throughout their western front—Baltics, Ukraine, even Poland. They're also moving south in a pincer movement along the Caspian."

"Toward Iran?"

"Toward Iran," Olivia confirmed.

"But they were just *helping* Iran's nuclear program," Garin said, thinking out loud. "But really, unbeknownst to Iran, the Russians were using them to hit us with an EMP. The mother of all false-flag operations."

"And now they're about to invade their ostensible ally," Olivia continued. "An ally whose military defenses have been utterly devastated by weeks of massive bombing."

"So we've essentially prepared the ground for Mikhailov." Garin whistled slowly. "He causes us to bomb Iran into oblivion and then he waltzes in and controls their oil reserves."

"Not to mention the Persian Gulf and the Strait of Hormuz," Olivia added, speaking rapidly again. "Fifteen million barrels of oil pass through the strait every day. Combined with their own reserves, the Russians would control more than a third of all the oil on the planet."

"Holy—"

"Nothing holy about it, Michael. He's gambling that this doesn't result in a world war. This is sheer insanity—"

"Maybe not," Garin interrupted. "If Bor hits the sites, the probability of war is certain, but war with *jihadists* and their state sponsors. It will look like *they're* the ones who hit us, not Russia. On top of everything, it will look like Russia's doing our dirty work for us by invading Iran— the world's greatest state sponsor of terrorism."

Garin tapped the brakes. He'd gradually sped up during the exchange with Olivia. He drifted back another fifty or so yards.

"Still a big risk," Olivia insisted.

"We can debate that all day, but it's happening. The suicide bombers are proof."

"What do you need from me, Michael?"

"Tell Congo to stand down and allow the medical personnel to treat you," Garin said. "And call Brandt. Give him the flight numbers. The president will order them grounded."

"What about Bor?"

A dull wave of pain pulsed from his right ear to the other side of his head, clouding his vision. The sharp, piercing sensations, though less frequent than immediately after his encounter with the Butcher, remained just as intense. He focused on Bor's cab.

"I'll take care of him. Go." Garin disconnected. Several cars ahead of him he caught a glimpse of Bor riding in the back of the Red Top cab. Garin knew that the threat wouldn't be eliminated with a simple order from the president grounding flights identified on the list he'd taken from the man in the safe house. For all he knew, the list itself was a fraud, a decoy. If there was anything Garin had learned from Bor's operations, it was that even his backup plans had backups. And nothing was ever as it seemed.

Bor caught another fleeting glimpse of the black Explorer in the rearview mirror of his cab. It appeared Garin had just terminated a call.

Bor had been aware of Garin's presence mere seconds after leaving the consulate. Despite Garin having thwarted the EMP operation, Mikhailov, Stetchkin, and the rest still didn't fully comprehend the nature of the man they were dealing with.

Bor placed a call on his cell. When it was answered he spoke briefly in Russian before disconnecting. Seconds after that, two gray Jeep Grand Cherokees trailing Garin's SUV by several car lengths peeled off onto a side street to the right.

Bor leaned forward. "How much longer until we get there?"

"In this traffic, not long. Ten minutes. Fifteen tops."

Bor leaned back and counted the seconds subconsciously. They were approaching another intersection approximately a quarter mile ahead. If his timing was correct, it should happen there.

Thirty seconds later Bor's cab cleared the intersection. He saw Garin's Explorer in the right side-view mirror as it entered the same intersection.

Garin caught a flash of gray out of the corner of his eye less than a second before one of the Grand Cherokees slammed into the right side of his Explorer, driving it across the street and into a car parked against the opposite curb.

Garin's head ricocheted off the driver's-side window, rendering him momentarily dazed. Garin instinctively reached for his SIG. The doors of his car were sandwiched between the car on the curb to his left and the Grand Cherokee to his right, trapping him in the vehicle.

Garin shook his head to regain his senses, swiftly raised his pistol toward the front of the Grand Cherokee, and squeezed off six shots—left to right—across the SUV's windshield. Four of the rounds—two apiece—struck the two Zaslon operators in the front seats, killing both. Almost simultaneously, the third Zaslon operator sprang from the right rear door of the SUV, an MP5 submachine gun trained at the Explorer. Garin dove to the floor as a three-round burst ripped across the rear of the Explorer. Garin popped back up and returned fire with two rounds to the Zaslon operator's face, dropping him in the street.

Garin's eyes searched the interior of the Grand Cherokee for any additional targets. Seeing none, he swiveled to the rear, emptied his magazine into the back window of his SUV, and dove through the shattered remains, rolling onto the hatch before falling to the street.

A cacophony of screaming, sobbing, and whimpering pedestrians and squealing car tires swirled about him as he scrambled to his feet and the second Grand Cherokee screeched to a halt thirty feet behind the first. In one fluid motion Garin ejected the spent magazine, seated a fresh one, and fired seven rounds into the darkened windshield of the second SUV.

Garin swung behind the Explorer, using it as a shield, and paused for a moment, the only sounds the tinkling of broken glass and approaching sirens. He discerned no movement in the passenger compartment of the second Grand Cherokee. He saw no bodies, dead or alive.

Two Arlington patrol cars approaching from Garin's right skidded to an abrupt halt twenty feet from the second SUV. Two officers leapt from each of the vehicles with weapons drawn, shouting unintelligible commands in the directions of both the second SUV and Garin. A single Zaslon operator materialized from the rear door of the vehicle and with astonishing speed and precision shot each of the four officers with an MP5 before any of them was able to squeeze off even a single shot. Almost simultaneously, Garin fired five times at the Zaslon operator, hitting him three times in the torso and once in the throat.

The Russian was dead before he fell to the ground. When he did so, Garin saw a pedestrian lying on the ground on the opposite side of the street, Garin's fifth round having struck his upper left thigh.

Garin cursed, rose from his crouch behind the cab, and cautiously approached the second Grand Cherokee. The bodies of two Zaslon operators lay slumped in the front, dead. No one else was in the vehicle.

Garin sprinted across the street, and the wounded civilian's expression morphed from one of pain to one of terror as Garin neared. "It's okay, it's okay," Garin shouted. "I'm a good guy. Good guy."

Garin knelt to examine the man's wound. Although his left pant leg was bloodstained, the wound, though painful, was relatively minor. The bullet had merely grazed the man's thigh.

"You're going to be all right," Garin assured him. "More cops will be here any second. They'll get you to a hospital." Garin seized the frightened man's arm, tore a strip of cloth from his shirt, and wrapped it around the wound. "You'll be fine. Hang tough."

Garin rose and sprinted toward the closer of the idling police cruisers, the wail of approaching sirens in the distance. He climbed in, shifted into drive, and sped in the direction Bor's cab had gone.

Garin's intention was not to overtake Bor, presuming that was even possible at this point. It was to evade arrest and detention by the police, something that would take him out of play and thereby virtually ensure the success of Bor's mission.

Garin raced down Clarendon, light bar flashing, until he was confident he'd put sufficient distance between himself and the scene of the shootout. He needed to abandon the stolen cruiser before he was intercepted. A quarter mile in front of him was another intersection, three cars stopped at the red light. He swerved around and in front of them, blocking their path. Then he got out of the car with his SIG leveled menacingly at the driver of the lead vehicle and motioned for him to get out. The panicked-looking middle-aged man complied instantly, his hands raised over his head. Garin slid into the driver's seat of the maroon Ford Fusion and proceeded in the direction of Reagan National. A simple calculation to increase the odds. He had no hope of reacquiring Bor, but he knew the assassin was eventually headed toward Reagan National or Dulles. The odds of intercepting him there were better.

Garin picked up his cell and called Dwyer.

"Dan, Bor is likely going to Reagan or Dulles."

"How soon?"

"Assume immediately. He and whoever is with him cannot be allowed on any—" Garin stopped speaking abruptly, interrupted by an agonizing bolt of pain that shot from his outer ear through his skull.

"Mike?"

The intensity of the pain blurred his vision. Garin clenched his jaw and composed himself. "Call Olivia on Congo's cell. Tell her to tell the president he needs to order FBI SWAT teams ASAP to Reagan and Dulles, and to alert security at both airports."

"What for? Won't that tip off the mole? Tip off Bor?"

"Yes. No. No other options. We lost Bor. We're out of time. I've lost Bor. There, the attack is imminent . . ."

Dwyer's brow furrowed. Garin was babbling, incoherent. "Mike, what's going on?"

The garbled response from Garin was interrupted by the noise of violent impact and the sickening sound of twisting metal.

CHAPTER 84

Had any of his maintenance coworkers been paying any attention to him, they'd have immediately recognized something was wrong.

The look on Hassan Ali Daar's face was one of dread. After nearly a year of slow, painstaking preparation, the time had arrived. Almost every workday he'd bring in another small piece. Most of the time, the piece would be attached to his key ring. He'd disguised them as ornaments. Sometimes they'd festooned the bracelet he wore on his left wrist. Occasionally, one of the larger pieces would be strewn innocuously among the items in his standard-issue toolbox.

Each time, the component would pass through the scanner undetected, never even drawing a second look. Even if they had, the various unconnected items would have appeared to be inconsequential knickknacks, some obscure pieces of metal or plastic.

More than two hundred separate workdays. More than two hundred scans. A smile, a nod of acknowledgment to the screeners, then off to work down one of the concourses.

He'd get only a minute or two each day for assembly. The airport seemed perpetually busy. But a minute or two was all he needed. Spread over two hundred workdays, it amounted to several hours. More than enough. Enough to assemble two, if needed.

Late mornings were best. Air traffic, and therefore foot traffic, was lightest then. He would scan Terminal B for travelers, coworkers, and security, and when he'd assured himself he'd have a minute or two without interruption, he'd duck into the men's room. There, he'd first peek under the stalls. It didn't matter if one was occupied by a traveler.

After all, they couldn't see what he was doing, and even if they emerged, nothing would seem amiss. He was maintenance. He was supposed to be there. On the other hand, if he recognized the trousers of a coworker or security, he'd take a pass, deferring further assembly to another day.

One minute was all it usually took. Sometimes two. Never more than that. With a flathead screwdriver he'd remove the aluminum cover of the stainless steel waste receptacle set into the tiled wall next to the line of sinks. Behind the aluminum cover was a black plastic cover, which he'd pull away to reveal a small cavity in the wall hollowed out using the claw of his hammer.

And therein lay the assembly project. Undetected. Growing incrementally almost every workday, one piece at a time. Gradually beginning to resemble the finished project. Until one day approximately one month ago it was complete, sitting dormant, ready for use: a PP-2000 SMG submachine gun chambered for a 9×19mm round. A fierce-looking Russian cousin of the MP7, with a forty-four-round magazine capacity. It held an extra magazine in the rear acting as a stock.

Daar also stored several additional magazines with it, each loaded with armor-piercing cartridges because some of the airport's security personnel wore vests. The *ughaz* hadn't specified the rounds be armor piercing, but Daar was taking no chances. He was determined that everything be perfect. The *ughaz* frightened him. Not that Daar was easily frightened. Far from it. He'd grown up in the war-torn streets of Mogadishu during the brutal reign of General Mohamed Farah Aidid. Daar had seen mass slaughter and starvation on an industrial scale.

But the *ughaz* inspired fear on a plane of its own. Daar had witnessed him break the back of an *askari* who hadn't properly followed instructions. He'd picked the poor man up as if he were a small child and slammed him across his knee. Daar vividly recalled the sickening snap of the spine, almost as loud as a gunshot. He remembered the J-shaped scar along the *ughaz*'s right jawline just as vividly. The mark of the *ibliisku*.

So, although Daar had discharged his assignment to the letter, he remained fearful. The *ughaz* had called moments ago to confirm the location of the weapon. The appointed time was at hand. Untold infidels would die. Daar prayed it would be a success.

Taras Bor wheeled the minivan toward the parking garage at Reagan National, glancing in the rearview mirror at the five volunteers seated behind him. Their expressions were indecipherable to Bor, almost blank. Each carried a slim canvas backpack containing a laptop or tablet. Otherwise, they had no luggage. They would need none.

The assassin checked the digital clock on the dashboard. They were cutting it close, but they had sufficient time for each to navigate through the airport to the TSA checkpoint and toward their respective flights in Terminal B. The departure time for each spanned a thirty-minute window. The strike points spanned another two hours after the first plane took off.

So far, everything was proceeding according to plan. Well, everything within his realm of responsibility. He had, after all, been given the signal to execute his operation, the backup plan. That meant that the event had somehow failed, or at least been delayed.

No matter. Bor's operation would accomplish the ultimate objective. Provided, of course, they were not thwarted by Garin.

Bor held no illusions that Garin wasn't at that very moment doing everything he could to locate Bor and stop his operation. After all, Bor had received no word from any of the Zaslon operators he'd dispatched to intercept Garin. The probability that they would kill Garin was very good. They were in an entirely different league from most other operators: They were in an entirely different galaxy from Bulkvadze's men. But as formidable as the Zaslon operators were, Bor knew never to dismiss his former teammate until the last shovel of dirt was thrown on his grave.

And, in truth, Bor would be disappointed were it otherwise.

Accordingly, Bor would be prepared in case Garin somehow appeared. He had sufficient firepower at his disposal and he'd also provided a bit of misdirection: a decoy list of flight numbers and times that

Garin had taken from one of the Butcher's men. The actual flights departed from different concourses and earlier than those on the decoy—not by much, but enough to make a difference. Even if Garin could stop some of the volunteers, he wouldn't stop them all.

G arin awoke in a haze of pain. Instinctively, he tried to assess the situation and locate his firearm. He saw in his peripheral vision two handguns trained behind each ear. He didn't know if they were friendly or hostile. Either way, it didn't matter—he was ill positioned to respond.

Dwyer and Knox came to an abrupt stop approximately one hundred feet from a mangled maroon Ford Fusion, the hood of which was nearly wrapped around a large oak on the tree lawn.

Three Arlington police cruisers surrounded the vehicle at various angles and an EMT was stationed no more than a dozen feet to the rear. It seemed one million lights were flashing. Six police officers, weapons drawn at the low-ready, were slowly, warily meandering about the Fusion, assessing the damage and any potential threats within. Concentrating on the wrecked vehicle, they appeared oblivious to the presence of the DGT SUV behind them.

Dwyer and Knox got out of the black Explorer, each with an HK416 at the ready. Dwyer motioned for Knox to flank to the right. Knox nodded and both men crept slowly behind the officers, weapons tracking the movements of the officer who appeared most primed. Dwyer identified the sergeant who appeared the most senior and advanced carefully to within a few feet to his rear, HK at nearly point-blank. Dwyer addressed the officer in a low, neutral voice so as not to startle him.

"Stand down. Lower your weapon slowly. Then look behind you."

The sergeant did as instructed, his eyes widening upon seeing the muzzle of Dwyer's HK inches from his face. The officer glanced to his right and saw Congo Knox with his rifle trained in the direction of the other patrolmen.

"We're friendlies, Sergeant. So is the man in the Fusion. Tell your men to lower their firearms. We intend no harm, but if you so much as flinch, we'll put all of you in the ground."

The sergeant complied immediately. "Holster your weapons," he commanded. The command disrupted the concentration of the other officers, who were startled to see Dwyer and Knox with the drop. Instantly they obeyed the sergeant's command.

Dwyer addressed the senior officer. "Sergeant . . ."

"Bowman."

"Sergeant Bowman, how often have you been told you were involved in a matter of national security?"

"Never."

"Right," Dwyer said. "Look at our weapons. Not your typical gangbanger pieces, right? You know about the bombings in the District, of course. So understand, the man in that vehicle is vital to stopping further damage to the national security interests of the United States. You can help. How cool is that?"

Sergeant Bowman nodded but looked conflicted.

"A healthy skepticism on your part is understandable," Dwyer acknowledged. "Congo, cover them."

Dwyer lowered his weapon, letting it hang from its sling as he pulled out his cell phone and tapped the keys for SecDef Merritt's cell. No answer. He placed the phone in his hip pocket and produced several plastic ties from his back pocket.

"All of you, please lie facedown on the ground." They complied.

"We could use your help. I just called someone to vouch for us, but no answer. I assume you good officers are not the trusting type and will try to stop us by radioing in. So you understand why this is necessary."

Dwyer tied their respective wrists behind their backs. "We could've used an escort to Reagan National. We're going to be driving a bit over the speed limit."

Dwyer heard a noise from the Fusion.

"Okay. We need to check on our friend. The crash looks bad, but if I know him, he'll want to be on his way as soon as he's able. Can I trust you not to do anything stupid?"

"Yes, sir."

"Good. Because all of you together are no match for my intense black friend over there."

Dwyer nodded to Knox and to the Fusion. Knox went to the driver's-side door, where Garin, pinned between an airbag and the seat, was struggling to get out.

"Slow down, Mike, slow down. Let me give you a hand."

Knox let his rifle hang from its sling, grabbed Garin's left arm, and eased him out.

"What happened?" Knox asked.

"My ear. I passed out."

It appeared as if he was favoring his left side. "Looks like you might've cracked some ribs. Does it hurt to breathe?"

Garin steadied himself on the tree lawn. "Time?"

"About 5:15."

"We're running out of time."

"No, Mike," Knox countered. "The flights aren't for at least another hour and a half. We can still get to Reagan in time."

"Wrong."

Dwyer grasped Garin's other arm to help steady him. "What do you mean, Mike?"

"The flights will leave earlier. Those departure times are fake. I didn't give it much thought before, but it was way too convenient. A handwritten list in someone's pocket? Bor plans every detail, anticipates everything. The list was just another safety valve. A decoy."

"Holy . . ." Dwyer whistled. "We better get moving."

Knox shook his head. "Where does a guy like Bor come from? What did they do to make that guy?"

"They raised him Russian," Garin replied.

Bor descended the escalator, strolling casually toward the Qdoba restaurant adjacent to the TSA checkpoints. The volunteers had been instructed to enter the terminal separately at five-minute intervals and proceed to the TSA line with sufficient space between them so as not to draw attention.

So far, so good. Although the TSA lines seemed interminable, Bor saw nothing else out of the ordinary. Security, though robust, appeared little different than usual. There were several armed uniformed personnel and Bor believed he had detected at least a few plainclothes security. Despite the bombings in the District, most flights were on schedule and security behaved no differently than on any other occasion. Indeed, Bor expected that security had been instructed to act in a manner calculated not to produce anxiety among travelers.

Bor had purchased a ticket to Miami under an alias so that he could pass TSA, enter the concourse, and monitor the volunteers until boarding. He entered the TSA pre-check line after the last of the volunteers had passed the scanners. A painfully skinny man by the name of Hassan Ali Daar had left a gift for him in the men's room across from Gate 8 on the concourse, and the assassin was eager to unwrap it.

They were within a mile of the access road to Reagan National Airport, Congo Knox topping ninety miles an hour as he wove the black SUV, Garin in the passenger seat and Dwyer in the rear, around slower vehicles.

"Try her again," Garin demanded.

Dwyer keyed Olivia's cell for the third time since they'd left the accident scene, again with no answer. They needed to confirm that the flights were grounded.

"Nothing."

"Try Merritt," Garin instructed, referring to the secretary of defense.

"Not picking up. Cell phone's off."

Knox careened onto the ramp leading to the airport access road.

"Airport security."

Dwyer dialed and keyed. "Nothing."

"FBI," Garin shouted over the squeal of the tires and blaring horns of drivers alarmed by the speeding SUV.

"No go, Mikey. Too removed from the chain of command. By the time they get the authority to ground the flights, it'll be too late."

Knox braked violently as the Explorer jumped the curb onto the sidewalk in front of the sliding glass doors leading to the United ticket counter. Dozens of people scattered frantically.

Garin considered the dilemma for a split second. They had to move immediately, no time for locating and engaging in protocols, niceties, and permissions with airport security. Besides, the moment they entered the terminal with weapons, they'd be deemed threats to be neutralized instantly.

Given the circumstances, Garin spoke with preternatural calmness. "This will likely be suicidal. Security will cut down anyone who enters the terminal with a firearm, and if they somehow miss, Bor won't. You're civilians. It's not your fight."

"Not your fight either, Mike," Knox said. "You're a civilian too." Knox looked at Dwyer. "We're in."

Garin considered the circumstances.

"Leave the rifles; SIGs only. Keep them hidden as long as you can," Garin said. "Dan, spare mags?"

Dwyer reached behind him into a small munitions kit and passed around several spare magazines, which they stuffed into their pockets. "How we going to play this, Mike?"

"No way to finesse this. They may be boarding as we speak. We need to stop them," Garin replied. "Any way we can."

"Mike," Knox said. "We need to go to security or air traffic control and tell them to halt all boarding."

"Time. By the time they verify who we are and get permission, some flights will have taken off. Once they're off the ground, Bor's agents can control them. But"—Garin opened his door—"you and Dan *are* going to security. Tell them everything and see if you can persuade them to ground all flights, or if you can't, get them to call the White House. On your way there keep trying to reach Olivia. *Go.*"

Garin stepped out of the vehicle.

"What are you going to do, Mike?" Knox asked.

Garin was already moving toward the entrance to the terminal, intensity covering his face. Over his shoulder, he said simply, "Speed kills."

Dwyer and Knox ran toward the first uniformed security guard they saw standing near the American Airlines ticket counter, the rapid approach of the two large men causing him to tense. Dwyer raised his palms to assure the guard he wasn't a threat. In a low but urgent voice he said, "I'm Dan Dwyer, CEO of DGT, the military contractor. I know you've heard of us. We have a national security threat emerging here. You need to alert the federal security director, who needs to alert the manager of airport operations that all flights need to be grounded immediately."

The guard appeared bewildered.

"Tell them to contact DHS if they want verification," Dwyer continued. *"Move."*

Bor calmly surveyed the gates along Terminal B, scores of travelers seated or milling about the boarding areas and ticket counters adjacent to Gates 10 through 14. Strapped across his left shoulder was a canvas bag. It contained a PP-2000, fully loaded with armor-piercing shells, and several spare mags.

Hassan Ali Daar had done precisely as instructed. The submachine gun was where it was supposed to be. Bor had no difficulty retrieving it. In a few minutes he would have no use for it. Most of the volunteers were in the process of boarding their respective flights or had already boarded. The flight to Chicago departing from Gate 10, for example, had already pulled back from the gate and would soon taxi to the runway for the two-hour flight to O'Hare.

It wouldn't make it. Shortly after takeoff it would bank slightly to the south, to the bewilderment of those on the flight deck and in the tower. Less than five minutes after that the aircraft would approach the Calvert Cliffs Nuclear Power Plant on the western shore of the Chesapeake, less than forty-five miles outside Washington, D.C. Two minutes later it would make a steep dive and its ninety-one thousand pounds of metal and composites would crash directly into Unit 2 at a speed of 520 miles an hour, instantly killing all 110 passengers and crew members and imperiling the health and safety of the nearly three million souls within a fifty-mile radius of the facility.

At Gate 11, to Bor's left, a group of college students laughed while boarding the United flight to Hartford, Connecticut. The Jetway door would close momentarily. It would become airborne at almost exactly the moment the sirens would sound along the Chesapeake. Forty-five minutes later United Flight 7174 with eighty-nine souls on board would obliterate the Hope Creek Nuclear Generating Station in Salem County, New Jersey, along with the futures of many of the six million people who lived forty-five minutes' driving distance from the site.

And on it would go. Two hours from now nuclear power plants, oil refineries, and hydroelectric dams throughout much of the eastern half of the United States would be destroyed. The lives of millions would be devastated.

Bor noticed a look of curiosity appear on the faces of a few of those waiting to board. Next he heard shouting coming from a distant area of the terminal. Then the low rumble and buzz of some kind of commotion followed by scattered shouts and an alarm. The monitors along the concourse flickered and went blank.

Taras Bor knew Mike Garin was on his way.

A minute earlier Garin had descended the escalator to the main level near the wine bar approximately one hundred feet from the line for the TSA checkpoint leading to Terminal B. The instant he came to the bottom he sprinted at top speed toward the checkpoint. Though the sudden movement immediately captured the attention of several startled security guards, they remained frozen for several moments before reacting. Two of the more alert guards—one a K-9 unit—instinctively gave chase. Alarmed travelers in the TSA queue scattered as Garin barreled past them and toward the scanning machines.

The screams of bystanders mixed with the shouts of the security guards and the barking of the guard dog in hot pursuit. A 280-pound blue-uniformed TSA agent stood obstinately in front of the scanner toward which Garin was heading, blocking his path. A mistake. Without breaking stride, the former all-state running back lowered his left shoulder and plowed into the doughy obstruction, driving him over a metal table and onto the floor.

An airport alarm sounded as Garin, having cleared the TSA checkpoint, veered sharply to his right toward Terminal B for no other reason than its departures were primarily toward East Coast and Midwest destinations. Farther destinations presented a chance, however remote, that there would be enough time to intercept and shoot down the subject planes, if necessary.

As he turned toward Terminal B, Garin glimpsed a Belgian shepherd, its leash trailing behind it, rapidly gaining from the rear. Just as the dog reached him, Garin turned and seized its muzzle with both hands until he could secure its jaws with his right hand. With his left hand he grasped the leash and wound it tightly around the dog's jaws several times, inserting the handle through the collar in a slipknot. The unharmed but stunned K-9 ran whimpering in circles as Garin resumed sprinting alongside the conveyor belt to Terminal B.

Within seconds, Garin entered the concourse. Three security guards, trailing approximately forty feet behind, commanded him to stop. Travelers scattered frantically; others froze.

Garin saw the unmistakable figure of Taras Bor standing at the far end of the concourse in front of Gate 11 and came to an abrupt halt. A couple of beats later the three security guards, brandishing handguns, also stopped, one flanking Garin's right, the other two to his left. Garin's SIG remained secured at the small of his back.

Bor stood no more than thirty feet away with the PP-2000 aimed in the direction of Garin and the guards. A girl of seven or eight stood directly in front of him. Many of the throng of travelers in the area instinctively dove to the floor. Others pressed against the walls of the concourse. The only sound was that of the alarm.

Keeping the PP-2000 trained on Garin and the guards, Bor wrapped his left arm around the girl and hoisted her in front of him, shielding his head and torso. No clean shot. Garin was vaguely aware of a woman screaming.

The look on Bor's face was eerily calm. He made a downward motion with the submachine gun, signaling the guards to lower their weapons. They didn't budge.

"Place your guns on the floor," Bor commanded. "Do it so this girl may go home with her mother. You have three seconds."

Whimpers and whispers wafted from the prostrate crowd. The guards remained motionless.

Bor counted down. "Three . . . Two . . ."

Each of the guards lowered their respective pistols to the floor.

Bor, in turn, gently lowered the girl to the floor. Then he fired a series of three-round bursts, killing each of the security officers.

Garin drew his SIG from the small of his back just as he was staggered by another spike of pain that shot from his ear to the center of his skull, clouding his vision. He fired at Bor, the round deflecting off the muzzle of the PP-2000. Almost simultaneously, Hassan Ali Daar emerged from the lavatory with his own PP-2000 and appeared in the rightmost edge of Garin's blurred field of vision. Garin dove to the floor a tick before Daar fired a burst in Garin's direction, the rounds slamming into the Gate 10 counter.

Prone, with his SIG extended before him, Garin fired repeatedly at Daar, striking him five times in the head, neck, and torso. The Somali's body flipped backward over a row of chairs in the seating area adjacent to Gate 11.

Still prone, Garin shifted his aim back to Bor . . . who had disappeared. Garin cursed under his breath, sprang to his feet, and bolted toward Gate 11, firing at the ticket counter to provide cover until he had expended his ammunition. When he was within a few feet of the counter, Bor sprang up with the submachine gun trained at Garin, who hurled himself over the counter and into Bor, slamming the Russian backward and onto the floor, Garin landing on top as his SIG clattered under the scanning station.

Garin seized the stock of the PP-2000 as Bor, momentarily stunned by the collision, struggled against Garin's weight to regain control of the weapon sandwiched between their torsos. Garin responded by pinning the PP-2000 against Bor's chest with his left hand and jackhammering Bor's face with several blows from his right. The weapon discharged in a staccato series of three-round bursts that shattered the windows overlooking the tarmac adjacent to the concourse, causing travelers to scream and scurry frantically in the direction of the main terminal.

Bor heaved and rolled to his left, throwing Garin, who maintained a grip on the weapon, off of him. Another series of three-round bursts fired, a ricochet catching a wailing gate attendant in his left thigh.

Garin now used both hands to attempt to wrest the weapon from Bor's grasp. As he struggled to maintain control, Bor's finger squeezed the trigger and he heard the hollow metallic click signaling an empty chamber.

Garin immediately released his grip on the weapon and pumped several savage punches at Bor's face, producing a torrent of blood from the assassin's nose and mouth. Bor countered with a brutal thrust of his knee to Garin's abdomen that caused him to roll away in agony.

Almost simultaneously, both combatants leapt to their feet. Bor, still grasping the empty submachine gun, swung its stock like a bat at Garin, who absorbed the blow on his left shoulder, pivoted to his right, and thrust his right forearm into Bor's bloodied face. The Russian barely recoiled, moving back a half step before driving the butt of the PP-2000 upward under Garin's jaw.

Staggered, Garin instinctively retreated a step to gather himself. Bor pressed forward with another thrust of the stock toward Garin's head but missed as Garin crouched under the blow and then sprang forward, driving the top of his skull into Bor's exposed face. The assassin grunted in pain and dropped the PP-2000, but barely moved. He spun furiously to his right in a complete three-sixty—elbow raised at shoulder level—to generate enough centrifugal force for a debilitating blow to Garin's head. In the fraction of a second Bor began the move Garin recognized his former teammate's maneuver, ducked under it, and pounded a hook into Bor's exposed ribs. Bor winced in pain, the blow cracking two of his floating ribs, but continued to spin rightward, slamming his left fist into Garin's head. Though jarred, Garin lowered his shoulder and drove Bor against the Gate 11 ticket counter, knocking the wind out of him. Garin quickly windmilled a flurry of punches at Bor's head and torso.

His arms pinned against the counter, the assassin thrust the edge of his right foot toward Garin's left knee. Had the knee not been slightly bent, the blow likely would've shattered the patella. As it was, the force of the blow threw Garin off-balance, causing him to fall onto his back next to a row of chairs in the waiting area. Bor dove atop him, seizing both sides of Garin's head, and began repeatedly slamming the back of his former leader's skull against the low table between the seating.

Garin tasted blood and noted the familiar sharp smell of ammonia that signaled concussion. Desperate to avoid unconsciousness, he launched a roundhouse at Bor's head, missed, then threw another that barely connected. As Bor continued to pound Garin's head onto the edge of the table, Garin twisted his head, dug his teeth into the middle of Bor's left forearm, and ripped off a chunk of flesh, generating a guttural cry from deep within the Russian's chest.

Blood spurted onto Garin's face as the assassin released his grip. Garin's eyes rolled in their sockets as he strained to regain focus. His survival instincts insisted on immediate movement—but his body struggled to respond.

In his right periphery he saw Bor beginning to stumble to his feet as he grasped his torn forearm. The piercing sound of the terminal's alarm imparted an even greater sense of urgency, and Garin responded by rolling onto his hands and knees. He shook his head and took two quick, deep breaths to regain his sense of awareness. His mental clock told him he had no more time to recover before his adversary would make his next move. He needed to engage now.

Down the concourse toward the main terminal he could hear the sound of officious voices, issuing multiple commands and directives. More security was approaching. To his right he saw Bor reaching for the empty PP-2000. Garin shook his head once more and craned himself upright. Bor had released the submachine gun's spent magazine and was slamming in a fresh one retrieved from a back pocket. Garin shot forward and with his right fist jacked two fierce punches at Bor's head while using his left hand to attempt to tear the weapon from the assassin's grasp. Bor stumbled backward as another blinding bolt of pain streaked from Garin's ear and through his head, causing him to double over at the waist, nothing in his field of vision but white light. He sensed the presence of several security officers immediately to his rear. There were several angry shouts, then staccato bursts from a submachine gun and the distinctive sound of metal striking flesh.

Though still staggered, Garin began to regain his bearings a couple of seconds later. He was surrounded by the bodies of four dead security personnel. Bor was gone.

Garin recovered the SIG from under the ticket scanner, released the magazine, and seated a full one.

He approached the gate, paused at the door, and darted his head into the Jetway. It was empty. Quickly but cautiously he slid down the corridor—weapon before him—hugging the left wall. The hatch to the plane was closed, the flight crew having secured it upon hearing the terminal's alarm. A baggage handler lay on the right side of the Jetway, his head blown off.

Garin looked through the gap between the Jetway and the plane's cabin to the tarmac below. Bor was nowhere to be seen. Behind him Garin heard a stampede of footsteps approaching down the Jetway from the terminal. Glancing back he saw a pack of armed uniformed and plainclothes security personnel led by Dwyer and Knox. Immediately behind Dwyer and Knox was a man wearing a suit with his weapon drawn, no doubt in charge of security.

Garin pointed to the tarmac. "The target's somewhere down there," he shouted. "Get your men and dogs down there *now*. Secure the entire airfield, including the area bordering the Potomac. Halt all traffic out of the airport. No cars, no cabs, no shuttle vans. Nothing."

The lead man nodded and barked orders into a radio.

Wincing from pain, Garin motioned for Dwyer and Knox to follow him before leaping down to the tarmac from the bridge. Immediately upon landing on the concrete Garin spun in a crouch, tracking 270 degrees. With Dwyer and Knox landing behind him, he moved to a nearby baggage cart and water truck, examining each before scanning the area under the concourse bridge leading to the main terminal. Dwyer and Knox flanked him at intervals of twenty feet. They began sweeping northward along the length of the terminal's exterior, an FBI helicopter appearing above. Far ahead, at the other end of the terminal, six SUVs screamed onto the runway and screeched to a halt. The doors exploded outward and within seconds a swarm of FBI HRT personnel in SWAT gear was busy searching and securing the airfield. Seconds later a horde of K-9 units emerged from the maintenance doors near the junction between Terminal B and the main terminal.

The speed with which the various teams had arrived and the proficiency of their respective maneuvers was impressive, the product of innumerable tactical drills and exercises. As they proceeded to move, scores more began to arrive from nearly every direction. The airport was completely locked down, the surrounding vicinity utterly secure.

Garin took a deep breath, one not of relief but of resignation. He knew none of it mattered. They were, after all, searching for Taras Bor.

They were searching for a ghost.

CHAPTER 85

Garin heard laughter coming from down the hall. Raucous laughter. Familiar laughter. And from the looks on the faces of several of the physicians, RNs, and techs walking in the corridor, unacceptably loud laughter, for it clearly disturbed the other patients.

But nothing would be done about it. Because no one dared to do anything about it. Earlier a charge nurse had poked her head into the room to admonish Olivia Perry's visitors to keep it down. Upon seeing the intimidating forms of Congo Knox and Dan Dwyer, she quickly concluded that the hospital could use more sounds of levity and mirth.

Garin entered Olivia's room and saw Knox and Dwyer sporting enormous grins at the foot of her bed. Next to Knox, in front of the window, was a beaming Luci Saldana.

Glimpsing Garin out of the corner of her eye, Olivia turned. Even after several days in a hospital recovering from the trauma of an explosion, she somehow managed to appear stunning. The only outward signs of injury were a small bandage on her left temple and a few discolored bruises on her face and neck.

Olivia smiled broadly and Garin felt an electrical charge.

Dwyer was the second to notice Garin, taciturn as usual. "Uh-oh. Fun's over. Undertaker's here." More laughter. Luci came over and gave Garin a hug.

"Saved the world twice this summer," Knox said. "What's next, Mike? You going to Disney World?"

A flicker of a smile crossed Garin's face, everyone in the room taking a mental snapshot before it vanished.

"Whoa," Dwyer said, "I haven't seen him this happy since we described Hell Week to him at BUD/S. What happened? Did the CIC convince you to come back on board for more mayhem in the service of truth, justice, and the American way?"

"We'll talk about that later," Garin replied. "I'm leaving tonight to see Clint Laws."

"Outstanding. The Professor of Death and Destruction. Sounds like the band's getting back together again."

"We'll see."

Dwyer affected a gravelly British accent. "We sleep soundly in our beds because rough men stand ready in the night to visit violence on those who would do us harm."

Garin leveled his gaze at Dwyer. "He's still out there." The gravedigger's voice had returned.

Dwyer rolled his eyes. "Geez, Mikey. Give it a rest. You've stopped him twice now already."

"Have I?"

There was silence for several seconds.

"Clearly you have, Michael," Olivia assured him.

"He didn't shoot me," Garin said flatly. "Why not?"

"Because you didn't have a weapon drawn. The others did," Dwyer answered. "Respectfully, Mikey, you're overthinking this."

"No. There was something else. He let me live for a reason."

"Probably to aggravate the hell out of the rest of us."

"Bor not shooting me means something, Dan. It should worry you."

"*Hell yeah,* it worries me. It means a guy with exceptional shooting skills but piss-poor judgment is running around loose out there."

"I have no idea what you guys are talking about," Luci interjected cheerfully. She took Knox's hand and pulled him toward the door. "But I'm pretty sure Captain Sunshine didn't come here to talk about death and destruction."

"Obviously, you don't know him as well as we do," Dwyer retorted.

With his free hand Knox grasped Garin's. "Mike, if I can be of service, just let me know. I'm with you."

"Ho, Deadeye," Dwyer said, following the pair. "I'm paying you a gazillion dollars and you wanna run off and join *this* guy's circus?"

Knox pumped Garin's hand once. "You know how to reach me."

The merry trio left the room. As they retreated down the hall, Garin heard Dwyer say, "Beer at my place. I think that nurse liked me. I'm gonna invite her, too."

Garin turned to Olivia with eyebrows raised.

"A couple of more days," Olivia said, answering the question on Garin's face. "I had a concussion, a couple of hairline fractures, and some internal bleeding. I'm okay now. They just want to keep me for observation. After President Marshall called to check on me they're clearly not taking any chances."

She leaned back on the pillows propped behind her. Her impossible abundance of hair fanned in a halo around her head and shoulders. She took the killer's hand, ambivalence yielding to attraction. Now both of them felt a charge.

"How is your ear?"

"It's an ear," he deflected. "I'm on antibiotics and steroids."

"It's more than that, Michael." She patted his forearm wrapped in bandages. "And the burns?"

"We'll see. Maybe some skin grafts."

"You owe me a spaghetti Western marathon."

"As I recall, it was a Dirty Harry marathon," Garin replied.

"We'll alternate. *A Fistful of Dollars, Magnum Force, For a Few Dollars More, The Enforcer*..."

"I'm not sure I can last that long."

"I'm absolutely certain you can." Olivia blushed at her own boldness.

"Did the president thank you?" Garin asked.

"He was very nice."

"Without your analysis, we'd be in the middle of a catastrophe."

Olivia blushed again. A compliment from a killer. She shouldn't have anything to do with someone like him, she thought. She was a Stanford PhD—a rising policy star. She should be seeing Senator What's His Name. Insufferable, but safe and predictable. Garin, on the other hand, was all chaos and almost certain heartbreak. Yet she savored the sound of his voice.

"So, it's a date, Mr. Garin?"

"I believe it is, Ms. Perry."

She released his hand. "Call me when you return from seeing Clint Laws. Dan can give you the number."

"It may be a few days after I get back," Garin said. A chilling look came over his face. "I have to tend to some unfinished business first."

Then Garin turned abruptly and left without another word. Olivia gazed at the broad shoulders tapering to the narrow waist as he disappeared around the corner. Moments later the nature of his unfinished business began to dawn upon her. And it occurred to her it was possible, quite likely even, that she would never see Mike Garin again.

R uth Ponder was sitting in her living room watching the news when the phone rang. Most of the folks who had been with her from the outset were sitting with her. A talking head was describing the events that had occurred in Washington, D.C. Her daughter Barbara answered the wall phone in the kitchen. After a long pause Barbara called Ruth with a tone somewhere between anxiety and awe.

"Mom. Telephone. Come quick."

Ruth rose and was followed by Rev. Broussard and several of her neighbors, concerned about the sound of Barbara's voice. Barbara, wide-eyed, handed Ruth the phone.

"Hello?"

"Mrs. Ponder. Please hold for the president of the United States."

"Pardon?"

A second later: "Hello, Mrs. Ponder, this is John Marshall."

"Goodness. Are you sure? I mean, I'm sorry, I don't know how I'm supposed to address you, sir."

"John will do just fine, ma'am."

"Oh, I couldn't do that, sir. Would you mind terribly if I just called you Mr. President?"

"You can call me whatever you like, Mrs. Ponder."

"Oh my goodness. Oh my. Mr. President, you should know I voted for you last fall, as did my late husband, Amos. He said he didn't always agree with you but he could tell you loved America."

"That I do, ma'am."

Ruth Ponder's family and friends were gathered around her with expressions of amazement.

"Matt Colton tells me he promised to call you back, but I asked him if I might have that privilege. Matt informed my staff that the information you provided was critical to our ability to protect the country. In a true sense, without your husband and you, this nation would have suffered an attack far more devastating than the one it has."

"Oh, Mr. President, thank you very much, but I just gave Matt a tiny bit of information in the hope that Amos's killer would be found."

"Mrs. Ponder, your information saved untold lives. I cannot express my appreciation deeply enough. You are a patriot, ma'am. On behalf of the United States of America, thank you."

Ruth Ponder clutched her chest. "Oh my. Oh my goodness. On behalf of Amos and my family who are here with me right now, as are Reverend Broussard and some of our friends, thank you, Mr. President."

"If we can be of any assistance, Mrs. Ponder, just let me know."

Ruth Ponder paused. "Mr. President, did they by any chance get the man who shot my Amos?"

"I'm sorry to say we did not, ma'am."

"Oh. Yes." Ruth's voice became a whisper. "Well, I do understand, Mr. President. I understand how difficult these things can be. Matt said as much."

"Mrs. Ponder?"

"Yes, Mr. President?"

"It's true we did not capture your husband's killer. Yet. But I know a man who I suspect is doing something about it as we speak. I'm sure Amos would've liked him a lot. I feel sorry for anyone who is in his sights."

CHAPTER 86

**BETHANY BEACH, DELAWARE,
AUGUST 29, 8:14 P.M. EDT**

A cooling breeze lilted off the ocean as the eastern horizon shaded midnight blue and threads of yellow and orange rays played across the ocean as the sun set to the west. The heat from the blistering day radiating from the white sands of the beach below belied the fact that fall would soon be approaching.

The lone figure standing on the second-floor balcony of the sprawling beach house on the northern end of Bethany stood tall, drawing from a Winston and savoring the calming sounds of the crashing waves.

They'd been thwarted. The meticulous planning, the Machiavellian maneuvering, had all come to nothing. Worse. After the finger-pointing and recriminations were complete, heads would roll. Almost literally. In fact, several had already been executed and more would follow in the immediate future.

He would be safe. He had performed all of his tasks flawlessly. Besides, other than the assassin, he was Mikhailov's most valuable aide. And Mikhailov, despite the debacle, remained secure, in large part because he'd eliminated almost anyone who could mount an opposition. The ruthless typically survive.

He was still trying to determine why the event had failed. The consensus among the forensics examiners was that it must have been due to an extraordinarily sophisticated worm of some sort, but thus far not a trace of such a worm had been found. The most accomplished cybersleuths in Russia remained stumped, and it was whispered that only one person in the country, perhaps in all the world, could've designed such a thing, and that person was dead—found murdered in the famed Tatiana Palinieva's luxury apartment.

Perhaps even more extraordinary was the failure of the secondary plan. The assassin had, as usual, performed with nearly supernatural efficiency. Yet the American operator, the one the assassin adamantly insisted be eliminated, had intervened. The assassin had been proven right. The entire operation should have been placed on hold pending the death of the former leader of Omega. But for the American, the world today would be a vastly different one. For all intents and purposes, a Russian one.

Now they were checkmated. By idiot Americans, no less. Marshall had convinced NATO that the troop buildup along the Baltics, the incursions into eastern Ukraine, and the movements toward Iran merited a response almost akin to Article 5. Even the weaker sisters in the EU reluctantly concurred. As a consequence, several divisions of NATO troops were deployed in the Baltics and Poland, and an armada of naval vessels supplemented the US Fifth Fleet in the Persian Gulf.

Several Western European nations, sufficiently alarmed by the Russian aggression, began to shift to more US-produced oil and gas, something that would pose a threat to the Russian economy and, unless he found other means to float such economy, to Mikhailov himself. Marshall was shrewd enough to employ that as a lever against Mikhailov, gaining concessions and keeping him in check. The patrician was sure Marshall would do just that.

The debacle, however, could have been worse. There was no evidence of Russian involvement in either the suicide bombings in Washington or the planned hijackings. All evidence pointed to jihadists as the culprits. The captured volunteers believed they were discharging their missions on behalf of ISIS. They had no inkling whatsoever who their real leader was. The assassin had shrewdly altered his appearance sufficiently to frustrate facial-recognition software. Any surveillance cameras that captured his image—whether at the airport or elsewhere—would be unable to identify him as a Russian operator. And the Zaslon operators the American had killed were all functional cleanskins—utterly untraceable. Even Stepulev couldn't be linked. The volunteers too. All of their flights had been grounded, all had been seized by the American authorities, and all believed they had been prospective martyrs for ISIS. The only evidence of Russian involvement was the Butcher, of whom the DIA had long been aware—but only by reputation, not by identity. Regardless, that piece of evidence had been eliminated when a potential crime scene in Lorton, Virginia, had been reduced to rubble due to an inexplicable gas-line explosion.

The infernal American operator knew, of course. He knew the signature of a Russian operation. And he knew the assassin. Thus, the American president knew. But mere knowledge was immaterial in international relations. Nations couldn't, and didn't, act *publicly* based on knowledge. They acted on proof—especially when a nation's allies assiduously resisted anything that might involve tough choices, let alone the possibility of military reprisal. No one wanted to go to war with a nuclear power over suicide attacks that, by all accounts, had been perpetrated solely by jihadists untethered to any nation-state.

Nonetheless, the West's reaction to the troop buildup was ample sanction. Russia was worse off now than before the entire operation, including the EMP affair. There was no denying it was a disaster, all because of that abominable American operator.

The patrician, however, remained unaffected. Throughout, he had performed his role brilliantly. Indeed, the aspects of the operation for which he was responsible proceeded precisely as planned, despite all of the constraints under which he labored. Mikhailov recognized this. Indeed, Mikhailov had quietly rewarded him for it—both financially and with an even more trusted role in the Russian president's orbit.

Perhaps just as important, he remained a trusted confidant of the American president.

The patrician flicked the cigarette onto the beach below and opened the sliding screen doors leading to his darkened study. Somewhere outside he could hear the radio belonging to members of his protective detail broadcasting the Orioles–Indians game. It was the middle of the seventh, the Indians with a 5–3 lead. Stretch time.

He padded to the bar next to the bookcase and poured himself a glass of Smirnoff, room temperature. Then he sat in a high-backed leather chair facing the balcony and took a long, slow sip—but not a mournful one, not one prompted by failure and dejection. Rather, a contemplative one—one to slow, order, and distill his thinking.

They had suffered a crushing defeat, even if their adversary didn't fully realize just how big a defeat it was. But they had suffered seemingly crushing defeats in the past, only to emerge the victor in the long run. And so it would be once more.

Because it wasn't over.

The Western powers, having imposed sanctions and deployed military assets, would be satisfied that Russia had been dealt with, the matter concluded. They would then turn their attentions to the latest frivolity, convincing themselves it was some matter of importance.

The patrician, however, knew that the West's demise lay dormant here in the United States, somewhere in a rural county in the southeast part of the country. And every single person in the United States but the patrician was oblivious to it. In fact, only two others in the entire world were not oblivious to it.

Consequently, no one would find it. It would remain hidden until unearthed from deep beneath the floorboards of a rickety wooden barn that stood approximately two hundred feet from a pile of cinder blocks and ashes that had once been the home of Oleg Nikolin of Leningrad and Aleksandra Ivanova of Moscow.

And shortly after it had been unearthed, Russia, ever destined to rule the world, would finally do so.

EPILOGUE

All things considered, matters could hardly be better. Perhaps not for Russia. The event had been a disaster, and the subsequent sanctions, recriminations, and retributions were severe.

But for Aleksandr Stetchkin, life was good and the future promising. After all, ruthlessness and treachery were irreplaceable assets.

Within days of the debacle, many of those associated with it had disappeared. The more fortunate were merely fired or demoted.

Stetchkin personally supervised the unceremonious execution of Major Volkov. A single shot to the back of the head. The idiot had guaranteed the success of the event. He deserved the appropriate consequences for its failure.

Stetchkin had, understandably, been anxious after the event had failed. More accurately, he had been petrified. Mikhailov had excoriated him for eliminating Piotr Egorshin, and Stetchkin was afraid the Russian president would, therefore, hold him responsible for the failure of the entire plan.

But as the days passed, it became clear that Mikhailov needed him. A man with Stetchkin's talents was invaluable, especially given Yuri Mikhailov's grand ambitions. Besides, he and Mikhailov were longtime friends, former KGB colleagues. Those who had disappeared were cyphers.

Stetchkin—as well as everyone else associated with the event for that matter—remained mystified as to what had gone wrong. Stetchkin was convinced, however, that Piotr Egorshin had somehow sabotaged it. The supposed genius had done or failed to do something to make the computers go awry. The other imbeciles didn't believe it. They thought Egorshin a patriot. Besides, he was already dead by the time of the calamity.

But the devious are difficult to deceive. Stetchkin was convinced that Egorshin's uncle, the SVR man Morosov, was somehow involved.

No one could find any evidence that the computers had been tampered with. They'd devoted several teams of the best and brightest to the endeavor, only to find nothing whatsoever. The failure was inexplicable.

But Stetchkin knew better. Nothing is inexplicable, and if it appears inexplicable, it's the result of human intervention. So Stetchkin had ordered surveillance videos of the operations room from the time of the last simulation to the time the event was to have been initiated. Over and over he reviewed the videos for any peculiarities or anomalies, but nothing seemed amiss or unusual.

At one point in the video Morosov appeared. He spoke briefly to two supervisors and then entered Egorshin's office to retrieve personal effects. He hadn't lingered and it didn't appear as if he had disturbed anything or taken anything he shouldn't have taken. Throughout, he was under the close scrutiny of a number of security officers.

Nonetheless, Stetchkin persisted. He slowed the video to a crawl and viewed it second by second. He studied still images and scanned from every angle available. Everything Morosov did, every move he made, appeared innocuous. At another point he'd left, only to return to collect a photo of Tatiana Palinieva.

Frustrated, Stetchkin only became more suspicious. He decided, admittedly without evidence, that Morosov *must* be the culprit. Accordingly, he decided Morosov *must* be eliminated. And Stetchkin planned to have Morosov eliminated later tonight.

He sat comfortably in the rear of his armored Kortezh SUV, his driver and a bodyguard in front. It was a beautiful evening. There was a slight chill in the air, but otherwise it was still. A short distance ahead he could see the carriage lights atop the posts flanking the wrought iron gate leading to his residence, which gates swung open upon the SUV's approach. An armed guard emerged from a kiosk just inside the gate and waved in deferential acknowledgment.

Palinieva. She was afraid of him, naturally. She was smart enough to surmise that he may have had something to do with Egorshin's death. And that was a good thing. Fear was a good thing. It would make her compliant, if not willing. With time she might even grow to like him. A man with his power and wealth could do wonders for her career. Either way, it didn't matter. He would have his way.

In the darkness of the back seat Stetchkin smiled. He decided he'd pay a visit to Palinieva a bit later this evening. It was still relatively early, after all. He'd grab a quick shower and then have his driver drop him off. He smiled again, more broadly.

The vehicle stopped at the front door, which was opened from the inside by a large bodyguard, who retreated to a small room containing an array of surveillance cameras. Stetchkin stepped inside. There wasn't a single inch of the grounds that wasn't under observation at all times. In addition to his driver and bodyguard, a dozen other armed security officers were stationed about the grounds and residence.

Stetchkin approached the steps to the upstairs bedrooms and bath before changing his mind and proceeding down the long, broad hallway to his study. A quick drink before showering.

The stately wall lamps along the corridor shone a soft yellow glow upon the photographs of Stetchkin that hung as reminders of his journey toward extraordinary power and importance. There he was as a young KGB lieutenant standing behind Yuri Andropov. Then standing next to a desk pointing to a document in front of a hunched Mikhail Gorbachev. Yet another clasping hands and laughing with Boris Yeltsin.

He paused for a moment in front of the Yeltsin photo. The entire corridor was a chronology of his inexorable advancement, his accumulation of wealth and prestige. But the Yeltsin photo was his favorite. It made them appear as two historical figures, as equals.

He swelled with satisfaction. He was indomitable, in control.

He strode to the entrance of his study, the door locked because it sometimes contained sensitive documents. He withdrew the key from his pocket, unlocked the heavy oak door, and flipped the light switch just inside, illuminating a small desk lamp in the far corner of the room.

A second later his chest seized with terror, for in the dim light of the desk lamp was the most ominous sight he could imagine: a J-shaped scar along the right jawline of a face otherwise cast in shadow.

ACKNOWLEDGMENTS

Once again, thanks to the entire Dutton team, with special thanks to my marvelous editor, Jessica Renheim; eagle-eyed copy editor, Eileen Chetti; and publicist, Jamie Knapp. I'm also grateful for the hard work and insights of my agent, Scott Miller. Collectively, they make writing a breeze.

ABOUT THE AUTHOR

Peter Kirsanow practices and teaches law and is an official of a federal agency. He is a former member of the National Labor Relations Board and has testified before Congress on a variety of matters, including the confirmations of five Supreme Court justices. He contributes regularly to *National Review*, and his op-eds have appeared in newspapers ranging from *The Wall Street Journal* to *The Washington Times*. He lives in Cleveland, Ohio, where he is wrapping up his next Mike Garin thriller.